C000104576

Trigger Warnings

Blood & Gore

Kidnapping

Death & Murder

Mentions of Mental Health

Drug & Alcohol Consumption
& Use of Weapons

Mentions of Sexual Assault

Inappropriate Language

Mentions of Suicide

Pronunciations

Names

Haakon – (Ha-con)

Abizer – (A-bee-za)

Keita – (Key-ta)

Arista – (Ar-ee-sta)

Nephus – (Nef-us)

Emmita – (Em-ee-ta)

Places

Adira – (Ad-era)

Ellwey – (El-wee)

Anaphi – (Ans-roo-tas)

Tinos – (Tee-nos)

THE NORTH SEA

FAERDRE

OCTOPUS BAY

HAF

AMBRE

HESPER

TINOS

SCARRED LANDS

LOCHWOOD VILLAGE

SUNNE

MOUNT ADIRA
MOUNT CHASIN
LARISSA
ELLWEY
ANAPHI
KOS
ANSRUTAS
LEFKI
THE AVAK

*To all those nervous, shy kids who grew feeling left
out or never good enough.
You are.*

PROLOGUE

The night is cold, freezing actually, winter has well and truly set in in Hesper, a city named for the evening star. Where snow should fall, rain has taken its place, and the stars twinkle brightly in the sky miles above, looking down on the still buzzing city and the dark clouds that surround the metropolis from all else.

Within minutes the concrete paths and the brown brick buildings are drenched in water, droplets race each other down windowpanes and soon even the streets are running with small streams of water that flow into nearby drains.

Besides the incessant patter of rain droplets, shaky breaths accompany the silence in the icy, damp alleyway.

Hounds bark in the distance, coupled with the screeching of cats as they fight over territory, and the rumble of cars and vans, each noise only accomplishes grating on the young males' nerves.

The youth is barely twenty years of age and stands shivering with his hands tucked tightly into his pockets helplessly trying to keep himself warm; his navy-blue cotton jacket absorbs the water that falls from the gloomy night sky. His oversized hood is up and hanging over his face striking an almost deathly silhouette. His nose ring shines in the dim light of the alley as rivulets of rain run down his tanned face, his rich deep brown eyes scan his surroundings quickly, like a timid deer watching for a predator lurking in the shadows.

He blows out a breath desperate to calm his racing heart, sending up a plume of hot air that whips its way into the night.

Nights like this have become familiar to him, and yet the threat of detection always makes these drops an anxiety-fuelled few hours.

It started months ago. He had walked in on his friends at a party taking Mica Glitter, snorting it off the bathroom counter, all drunk off their faces, they looked up as he entered smiling goofily. He hadn't taken any himself. Not that he could remember anyway. But that was how he had found himself quickly in possession of bags of it. Having to be the stand-in on the few occasions when his friends couldn't make the drop themselves, most likely from having taken it.

He'd hated doing it. Hated being the reason that the drug was so widely spread in the city. But the money is good, so morals be damned, right?

Sirens from emergency services echo throughout the many streets, fuelling the already restless and cautious feeling that sets his senses on high alert.

He tugs out his phone checking the time.

"Late as fucking usual," he mutters to himself. He pulls up his text thread and types out a quick message.

'Where the fuck are you guys?' It's sent with a swoosh and the phone is promptly stuffed back into his pocket while he waits impatiently for the reply, his foot tapping quickly against the wet concrete.

A stone scrapes across the floor at the end of the alley catching his attention, the sound muted as though it's wedged between the pavement and a boot. The male's head quickly whips in the direction of the noise, his breath catching and holding itself in his thin, quivering chest. A thin fog crowds down the alley, produced by the close-knit buildings, making it hard to see exactly who it is he is looking at.

The shadow takes a step closer.

Prying his tongue from the roof of his dry mouth, he swallows and licks his lips to moisten them.

"What's the word?" he calls.

If it's his drop 'client,' they should know to reply with their predetermined codeword.

He gets no reply.

Instead, the mysterious shadow tilts its head to the side, like that of a dog listening for a command, but moves no closer, its attention never wavering from the male's face.

An eerie silence descends like a blanket over the two figures for a few moments. The male squints his eyes to try and get a look at their shadowy face, only for him to see that the wraith-like figure is wearing some type of fabric mask fastened close to their jawline and nose, with a large hood covering the top portion of their face; the leather fabric sags a little under the weight of the rainwater.

They wear no coat but instead a flexible waterproof cloak, leather gloves, and pants, along with knee-high lace-up boots. A gun strapped to each thigh, and a combat knife tucked into their boot.

His heart rate increases, thudding strongly against his rib cage upon realising that this person is in fact a complete stranger.

The shadow takes silent steps forward, each movement filled with lethal intent.

"Shit!" he curses, willing his stiff muscles into action. He sprints down the alley in the opposite direction, his hood flying back revealing his head of dark and thick curls. His breathing quickens becoming uneven as he pushes himself faster and faster, away from the stranger, looking back only once to see if they were following. He stumbles around a corner and comes face to face with a tall, red brick wall, blocking him from the street beyond. He curses again trying to find something to climb on, but promptly gives up when he finds nothing.

In a panic he whirls around and doesn't see the stranger pursuing him, he pants out some relief and rests his hands on his knees catching his breath, the rain begins falling heavier now saturating his soft hair.

He takes one final drag of air and stands up right before taking a step forward, pausing when he once again sees the imposing figure at the end of the alley.

"Fuck," he breathes, backing away. One step, then two until his back thumps against the wall. The figure advances quicker now evidently enjoying the cat-and-mouse chase.

The male rests his weight against the wall shaking so much that he begins crumbling in on himself.

"Please," he pleads, hands raised as he slides down to the filth-ridden floor.

The phantom doesn't stop until they stand just inches from him, slowly crouching down to his level, they reach out a hand toward him moving methodically; he whimpers awaiting the contact.

The stranger starts to rifle through his pockets deliberately taking their time until they find what they came for.

A fifty-gram bag of finely ground sparkling silver powder.

The figure stands back up and moves under the dim light in the alley, checking the bag's contents.

"T...take it," he sobs, curling in on himself, his palms raised.

He'd heard stories of what stood before him; the type mothers tell their children to get them to behave. Of monsters, mere whispers in the night would come to snatch away misbehaving children and take them back to their lairs. He'd lost several nights of sleep over these stories as a child. His own mother for the gods' sakes, had told him these same stories, as he grew older however he'd brushed them off as nothing more than folklore. Now he wished he hadn't.

Time seemed to slow, and his eyes went wide as the stranger pulled out a gun from its holster, dangling it in their hand against their waterlogged pants, taunting him.

"Please, don't," he pleaded, crying harder. "I have a family, I...m...my sister, she needs me!"

The assailant's hood sprays water in every direction as they whip their head to face him again, almost as if they had forgotten he was even there, they lift their cloak and put the bag in one of their pockets, and raise their weapon.

A flash of lights brightens the alley and an ear-splitting bang before the male can utter another word. His body goes limp and his head slumps back against the wall, his eyes are open to the sky and his unshed tears roll down his face mixing with the rain.

The stranger re-holsters their gun and without another glance at the corpse beside them, they walk away.

Lights from the nearby buildings flick on as people wake from the gunshot, but the figure is nothing but a whisper in the night.

CHAPTER ONE
THE UNCONQUERABLE

"Do you have eyes on the target?" A deep, gravelly voice rumbles through my earpiece.

"Yes sir," I reply, staring down the scope of my rifle, tracking the amber-eyed, deer shifter wandering through her lavish apartment.

Chancellor Abigail Dyani steps foot into her clean, grey and white kitchen, after having kicked off her shoes upon entry. Showing no hesitation, she reaches for the amber filled decanter, in the centre of several other crystal bottles before pouring herself a drink, draining its contents, refilling the glass before the first has had a chance to settle.

She walks leisurely through her modern apartment, sipping from her drink all the while, her short auburn hair wafting with each movement, not even an inkling of being watched through her floor to ceiling windows that reflect the city's lights.

The earthy tonal colours bring an even grander feel to this expensive home, multiple sculptures decorate glass topped tables, partnered with flower arrangements that are spread around the open plan living room and kitchen.

I observe each detail of her house as I sit perched on a roof opposite her building. A soft breeze wraps itself around me as I sit here, having not moved since early this morning, waiting for the moment she arrived home.

Miss Dyani's outstanding professional political reputation has since come into question as of late, after she was spotted with some local dealers clearly partaking in some nefarious dealings. Not only was she caught, but she was also photographed. An investigation was opened up by the metro-police immediately.

She is the financial chancellor for the city of Hesper and her colleagues became concerned about her private activities. Worried only for their own reputations and political images, but still, the media has since picked apart her life and shone light on things best left in the dark – making her a liability.

Chancellor Dyani had contacted the Fort once in the past, to help deal with a certain competitor. Something I believe she regrets dearly. Once you participate in our services, you become part of the fold, and there is no way out.

The information that I have been given is that MG is directly involved. MG being the street name for Mica Glitter. A glittering white and delicately powdered drug that I've had several unfortunate encounters with, providing the user with graphic hallucinations that can last for hours, it can be taken in several different forms, but one thing always remains the same, the drug always has its signature glitter-like component.

Tyres screech down the road a few moments later and several black, unmarked cars come racing down the street, skidding to a stop outside the chancellor's building.

"We have movement," I murmur into the communications receiver secured in the fabric of my left sleeve. Twenty or so agents spill out onto the street dressed in black bullet proof vests, all carrying rifles, helmets, and masks to hide their features as they storm the building.

"What kind?" Callum's voice comes through my earpiece again. Callum is my handler for this particular mission, having trained to work with me and my sisters-in-arms for years, he is specialised in how to *control* us.

"A unit of special forces has entered the building."

"Well, there's only one thing they're here for," he sighs, "hang tight." His voice is muffled as he seems to speak to someone next to him, I screw a silencer on the end of my weapon, waiting patiently for him to give the order.

"Alright, finish it," he speaks, finally.

Without hesitation I squeeze the trigger and the bullet whizzes through the air, shattering the glass before piercing through Abigail's skull. A splatter of blood and brain matter bursts through the hole as her body drops to the floor, her glass of whiskey splinters into pieces from the impact, the contents mingling with the growing pool of blood.

A knock at her apartment door sounds at that moment, as I pull back and start to disassemble my weapon slowly, placing each piece back into its carrier carefully, whilst watching the scene play out in front of me.

The door is breached, disintegrating from the force of the battering ram and the special forces team charge into her apartment, guns raised.

I sling my gun bag over my shoulder, getting up swiftly just as they discover her body in her bedroom. I turn, walking away so they don't have time to investigate the room and the cause of her death.

Climbing down the ladder, the breeze strengthens, blowing my hair every which way, until my boots touch down into the alleyway below and I find my way back to the street, to the team that I know is awaiting me in a blacked out car at the end of the street

"Well done Three-Nought-Nought, excellent work." Callum's voice comes from the passenger seat, as I slip inside, situating myself in the backseat next to a suited guard. I watch as he finishes the call he was just on; another guard sits behind the wheel, starting the car. I turn to see the male in the backseat has his eyes on me with quizzical interest, we lock eyes, to which he turns away his cheeks flushing with a blush of the softest pink, but neither say anything to me, as we pull away from the curb and depart from the chaos that will surely ensue tonight.

"Another successful mission, Three-Nought-Nought." Her words are the

closest thing I'll ever get to praise. Not that I need it, I enjoy what I do.

Madame K's face is tight with disdain, her slender nose creased at the sides from her scrunched up scowl and her icy blue eyes harden, as they flicker from me to the mission report she holds in her hands.

Her blonde hair is tied tight in a bun with shimmering streaks of grey that have started to break through her natural colour, making her look older than she is.

I stay silent as she reads.

I'm trained to only speak when spoken to.

A faceless and voiceless weapon.

We sit there in the lengthy silence as Madame continues to read through my report as I sit in front of her plain pine coloured desk, watching her eyes rove over the paper.

The office itself is no pretty thing. Just the barest of necessities, the desk takes up most of the space

"Mica Glitter?" she asks, lifting her eyes to look at me through her eyebrows, she doesn't look happy about that snippet of information.

"Yes, Madame. I was only informed of that when we reached the target. I had no previous knowledge that there was any direct connection to the drug," I reply flatly.

She scoffs in response but says nothing more.

Madame K has been my program leader since I have been able to walk, she knows everything about me and every detail of every mission that I have ever completed.

In my most recent years I've been tasked with nurturing the drug trade, helping it to grow and cutting branches off should the competition start to get out of hand. Mica Glitter is the newest addition to the ever-expanding market.

Once she's finished, she rearranges the papers and tucks them into a beige folder, rising to place them into one of her many filing cabinets at the side of her office.

"You are dismissed," she says, turning back around, moving to her desk. Her gaze does not find me again.

I bow my head with my arm across my chest and rise, leaving at her request.

With my team having gotten back from the city at such a late hour, the corridors are empty of the usual bustle of the waking hours. Most of the night shift guards have finished their sweeps of each floor and have now moved to the lower levels, including the garages and the dungeons. There's always a few in the control room, where they monitor the cameras that are spread throughout the base, there's even a few dotted across the mountain range, watching and waiting for any sign of trespassers.

I head for the stairwell, only passing two guards on my way, and take it down a floor to the Furies quarters. A series of small rooms only big enough for one bed and a wardrobe. If you're lucky enough some rooms even have a small window, but they are so deep and narrow thar they barely allow in any light at all.

I lock the door behind me and flop down in my uncomfortably hard and lumpy bed, the exhaustion of the day finally catching up to me.

Peering over at the clock on the tiny nightstand, the bright green numbers tell me it's a little after three in the morning. I groan and throw my arm over my eyes willing myself to sleep, knowing that in just a few hours I will have to wake and start the day. I pull my long blonde hair out of its high ponytail and kick off my boots, not bothering to change out of my clothes.

"Again!" Her sharp voice sounds throughout the room, reverberating off of the walls as we stand in formation, one girl to a mat. Two of the walls are made of the natural stone that forms the mountain core, and the other two are made entirely of glass.

One overlooks the garage below us, the other shows the dark-painted corridor that leads down to the elevator; of which only a select few have authorisation to use – with the help of a security badge – leaving the rest of us having to use the stairs.

Sweat pours from my body as I concentrate on my balance, this particular sequence focuses on being both balanced and swift. A hard combination to master.

The Unconquerable

With thirty of us all spaced out equally in the rectangular training room, this group is the largest group of Furies ever to be trained together, all of us under the meticulous guide of Madame K, who's training methods are known for being brutal. She thrives on the competition from the other program leaders, so much so that one of our sisters has already been escorted from the room and down to the dungeons a couple of floors beneath us. She had failed to keep Madame satisfied. Not that Madame is ever satisfied with our performance, but to disappoint her is to disrespect her - and you do not disrespect Madame Killick.

I balance on my left leg, my right is up in front of me, bent at the knee. I move my arms sharply, picturing in my mind a blade whispering through the air, all the while making sure my ankle doesn't wobble unsteadily. Madame K weaves in between us, her hands clasped together in front of her, her almost wrinkled lips in a pout as she judges our forms.

My reputation is something that I have never cared for. But I have noticed that I am usually scrutinised more heavily than the others. I have wondered if it's because I can sometimes be more ruthless than any of my sisters.

Killing is what I'm good at, and a sadistic part of me enjoys inflicting pain on those who deserve it. I've been trained to do this since I could hold a gun in my hand, and that dedication is what makes me invaluable to them.

The last significant mission I had been sent on had gone spectacularly wrong, and I ended up with a broken leg, some fractured ribs, and a hairline fracture in my skull.

That was nearly two years ago now. But my time away has driven me nearly insane with boredom. I've been chomping at the bit, at the chance to perform my duties again.

"Rest!" K shouts again. In near perfect synchronicity we lower our legs, and take the guarded stance, clasping our hands together behind our backs. Our collective breaths come out more like heavy pants.

"Break!" Her voice is sharp and authoritative, most fumble towards their bags. Searching for their water bottles, taking mouth full after mouth full.

"Move to your next session," she says, after allowing us a few minutes of reprieve. Everyone slings their bags over their shoulders, moving to the pine wooden doors at the other end of the training room, sourced from the local trees that encompass the base of the mountains.

Beyond those doors is the armoury, and a giant of a man resides within.

His official title is Weapons Master.

But we just know him as Gregory.

His hulking frame towers over most people in any room he's in, but he couldn't be more of a gentle giant if he tried. Despite his speciality in weapons the most disarming thing about him is his smile. His crooked grin is so kind, in a place that is such the opposite, it's the smallest ray of sunshine in the darkest of nights.

His shoulder length blonde hair gives way to an even longer scraggly beard, and despite his innocent smile and still bright eyes, his history can speak for itself. It's not easy to become a member of the Fort, let alone to become its Weapons Master, but Gregory did. And I know that history still haunts him to this day.

Madame watches on as we all make our way to the other side of the room. She steps up behind me, following us to our next class.

She closes the door behind me as we are the last to step into the armoury.

Gregory watches as my sisters all march through the doors, heading straight for the locker room, but spots us quickly enough for that signature crooked smile to grace his face, his gold rimmed glasses folded and tucked into his navy plaid vest, his safety goggles high up on his face, accompanied by his noise cancelling earmuffs.

"Well, if it isn't my favourite lady." He slings an arm around Madame K, hugging her tightly - who accepts it begrudgingly - whilst he winks at me.

"Come on Siren, let's get you set up. Put your stuff in one of the lockers, I'll grab a selection of guns for you to play with." I nod walking into the small locker room and throw my bag down onto the bench, the only available space left, before I take the last booth at the far side of the room.

Gregory places a selection of weapons down in front of me. A couple of the new handguns were delivered only a few days ago and one of the new semi-automatic rifles.

I pick up one of the few handguns Gregory has placed in front of me, like second nature I load it and aim for the central point on the paper target at the other end of the room;

"Girls!" Everyone's attention shifts to him, "Load." The sound of several guns clicking at one time through the room. "Take aim," he directs. My sisters and I raise our weapons in synchronisation. "Fire!" he shouts as the boom of several guns fire off at the same time.

Perfectly in tune.

We fire in quick succession, do an even quicker reload and fire again emptying the clips.

I place my own gun down and pressed a button off to the side of my booth, pulling the paper forward on a track right up to my booth. The others continue practicing, now going at their own paces as Gregory walks up and down correcting those that need it.

I pull down the paper and hand it to Gregory when he reaches me. I put another piece up and press the button pushing it back into position before picking up another gun, ready to repeat the process.

Gregory holds up my first piece and shows it to Madame K, a smiley face made from holes smiles at her. Gregory laughs loudly at what I'm assuming is a disapproving scowl on her face, but I'm far too focused on my next target to care, he walks into the other room, where he keeps all the weapons locked up in metal cabinets, chuckling all the while and comes back out carrying something.

Madame shoots him a glare stepping up behind me. "Show some decorum or you'll be joining Three-Seven-Six in the dungeons tonight." Her heels clack against the floor as she walks away and I fire off some more shots, this time from the semi-automatic rifle creating another piece of artwork, hiding it from Madame I hand it to Gregory, who in turn places something down on the counter before me.

I give him a glance, but he only nods to the black box giving nothing away.

Choosing to trust him I open the wooden lid to see a combat blade placed delicately on a foam mat.

The steel blade is engraved with a feathered wing on either side sweeping up from the base to the tip, the handle itself is made from the finest ebony wood. The cross-guard is engraved with words in a language I've never seen.

Fascinated, I run my thumb over it feeling each groove.

I look at him trying to understand. He leans toward me so close that I can feel his breath tickle my cheek.

"It's written in the old language." He winks at me with a friendly smile on his face.

"I came across this a long time ago. So long ago I had forgotten where I put it. It wasn't until recently that I stumbled upon it again." He picks it up examining it. The look in his eyes is tender, as if he was looking at a family portrait. "It deserves to go to someone who knows how to use it." He smiles, flipping it so he holds the blade in his hands, the handle reaching out towards me.

"There are plenty here that know how to use such a knife," I grin, even as my fingers curl around the handle, eager to get a hold of it. The wood is smooth and cold. The weight is perfectly balanced and fits just right in my palm.

"You know what I mean." Again, Gregory is solemn, I bow my head in thanks and say nothing more. Instead, I sheath it in the hidden leather-bound holster under the rim of my boot.

"And I thought you weren't allowed favourites," I tease, just loud enough for him to hear as I reposition the rifle against my shoulder.

He huffs a laugh and places his headphones back over his ears walking away without another word. Madame K – having seen the whole thing – gives him another judgmental scowl but stays quiet.

Gregory only shrugs his shoulders and continues with his lesson.

CHAPTER TWO
TRIAL BY FIRE

The Furies all stand together in a circle hugging the walls of the training room, the new recruits stand in front of us. Today is challenge day. Where the latest batch of fresh faces fight for the chance to join the more advanced groups.

"Fury Five-Seven-Nine!" The young girl in front of me flinches as her name is called. Her breathing had been heavy from the beginning of this meeting. Whether it was because it was me, she was standing in front of, or the possibility of her fighting today, I can't say, but she steps forward, keeping her head high. A false confidence, something she so desperately needs to portray.

She bows to Logan, and the Madame's before placing herself in the centre of the room within the confines of the yellow circle there, stark against the black padded flooring.

Madame Valentina steps forward and begins to wrap her hands, readying her for the fight to come. Madame Valentina is the new recruits program leader; she takes pride in her work. She claims her role is more vital than the other Madame's because she prepares the 'fresh meat' for the more advanced trials that await them as they progress.

"Fury, Six-Nought-Nought. Step forward," Logan calls out again.

Logan Hunter-Findlay, the overseer of the Fury Program. His gaze scans the two females from head to toe with an all too pleased twinkle in his eyes, before they sweep the rest of the room. I take note of his dark features, his neatly trimmed black beard matches his equally kempt black hair, swept back showing his pointed fae ears filled with a multitude of glittering earrings. Tattoos in swirling patterns, decorate one side of his neck, creeping out the collar of his black button-down. A lazy smirk brightens his face, and his deep brown eyes latch onto mine for a brief second and I swear I detect a hint of fear in them before he breaks the connection. He not so subtly looks at another point in the room.

A girl with beautiful white hair steps forward, her gaze nervous as she sizes up her opponent. Both dressed in tank tops and breeches, she too has her hands wrapped by Madame Valentina. Who shares some harsh words with her by the terrified look on the girl's face.

As soon as Madame V steps away Logan steps forward, eyeing both of the girls in the ring.

"Now we need a clean match. Use the skills and knowledge you have been taught to achieve your goal. The loser of this match will be going to Madame Tuli." Madame T shows a vicious smile, the one you'd see on a wild cat right before they pounce on you. The girls both swallow.

"And the winner will be joining Madame C's group."

I look to my own group leader, Madame Killick. Her face is impassive and shows no disappointment, but I had known she was wanting to introduce a new girl to our group.

"When the bell chimes, you begin," Logan says, looking at both of them once again. He turns and takes his place once more between the Madame's and nods to one of the guards. The bell chimes and the girls all but dive towards each other.

Neither can be older than ten years and yet the skills they have learnt have already made them deadly little creatures. Punches are thrown with arrow-like precision and before long the two are dropping to the floor wrestling, in a tangle of limbs and fair hair. The duo, scratch, and kick at each other whilst everyone watches the girls before us, I think back to my own time on the mat. The haunted expressions on the girls' faces each time they faced me. I still see them in my dreams. Of course, back then, it was different. We had to fight to the death. Now they fight for higher-ranking positions. It became too much strain on our resources to train so many to lose them in the monthly challenge.

I was brought back from my thoughts when Logan finally announced a winner. The blonde girl who was in front of me earlier is sitting on top of the white-haired girl. With her hands around her throat; the girls cheeks are tinged a bright pink.

"Fury Five-Seven-Nine, release," Logan shouts, presumably for the second time, given the look on his face. She does just that before standing, with her hair in disarray. She offers a hand to her opponent, and they bow to each other. Before parting ways, to join their new groups. Tuli looks all too pleased to have the more innocent looking of the pair and I have to fight the shiver that rolls down my spine at the violent twinkle in her dark eyes.

"Madame Gina's group you will be staying here for your balance and core training. Madame Campbell's you will be heading next door for your muscle and agility training. Madame Killick's group you will be heading up to the lab for your monthly check-up and injections and last but not least, Madame Tuli's group, you will be heading over to the tactical training centre over the bridge across to the sister mountain," he calls out, listing us off from a clipboard.

As if the actual main section of the Fort wasn't big enough already, we have - in the last fifty years - expanded into the sister mountain of Adira. Where our tactical skills such as field medical training; navigation, situational awareness, and digital competency, are honed to a fine point. They built a series of rooms and winding corridors into the heart of Adira Mountain, using the stone removed to create a bridge between the two; the high altitude and cold winds make for an unpleasant walk.

Madame K leads us to the stairwell and up the four flights of stairs to the lab.

Upon opening the doors, we are greeted with the sound of classical music, violins and cellos drifting through the sound system above us, providing a soothing atmosphere despite what is to come.

The lab itself is incredibly modern — only the best equipment for one of the best scientists on the planet. The pure stone walls are in keeping with the rest of the Fort. Glass doors allow one to see into each room as you pass by, some with plants in to study the different properties of each species. Another room is home to multiple whiteboards and desks; I can only assume they are the offices of Dr Feng's assistants. Walking past the only room with a wooden door, a golden name plaque drilled into the wood, Dr Lei Feng.

The door opens and out comes a very small, albeit authoritative, female.

Her head tilts up to look Madame K in the eye since she barely reaches past the average female's torso. Her thick black glasses fall back up her nose with the angle, and her short black-haired bob shifts with the movement.

"Dr Feng," Madame K greets, breaking the silence first.

"Yvonne," she snipes back, narrowing her angular eyes; the green surrounded by brown colour of her irises, look menacing under her thick eyelashes that are only magnified further by her glasses.

She says nothing more as she looks at each of us and walks away slowly towards another room, this one larger and more clinical, that houses cabinets and a chair with leather straps attached to it.

"You know the drill girls; I call out a name and the rest of you wait out here. Quietly," Madame K calls down the line, with her having the biggest group of nearly thirty under her care, only half of us are here at the moment and the other half will be presented this afternoon.

"Fury, Three-Five-Nine," K calls, and Aria steps forward. Her ebony skin sparkles under the fluorescent lighting, and her black braided hair sways with the movement revealing her pointed fae ears.

She strides into the room with a forced confidence that I know all of the females here are trying to replicate.

Dr Feng's assistant helps tighten the straps across Aria's torso, wrists and ankles, her face giving nothing away even as she eyes Dr Feng as she prepares the vials and injections for each of us. The door closes and just a few minutes later Aria groans in discomfort.

After several more minutes, the door reopens to uncover a sweaty and washed-out looking Aria, who stumbles back into line.

"Fury, Three-Four-Seven!" Madame K yells. Surya, the black-haired mortal steps forward, her ponytail bouncing, and her caramel skin seems to glow from within. She too walks confidently into the room and minutes later comes out looking tired and ill.

This continues for the better part of an hour, each screeching as the drug is reintroduced into their systems.

Until it's my turn.

I walk into the room and flop down onto the seat, strapping my ankles down.

I know the process.

There's no point in fighting it.

Dr Feng turns around to face me after having changed the needle and the liquid in the syringe, her face draining of colour slightly. Her legs dangle comically off her stool that I don't doubt, she struggled to climb up.

My chest is then strapped down and my wrists next, she squeezes my arm in hopes to find a decent vein and doesn't hesitate to get it over with. I don't look as she pierces my skin with the needle and neither do I wince, but the feeling of the serum is always shocking as it rushes through my system. The cold invades my blood, and my muscles begin to tense of their own accord.

Almost immediately my eyes pick up on different colours, my nose on different smells, the antiseptic in particular. My ears can hear the sounds of the girls groaning outside as the serum focuses on heightening my senses one by one.

My muscles tingle as it strengthens them, it's almost like I can feel my cells replacing themselves over and over. My head begins to spin with all of these sensations attacking me all at the same time.

Closing my eyes, I hold on tight to the arms of the chair, the leather creeks under my fingertips, and I take several deep breaths.

A hand squeezes my own and my eyes fly open, to see a small hand wrapped around my fingers, and Dr Feng's sympathetic eyes boring into mine.

"These always did affect you differently than the others and I still don't know why," she murmurs quietly, watching me closely. It's then that I realise we are completely alone now, no assistants to witness.

I groan and flop back into the chair and she goes to unbuckle the leather straps from my ankles, always leaving my wrists for last.

Madame Killick comes rushing into the room then, a stern look on her face, which appears to soften ever so slightly when her eyes fall on me. Sweat drips from my forehead, my skin is flushed from the fever that is burning under the surface of my skin and my veins bulge from the strain as I fight against the leather cuffs.

"Retire to your quarters, I expect you all recovered tomorrow for the training session," she calls out the door to the others, who shuffle and groan loudly, heading back towards the stairwell.

She's at my side in an instant, her hand on my forehead, but her face shows no concern.

"Can you not synthesise a different dosage for her, rendering her useless like this for days is inconvenient," she snaps, at Lei.

"Yvonne, you know that I have been trying, I still don't fully understand why she reacts this way when all of the others have the same symptoms that they can overcome within an afternoon," Feng snaps back, hopping down from her stool, she throws the needle and vial into the medical waste bin. "Even when I've had samples of her blood to experiment with, it still reacts the same."

Killick only shakes her head, "what are we going to do with you?" she mutters quietly, so only I can hear as she strokes my hair.

"Do you need me to call a guard to carry her back to her quarters?" Dr Feng asks from the open doorway.

"Call Gregory," she replies, not taking her eyes from my face, even as I blink heavily.

"I'll have one of my assistants check on her every few hours and put a drip in her arm." With that, Dr Feng leaves us.

Madame pulls up a stool and sits next to me, my breathing deepens, and my eyes become heavy, pulling me into total darkness.

A trail of hot puffing air follows behind me, drifting skyward into the freezing winter day as I battle through this freshly fallen knee-deep snow. The sky is a brilliant white that has gentle flakes fall heavily from it, the north wind blows against me fighting my every step, whipping the gentle flakes around in tendrils through the dense frozen forest.

It's been three days since my injection. Three days of missed drills and training sessions. Three days in and out of consciousness. The effects of the serum have lessened and Madame has once again cleared me for duty.

My breathing starts to become uneven as I shove past centuries-old pine trees that droop with the weight of the snow and ice that clings to their branches, being careful of each step I take without slowing.

I race towards the vast frozen lake – my long-sleeved shirt and breeches doing nothing to keep out the cold - that has carved itself into the once grassy plain beyond the mountains, each crunch of the icy crystals louder than the last. I charge forward fighting my way out of the last row of stagnant trees, bursting through the snowdrift like water from a breaking dam.

My speed does not falter as the terrain changes from silky soft snow to crushingly hard ice as I begin sprinting across the thick layer that separates me from the freezing water below; my feet thump against it, the sound vibrating through the entire sheet.

My mind is focused but my heart beats like a wild stallion. The goal is to outrun the others whilst also outdoing myself. To do that effectively, I've got to quickly find the hole carved into the ice - like that of an ice fishing hole, perfectly round and small enough for only one person. It's no easy thing to find, especially at this speed. But it's the challenge I thrive upon, becoming the best at what I do has always driven me further, faster. I'm stronger than I have ever been, my senses – now heightened due to the serum – help me feel near invincible.

Something notched in the ice to my left catches my eye and I change my direction, adrenaline coursing through my blood while I desperately try not to slip.

Footsteps hit the ice behind me beating harder and harder, they're catching up. The twenty or so females charge across the ice unsteadily.

I don't dare to look behind me, not even to check the distance between me and them, it would only prove to slow me down; and speed is everything out here in this frozen tundra.

Thankful of my intuition I make it to the opening, slowing only to check out the circumference of it.

Without thinking, I jump, gliding through the air and slip seamlessly through the surface of the water, into the frigid temperatures below. The initial shock threatens to steal the breath from my lungs, but I don't give my body a chance to react. I immediately begin kicking my legs in an effort to propel myself through the water.

There are those in this world who are faster and stronger. We are taught how to exploit those traits. Both shifters and fae live amongst the mortals, it's been that way for centuries. The fae though older and near immortal, living for centuries has taught them many things, some things have been passed to mortals but fae mostly keep to themselves after the civil wars of old.

Shifters are different, able to change into animal forms shifter have been hunted to near extinction. Feline shifters for their unpredictability and canine shifters, simply because the king degreed it, without explanation causing thousands to flee from their homes and the people they love in order to protect themselves and their species. Others weren't as lucky.

Some have taken to only care for themselves.

Dividing colonies and living away from civilization.

Like the little folk who live high in the mountains separating North from South – relying only on the land – or the merpeople who live in the deepest oceans. No one I know has ever seen one above ground, not for a few decades at least.

The cold of the water caresses my flailing limbs and goads me into looking down, toying with me like there's something foul hiding within the depths, waiting to snatch me up. Despite the bright white sky, it's dark under the ice, looking below myself is like looking into a dark abyss that could easily swallow me whole if given the chance. I feel insignificant in the face of the void below.

The air in my lungs begins to burn the more I power through the water, the fire spreads up my throat and the cold seeps through my muscles and caresses my bones, promising a slow death. Ignoring it is difficult, and refocusing my mind is even more so, but trusting my body is second nature so I push it harder still; my body begs for air and the instinct to draw breath grows insistent.

The twin hole to the other becomes visible to me then as the muted sunlight streams through it, almost like The Golden Fields are calling me home. The water's surface behind me breaks as my *sisters* enter it, creating ripples that blub under the ice. I push faster still until I burst through the surface on the other side, gulping down mouthfuls of sweet frosty air, coughing and spluttering at the water trying to force its way into my mouth and up my nostrils.

I waste no time clambering clumsily onto the ice. Taking only a few seconds pause to breathe, I stand and begin pushing forward, my body crying for mercy as I try desperately to move past the biting cold from the wind as the water soaks deep into my clothes. I sprint for the other side of the shoreline, my breath coming out in frantic pants. The short run through more trees feels like an impossible task with my clothes freezing to my skin, my thighs and calves burn as I look up to my final obstacle. A two-thousand-foot climb up the side of a frozen, snow-covered cliff.

A laugh bubbles up from my throat but I catch it before it's given sound. When I reach the bottom of the cliff I look up at the daunting height and swing my leg out in front of me which, naturally, finds purchase in one of the grooves that cuts across the cliff face. The jagged stone is cool to the touch and chips of ice are sprinkled across every crevice and ledge. Within minutes my fingers become numb making it harder to pull myself skyward. A bone-deep cold has long since overcome my tendons and limbs. My wet hair, in a knot at the nape of my neck, has frozen together; the falling snowflakes sprinkle across my eyelashes.

Trial by Fire

Blood rushes to my cheeks and it's the only thing I can feel while I climb higher still. My muscles protest with every push and pull, the strain of just reaching the tops of the drooping pine trees has me panting heavily. It's here that I finally hear the breaking of the water's surface and the gasping breaths of my comrades emerging from the lake.

Our handlers call these mountains *'The Playground'*.

An icy death trap is what they should be called.

The lesson this exercise teaches us is that only the strong survive. It's a lesson taken all too literally.

The north wind whips around me like it's playing a game

It whips around joyfully, toying with my life as I climb higher still. To fall now would be to die. My grip tightens on a sharp rock ledge, and I curse the gusts as they blow harder.

There are no wires up here, no ropes to catch you.

If you fall, you die.

A few agonised whimpers leave my lips as I plead with my fingers to move, begging for some feeling to return to them, looking down I see my numb foot grip onto a section of gritty rock and note the first of my sisters begins her own ascent.

My left-hand slips whilst grasping onto a clump of broken rock and I watch as it crumbles in my hand, clattering against the cliff face as it falls away. My legs flay as my feet slip from their icy nooks, my heart pounds wildly in its cage, I feel its strong beat in my throat. Desperately I try to clutch onto anything that I can, and notice the wind seems delighted with my struggle; it appears stronger and louder.

Grunts come out of my mouth as my fingertips grip a small crevice and I draw myself up further, my feet reattaching to the wall. Leaning my head against the cold stone I close my eyes and begin taking deep breaths, trying to calm my thundering heart and once more steadying my panicked mind.

It takes everything in me to drive myself upwards to the top. Easily an hour has past, by the time my fingers finally reach for the ridge, clasping onto frozen grass. I allow myself only a moment of relief. Groaning as loudly and obnoxiously as I can I pull myself up dragging my frozen body over the cliff's edge and back onto solid ground once more.

Lying flat on my back with my face to the sky, I watch the snowflakes float towards me covering me in a soft layer of fresh snow. The pride and the relief I feel are short-lived when I look to the side and my gaze is met with disappointed stares. Panting hard I stand quickly on shaking legs like a newborn deer taking its first steps. Every part of me wants to lie back down and stay there until I'm frozen to the ground, but I stand. I show no weakness.

"Finally. At least *one* of you has made it, I thought we'd all freeze out here." Snickers from the masked, fur-covered guards are heard, but it's not them I'm looking at. Seeking out the owner of the voice I turn to Madame K. "Well, I'd like to be able to give you praise, Three-Nought-Nought but unfortunately I cannot." Her skin is almost as white as the icy landscape surrounding her, and age-defined wrinkles bracket the sides of her mouth and nose, cutting fine lines on her face, most likely from all the years she's spent scowling.

Her thin blonde hair, speckled with grey, is tied tightly into a bun at the base of her neck with a white, wolf fur hat covering the rest.

"You're getting sloppy," she comments as I hold her gaze. Shifting uncomfortably, she pulls her tan, oversized fur coat tighter around herself and levels her eyes on me.

"Apologies, Madame," I pant with a small bow of my head.

It's almost as if the wind itself has stopped howling just to hear her response, it's then I realise what I've done. The guards shift their weapons, each one looking to her for permission. But her eyes never weaver from mine.

Her unrelenting ice-blue eyes bore into my own.

I've made a mistake; one I'll pay for later. I drop to my knee, my arm across my chest and my head lowered in submission.

"Up!" she hisses, "And get into line."

Nodding silently, I walk past her and the armed guards – some shivering with the cold – and head straight to the dog-led sledges.

The guards of the Ajay are all male and have all been professionally trained by our *Dungeon Master – The Captain.*

His birth name is Cornelius Anderson, and he's a sick son of a bitch. Even by my standards.

I've always enjoyed my job. There's nothing I'm better at. But Cornelious is a different breed entirely.

He doesn't quite understand the distinction between acquiring information by any means and disfiguring his targets for life.

Whenever a target is being particularly different to squeeze information from, we bring them home and hand them over to Cornelius. He has never once failed to pry information out of anyone. He's the Director's right-hand man for his ruthlessness alone. The guards are so well trained that enough of them could overwhelm a lone Fury, but not enough to take us all at once. At least they seem to understand that. They never do get too cocky in our presence.

Several of the dogs with tri-coloured fur of silver, white and speckled black and deep brown eyes seem to perk up at my approach, twitching their fluffy ears and wagging their bushy tails. The drivers of the sledges, each covered head to toe in furs and animal skins, watch me warily as I stand close to them, my arms behind my back, my clothes now thoroughly frozen to my skin.

None of us speak for a long while. I stand there in the middle of a clearing filled with deadly males and a scornful female, shivering quietly watching my already pale skin turn blue. The silence is only broken by the whispering sound and howls of the wind as it whips violently through the trees taking with it the gentle falling snowflakes and not even allowing them to join the already substantial blanket spreading across the ground.

An ear-splitting scream suddenly rips through the freezing wild wind, followed by shouts that echo around the Northern Mountains for miles. None of the guards bat an eye at the sound; they only seem to care about keeping themselves warm. Madame Killick is no better, moving only to brush a stray hair away from her face that has come loose in the wind. We continue to stand in silence, waiting for the others to join us. For long and bitter minutes, we stand there, my mind reels to know which of my sisters fell. I have learnt, over the years, to not form any emotional attachment to anyone, even ones I've spent my entire life with. Nothing lasts. Everything comes and goes. And to the Fort, girls are expendable, when one dies another takes her place. Emotionless, faceless weapons.

That is all we are. That is all we'll ever be.

Finally, the first of the group pops her hand over the edge.

The first female, after me, to finish the course is Three-Five-Nine, otherwise known as Aria. Although I'm not allowed to call her that. It would only serve to put us both in The Captain's sick path of torture and mutilation. Three-Five-Nine is the second oldest Fury, the last one from my original group to still remain. The rest perished. Either from the training or the missions.

The dark-haired fae drags herself over the lip of the cliff, agony in her chocolate brown eyes and sweat glistening on her dark skin. She rests back on her heels, panting heavily as her body trembles.

"Who was that?" Madame Killick demands, not even looking at the panic-stricken female. Aria glances at me. I can see the misery in her eyes. I know before she even opens her mouth. Her emotions are shut down within an instant, that disinterested film glazing over her eyes. A mask each of us has perfected over the years. She turns her attention back to Madame Killick.

"Surya," she puffs, standing, taking in rapid deep breaths. "Surya fell."

Madame Killick rolls her eyes, "Three-Four-Seven." She stares pointedly at Aria telling her the mistake without using her words. Aria drops to one knee, her head bowed. The same position I took, "will be greatly missed, I'm sure. But you know our creed. Only the strong survive," she proclaims, raising her chin higher, pride radiating from her very pores. "I'll have Three-Four-Seven collected later." She waves her hand again dismissing Aria.

Aria nods solemnly and gets up to join me by the sledges, standing in unison with her arms behind her back and her chest thrust out standing up straight, I can see the muscles underneath her navy-blue long-sleeved shirt quivering. I spare her a quick sideways glance, but she only looks to the cliff edge, I see the horror in her eyes, and I know the battle she is facing. Not from personal experience but her eyes go in and out of focus, she is trying to stay present for her own salvation, yet she cannot help the images flashing across her vision.

The rest of the faction eventually make their way up the cliff and onto the frozen ground before us, a diverse group of fae and mortals alike, each pitifully trying to catch their breaths, watching them struggle to stand is more painful than sitting to watch paint dry on a wall.

Madame barks an order and they come rushing over to stand in formation.

One of the youngest guards, standing closest to Madame K, leans into whisper in her ear. Although my eyes are forward, looking out at the mountain range beyond the cliffs, and the lake at the bottom of the frozen valley, I feel their gazes on me, burning into my skin like a brand. She nods and steps forward looking at each and every one of us, taking her time without a care in the world that some of us are struggling to stand. We'd freeze to death out here and not a single one of these guards, nor our program leader, would so much as bat an eye.

"Disappointing girls. Truly, disappointing. I expect better from my class. This..." She waves her hand over the side of the cliffs to the scenery in the distance, "This is child's play, and you can't even measure up to that." She stops walking when she reaches the middle of the line, her furry boots sinking into the deep snow, nearly to her knees. She seems to ponder her next words as she looks up to the sky as if inspiration will just fall from the clouds and land in her lap. "Maybe I should just put you all out of your misery now."

Clicks all around us sound as the guards take the safety off their weapons.

"But then I would have to replace you and teach new ones, which would take far too long." The deadened twang in her voice tells me that that's far too much effort for her to go through. "Not to mention I would have to explain to the Director why I did what I did."

Now that *is* too much effort.

At the sound of his name, my spine straightens even more and my breathing picks back up.

"I've already lost one of you today," she mumbles, looking over the edge at what is sure to be just a splotch of red shattered in the snow below. "I suppose you can live another day." Her disinterest in the situation is clear. I know her well enough to know that all she wants to do now is get out of this weather and into a hot bath. She's rushing through this usually longer lecture.

"As punishment, you will all run back." She crosses the clearing and situates herself under the thick animal skin blanket that rests on the top of one of the sledges, pulling it up high so it lies just under her chin and tucks her arms under it also. "You have one hour. After that, the doors will be closed, and you can fend for yourselves out here."

She says nothing more.

There's no need for her to.

Her words are a promise.

Her sledge pulls away at the wave of her hand. The rest of the guards, as if puppets on a string, follow in her wake moving to their own sleds and departing in a flurry of sparkling snow dust. My sisters-in-arms and myself, all bow our heads and cross our arms over our chests and watch as they leave.

White flakes that have been whipped up from the ground caress our skin and for some of the females even that is too much extra weight to bare, and they collapse where they stand. Some groan as they lower themselves gently to the ground, others try to haul them back up and beg them to keep going.

I offer Three-Five-Nine a weak smile before she walks to the edge, looking down over the cliff side, her dark braided hair whipping at her face from the strong upwards gusts. I watch her for mere moments before following in the direction of Madame Killick, heading back towards the guild. I liked Surya, but in this line of work, it doesn't pay to have friends. Instead, I shake my head of any thoughts of her and begin the trek back to the unconquerable Fort of Ajay by myself.

CHAPTER THREE
THE DEMONSTRATION

Armed guards stand at the only door in and out of the colossal mountain, likely having been made to wait for us out in this blizzard by the looks on their faces, and the thick fur coats over their shoulders.

I made it back a little over twenty minutes after Madame had left us there. I charged through that snow like a bear chasing an elk. It's possible my body will suffer for it later, but feeling the heat streaming from the Fort's open doors makes it hard to care about later.

After an almost scolding shower, I'm washed and dried. My long blonde hair is tied up tight, in a high pony that swishes across the back of my neck whilst I walk to my destination.

A note was left in my chambers, from Madame K, asking me to seek her out. Me heart beats madly, fluttering like a thousand butterflies trapped in a bony cage, but my face gives not such turmoil away; my arms swing gently at my sides as I walk down the empty, long, white marble corridor. This is likely to be about my punishment for my speaking out of turn earlier.

The silence of the space almost suffocating and is only broken by my polished boots squeaking on the freshly cleaned matching marble floor, so shiny you can see your reflection staring back at you.

Two guards round the corner, their chins raised, arms behind their backs, as they stride past me side-eyeing me as they go.

Another two follow them shortly after, stopping just outside the doors that I need to go through. They don't turn their heads, as I approach but I know that they're not here to watch the empty room behind them, they're within earshot of Madame in case she calls out for help.

They're here to protect her from me.

Both of them are wearing matching black combat gear, decorated with an array of stars, dependent upon the rank of each officer and tightly laced boots that shine just as much as the floor. Similar to that of my own outfit, a long-sleeved black cotton shirt and combat trousers with laced-up boots reaching up to just under my knee, with a tight yellow armband on my upper arm. To signify that I'm a Fury. Like that wasn't already obvious by being a woman.

Being trained here, or rather, raised here has its perks. I am one of the few who is allowed to walk the halls without an escort. Aria – no – Three-Five-Nine is another.

At the end of the corridor, I make a sharp turn left and come face to face with a double doorway. The pine wood doors are stained in a brilliant white, to match the rest of the cleansed hallways, the doors are extraordinarily large. They could easily fit four people abreast through them and there would still be room to move. The doors have been expertly carved into, with trees and hanging vines, sprouting flowers and even a free-flowing river through the middle. Amid all the beauty of nature, there are hidden elements of danger. An archer in one of the trees, his bow string pulled tight as he aims at a deer, drinking from the aforementioned river; a wolf in the brush stalking that same unaware animal. The vines are curling around swords and daggers as if the plants are intent on using them and a hawk hovers in the air searching for its next meal.

Truly a work of art, if ever there was such a thing.

The Nursery.

This is the place where the new recruits are taken on their first few days. Each new female will be organised into their factions, dependent on their age. They will stay with those groups and learn, as one, the ways of the guild that they have been brought into.

Madame likes this place. I have yet to figure out whether it's because of the beautiful door, the homey interior, or the fact that fresh faces come in from the outside every year. Never once have I seen her smile, but I know that she enjoys helping Madame Valentina sort the new girls into their factions. She almost always volunteers, even though there are other program leaders that are subject train, what she likes to call *'fresh meat'*.

This room doesn't tend to bother me, but the stark contrast between the clean and sanitary white of the hallways and the cosy wooden interior of this room does fill me with a pinch of unease.

Upon opening the doors I'm surprised to be greeted with an empty room, Madame, being the more punctual of the two of us, is usually at our meetings first.

I take a few steps into the grand room, the doors drifting close behind me. The room itself looks like it belongs to a wealthy governing body as their study. Two dark red wood desks on either side facing the centre of the room, and four other sets of doors. Each one leads to a corridor that will take different factions to their sorting chambers. In due time their lives from the outside will be erased, if they had any history to begin with. They will be given a number and new clothing before being designated a room and bunk. Any personal items will be confiscated and later disposed of by the guards.

Everything they know and love will no longer be of consequence, they will become nothing more than what they will inevitably be trained to do.

Become a killer.

The dark panelling climbing the walls, I realise is what makes me feel uneasy. The warmth of it, it's so different from the rest of the guild that it makes me almost nauseous to be in here. This room and the Director's rooms are the only places that would actually feel like a normal homestead, they're the only places that have furniture as decoration and not just for a purpose.

Three beige rugs span across the dark wooden flooring, and an opulent limestone fireplace is what gives the space a sense of comfort.

The stone of the fireplace is chiselled to depict helpless animals being hunted and eaten by horrifying predators. The irony of such a sculpture was never lost on me. Neither was the message.

Kill the innocence, become what they fear.

It's the fireplace I stand before, looking at each of the realistic statues when the door opens and in walks Madame Killick; her high heels clicking on the polished wooden floor.

"Three-Nought-Nought," she says, claiming my attention as if it was on anything but her. Now wearing a cream-coloured blazer, buttoned at the waist, with a matching pencil skirt, just grazing the lower portion of her knees and a freshly steamed white blouse, with soft ruffles down the breastbone, all topped off with matching three-inch white heels. Her hair in a simple twist behind her head shows off her delicately pointed fae ears.

Whilst dressed like this it would be hard for an outsider to see her for what she is. She almost looks like a porcelain doll. Delicate and beautiful.

Almost as if she doesn't belong here.

But monsters do come in all shapes and sizes. And this Fort is full of them.

She walks over to one of the large desks and perches herself on the edge, her fingers curling around the lips of the desk, pinching her arms close to her sides, and crossing one ankle over the other.

"We have a job for you," she speaks almost solemnly. I nod my head but keep silent. Not exactly where I thought the discussion was heading.

Since having lived here all of my life one quickly learns the way of respect, of how to obtain it and how to keep it. One of the first and most important lessons they will teach you is to not speak unless directly spoken to. Until such a time you are to remain silent. It is seen as an act of disrespect to speak before being given permission.

With the exception of earlier today, the last time I spoke out of turn, I had been left to hang by my wrists in a steamed room without light, defecating where I hung, no food was brought, and I was barely allowed enough water to counteract the amount of sweat that poured out of my body. For three days I hung there without relief.

"There have been numerous reports of active terrorism in the south."

Her icy eyes bore into mine. "It started months ago as peaceful protests but has since led to violent riots that have wounded the beautiful city of Ansrutas. There have been a few reports of casualties." She pauses for a moment, looking down at the floor as if to choose her next words carefully. "His Majesty has already sent a large team from his Stratos military group, but they have since asked for further aid. Apparently taking care of a few wannabe rebels is too much for them to handle," she mocks, grinning maliciously, "The main problem is, more and more civilians are joining the cause, and we are now being forced to intervene, to help squash any rumours and *'misinformation'* before this goes any further." She clears her throat before continuing, "His majesty has done his best to help the people in the southern city since the war began, but it appears the people have lost faith in his abilities and leadership." She smirks at me then, a devilish grin that I've only seen on a handful of occasions, "Your assignment, Three-Nought-Nought, is to find and kill the ringleader of this *organisation* and to reaffirm the people's faith in the Stratos and his majesty." She stares at me again for a few breaths before speaking quietly, "I trust this is something you can do."

"Yes, Madame." I bow my head and hold it for a heartbeat, before looking back up at her.

She sits there unblinking; her eyes glaze over softly before a knock at the door breaks her out of her reverie. She stands, "You leave at first light. Prepare yourself, you will be gone for some time. As you are aware of our protocols you are to check in once a week, at a *minimum*.

You will have two handlers for this mission. They are there to assist you in any way they can, but remember Aella, they are not to do this for you." She levels a glare at me and opens her mouth to speak once more, "It is a shame that you will miss our end-of-month fight. The girls chosen are sure to be a spectacle." Her eyes light with fire, the icy blue deepening. "The winner will be joining my group. We only have to wait and see if she can keep up with you." She walks to the door then, while I stand there surprised at the use of my name, her hand rests on the knob. "Oh, one last thing, take it easy on these new handlers of yours, apparently they've just been transferred." She grins at me showing off her gleaming fangs. "I know how you get." She winks and leaves me alone in this vast room.

After the meeting, I take the stairs two at a making my way to the dining hall.

A strange air of trepid excitement has wrapped itself around me. Having a purpose, a goal has made me feel increasingly calm and motivated. Not even the thought of being bound, gagged, and left in the hands of The Captain could falter my mood at this moment.

Well maybe *that* could.

Walking down the busy corridor, I weave my way towards the cathedral sized hall in which most of the on-duty guards are already enjoying their afternoon breaks. The room itself is grand in size and by size alone, the exposed stone walls provide little warmth, in both respects of the word. Two protruding stone fireplaces take up the middle portion of the walls on either side, with fires that stay lit even in the height of summer. Being this high up in the mountains has its advantages, the terrain is so perilous most trespassers don't make it from one side to the other and none have ever found us, but for those that do live here, you really have to like the cold.

Criss-crossing arches overhead seem to add more height to this already monumental room and have been beautifully hand-painted with a mural of the gods at war. The art is both ethereal and horrifying, casting the gods a fight for power. No one knows if the depiction is real or a designs of the artists' choice.

The white tiled floor is absent of rugs and is littered with scrapes and chipped faces from the many years of abuse.

Four bulky wooden tables, each easily seating up to thirty or more guards, with matching wooden benches, which stretch down the sides of the room with a small break in between for the fireplaces. Four smaller sister tables take up the centre of the room currently unoccupied. These are reserved for the Furies and the program handlers.

But it's the two-story arched windows that always catch my eye, depicting a breathtaking view of the snow-capped mountains. The view, whilst stunning, is obscured slightly by the metal bars that run the length of the glass, something that I've long since grown to ignore.

Some of my sisters walk in then, yet the guards pay no mind; they continue with their lively conversations and tell each other tall tales of their past experiences.

Walking the length of the hall I stop in front of the windows next to the buffet tables that lay beneath.

Madame Campbell's, much smaller, group of Furies fill their plates in silence and take their seats in the middle of the room. I follow their lead filling my plate, and just as I'm about to take my seat I notice the snow on the tops of the mountains being blown off the peaks and disappear into the wind. I watch the charming scene for a breath before a presence appears at my shoulder, without turning I know who it is.

"My condolences for your loss. I know you two were close," I say to Aria – no, Three-Five-Nine – as she steps up to my side, her eyes full of sorrow, but she gives me a small smile in return. I turn to leave and choose an empty table to sit at by myself.

Taking my first bite from the selection of steamed vegetables on my plate, I shudder when a shrill voice calls my name.

"Siren!" Madame Valentina, squeals. The hairs on the back of my neck stand on end at the sound emanating from her tiny form.

Although she's younger than Madame Killick by a decade or so, you would think that they are the same age. That's what years of stress and conditioning will do to the body.

I look up to see her in the doorway of the dining hall, arms open wide with a bright smile on her face. Those present in the hall have each taken their turn looking between us.

Something that greatly annoys me the most, is how she thrives on being the centre of attention and how she continually tries to drag me into the spotlight with her.

I'm happy staying right where I am.

Resisting the urge to roll my eyes I stand and walk over to her to see what she wants of me. Her glossy dark brunette hair is pulled back into a simple twist and is held together with small golden floral pins. Her face is much more supple than Madame K's, and like all retired Fury's turned handlers, she holds herself proud, her chin high and her shoulders squared, accentuated further by her freshly steamed, matching black blazer and knee-length black skirt, her white shirt holds not one crease, and the look is completed with her small black pumps.

"Madame," I murmur when I finally stand in front of her, bowing my head and she drops her arms to her sides.

"Three-Nought-Nought once you've finished, I wonder if we could have a chat. It's about this year's new recruits. I would like for you to set an example for them, a little *demonstration* if you will."

I nod my head, and her smile brightens some more.

As if I have a choice.

"Fantastic! Come to the nursery. We will be in there for some time." She leaves, her heels clicking down the hall and I move back to my table to finish my food in peace. I note the wary glances directed my way from the guards and the longer I sit there the more uncomfortable they feel, some stop talking, and some even get up to leave the room entirely.

Finishing my meal quickly I get up to leave for the nursery again when another voice calls out to me.

"Three-Nought-Nought!" I turn to see Madame Killick strutting down the hallway towards me. "Where are you off to?" she queries, her face the picture of scepticism.

"Madame V has asked for my assistance," I reply, bowing my head to her.

"Ah, the demonstration she was asking about earlier." She pauses looking at me for a heartbeat, weighing something up behind her icy gaze, "Needless to say do not take all day, I am aware that you still need to pack. I've left the files for your assignment on your cot. Read through them before you leave." She turns to leave but pauses once again. "Oh, and before you go make sure to pop into my office, I still have your punishment to dole out." Her eyes are hard as she looks at me.

I nod once and turn on my heel, marching down the stairwell, to the floor below.

My knuckles rapt loudly on the door before I let myself in. Hearing Madame V in the middle of her well-rehearsed speech takes me back to some of my earliest memories of this place.

"The name *Fury* is only given to those special females who graduate from our elite program that we place you under. You will undergo a series of intense training and psychological conditioning to achieve the goals that we have set for each of you."

I slink around the outside of the group of young females sat on the floor watching her with fear in their wide eyes, to the back of the room where I lean against the back wall and cross my arms over my chest. A small handful of guards line the walls, arms joined at the wrist behind their backs, and they preside over the introduction.

I know that they're not here for anything other than this demonstration that she has in mind.

"Some would call us assassins, or spies, perhaps." She walks back and forth in front of them, "But we are so much more than that. Without us, governments would topple and whole countries would fall. Nobody and absolutely nothing moves without our knowledge or intervention." She pauses for a breath looking at all the young girls, some of whom are barely keeping themselves together. I can see that most want nothing more than to go back to wherever it was they came from, even if it was back to the streets.

"Despite what is said about our *reputation*, we do control nearly sixty per cent of the world's major governing bodies. We pull the strings for their laws, for wars and even occasionally for peace treaties." She says it as though it's a mercy. "But like everything we do, we do from the shadows. Never giving a face to the name. Ajay is only as strong its weakest member. Remember that should any of you make it to the graduation ceremony."

I roll my eyes at some of the girls that whimper from in front of me, and that's exactly the moment when all attention circles to me.

"Three-Nought-Nought if you please, to the front of the class, it's demonstration time," Madame quips, the muscles in her jaw flex as she grinds her teeth.

Oh, she definitely saw the eye roll.

The cowering girls quickly shuffle to the sides creating a narrow aisle for me to walk down.

Looking out at the sea of terrified eyes should have me feeling sympathetic towards these girls, but I lost the caring side of me long before any of these girls were even born.

"This particular female, girl's, is someone you should aspire to become." None of them react in any particular way, clearly having no idea who I am from the look of me.

"This is Three-Nought-Nought. Although from that, you won't know just how important she has become to this organisation. Her reputation is something that I'm sure most of you have heard of. The *'Siren'* and I have organised a short demonstration for you all, one that will allow you to get a better understanding of what it is we are asking of you."

Gasps sound through the room as my alternate name is revealed, and that pulls a sly smile from Madame Valentina. "This girls is our very own mythological creature. Capable of great things. If you've heard the *ghost stories* that people tell of her than you know just how capable she truly is. A myth turned legend before your very eyes." She looks about the room, the wicked light gleaming in her eyes.

"Our goal for you young ladies, is to be an equal match to our Siren." V puts her hand on my upper arm as if she's proud to be able to touch me and show me off like some prized mare.

I didn't go through years of training to become a show pony. I bite my tongue at the thought and resist the urge to roll my eyes again.

"Right! Now to the demonstration," Madame claps her hands together in excitement and ushers the girls to the far side of the room, setting them up as though they are about to have a class photo, but at least she's given me a large space so that I don't accidentally hit one of them. She turns to face the front again, tucking herself off to the side of the room, beaming with excitement like this is some play she's paid for.

"Joel if you'd be so kind." She waves over to the youngest of the guards amongst us; determination set in his grey eyes and maybe just an inkling of fear. His black hair hangs down to the tops of his pointed fae ears and over his pale forehead, brushing his eyebrows. He shifts into a fighting stance his fists raised, and his feet squared; he shakes the tension out of his shoulders and takes a deep breath.

I stand with my arms crossed over my chest, scrutinising his movements and assess his body and stance for any weaknesses.

Finding none, I scrunch my eyebrows as I figure out the most efficient way to take him down.

A giddy squeal comes from my side, and I already know it's Madame Valentina. She has taken it upon herself to monitor my progression throughout the organisation, ever since I had been given my first mission at six and I played the role of a poor homeless girl begging for scraps. All the while I had an intricate system of informants passing information back to me, which I then passed back to the guild. My first mission had not only been a success, but it became the cornerstone of my career. I was given only the best assignments.

I watch as Joel starts bouncing on his toes, psyching himself up, as if that'll help him.

I know what's coming.

He knows what's coming.

This whole demonstration is pointless.

In all actuality, she could just put on a video of me fighting and have done with this. But instead, here I am, about to beat the shit out of a guy who is bouncing on his toes and shaking out his fists.

And I'm done with waiting.

I take a step forward catching him by surprise and feign a punch to his head, which he easily dodges only to be caught in the stomach by my other fist. He grunts but isn't deterred, my guard is up within a split second as he steps forward jabbing with his right hand and stepping with his left foot.

My fingers curl around his wrist, giving it a sharp tug, the motion twirls him around quickly, his back is to my chest. I lock his hand between us. I push his arm up his back, straining the muscles. He grunts out his discomfort slamming his head back into mine, crunching my nose. His distraction is enough to force my hand open; he takes the opportunity to steps to twirl around and throw more precious punches, ones I can barely just manage to block.

Blood begins to pour freely, running over my lips, spitting it on the floor in front of his feet.

He doesn't take his time now; he steps forward over the blood; wild determination and anxiety fight within his grey eyes. One fist flies towards my face, I block with my forearm as the other goes for my rib cage. Ducking to the floor I swing my leg out catching his ankle. He stumbles back pinwheeling before hitting the floor like a sack of potatoes.

Winded but not out for the count.

He stands quickly mimicking my guarded stance.

Joel steps forward again, instantly throwing another punch at me. I dodge and take a step backwards, he follows. With each step I take, he's right there chasing me. My back hits the wall before I know it and Joel is right in front of me. He throws another punch, one destined for my nose, I duck, and his flesh meets the wall. The wood panelling cracks, splintering before my eyes. Blood gathers over his knuckles but that doesn't seem to deter him.

My quickness seems to stun him for a second and I take advantage of that by throwing a quick combination of punches to his face, chest, and ribs. He groans at the rapid hits to his torso dropping his guard slightly and I don't hesitate to punch him square in the face, his cheekbone crunching under the force.

He yelps stumbling away from me clutching his cheek, the skin split from the force of the impact.

"I yield," he hisses, forcing the words out through clenched teeth.

Madame V, beams with pride, "Excellent!" She claps her hands again and looks down at her flock of stunned and terrified girls, ignoring their wary stares as she says, "But I think we can do a little better than that though can't we?" She nods to another guard, and I watch as he steps up to the front, again looking for any sign of weakness that I can exploit.

This guard I've seen around before.

Maddon.

He's been around the Fort for a while – and that's saying a lot for a human guard - the fact that he has greying hair dappled through his dark brown locks shows just how long her been employed here. I appreciate his well-built physique as he steps into his well-acclimated fighting stance, and just like Joel, shows no sign of injury or feebleness. Before I can finish the thought, he's lunging at me, I dodge and defend against his violent fists.

Now I know why he's lasted so long.

He's relentless.

One of his fists comes reeling towards my face whilst the other one swings towards my side, I throw myself over one of the large mahogany desks, rolling across the wood, pens, and paper fly everywhere. He steps to the side moving around the table, I mirror him, the desk still between us. The items left on the desk are not heavy enough to create any real damage.

So, I rely on the only thing I can.

I hop back onto the table, using that momentum to throw myself back across the desk, a leg out in front of me like a spear.

My foot finds its mark, buried in his gut.

He grunts and flies backwards losing his footing, he lands next to the bookshelf on the opposite side of the room, the impact so heavy a few books fall from the shelves.

Maddon groans but sits up quickly, a fire blazing in his brown eyes.

Within seconds he's on two feet charging at me, a snarl on his face, his knuckles nearly white with how firm he holds his fist. His war cry of rage is almost intimidating as another series of punches are thrown at me. Some of the girls whimper and cower away, I can practically smell their fear.

He dazzles me with his upper body strength, and I'm so focused on defending my head, that I don't see him duck down, swiping my legs out from underneath me. Not until the air is forced from my lungs and I'm looking up at the ceiling.

His movements are quick.

He has me pinned beneath him, sitting on my chest, his legs on either side, raining hellfire down in the form of quick, sharp hits.

It's all I can do to block each one, to let him think he has won until he tires himself out.

That golden opportunity comes quicker than I would've expected.

Maddon's hand rises once more but he holds it there for a breath too long. Enough for me to throw out my elbow catching him squarely in his manhood.

The air whooshes from his lungs and he crumbles to the floor rolling to and fro on his back, hands cupped in between his thighs.

I roll away creating distance and stand. He tries to catch his breath, but I feel no remorse for his pain.

Madame V claps her hands in delight, dragging my attention away from the groaning man on the floor, relishing in the display of what years of selective training can create.

"Wonderful, just wonderful, see girls you'll be able to do just the same if you throw yourself into your studies."

Madame saunters over to me a fake grin plastered on her face before she whispers in my ear, "I don't appreciate the attitude, but you did put on a good show. Do not disappoint me like that again." She looks around the room, at the frightened little girls and she grins with delight, like a spider when it finds a fly tangled in its web. "Go clean yourself up," she hisses, and I respectfully bow my head, my arm crossed over my chest before stepping out of the room.

"Gather round girls. Now... Maddon quit your whining and get up! Now I'll help you to understand why you have been selected for this program. Girls and women alike are often far more overlooked in society than any other. That makes it easier for us to come and go, rather unnoticed..." she begins, but I'm through the doors before I can hear the rest of the age-old speech, the very same that I heard when I first began my own training.

I walk to the stairwell and head up to the Furies quarters, two floors above the Nursery. With the Fort being built into the heart of Mount Chasin, thanks to the sheer determination of our forefathers, this place has earned its name 'The Unconquerable' and is the largest mostly natural structure in the country.

There will come a time when the mountains fall to the sea and the stars fall from the sky, but for now, this mountain protects all those who call it home.

This particular floor of the mountain has been dedicated to the Furies. Graduates from the courses and trails that they put us through. Separate bedrooms are reserved only for those who are more seasoned in the arts of espionage, or rather, those that are allowed to leave for missions across the globe; to come and go as our program leaders see fit.

The young ones, all share quarters with their respective groups. Bunk beds are set up in rows upon rows, with up to twenty girls in one group all sharing the space. Those group rooms are on the other side of the mountain away from the private rooms. The graduated Furies have minimal contact with the new recruits until they are old enough to join the more advanced groups.

In recent years these rooms have seen Furies come and go like the changing of the seasons. The outside world is becoming harder to navigate as the years go by. Only those apt at adapting will survive to see another moon cycle. The private quarters haven't been full in a very long time since I was freshly graduated myself. Those left have been deployed all across the world in order to bring it to heel.

The floor above is the group leaders' quarters, a handful of meeting rooms along with the control room and the mission control room, the only time that we are allowed to enter there is when we get debriefed on an upcoming mission; it's also where they can assist from afar if needed.

Above them is the lab where each Fury gets their monthly injections. I'd say they help us become more compliant but that would be too simple of an explanation. What the serum does is alter our brain function to perform at our best and keep us under control. They have been experimenting recently, determined to synthesise a new way to keep the change permanent.

Having been raised here, I was taught the ways of psychological conditioning, along with Three-Five-Nine but this serum chemically alters the brains' function. Neither of us need the injection the same, but in order to make the process *fair* for the other girls, we are made to have that crap pumped into our systems every other month.

The younger girls have theirs every month, and at every month's end we are forced to hear about how they hate the burn of the serum.

The Director has two floors above the lab. One in which he works and the other as his personal quarters. Below the Furies' quarters is the dining hall coupled with the guards' rooms. Below them are the training room, gymnasium, and armoury. The garages are below that, classed as 'ground zero', that has the only exit - a large bomb-proof steel door - and further down still are the dungeons.

It takes me a while to make it to my own quarters, making a stop at the joint bathing chambers to wash the blood from my face. The bathroom is large enough to comfortably house at least thirty of us, and decorated in an array of light blues, silver and white. A series of carved, naturally heated pools are used for bathing in, private showers fill one corner, along with toilets and sinks. This is one of the few rooms to actually have any windows and even so, like the ones in the dining hall, they are bracketed by bars.

Passing door after door until I make it to my own private quarters, a silver number drilled into the soft pine door, Three-Nought-Nought. The number isn't dictated by which room you occupy but by which number you are given upon your arrival.

I close the door softly behind me after I step in and look at the basic space. The walls are grey, painted that way to match the two natural stone walls. The space is no bigger than a storage cupboard. A single bed is pushed up against one wall, the very same I spent the past three days holed up in as I fought back against the effect of the serum. The scratchy blanket tucked neatly across the width of it. The three-legged wooden stool takes up one corner. A narrow wardrobe tucked into another, and a small table sits next to my bed, with a light and an alarm clock. A worn, beige rug is the only decorative piece that I have been allowed. Natural light streams through the tiny window no bigger than the slits in a Rise that archers use to fire arrows through. The size nor the simplicity of the room bothers me much, any free time that I have is usually spent training.

I immediately go to start packing clothes and upon opening my wardrobe, which has been crammed into one corner, I see my all-black clothes staring back at me. I pick out several, long-sleeved t-shirts, with multiple matching pairs of breeches and fold them neatly into a pile then pack them into my large backpack. It only takes me a few minutes to pack up my clothes and footwear, yet a nagging feeling gnaws away at me. I check and check again that I have everything when it hits me.

Weapons.

Madame said that I will be away for a while, but I won't be able to carry months' worth of ammunition and weaponry. I need to pack light and smart.

Within minutes I'm striding through the glass doors of the training room, the sound of my fellow sisters practising their forms on the black and yellow mats resonate down the hallway. Each of them move in sync with the other. Madame Tuli grants me a nod as I pass by, barking out orders for them to start again and to do it better this time.

None of the program leaders are to be messed with. But Madame Tuli is one especially you don't want to get on the wrong side of.

She comes from the East, where the land is barren and covered in towering dunes of sand, the sun beats down mercilessly, and where only the toughest make it out alive.

The back door to the armoury lies on the far side of the training room, and the stares of some of these girls don't go unnoticed neither by me nor Madame T.

A whip is cracked, drawing their attention back to her. Her signature weapon is a bullwhip. Tuli has a varied selection, ones made from leather, ones with claws attached to the end, some short and some impossibly long. She's rarely seen one without one coiled on her hip.

They're just lucky she didn't decide to turn it on them.

With the click of the lock, I slip soundlessly into the armoury to be greeted with the sound of heavy rock music punishing the sound system.

Gregory is hunched over one of his many countertop spaces, the intricate pieces of a weapon spread out in front of him. With a dirty rag in one hand and a cup of coffee – no doubt with a splash of whiskey – in the other. He looks up at the intrusion, his blonde hair loose and flowing down the back of his neck, a few strands fall across his face and his bushy blonde beard splays across his chest. His blue eyes meet mine through his thin, golden-framed glasses and a small smile graces his face.

"Ella," he greets, "what can I do for you?" He sits on a high stool behind the counter, scrubbing rigorously at the barrel of one of the new pistols.

"Gregory," I reply by way of greeting as I bow my head with a voice that is devoid of all warmth. "I've been given an assignment and require a weapons cache."

A look of confusion crosses through his eyes. "Assignment? The Director didn't tell me he was sending you out again." He sits taller looking ruffled.

"I believe it is 'impromptu.'"

"Impromptu, my arse. Nothing they do is impromptu." He rolls his eyes clambering, ungracefully from the stool. "Right then. When do you leave?"

"Tomorrow morning at first light."

"Fuckin..." Anger laces the word, but he sighs and calms himself once again, "Right, you want your pistols?" he asks, as if I can truly want for anything. Without looking he turns around facing the mesh metal cabinets behind the counter housing a remarkable number of weapons. Gregory has once referred to it as his 'sweet shop'. I didn't quite understand what he meant, but I smiled all the same.

The click of a key in the lock and groaning of the cabinet door force my attention over to him, where he pulls out a case, my number embellished on the top. With a skull and two crossed daggers underneath.

"How long are you gone for kid?" he asks, walking over, placing the case down on the counter before opening the lid.

"The date is undetermined. Madame made it sound as though it could be months."

He stills and both of us stare at each other unmoving. Gregory clears his throat and turns away without saying a word. There's something unspoken and all-knowing in his eyes. Something he's not likely to share. Open my mouth to ask the question.

"Well come on then, let's pick the rest of them out." He cuts me off, not so subtly changing the subject. Lifting the upper part of the countertop he allows me through to the back room.

I peruse each cabinet, my hands clasped together behind my back, coming to a stop in front of the glass case full of wicked-looking knives. A grin savagely splits my face, until I see Gregory in the reflection of the glass, only one step behind me.

I'm trained in all of the weapons in this locker storage, having had nothing but time in my two and a half decades of life but training, and the opportunity to expand my knowledge and skill – and whilst guns are fun, there's something far more intimate about a knife.

There's nothing more satisfying than holding the power of life and death in your hands, getting to watch the life drain from their eyes.

A shiver runs down my spine, sending goosebumps across my skin.

Gregory opens the glass case; a small draw pulls out at the bottom a sheathed combat blade rests on the velvet-cushioned interior.

My blade.

The ebony handle sucks in all the light that touches it, while the wing-engraved blade reflects it like a mirror.

He chuckles at me, "You did always have a fascination with knives, didn't you kid? You want any of the others?"

I brush my fingertips over a few of them before taking them out of their moulds, three in total. A classic combat knife as long as my forearm, a sickeningly curved blade that looks like it belongs on some evil, demonic creature's paw, and a small knife that looks like it could be used as a letter opener. I waste no time in sheathing them into my belt holsters and one in my bootleg.

I quickly pick out some of his best guns. A sniper rifle for those long-range shots, two of my favourite assault rifles – for well, you know, just in case – and a few extra handguns. Two weeks' worth of ammunition is also shoved into my hand.

"Good choices, as always," Gregory notes, his tone solemn. I watch him move to re-lock the cabinets and grab a large duffle bag for me to use.

"Right, sign your name on this form, you know the drill." He points to the clipboard hanging from a rusty nail on the wall.

I scribble my name on the paper and bow my head, my arm across my chest.

"Aella." Gregory is the only other person beyond Madame K, to use my name. It still surprises me to hear it from her, but Gregory had always made a point to learn everyone's by heart. "Be careful." Concern flashes across his face, but the emotion is lost on me. I bow again and turn to leave, to complete the last thing on my list.

Find Madame K.

CHAPTER FOUR
IT'S ALL ABOUT THE OUTLOOK.

My soft knock is the only sound down the otherwise empty corridor, even though I know no one truly lurks in the shadows my eyes still scan my surroundings as I wait for permission to enter. Madame, sitting at her small desk, looks up as I enter, her attention temporarily taken from the stack of papers spread out in front of her. Madame's face is impassive as she waves her hand towards a seat in front of her desk.

"Are you ready?" she asks, eyeing the stuffed duffel bag slumped on the floor beside the chair I occupy.

"Yes Madame, I'm just getting back from the armoury now."

"Good," she nods, her gaze icy as it latches onto my own while she stares at me and at nothing, all at once. "You will not be receiving punishment. We do not have the time to carry it out. But do not mistake me, I do not want to hear you speaking out of turn again. Do you understand?"

I nod. Feeling indifferent to the whole situation as it already is. I do not fear punishment, no matter the method. Each time is another lesson learned.

"Aella," she clasps her hand together and leans against the desk, "There is something I feel you need to know about this mission. Now this is confidential information. Only the Director and a select few know. Not even I'm supposed to know. But I believe this could affect the outcome if you are not told." A knock strikes against the door cutting her off. Her eyebrows scrunch in annoyance, she snaps her mouth shut and I can almost hear her teeth grinding together. "Enter," she calls.

Madame Campbell pokes her head around the door, her fiery red hair tied back in an elegant curly updo. "Oh, my apologies Yvonne, I thought you were alone. Don't forget we have the monthly meeting in a few minutes."

"Yes. Thank you, Michelle," she replies, her temper slipping through into her tone, as her muscles flex in her jaw, an action Madame C either doesn't see or chooses to ignore.

"Three-Nought-Nought. I have to go, but if there's time in the morning, come see me again." I nod and collect my bag getting up to take my leave.

I bow to Madame C on my way past and make my way down the hallway and back to my quarters, to place the weapons bag in there before joining the others for dinner.

Morning comes quickly, the howling wind forces itself against the glass of the tiny window in my room, and through the cracks of the sealant. My alarm blares, waking me before the sun has even risen. Slamming my hand down against the screaming alarm clock, I roll over onto my back, looking up at the ceiling; the silver of the morning light is the only indication that a new day has begun. Everything else is still painfully plain and dreadfully the same.

I throw the covers off and quickly dress myself not knowing when exactly my transport will arrive. Brushing through my hair, I pull out the knots before braiding it and let it dangle down my back. The cold of the morning has me buttoning up my fur-lined winter coat before I've even made it outside the blast doors into the wilderness beyond.

Hauling my backpack up onto my shoulders, I pick up the duffle bag and decide to try and find Madame Killick once more.

The squeak of my boots on the polished floor has me internally cringing with each step. My hand is raised ready to knock on her office door, when Madame C's head pops out from around her door, looking as though she has been up all night. Her tired eyes and dishevelled hair allow me to peek behind the meticulously kept mask she always wears.

Just like the rest of them.

She's usually the picturesque aspiration of perfection.

Not today, however.

Today she simply looks tired.

"Yvonne is not in. I would know." The venom in her voice doesn't go unnoticed. "What are you doing here at this time?" She looks behind her, her eyes widen for a brief second then turns her predatory gaze back to me. "Well? Answer me."

"My apologies Madame. She asked to speak with me before I departed, but I can see she's not here." I bow my head holding it there.

"So? Go! Don't let me hold you up," she hisses. I pick my head back up and turn without another word.

"Has she gone?" A harsh male whisper comes from behind her door.

"Shut up, you imbecile!" she snaps back.

I take several flights of stairs down to the dining hall, the smell of different meats cooking, and eggs makes my stomach grumble loudly. I fill my plate quickly, sitting alone in the hall, only a handful of guards are in here doing the same as I, those who are just finishing their night shift and those who are just beginning the morning one.

I eat quickly checking the clock every few minutes, my foot taps against the stone with a much-awaited anticipation.

A beat-up four-wheel drive is parked in the middle of the vast room. More vehicles line the sides of the room, buggies, armoured cars, and off-road motorbikes. All painted black with a single number at the rear. None carry plates, making them perfect for a much-needed escape.

The blast door is already open and the blizzard outside has calmed enough that I can see beyond my nose, the flurries of snow find their way inside decorating the stone tiles in patches of white. A few on-duty armed guards stand beside the door, their attention split between watching the landscape beyond and the rumbling bright red vehicle, with flecks of paint peeling from the bumpers.

There's no one here to see me off.

Not only is it too early for such a thing, but it's also not like I'd know what to do even if someone were.

I turn back to get the last glance that I'll get of this place. The only place I've ever called home, at least for a few months anyway.

Movement from the floor-to-ceiling glass windows above drags my attention to the training room that overlooks the garage. A broad-shouldered male silhouette stands over the space like a king in his castle.

I suppose he is in reality.

His sharp features are obscured by the darkened room, but just by his shadow alone in know who it is. He stands there in his classic three-piece suit with his hands in his pockets. The material is expensive and luxurious, not a single crease will be in sight and all of that I can get just from knowing who that male is. The endless black eyes stared down at me.

The Director.

He takes one of his hands out of his pockets and presses it against the glass. The disgust I feel does not mar my face, but my heart still feels it. That is something that they cannot control. I may not be in control of my own body but that does not mean I don't still have one hand on the wheel internally. Before I know it, my knee is pressed to the tile of the garage floor and my head is bowed in submission with my arm across my chest. An act of respect that is always due to him.

The door to my transport opens.

"Come on then, Siren. The road isn't going to be easy especially in this blizzard, so we'll need to get a head start if I'm going to get you there on time."

I rise at the sound of a masculine voice and turn to see my driver approach me, his name tag reading, Warren. I nod my head to him, and he picks up my weapons bag. "Gods, what do you have in here?" he grunts, lifting the strap over his shoulder; he stumbles back to the car. I place my backpack next to it and climb in the backseat, strapping myself in.

Warren joins me moments later behind the wheel.

"Ready kid?" He smiles at me through the mirror, the wrinkles around his eyes deepening with the action. His salt and pepper hair makes me question if he should be driving us both down this mountain, but his still shining brown eyes tell me he's not as old as I think.

He needs no confirmation from me to begin driving.

Moments later we pass through the gigantic weatherproof garage doors, and I grant myself one more glimpse.

The Director stands there as still as a statue, I can just barely make out the rise and fall of his chest. His hand falls away from the glass, allowing it to simply dangle by his side.

The sun blinds me once again as we turn around the corner of the pass we are travelling down, telling me that we have already been on this descent for a few hours now at least. Warren had made several attempts to make conversation with me at the start of the journey to which I gave him minimal answers. Something he already expects from the Furies, but it's still something that doesn't get easier with time. Watching him deflate tugs at my heartstrings. But there is nothing I can do.

Protocol is everything.

My nerves are shot by the time we make it to the halfway point, where thankfully Warren suggests we take a break. The fresh air is a blessing, and I remember why I and the other Furies enjoy being deployed so much. The forest at the base of the mountains stretches on for miles before us. Warren explains the rest of the route to me, using the ridges of the mountain as his guide. I nod and smile in all the right places, but the only thing I can truly focus on is the gushing waterfall that feeds the equally impressive river below, moving rapidly, snaking off into the distance and the valley's reservoir.

The engine rattles to life once again and is just as deafeningly loud as it was when we were amongst the peaks of the twin mounts.

The fact that Warren has even made it up the savage mountain passes is a blessing from the Gods all in itself. From somewhere deep inside, I bring myself to pray to the God Faramund, who protects and guides those on the road. Known sometimes simply as, 'the wanderer'.

I've never been the religious type.

But heights really aren't my thing.

The wind itself is still stirring up a violent storm, shaking the car on all sides. I'm silently impressed with Warren's skill at keeping us on the road. The terrain isn't the easiest to navigate, especially in the ice and snow, where passes have been blocked by fallen trees and broken rock.

I suppose this wouldn't be a bad place to die.

Just not right now.

Spring approaches in the south and a small part of me is looking forward to being warm when I walk around and not constantly having to deal with numb fingers and blue lips. The temperatures up here won't change much until it gets closer to summer in the flatlands. For now, up here we still have a few more months of staring out at the snow and can relish the feeling of the ice-cold winds penetrating through to our bones.

That's what I think about as I try desperately to ignore the thousand-foot drop that is less than one metre away from the car, as it rumbles on over rocks and bumps over crevices and cracks.

The sun is high in the sky by the time we make it to the bottom. Each of my muscles aches with tension as I exit the vehicle.

The feeling of the spongy mossy ground underneath me feels more energising than I thought it ever could.

I nearly fall over my own feet, in my haste to stretch out the soreness from my limbs.

Pine trees, as tall as most buildings, tower over us as I take in the surroundings of the forest. The birdsong is something I've secretly missed about being in the mountains. Sure, the birds flock to the forests further north when the weather gets warmer, but they leave just as quickly when the first frost comes back.

Warren, holding both of my bags, takes the lead and guides me along a hidden moss-covered path through some dense, moist brush, the noise of conversation and the smell of cooking meats greet us before they come into view.

Multiple wooden shacks built in a circle all surround a campfire in the centre and log seating borders the large bricked-off fire pit. A couple of tall wooden watchtowers are hidden further away from the main campsite, barely visible through the mass of thick tree trunks.

Around thirty male guards are situated down here at the outpost. Their singular job is to deter people from asking questions. I can imagine it can get quite boring here. But no one stays here long enough for boredom to become a problem, each month they are carted back up to the peaks and fresh guards are brought down. A healthy mix of fae and mortals call this place home and not a single one of them bats an eyelid at our approach.

Warren turns to me and tells me to stay put, I nod looking around at everyone's faces and the scenery beyond. From the corner of my eye, I watch him walk over to a sandy blonde-haired fae, leaning forward to whisper quietly in his ear.

That catches my attention.

The fae's eyes lock with mine when I turn my head to watch the interaction between the two. He looks me up and down and nods to Warren before standing up. Warren gives me a small smile and follows the fae back over to me.

I observe this stranger cautiously. He seems confident in himself; he holds his chin up high and he too, gives me a gentle smile as he nears.

His muscles are visible underneath the thin dark grey t-shirt he wears.

It's warmer down here than in the mountains but I wouldn't have thought t-shirt weather.

But who am I to judge?

Tattoos decorate his throat and the sides of his neck, and the intricate designs are so large I'm sure they expand down onto that well-toned chest. Every inch of his arms are covered in them and each time his muscles move the designs contort and swell.

My eyes roam farther down still, to his hands. His hands where the veins are visible.

Something unknown warms me from within.

"Siren, a pleasure to have you with us. I'm Darian, I'm the commander of this outpost and if you need anything please feel free to ask," he introduces himself, breaking my train of thought. I look down to see his outstretched hand.

"Oh, my apologies. I forgot. It's been a bit of time since we last had a Fury pass through. I almost forgot the *no touching* rule of the code." He grins and a faint blush spreads across his cheeks and he retracts his hand. "If you'll follow me."

We pass by cabin after cabin, until we come to the smallest one, devoid of light. A swinging chair creaks softly in the chilling breeze, my eyes instantly go to the shadows of the forest beyond, scanning the bushes. Even these guardians have this outpost under control, being aware of my surroundings had become second nature to me.

I follow him up the wooden steps that groan loudly under our weight.

"Yeah, we need to get those fixed," he excuses pushing the door open. "I'll quickly light this fire for you, we weren't sure what time you would be joining us, otherwise this would've already been done."

"Thank you," I murmur, taking in the room.

Because that's all it is.

One room.

It's a small and quaint space, well in keeping with the forest outside. Small potted herbs are the only spot of green on the inside, and tired natural wood counters take up most of the back wall of the lodge. A coal stove splits the counter space, and the small window above it looks out at the daunting trees behind the cabin, letting in the only glow of natural light.

Built into one of the side walls is a set of bunk beds, only two in this cabin, not that we need more than that, but the cabin does look a little sparse.

In front of the fire, a large suede-covered couch sits draped in a beige and brown, colour-washed throw with two miserable-looking cushions, a similar-looking armchair sits closer to the fire and a fraying, deep red rug lies beneath it all. Above the splintering mantle, a stag head mounted on the wall looms, forming a spine-chilling shadow that devours most of the floor.

After he lights the fire, Darian turns to me with a smile, his bright green eyes glow in the low light of the flames, his pale skin a sweet pink from the cold and a small barely-there scar cuts through the otherwise immaculate skin of his jaw.

He has a youthfully handsome face with a muscular build. But he could still be several decades old, if not older. Damn those fae genetics.

He's dazzlingly handsome, there's no doubt about that.

"Your handlers have checked in at their latest checkpoint. They're travelling in from another job, otherwise, they would be here to greet you. There's a few more hours in the day yet but I don't doubt that they will be here before sundown."

I nod in understanding, unbuttoning my coat and I throw it over the back of the sofa.

"I don't expect you to sit in here all day. It's necessary to ask that if you go for a walk, you don't go too far. There's a small stream nearby where we collect our own water, so if you want to wash up or drink, which will have to do."

"I'll just put your bags down here kiddo," Warren huffs, and I turn to him, having completely forgotten he was here.

"Thank you," I reply, and watch him go unnaturally still.

"You're welcome," he clears his throat, regaining his composure.

"Lunch is being cooked, I'm sure you smelt it on your way over. I'll set a plate out for you whilst you get settled or you won't get any with these animals," Darian grins and the warmth behind it nearly knocks the breath from my body.

I bow my head and an awkward silence blankets us.

"Come Warren, let's get you fed as well," Darian says, ushering him out of the door. "We will be out here if you need anything, Siren."

A small wooden bucket sits next to the cool box in the small kitchen. I pick it up and head back outside. The twenty or so guards all sit around the lit campfire eating and laughing with one another. Warren amongst them.

Without wasting time, I take the bucket and head into the forest, past one of the guard towers and further still, scaling over logs growing fungi and moss-covered stones, until I hear the sweet trickle of running water. The smell of the damp ground is more potent here, the foliage around, greener. Taking the bucket, I dunk it under the running water, careful not to swipe up any little fish or swimming frogs. A rustle in the bushes gives me pause. My hand slides slowly to the blade at my side, my fingers curling around the hilt. When I don't hear it again, I stand up, looking around. My search comes up fruitless and I decide to head back towards the camp.

Upon my arrival, my name is called.

"Siren, come over here! I saved you a seat." Darian waves animatedly.

I nod and place the bucket down beside the door to my cabin and make my way over.

"Here." He hands me a plate piled high with deer meat and home-grown vegetables while I take a seat on one of the uncomfortable logs.

"Thank you," I reply.

"Noah is our resident chef, so apologies if it's burnt." He grins, his smaller fae fangs peeking out from underneath his full lips.

"Hey, if you don't like it. Don't eat it." A white-haired mortal says. His blue eyes warm with amusement, presumably Noah.

"I'm sure it will be amicable," I answer, taking my first bite. Riotous laughter bursts forth amongst those around, and my brows scrunch in confusion.

It's not until the flavours hit my tongue that everything else fades away; the herby, salty, juicy meat melts in my mouth and the soft buttery vegetables partner up in a way I've never tasted before. Food has mostly been used as a basic need, with no grandeur about it, but this has made me experience it in a wholly different way.

"Thanks." Noah quips back he appears deflated.

Darian nudges my side, his face alight with humour, something I couldn't even begin to process. I turn back to my plate and finish my meal in silence. Before long I retreat back to the solidarity of my empty cabin.

I drop down onto the lumpy sofa and dig out my phone from my pocket, after having retrieved it from my lockbox back at the Fort, I fire off a quick text to Madame K, informing her that I made it to the outpost in one piece.

I take off my boots and pad over to my bags, grabbing out one of my many books and one of my dual-wield pistols. The matte black of the paint swallows the flickering light of the fire as I run my thumb along the barrel, it's been too long since I saw these last. The embossed skull and daggers design protrudes from the otherwise sleek surface of the weapon, the depiction matches that of its twin that still sits inside the case at the bottom of the bag.

Shaking off the dust from the knitted throw on the back of the couch I tuck myself under it in front of the fire, my pistol balancing on my knee as I open up my book and slide out the bookmark, carrying on from where I left off last time. A book that is not for educational purposes is usually forbidden back at the Fort. Madame K has beaten me a handful of times for bringing them back, claiming if I had time to buy books, I clearly wasn't doing my work to the standard they have come to expect. Even still she has since confiscated the books from me. I thought that it would be the last time I saw them until I opened my numbered lockbox only to find them neatly stacked there with a note from Madame K, telling me to keep this quiet.

The sun is low in the sky when a knock at the door sounds, kicking off the blanket I hop up and open it to reveal Darian. All traces of humour gone from his face. "I've just had word from your handlers. They're running late and have decided to stop off in Ellwey for the night. They have asked that I escort you south to meet them there." He gives my face a once over and a polite smile. "I'll come and collect you in the morning but for now get some rest and I'll see you in the morning, Siren."

I nod and close the door.

As the hours tick by and the sky darkens further, tender taps pat against the roof and windows as a slow, drizzly rain comes down and the wind picks up whipping down the chimney and fighting with the fire. I place another few small logs into the flames, before putting my book back in my bag. I change quickly and crawl into bed placing my pistol under my pillow, my mind overcome with exhaustion.

Blinding light and a deafening ringing in my ears wake me from a deep slumber.

Muffled screams surround me from all directions. Explosions silence each voice and sends debris soaring through the air. Instinct flares, telling me I need to move and to do it now. Pulling myself up I nearly scream at the pain throbbing through my leg. Looking around I see myself lying in a patch of claggy mud, trees are catching fire all around me and bodies lay scattered throughout, what can only be described as a battlefield. My hand flies to my thigh trying to stop the agony as I try to stand once more.

Another boom is heard, louder this time.

Wetness dampens the sides of my face. Touching my ears I find blood coating my fingers.

Forcing myself to sit up, I see mounds of earth all around me and bodies lie at my feet; soldiers Anaphi's colours of red and gold surround me like some sort of mass grave. The one closest to me, a mere boy, barely of age, lies across my leg, his eyes stare up unfocused towards the clear blue sky. With my uninjured leg, I kick the too-young male off my feet, praying for forgiveness from the Mother of Gods, Emmita.

Using whatever strength I have left; I turn myself over onto my belly and start dragging myself up the first mound. Only to find it's not made of earth like I thought. Body after body has been piled up, putting me in a crater, made from the corpses of men and women alike, giving their lives in service to their country.

Fire begins to burn through my veins, starting from my leg and travelling all the way to my shoulders and neck, white light blares behind my eyes and a scream like no other tears through my throat.

Broken, it's definitely broken.

Gritting my teeth, I haul myself over the pile of bodies, gripping onto whatever I can. The mud coating me from head-to-toe acts like a second skin. No one will be able to tell I'm out here.

No help will come for me. A flicker of dread spears through me mingled with a hint of relief. Even as I crest the mass of armoured soldiers.

Looking around at the clearing, panting hard, I see purple and red-covered bodies smeared into the thick claggy mud. Soldiers and horse carcasses from both sides lie dead across the muddy landscape.

Rolling down the other side of the mound was a bad decision, but one I made all the same. Tears flow freely from my eyes. I begin to drag my broken body through the cold blood-soaked sludge drowning me, weighing me down.

A wet squelching sound rings clear in my ear; dullened screams echo, drowned out only by the sound of thundering gunshots, and the boom of grenades, as the fighting continues.

Trampling footsteps slogging through the mud suddenly fill my ears and shouts ring out, the words muffled and quiet

Warm hands touch my sides and I'm abruptly turned over, my gaze locked with midnight black eyes, flecks of silver are the only thing that breaks up the all-consuming abyss.

The cold of the floor leaves me as I'm lifted into the air into strong warm arms, pain tears through me but it's the unusual sense of safety I feel from this stranger, which allows me to close my eyes briefly as my vision begins to blur. The shock of my injury finally begins to take over and my blood runs cold until I'm shivering in the arms of my saviour. The male's mouth moves but I can't hear what he says.

My body feels heavy.

Limb by aching limb of my body begins shutting down.

Death has come for me after all.

I scarcely register the rocking of my body, my legs swinging back and forth as he starts to run with me coddled in his arms, my breath starts to slow and my eyes close with it. The beating of his heart is frantic. He talks again this time to someone else, but my eyes are too heavy to open. The only thing I can think to do now is pray to Death, to Damien, for safe passage to the other side as darkness claims my soul, dragging me deep down into his warm embrace.

I wake early the next morning just as dawn has broken over the horizon, the light filtering through the many trees along with the waking birds that sing happily from high in the branches. Raindrops drip noisily from the roof, splashing down on the already-soaked ground.

The warm light of the sun is what coaxes me out of bed, that, and the smell of bacon cooking in a pan outside. Some of the guards' voices can already be heard chatting amongst themselves as they cook breakfast.

Changing quickly, I check my bags not once but twice to make sure I haven't left anything and place them on the porch outside. I move to make the bed and wash my face before joining the still-sleepy males outside, with my coat buttoned to as high as it can go.

"Good morning, Siren," Darian greets me with a yawn, a steaming cup of coffee in his hands.

I nod to him and sit.

Noah, the white-haired guard from the night before, hands me a plate with bacon, eggs, and toast on it.

"I hope this is more than 'amicable' for you this morning," he grins, throwing me a wink.

"I'm sure it will be acceptable," I reply, taking the plate.

A choking sound comes from my right, I turn to see Darian laughing into his coffee.

"Come on Siren, you're killing me," Noah moans.

"Not quite. You wouldn't even know I was killing you or not, because you would not see me coming." I take my first bite effectively ending the conversation.

"That's unnerving," Noah retorts, biting his lip, looking for sympathy from his companions.

"Man, give it up," Darian chuckles at Noah's shocked expression.

The guys chat happily amongst themselves, and I sit there observing until Darian stands.

"I'm going to run some quick checks on our transport, I'll come and grab you in a minute." I nod watching him walk away. He really does have a great physique; and his perfectly round behind...

"Morning Siren." Warren sits down next to me, pulling my attention away from ogling Darian.

"Morning," I reply, my voice a little gravelly from lack of use.

Noah approaches once more, handing Warren his own plate of food and again a comfortable chatter takes over. I listen whilst scanning the ever-extending shadows in the tree line. The bushes rustle slightly. I can't tell whether it is from the breeze or something else, but whatever it is, it's gone before I get a good look.

"Siren!" Darian calls from the other side of the clearing, "Time to go."

"See ya, kiddo. Good luck," Warren says, giving me a soft smile. I nod and stand; grab my bags and follow in Darian's wake.

The bonnet of the vehicle is open when I get there, Darian leans against the side of the car talking to someone at the top of the watchtower. I clear my throat softly to let him know I'm here, to which he practically jumps out of his skin, his wide-eyed stare says it all. Trying not to laugh I point to my nose; he mirrors the action pulling his hand away to look at his fingers finding oil there. I throw my bags in the back of the matte-black car and buckle myself into the passenger side.

The bonnet drops a minute later and Darian waves goodbye to his comrades and climbs in beside me.

"Ellwey is a few hours away so get comfy," he says buckling his safety belt around him, starting the engine, "you know any good car games?" he smiles, pulling away from the camp.

CHAPTER FIVE
SMALL TOWN PRIDE

The trees began thinning out by the early afternoon. We stopped only once to stretch our legs.

Noah packed us some food for the journey and Darian's chatter had helped pass the time. I answered what I could, where I could, but some things I had stayed silent on.

Coming to the end of the forest surrounding the foot of the mountains gave me little relief, I haven't left the Fort in well over a year, even to do what I was trained for.

After I made my way back to the Fort by myself despite my broken leg and other injuries, it took weeks for the program leaders to make a decision on what to do with me. I was put on bedrest in the end, not even allowed to do basic training. I'm unsure whether the decision was enforced by Madame K or the Director, either way, without it I would be six feet under in the frozen tundra. I watched as my sisters came and went, and slowly began questioning when it would once again be my turn. I love my job and it became unbearably to watch them succeed when I could do nothing.

The sun shines bright in the apex of the clear blue sky. After lunch words were something hard to come by, at least for Darian. So, I've taken to staring out the window at the scenery flashing by. The cold and miserable morning has given way to a truly stunning afternoon, the sun shines down and dries up the moisture from the night.

We travel south-west for several miles skirting by the young trees bordering the widespread woods and we start to pass by wild, flower-filled fields, with bees and butterflies fluttering between the grasses and birds dancing up high on the breeze. Before long, neater upturned fields spread out in front of us. Farmers working in those fields have already begun planting new crops for the harvest season.

The expansive village of Ellwey resides at the bottom of a deep, green valley split in two by a wild, winding river that snakes in and around the town, bringing both land and water together in graceful harmony. White fluffy tufts wander the fields that scale up the hills, the mass of sheep makes it look as though the clouds have lowered to brush gently against the tops of the rolling fields.

The centuries-old stone buildings are swarmed with decades-old plant life that scales up walls and fences throughout the town, in an array of beautiful flowers that bloom from each twist of the vines and free-standing bushes.

The same families that have lived here for generations have passed down the legacy of agriculture and prosperity, making this the oldest town in Anaphi. Those same families have devoted their lives to pleasing the Goddess of the Harvest, Arista, paying homage to her to protect their crops and bring them a profitable harvest. Her statues line the streets, adorned with flower garlands and multi-coloured ribbons that flow gently in the fresh spring breeze; candles are lit for her in the temples' windows, with the eccentric wooden doors bordered by beautiful spring flowers.

Upon reaching the main road through the town, we drive slowly taking in the decorated village. Bedecked with large flower planters on each side and bunting hanging across the width of the street above us, with chalk signs standing proud outside of a variety of shops drawing customers in; from the blooming flowers outside of the florists, to the hanging meats in the butcher's glass window, even down to the cobbler's emporium with shoes mounted on stands. Children playing in the street help make this place feel joyful and free, but when they abruptly stop and stare at us passing through, a sinister shiver rolls down my spine.

We turn off the main road onto one of the many side streets, the stark difference is mind-blowing from the civilised almost sweet, cobblestone main street, to the much smaller eerie dirt road lined with terraced houses, with roofs that bow from years of water damage. It's like stepping into an entirely different town. The few people out on the street stop whatever conversations they were engaged in, to glare at us through the slightly tinted windows. At first glance, I can tell that this community consists of mostly mortals. Few of them have the pointed ears of the fae, and not a single shifter in sight.

"This is odd," I murmur, scanning everyone.

"What is?" Darian eyes the people, as we crawl by them looking increasingly uneasy, his grip tightening on the wheel.

A small girl stands just off to the side on the walkway, one hand laced through her mother's as she watches us glide by, her other hand clutches tightly onto a stuffed pink pony toy. Her eyes glow a fiery amber, with a pink button nose and shining auburn hair, the same as her mother's; freckles dot her cheeks and nose.

We come to a stop at the front of an old-fashioned inn, with exposed wooden beams and faded stone walls, decorated with little flowery window boxes under muntin-style panes.

Darian is the first to exit the vehicle, groaning as he stretches out his stiff muscles before moving to the back of the car, popping open the back. I join him quickly and he offers to help carry in my bags, he nods towards the front door, allowing me to walk in before him. I can see him looking up and down the street, as I walk by him.

"Not a friendly bunch are they." He leans in to speak quietly to me.

I shake my head, agreeing with him.

Upon stepping inside, I scan the area to see a large assortment of chairs and tables residing throughout the main bar area, in varying degrees of style and decay. It smells of off ale and damp timber, a lingering stench of vomit stales the air and the sconces on the wall are engulfed in years of grime.

The outside is a total façade for what resides inside.

Following the sound of hushed voices, I follow Darian further into the room and he begins conversing quickly with two familiar faces. I place my bags on the floor and offer the pair a respectful bow with my arm crossed across my chest meeting their eyes as I rise

I latch on to the fathomless black eyes with flecks of welcoming silver. The male rises from his table and walks to me, his dark skin glowing even in the low light.

"Three-Nought-Nought." His voice drips with honey, "It's good to see you made it in one piece." His alluring scent of amber and vanilla fills my nose and that unfamiliar sense of calm I didn't know I could feel. My heart swells to see him once again. Happy and healthy.

Something flickers in his eyes, but it's gone before I can get a read on it.

His partner is busy talking to Darian, standing with his back to me.

I meet the black-eyed male's glare once again and he offers me a small familiar smile and stays by my side until Darian shakes the second male's hand.

"Siren, it has been an honour. I will be departing shortly; I wish you luck and no doubt I will see you upon your return."

I bow to Darian, my fist across my chest. He smiles and leaves the inn without another word.

The second male turns to me then, tension bracketing his mouth.

"Let's get these upstairs," he grunts, taking my duffle bag from my hand, he turns to leave before I can take it back.

We walk past the receptionist's desk, where a young girl sits, twiddling her thumbs. I don't miss the way she ogles both of my handlers as we pass, with a twinkle in her eyes. When she turns to me, her eyes widen slightly, the smile drops as she looks away.

Each step creaks louder the higher we climb, following behind the dark-haired male silently until he stops outside a numbered room.

"This is your room, Ae..." he cuts himself off, snapping his mouth shut and a muscle ticks in his jaw, "Three-Nought-Nought," he hisses through clenched teeth.

I nod and step into the room and stop dead at the sight, utterly astounded. The sickly-sweet scent of floral potpourri forces its way into my nose, trying to mask any trace of mould that I already know grows in every corner. The draft through the floorboards is strong and wafts a cold breeze throughout the lace curtains, the crumbling windowsill doesn't look like it can hold the windowpane for much longer and the pane itself is grimy through and through, distorting the view beyond of the quaint little village.

"Surprisingly your room is nicer than ours." I turn at the sound of a melodic voice.

"Don't look so surprised. He's right," the hazel-eyed handler says. The first, with unmistakable black and silver eyes, strides across the room to sit on the narrow and probably lumpy bed. His long lean legs stretch out across the coloured-washed comforter as he rests back against the headboard.

The other, broader, male stands in the middle of the room looking around, my duffel bag forgotten by the door. He grunts as he looks up at the sagging ceiling speckled with watermarks and something brown that I'd rather not know about. "I take that back," he mumbles, closing the door.

My head tilts to the side and my attention flickers between the two of them.

"It's been a while." The one on the bed states, keeping his gaze connected with my own.

I nod my head and turn to the second. Hazel eyes latch onto mine, but neither of us says a word to the other. The dullness of his eyes gives me pause until the first speaks again, breaking the intense stare down.

"It's nice to see you too, Aella. It's been a long time, how are you?" Sarcasm rolls off of his tongue like waves against the shore. I tilt my head to the side trying to find a viable response, but promptly come up empty.

A little over a year ago, on my last mission from the Fort, I became tangled in a particularly brutal battle in the midst of the ongoing war. In which I had broken my leg and became stuck in a vulnerable position, these two males had been running to and fro rescuing those they could.

I still dream of that day. It was the day I thought I lost everything until they found me, covered head to toe in mud and my own blood.

Somewhere deep in my mind, I can almost recall the memories from all those years ago, even if the images are hazy as if I'm watching them through a sheer curtain. A part of me feels bound and gagged in the background in the farthest reaches of my own mind screaming to get out, feeling the connection between us twist and strain.

That painful stabbing ache throbs across my forehead reminding me that no matter the familiarity amongst us all a Fury cannot have attachments and I'm only here to complete the mission that I have been assigned with.

With time, it's possible the effects of the drug will wear. Likely the body will attack the unknown biological intruder and I will slowly regain pieces of myself each time it does, even if each time it's injected into the bloodstream, it becomes harder and harder to fight back.

The hazel-eyed shifter stands before me, his arms crossed over his broad chest, his olive skin like satin pulled tight over his exquisitely formed muscles as he stares down at me. Something akin to disgust swirls in those irises. He turns to his partner, who watches the exchange from the bed looking between us, his attention unyielding.

He stands and walks towards me.

His long lean legs eat up the distance and before I know it, he's standing before me searching my dead stare.

"What did they do to you?" he demands, his jaw set, looking far more menacing than I've ever seen him.

Finding the right words, I open my mouth to explain. "I have recently had my dose of the enhancement serum, sir." My tone is flat.

He straightens his posture, standing impossibly taller, towering over my much smaller frame.

"And what does that entail?" he asks, his voice a pitch darker.

I note the broader male has perched himself on the side of my bed disinterested in the conversation, as he stares out of the window behind me.

"Tell me what this injection entails, *Siren*." He spits the name like its poison on his tongue, but the silver in his eye's glows brighter.

"A chemical is implanted into the bloodstream, where it seeps into the cells and replaces certain elements that make up the genome. It reenforces compliance by chemically altering the brain's function."

His body tenses, his jaw slackens as though I've struck him, an uncomfortable silence follows suffocating me.

The brunette on the bed turns his attention back to us, but the surprise that was sparked to life at my candour is quickly snuffed out by the glance he gives me, like is trying to peel back layer after layer. Wondering what kind of threat I pose.

If only he knew.

"It does what now?" the darker-skinned handler asks. I open my mouth to repeat myself. "No. That was a rhetorical question. Do not repeat what you have just said to me." His tone suggests he is either uncomfortable or angry. "Declan, what are we going to do?"

Handler Keita stands before me, his eyes wide and mouth pursed. Declan, still sitting on the bed, scowls over at me in disgust. A little flicker of something dark springs to life deep in my chest.

Is it disdain?

Hatred?

Either way, the feeling is mutual.

I clear my throat and turn back to Keita, "permission to speak freely?" I ask. He nods, "Whether or not you accompany me. I have been given an assignment, and with that comes an obligation to follow the codex. A handler must be present when we leave the Fort, in some capacity. But should it come down to it, I can, freely, leave you behind. It is my duty to complete the mission with or without you, no matter the repercussions of my actions. So, I advise that we continue as planned," I answer.

Silence greets me. Soft and intangible, I tuck my arms behind my back clasping my hands, waiting for instructions. Keita turns to his partner, throwing his hands up in the air, silently asking for help.

"Don't look at me," he growls standing up, he brushes his hands down his thighs, straightening out any creases. "This was your idea Rich, not mine. Don't drag me into this more than you already have." Declan walks to the door and sighs heavily, reaching for the handle.

The empty void in my chest feels fathomless, a never-ending desert of isolation and darkness that I can't seem to shake. Helped along by the helpless expression on Rich's face.

"Maybe we should just all go for a walk and get some fresh air where we can just take some time to figure it out," Declan suggests, Rich seems thankful for the distraction but that quickly switches to annoyance.

"Declan, she's not a gods' damned dog!" he snaps.

"Well do you have any other alternative or do you want to keep her locked in her room all afternoon?"

Rich glares at his partner, before rubbing his hand down his face, "Fine." He turns back to me, "Ael..." he cuts himself off. "Three-Nought-Nought, you will stick close to us whilst we are out there. Do not stray from our side.

"Of course," I reply bowing my head. Rich's discomfort shows on his face, but he doesn't seem to want to question my obedience.

"Are you done?" Declan grumbles from the now-open doorway.

Rich rolls his eyes and seems to wait for me to step forward. "Yeah, let's go," he answers.

The sunshine warms me down to the bone, despite the cool spring breeze, when we step outside only a few minutes later.

I watch each person carefully as I pass them by, given the reception we received earlier, I wouldn't trust any of these people to not do something incredibly stupid or impossibly reckless.

Following in the shadows of the two broad-shouldered males is far more tedious than one might think. They receive appreciative glances, especially from the residential females, bringing too much attention our way, but most shy away when they see the resting scowl on my face; it's only when I pass by the windows, so clear they are a near perfect mirror, that I finally see what they see. And I to would shy away from that glower.

We turn again down a similarly decorated street with some small pop-up shops, the owners of which call out to onlookers each trying to sell their wares.

Undeterred by Rich's earlier warning, I drift towards the stalls and away from my two handlers, blending through the crowd, some shops are overflowing with freshly picked vegetables, some with rolls of fabrics and leathers; the one I drift closest to showcases a variety of handmade jewellery and beaded trinkets.

An elderly female stands behind the stall's makeshift counter a gaps leaves her mouth, and she watches closely as I approach. Her curious gaze tracks each of my movements, stopping to stare at my face for far longer than I would like. My fingers twitch, desperate to get a hold of the weapon tucked in my boot but I refrain and instead show interest in her selection of handcrafted accessories.

Her silver hair is tied up loosely at the top of her head, revealing her pointed fae ears, some of the shining wisps fall down to the sides of her face brushing against her cheeks, she watches me with a kind smile, her golden eyes alight with curiosity.

The tips of my fingers glide over the bracelets at the front of the stall, some decorated with crystals, while others have feathers of every shape and colour.

I smile as my hand hovers over something that seems distantly familiar; a small yellow opal, beaded bracelet, there's nothing particularly special about the gemstone, nor about the bracelet at all. But as the beads glint in the sunlight, they look to be glowing, soaking up the sun's light and claiming it as their own.

"That is a rare gem, where I come from," the older fae says to me.

I look up at her through my eyebrows and without missing a beat I ask, "and where exactly is that?"

She seems unfazed by the scathing question, showing me her wrinkled yet still bright smirk across her thin lips.

"It is said that those who wear such a charm are guided back home. If I may be so bold, I sense you've strayed from your own." She leans forward and looks me up and down.

"Not strayed. I will be returning shortly, but there are a few things I must do first." I sidestep her statement as much as I can.

Her smirk falls outwardly projecting her distrust. I step away from her stall, bowing my head, "Thank you, for your time."

"The little folk of the mountains imbued this trinket with their own subtle brand of magic, and they say it will choose its wearer," she rushes out, stopping me from leaving. Reaching out for the bracelet herself, her sleeves rolled up just above her wrist, revealing a tattooed number on the underside of her arm. I study the brand with open interest.

I have never met a survivor of the war camps.

My mind travels back to some of the more worldly-educational lessons that out program leaders thought should be mandatory of us to take, and to the stories Madame would tell us. About how, just as many innocents lost their lives every day in those camps, as those who are fighting on the battlefields. The men were slaughtered, the women assaulted and branded, and the children were used as slaves. Upon Anaphi's interference, those camps were the first things to be burnt to the ground.

Civilians lost homes from the battles and village wildfires, and those that survived that form of conflict were rounded up and committed to the camps.

She notes my tense posture and follows the path my gaze is blazing, down to her wrist. She clears her throat and quickly tugs her sleeve back over her wrist.

"I have lived many lifetimes, Siren. *That* was but a small portion of it." My attention snaps back to her face, she's looking right at me, at my clenched jaw and I begin to wonder how in the seven Hels' she knew who I was when someone grips my upper arm twirling me around. With my fist clenched I swing at the stranger only to have my fist caught by Declan. His face contorted with anger, but he doesn't let me go.

"What do you think you're doing?" he snarls, his grip tightening.

"Release me," I hiss back, pulling on my arm.

"The pair of you, stop it." Rich comes charging through the crowd. Only then does Declan release his hold on me, "apologies," Rich speaks to the old fae vendor, who is glaring at Declan's side profile. She turns and smiles at him, quietly accepting his amends.

"I think that's enough excitement for one day," Rich mumbles, shoving me in front of him.

Sitting in the main bar area back at the inn come dinner time, we take a table close to the entrance under one of the windows that looks ready to fall out of its frame. The draft coming through the sealant offers little hope for getting a good night's sleep, I have trouble fighting back against the cold.

The food we've ordered does little to lighten my dulled mood. Nor Declan's as he stares down at his bowl as if it's personally offended him in some way. Salted beef and, not nearly fresh enough, vegetables make up a watery stew with a crusty bread bun on the side. Rich can't seem to get the broth in him fast enough, while I push the soft vegetables around the bowl. My appetite disappearing into nothing.

The petite, wide-hipped brunette waitress saunters over to the table, her hair up in a simple twist with kohl-lined eyes, she flutters her eyelashes and rests one hand on her hip as she asks, "How is your food this evening?" She plasters on a dazzling smile as she shifts her hooded gaze between Declan and Rich.

"Great thank you," Rich replies politely. Her cheeks are dusted with a little blush at his attention, making her freckles appear darker.

"Are you two here for the games this week?" She leans forward, whether deliberate or not, but the action shows off more cleavage than is considered necessary.

Without missing a beat, Rich replies smiling politely at her, "The *three* of us are not here for the games, we are just passing through."

"Oh, well that's a pity, two strong males like yourselves would surely best the others without breaking a sweat."

Intrigue sparks at not only where she is going with her game of cat and mouse but also these games she speaks of. Yet I say nothing. Rich side-eyes me, humour lighting his eyes that fades just as quickly as it came when he sees my expressionless face.

Declan puts his spoon back in his bowl and turns to her, grinning wildly, "You think so?" He flirts back, much to Rich's annoyance.

"Oh, I know so," she grins, biting her lip, as she eyes him up like a delicious dessert ready to be devoured. It takes everything in me to not roll my eyes when she pushes her breasts together making them look much plumper.

Before I know what I've done, I've opened my mouth, "What do these games entail?"

Rich chokes on a mouthful of broth, his eyebrows shoot upwards creating grooves on his forehead and he watches me with open curiosity, a grin on his face. Declan turns to me also, his smug demeanour evaporating in the grimy air. Dread curls in my belly, I've spoken without permission, showing interest in something in a world where I don't belong. In a world where I have no place. I sigh through my nose.

The petite female turns back to me with a bright smile on her face, though I can sense her apprehension, she swallows audibly, "There's a tradition here in Ellwey, where the community gathers together to celebrate the new crop year. New seeds are planted that morning and in the evening we all gather in an open field around a large bonfire and play various games, for example, the males pull off feats of strength by throwing tree trunks, and heaving weights over a raised bar, and there a few eating competitions, and things for the children to enjoy. It's a way for us to celebrate spring and our Goddess Arista," she answers.

My lips purse slightly before I nod and thank her, and she retreats back towards the safety of the kitchen.

"My apologies I didn't mean to speak out of turn," I say, looking down at the grainy table, even though I can feel both sets of eyes on me, "I will gladly accept any punishment you deem worthy of such disrespect."

Declan spits out his drink and Rich sits there with his mouth hanging open.

"Excuse me what?" Rich hisses, clearly taken aback. I tilt my head to the side analysing his emotions.

"I said..."

"Yeah, I know what you said, that was another rhetorical question, Aella," he snaps, ignoring me when I wince at the use of my name.

"Sir, may I ask a question?"

"Do not call me sir." I can hear his teeth grind together.

"It would be an act of disrespect if I didn't, *sir*," I grit out. I feel Declan's contempt towards me, but I bite my tongue from saying the wrong thing once again, no matter how much I want to take out my growing frustration on him.

"Would it not be an act of disrespect if you went against my wishes?" Rich shoots back, a fire in those endless starry eyes.

I stay silent, clenching and unclenching my jaw. Neither of the two of them seem to understand the severity of the situation that we find ourselves in. The Fort of Ajay has its rules for a reason, and they are not something to take lightly.

Yet, it appears that neither Declan nor Rich can recall their training. They can't have just fallen upon this job, given both of their backgrounds. They would've had to go through the program like everybody else.

"Answer my question, Siren." I glance sideways at Declan, even though I know not to ask for help from him. I'm the last person he'd be willing to cover for.

"You know the rules. You should've been taught them in the program. I suggest you abide by them lest you get us all killed." I stand from the table, leaving the rest of my food untouched.

I make it back to my room with my hand on the handle before Rich catches up to me. A hand on the door preventing me from closing it.

"You never answered my question, *Siren*." I roll my eyes and invite him in. It closes with a soft click, and I turn to see him standing in the middle of the room, with his arms crossed over his chest. The same stance his counterpart held only hours ago.

"Are you going to start, or am I?" He asks.

"Why are you so persistent in what I call you, *sir?* I'm here to do a job, not make sure your feelings are intact." I grip my hands together behind my back.

"You're awfully talkative for someone who's not allowed to speak freely, *Siren*."

My teeth begin grinding again. "You have already given me permission to do so. Until such time as I am told not to. I will talk when you ask me a question."

"What about Rich?"

"If you remember your training, *Handler* Keita, you will know that as a 'project' I am not permitted to call my handlers by their first name."

He doesn't speak. In fact, I'm not quite sure he's breathing. "A project?" He murmurs.

That small flicker of dread that sparked to life has started to grow.

I step up into his space and regardless of his height I still manage to look down my nose at him. "How was it you came by the Fort?" The question stuns him, I catch his eyes widening slightly before he sets his jaw.

"Are you questioning my integrity, *Three-Nought-Nought*?"

"Someone has to. Because clearly, something is going on here." I pause, finding the right words to express my confusion. "Why did you appear shocked when I talked about punishment? My other handlers have never once questioned it and yet you seem off put by the simple notion of it."

"Maybe they should have because the mere idea of punishing you for speaking is *off-putting* Aella." His face is completely serious, devoid of humour or anger. One that bears his humanity unmistakably with emotion, "I have a question for you."

I nod.

"Does this serum stop you from wanting?"

It's my turn to be shocked. Of all the questions he could've asked and that was the one he went with. One I'm not sure how to answer. One I'm not sure I could give an answer to if I wanted. But there it is again. That word. Want. Have I wanted for anything? Do I know? Maybe. I know I want this conversation to be over already. But he's posed the question and now I have to answer. So, I give him what I can. Not what I *want*.

"The serum enhances cognitive function to a level where I do not want for anything, I am simply content as I am." My mouth dries just saying the words that have been beaten into me. Words that are not my own, but at the same time I suppose they are. The Fort is my home. It always has been and will continue to be long after this assignment has ended.

"So, brainwashing then," he drawls, "that's good to know."

I roll my eyes and step away, opening the door to see Declan and the waitress stumbling into the room adjacent to mine, giggling and laughing all the while. Too busy traipsing their hands over each other, they don't notice me usher Rich from the room. Their door closes on a slam and Rich turns back to me.

"Are you going to kill me in my sleep if I stay in there with you tonight? Because I am not listening to that."

I huff, there goes my shot at a peaceful night, I push the door wider, and he steps back in.

"So, who's taking the floor?" He asks as I flop down on the bed, "ok I've got the floor."

CHAPTER SIX
THE PAST AND THE PRESENT

Two Years Prior

Whimpers and screams wake me from a dreamless sleep and back into the waking hours. With too much blinding light, my hand automatically moves to cover my face, groaning loudly at the slow but powerful burn of pain behind my eyes.

The rustling of clothes and yet another cry of discomfort jumps me, I turn my head to the side and see healers trying to stop the blood pouring from a boy's leg. The very pale dark-haired boy, in unexplainable agony, who looks like nothing more than a living corpse.

My chest rattles fiercely with my too-rapid breathing; my throat constricted and dry like I've had gravel for breakfast.

Or dinner.

Whatever time of day it is.

I look down at my body to see my leg is elevated on several blankets and a tired-looking pillow, white bandages have been tied around and around so much that my leg looks double its normal size and is supported by a flimsy-looking wooden splint.

Tearing my gaze away from my ruined leg I finally take a look around to see just where the Hel I am.

White-linen tent has been erected around me, with a red cross on all side, a damn medical tent. Though I can't figure out how I got here. Fabric flaps noisily on one side – the entrance – maybe if I can stand, I can escape before anyone really notices.

Cots upon cots are organised in rows, and each holds somebody. Every person is in different stages of agony with missing or broken limbs, blood loss, or those that are simply being comforted and cared for until death comes to claim them.

Turning my head to the other side of my cot checking to see how many medical staff are around, only to see a broad-chested, olive-skinned male with deep chocolate-coloured hair dozing upright on a stool, leaning back against one of the tents supporting beams. His thick arms are crossed in front of him and his chiselled jaw rests against that lovely, toned chest, soft snores rumble in his throat. Curiosity gets the best of me, and I begin to lift myself up, fighting against the agony.

"No, no. Stay down." The male wakes abruptly and gently pushes against my shoulder forcing me back to the cot. Annoyed, I go to snap at him but when his sleepy hazel eyes connect with mine all words leave me.

Something about him feels familiar, warming, but I can't quite place him.

"Oh, you're awake," another voice says, a different, richer voice. I look over and I'm met with unyielding black eyes staring back at me.

The memories come back to me then. I was in the middle of a gunfight, surrounded by bodies. But he was there. He... saved me.

"Y...you," I croak before coughing violently, my throat dryer than the sands to the East.

"Here," he says, helping me drink the glass of water he brought. I start slowly sipping wincing at the rawness of my throat. "Easy," he hushes, one of his hands resting on the top of my head slowing me down and then he takes the water away when I try gulping down more. I study him while he puts the cup on the ground.

"Who... who are you?"

"I'm Rich Keita. Nice to meet you, well formally; and that ugly lug over there is Declan Angelos."

"You know, I've been shot twice today and had a building dropped on my arse, but *that* really hurt."

"Gods' above and below." The first male sighs and rolls his eyes, "it was a wooden shed!" Rich chuckles and Declan scowls at his friend but doesn't seem truly annoyed.

I scrunch my brows, confused by the interaction.

They both turn to me with smiles on their faces; it takes me a minute before I understand why.

"So, what do we call you?" Rich asks politely.

"My name? My name is, Three-Nought-Nought," I reply, shifting around in my tiny cot.

"What?" Declan asks, an amused smirk on his face.

"Three-Nought-Nought," I croak again, "that is my name."

They both look at each other for a moment, both not bothering to conceal their surprise. Declan's jaw works under his skin.

"That's not a name, it's a number," he grumbles.

Rich tilts his head to the side, the intrigue on his face builds with each passing second, I can almost see the wheels in his head turning.

"You know you don't have to be afraid of us," Declan says softly, his hand resting gently on my forearm, the contact is foreign, but I don't flinch away, even when something electric prickles under my skin.

They both observe me for a moment. But Rich looks to be peeling back the layers of my life. Something I can imagine will only leave him scarred. I say nothing as we watch each other, his attention makes me uncomfortable enough to squirm where I lie.

"I'd like to leave now," I mumble trying to stand once again, only to be pushed down once again, "stop manhandling me," I snap at Declan.

"You sound awfully grateful to the people who saved your life, princess," he grumbles back.

My eyes narrow on his hand on my arm. He quickly removes it.

"It's ok, you don't have to explain yourself. Not to us," Rich murmurs leaning in so no one walking by would be able to overhear us. I turn back to him with wide eyes, but my mouth stays closed.

"I would love to be on the same page as both of you," Declan mumbles, looking between us.

"Later," Rich replies, his eyes never leaving my face.

Anxiety spikes in my chest, my limbs run cold, and my breath quickens. I begin to wonder if he has figured out my secret. I have nothing on me to suggest that I was anything more than a mere bystander caught up in a brutal battle.

"Ok, I have a question then," Declan begins pulling all attention to him, "Why in the Abaddon were you out there in the middle of an active war zone without so much as a scrap of armour?" Declan asks commanding the attention of both Rich and I, the soft side of him hidden away of so carefully; he has some rank in the military with the way he holds himself.

"Wrong place, wrong time," I grit out shifting into what I hope is a more comfortable position only for my leg to flare up in blazing agony. Hissing wickedly, I grip my leg, holding back my curses as Rich reorganises the stack of fabric under it. "What the fuck happened to me?" I demand, throwing my head back into the flat pillow. Instantly regretting the decision when my head begins throbbing and the room spins in circles.

"A grenade."

The answer is simple and not all that surprising; it certainly feels like I've had a bomb dropped on me, no matter how small the parcel.

"It dropped about ten feet in front of you. We saw the whole thing actually; we expect the explosion broke your leg but you're lucky, another couple of feet closer and you'd have been flying about in little pieces," Declan shares. I blink at him, visually playing the scene out in my mind and wondering if that would've been better than having to be under his weighted scrutiny.

"I wouldn't call it luck, but sure," I mumble, "why save me?"

"We saw a person fighting to live. That is who we saved; we didn't actually know who you were at the time. You were just a person covered in mud and blood. You could've been the enemy for all we knew. But we saw your spirit. How, even with your injuries, you were still trying to live," Rich explains.

The enemy. If only they knew.

"But still, you could've left me. Or handed me over."

"Handed you over to whom?" Rich's dark eyes bore into mine, probing for more, and it was then that I saw little stars of silver in them, they seem to glow brighter the more I talk, as if those tiny stars are curious about me.

My silence speaks volumes, but I dare not say another word.

"We aren't the type to let people die, no matter their profession. You're still a person," Declan says.

I huff at them and close my eyes taking a deep breath seeking clarity, when I open them again both handsome faces are studying mine. Taking in every inch of my face as if they're memorising it for future reference, but I'm not used to such attention, so I turn away and look at the cot closest to me. A young blonde male lies there with blood soaking through his bandages, the steady rise and fall of his chest suggests he's asleep, at least for now, but his rib cage has a deathly rattle.

"Thank you. You know for," I sigh, "for saving me." In all of my life I've never had my life saved by another. The feeling is strange and foreign; something that I am not at all comfortable with.

Rich puffs out a little breathy laugh, grinning from ear-to-ear fangs bared, Declan's face is a mirror image.

My eyes splay wide, "You're a rare breed," I murmur astounded, in all my life I've yet to see a shifter. And now there two of you before me. How... coincidental."

"How so?" Rich queries, shuffling closer.

"Really?" I clap back.

"You're only just noticing? I'm kind of hurt," Declan deflects, his shoulders caving in. The honey-orange glow behind his eyes is more potent now and I wonder how I missed such a unique quality in both of them. Rich chuckles softly at the mock hurt on Declan's face, a tired but hopeful sound.

"There's only three kinds of shifter if memory serves me right."

"Two not three," Rich implies.

I grin but don't correct him, "So which are you?"

"Feline," Declan speaks first. The answer quiet; shifters aren't exiled but not openly discussed either. Especially not in Anaphi.

"Canine," Rich informs.

I blink rapidly, "King Theodore has declared open season on canine shifters."

"Don't I know it," he scowls.

"And you feel safe enough to share that with a stranger. Aren't you at all worried that I could tell someone?"

"Perhaps I see something in you that you don't see yourself yet?"

"How have you kept that a secret? You work for the king, don't you?" I ask.

"What gave us away?" Dec questions, grinning. He looks down at his armoured chest where the Anaphi crest is embossed into the metal, a stag standing proud on a hilltop.

Rich's is different. One I've seen, but a place I've never been to. My finger rolls over the cold metal, right over the crest. "The Southern Colonies," I murmur. He too sits a little taller, proud of his heritage. But given the war is between Anaphi and the Southern Colonies I raise my brow.

"Sormbay, not Duranda," he corrects, seeing my scepticism. "We've been working with Anaphi. Duranda's less civilised than the other countries. They chose to keep the old ways and traditions alive. They're bit more savage than the rest of us. But Sormbay and Salaria are the only ones that have the means to."

I nod my head in understanding. From the battle that I saw, I can say without a shadow of a doubt that his description of Duranda's forces is so incredibly accurate. Mounted on horse with nothing but curved blades and centuries of fury on their side, they are exactly as he said. Savage.

Rich laughs again.

"You know, there is one benefit of this meeting," Declan announces.

"What's that?" I sigh, almost afraid of the answer.

"Well, you princess, are now wrapped up in a life debt with us," he replies.

And there it is.

I roll my eyes groaning, whilst the two shifters wear the biggest shit-eating grins I've ever seen.

Present Day

The rays of the sun the next morning beam through my window, spread across the bed and begin warming me in this otherwise cold room. I groan still tired and have woken up with a pounding headache. Tugging the blanket, I pull it up further over my head wanting a few more minutes of rest.

A loud knock shakes the door.

"Wake up sleepy heads." Comes Declan's obnoxiously cheery voice from the other side of the door and I whine in protest, listening to his retreating footsteps. A groan from the floor startles me, and I sit bolt upright on the bed until I see Rich rolling over under his blanket, he too wants more sleep, even though the draft from the floorboards must have been killer through the night.

Incoherently grumbling I hoist myself out of bed, briefly looking out the window to see Ellwey still sleeping. A faint dewy mist hovers in the streets and over the hills where sheep still roam. I change into some fresh clothes and gather my gear quickly until I turn to see Rich smiling up at me from the floor.

"Good morning, liefling," he grins, placing his arms behind his head.

I grunt back and step over him to the door. "Not a morning person?" He asks with a chuckle in his throat.

I swing the door open narrowly avoiding his head and step out leaving him to gather his things and change, to prepare for the journey South.

We take our time through breakfast, waiting for the sun to rise further in the sky. Freshly cooked meats and eggs with warm bread and some newly harvested fruits are served within minutes. No one else sits in the dining hall, making me wonder if they have any other guests checked in. I heard voices in the night, and yet the inn appears deserted.

Idle chatter between the two males carries us through an otherwise quiet breakfast. Declan describes how flexible the waitress was during their *extracurricular* activities last night. I frown into my porridge listening to the pair of them. Rich rolls his eyes more times than I can count as Declan goes into too much detail, but the smirk on his face cannot be hidden and then we finally head to the front desk to hand back our keys.

The brunette receptionist behind the counter smiles timidly at me, a pink blush on her cheeks. Looking almost identical to the waitress from last night, Declan can't seem to help himself as he begins flirting with her. Clearly, the two are twins. She hands me a small parcel - a parcel she claims was delivered last night - and turns away speaking directly with Declan.

I hold the parcel in my hand like it's a live grenade before reading the note, my name written in cursive neatly on the brown paper.

Not my number.

My name. *Aella.*

Unease suddenly curls in my gut, and I step towards the doors, leaving my bags on the floor. Rich calls my name. The street is empty. I break into a sprint my mind warring with both the serum desperate for control and for me to remember my training and the other part that's wants to stop at nothing to find the owner of this parcel.

My breath comes out in swirling tendrils that float higher and higher in the mist. Behind me, Rich yells my name again but I don't stop. I follow the same narrow streets we took yesterday back to those surprising pop-up shops.

Skidding round the corner, I'm shocked to find the road completely empty, as if they had never been there at all. I come to a stop, breathing hard, looking around quizzically for even just a small hint that I'm not crazy. Nothing. It's all gone like a whisper in the wind.

Footsteps pound against the cobbles behind me. "What the Hel do you think you're doing?" Rich growls, grabbing my arm. I look down at the parcel still in my hand, ignoring him and rip the paper open. A little beaded bracelet falls out onto my fingers, the very same I'd seen the day previous.

"Siren, answer me," Rich's voice is a low rumble. He's not trying very hard to keep his emotions in check, I can feel his anger it's almost warming the air around us.

I hand him the note with my name handwritten, his eyes scan the scrap as he takes it and turns it over. Concern lashes across his face and he looks around, only now just seeing that the stalls have dissolved into nothing, and his own emotions match mine, confusion, and dread.

"Come on. You just scared the shit out of me, and we need to get on the road." He crumples the paper up and tugs on my arm.

I take one last look down the street, completely perplexed.

Rich leads me back to Declan who's already begun putting the bags into the back of their vehicle.

"Everything alright?" Dec asks when we get closer, his tone shows his disinterest. He glances at me from the side of his eye, the only concern he'd ever show.

"Yes." Is Rich's clipped response. I move into the back seats of the car the gnawing feeling of worry expanding with my many unanswered questions.

The sound of an infant crying fills my ears as smoke wafts above me. Weightlessness fills my body like I'm floating up in the air. I look around and see only darkness, an empty void stretching out before me.

A dot of white appears beyond my vision, growing rapidly. I'm paralysed against it as it hunts me, expanding wider and wider until it's all I see. A vast nothingness, I close my eyes feeling at peace. Allowing myself to drift into the void.

A soft breeze rustles the strands of my hair, and cheery birdsong cheeps in my ears. The warmth from the sun heats my limbs, I smile at the smell of the grass and the sound of a stream trickling not far from me.

My eyes open, surprised to see a warm glen, filled with blooming wildflowers and butterflies surrounded by pine trees tall enough to brush the clouds in the sky. Off to one side, I see a moss-covered log in the tall grass. Interest drives my feet to move, I notice that even the soil beneath my toes is warm. I draw closer to the log, only to find it's no log at all.

It's a body, I stumble over my own feet dashing for them, my knees slam down into the dirt beside them, and I use whatever strength I have to turn them over onto their back.

The chipper birdsong dies out and the warmth of the sun is no longer present as an icy blast of air sweeps over the glen. The air is punched from my lungs as I look at their face.

At my face.

My scream is drowned out when I'm once again plunged back into darkness, with nothing but the shivering cold for company. My body still lies at my feet, chest unmoving and I can't help but stare at the too-pale skin of my face, caked in dirt. At the too-blue lips cut and bruised. My heart no longer beats under my breast that much is clear. How long I've been dead I do not know, but I can see I've died alone.

A snarl rumbles around me, terror grips me, and my hands begin to shake. Something awaits me in the shadows, something deadly; and yet something pulls me towards it.

A shout cuts through my trance and a boom deafens me, a bright white light blinds me and suddenly I'm gasping for air, my eyes thrown open. The sky comes into view, a grey sky. My body feels heavy and cold, the wet slushy ground hugging me close. I push myself upright and before I can even move a muscle, I'm on my feet.

Mud and blood cover my skin when I look down at my hands.

I'm standing in the middle of a smoky, dark field; trees surround me. Shouts and screams draw my attention in all directions until I see them. The enemy line charging forward, draped in Duranda's colours of yellow and gold; blades drawn, their horses eat up the ground between them and I. I want to run, I want to scream, I want to do anything that will get me out of here. I try to lift my foot, but it's stuck too far in the mud. Panic wells within me. I shut my eyes again, so tight it hurts.

All sounds of battle die out, no trampling hooves no war cries. No nauseating smell of smoke. No booming of grenades or screams of agony. I peek through my eyelashes to find that Duranda's soldiers have disappeared, nothing but ash remains. Instead, around me now is a ring. A ring of bodies.

Six in total.

Three lay facing the sky, eyes glazed over. The other three lay face *down faces deep in the dirt. A musky thick breeze blows around us, moving their hair and parts of their clothing.*

Two of the bodies I recognised instantly their forms lay there with just a hint of colour still in their cheeks.

Declan and Rich. Blood covers their chests, a cavity in place of where their hearts should beat. My heart breaks at the manifestation before me. I want to scream but no sound comes out of my mouth. Falling to the ground I sob uncontrollably, while trying to crawl to them, to reach out my hand, they disappear in a cloud of dust blowing away with the wind.

The ground seems to move on its own, one second I'm crying and watching as my friend's ashes melt with the smoke and embers around me, and the next I'm standing before another body.

Surya. She too now lies at my feet, and just like Rich and Declan, she too faces the sky.

Her clothing is torn by her mangled body, ripped apart by the bones that protrude from her once caramel skin, her glossy black hair in knots and tangled around her neck. I drop down to my knees again and weep. I weep for Rich and Declan. I weep for the young girl in front of me. I weep for the lack of power I have to do anything about it.

I don't bother to wipe the tears from my face.

I'm suddenly before two more; these lie face down, until I reach out my hand once again. The body to my left turns over. A blonde female, her bone structure and widow's peak hairline shows she was beautiful in life. But in death she is featureless. Where her eyes should be there are dark shallow holes; where her nose should be, is smoothed over skin. Her mouth has been sealed with skin also, only a jagged cut line leaking blood is the mere suggestion of one.

No words come out of my mouth, nothing but a strangled sob, I'm not even sure if I know who she is, but no one deserves this fate.

A violent unruly tremor shakes my limbs while I quickly turn over the second body to reveal a brown-haired male, only to find the same, a featureless face with a grotesquely cut-out mouth.

My own salty tears drop onto the male's cheeks and an agonised sob leaves me before I can stop it.

Through blurry vision I see the sixth and final body behind them, with hair so pale one would think it's white. Mud clings to the strands sticking patches of it together. I raise my hand hoping to go to her when that vicious snarl rumbles again.

"Countless people die by your hand, Siren of Ajay. These are no different. You do nothing to stop it, even if it is poisoning us." It hisses, slithering around me. "You caused this. They're dead because of you." The words cut deep and true. Another sob escapes and more tears fall. "Let us see how you fair when all of those you know are dead before you. This is a mere taste of what is to come my child. To gain it all you first must lose it all."

A buzzing begins growing louder and louder, crows caw from overhead, circling the bodies, looking for their next meal. I put my hands over my ears trying to block out the noise and I go to scream again, and this time the sound finds me.

My eyes open abruptly momentarily blinding me with daylight, gasping loudly, my hands flail for purchase. With my skin covered head to toe in my own sweat, I greedily gulp in deep lungful's of air, feeling like I've run a marathon. I look around finding black leather seats, a field beyond the windows with quiet music on the radio.

The back door is open, and Rich's hand finds mine quickly. He squeezes it hard. Even if I don't return the familiarity.

"Ella, you're ok. You're safe here," Rich murmurs into my hair, as he cradles my head to his chest. Automatically I flinch at the use of my name.

My breath comes out in ragged pants, coupled with an uncontrollable beating heart. A deep sleepy haze covers my eyes, showing me flashes of my dreams, of dead bodies piled high. Of faceless people, covered in clay and blood.

"Do you normally sleep so much?" Declan grunts, snapping me from my nightmares.

"No."

Rich continues to rock me back and forth, and my heart begins to slow. Declan must see this and nods to Rich, who pulls my head from his chest to look me in the eye. A deep groove has formed on his forehead, imprinted by his concern.

"Is it because of the serum?" he asks in a hushed whisper.

Declan has already turned back to the wheel. Ready to continue on the road, having had enough of this distraction, and frankly, so have I.

"Handler Keita, I am fine to continue on." I sit up against the seat sitting taller, pulling completely away from him.

"And I don't think you are," he snaps back, climbing in beside me. "I want answers, Siren and you will give them to me."

I sigh and turn to him, still unsure whether these two have actually gone through the training to become handlers or not. Because they should know the answers to the questions they are asking. But even so, he has demanded I answer, and I cannot refuse.

"The serum has always affected me differently than the others. They have never understood why. But this isolated incident seems to be unrelated. The sleeping, however, could be."

"What does it do to you? Beyond all of the clinical bullshit. What does it do to YOU?" Declan asks causally, the surprise on his face gives away his train of thought. He's shocked even himself that his curiosity wanted to know so bad that he would dare to talk to me about something so personal.

"That is not something I can answer in too much detail," I muse aloud trying to find the right words. "It is an enhancement serum. So, it makes the body stronger; the mind more focused and our agility becomes almost inhuman."

Declan says nothing in return, falling quiet while he pulls away from the side of the road. Nothing but miles upon miles of fields stretch on before us. Untouched by farmers, and roads. Just pure healthy nature thriving under the blazing sun. He doesn't speak again, and that's fine by me. I turn to look out the window watching those fields pass us by. Praying the conversation is over.

That hope is crushed when Rich speaks again, "When did they do this to you?" His voice is muted and clipped.

"Several days ago, now, sir."

He scoffs and turns to look out the window himself, that thankfully, seems to be the end of it for now.

The sun has begun its descent in the sky by the time the white spires of Ansrutas peak over the horizon. The golden hour glow bounces off the spiralling glass roofs. The five identical towers have become quite the spectacle in Anaphi for being the tallest buildings ever built. They tower several stories over many of the other buildings that make up the ever-changing skyline, never to be overshadowed, not even by the magnificent and boundless sea glinting in the distance.

The closer we get to the city, the more and more buildings rise up seemingly from the ground, dwarfing the centuries-old sandstone wall that protects the city. Cypress trees line the central road leading to the gates, swaying gently in the sea breeze.

My eyes process everything in sight with fluid efficiency. It's been so long since I've seen something other than the grey walls of the Fort, or the white snow of the north, and I can't keep the minor flicker of excitement from bubbling up in my chest. Not that anyone would ever know.

Before long we are slowing down, merging with the lines of traffic, ready to enter the city through its centuries-old gates.

Border control stations have been hastily built outside the monumental wall and border the only two gateways in and out of Ansrutas.

"We've got to stop here for a minute, they need to check the car," Declan mutters to no one in particular but he still pulls over, driving down a carefully made dirt road, guided by a bored-looking male guard waving him down. The Anaphi flag is hoisted up high, not only on a flagpole but along the wall, the heavy material whips this way and that in the growing wind. The chains look to be having a hard time keeping the crest from falling to the floor.

"Well, we knew this would happen with the Stratos being in town," Rich reminds him, leaning forward and scoping out the station.

Several white linen tents have been erected in a circle.

The Stratos are the king's military, beyond his own personal guard, labelled as such. They are called to handle situations like this when the local police cannot handle it themselves. It is rare to see the king's guard away from the capital and the royal family. But sometimes he sends his elite selection of guards to do his dirty work.

Without the king having sent them into the battle for the border, I wouldn't have met Declan and Rich. They wouldn't have saved me, and I wouldn't have survived the night. Not with the injuries I acquired that day. I am now just wondering if our meeting was a blessing or a curse.

We join the line of vehicles waiting to be checked over and I take my time observing each guard stationed here, diverting everyone to different sectors. Some carry weapons and some carry clipboards. The car stops and we are asked to exit while they do their search.

A young male steps towards the car, an extendable mirror in hand. He places it under the vehicle and begins searching the undercarriage.

"Bomb squad," Rich leans in, whispering in my ear as if I didn't already know.

Kicking up the dried ground, I decide to stretch my legs wandering closer to the wall, listening to Declan speak casually with one of the female guards about papers and such, dropping in a few flirtatious comments here and there. Something she looks as though she could live without.

Rich stands close to Declan, rolling his eyes at what I can only assume is a very cheesy pick-up line - to which the guard scoffs and walks away - with his arms crossed over his chest, intensely scrutinising everyone that has descended on the car continuing their search.

The sandstone bricks of the wall have a thin coating of plaster covering the cracks and lines. The beige wall is faded and damaged, with the years of unforgiving weather and the brutal conflicts it's seen over its lifetime. Another gust of wind blows the Anaphi flag up, revealing a painted mural beneath. It's hard to make out in the flag's shadow but it looks as though fields of green used to encompass the land; creatures and beings of old used to live in harmony together amongst the forests and seas.

Looking further along the wall, even older art still subtly remains, depicting divine figures walking the paths we now take. Twenty-five in total. Each with their own unique characteristics. They used to live on this same land aeons before any mortal stepped foot here. The gods.

My heart thunders in my chest as I lock eyes with the mother. Emmita. It's not so long ago I prayed to her for forgiveness. Old dribbling graffiti stains the cracks in the stone just above her painting.

'The gods have abandoned us.' A shiver runs through me. Despite not being a religious type, I still don't believe that to be true.

My name is called, and I turn to see Rich waving me down.

It would seem I've wandered too far.

The search takes longer than most and I see them check, not once, but twice through my duffle bag, aggravating me. I know that they won't have left it organised, but once they are satisfied, we climb back in the car.

The giant wooden gates are already open, they've likely been like that for years. It saddens me to see such a gigantic structure wither away, the gates are no different, with the rotting wood and rusted age-old iron hinges, it would be near impossible to close them now without them crumbling under their own weight.

The sun sinks lower on the horizon, and the sky becomes a beautiful hue of purple, pink, orange and yellow that reflects off of every window.

The tall buildings have their own unique architectural beauty. Each has its own secret connection to nature, whether on balconies or hanging from the rooftops, or entire walls made up of green, each building incorporates some form of plant life within its architectural design.

Bells ring loudly in the distance scaring a flock of birds that take flight in fright. A temple that is surely bigger than most buildings here, is made from white stone, with matching stone pillars holding up the roof, like one epic offering to the many gods. Many much smaller and less exorbitant temples dedicated to individual gods, spread out throughout the city, but the pantheon is the only sacred space that depicts all of them in one place.

We finally pull up to the side of the road. A tall brown brick building looms over us. Flaking mortar and crumbling windowpanes don't exactly fill me with confidence, if the inside is anything like the outside, I'm not exactly overflowing with joy.

The three of us bump and bang into each other carrying our luggage up the narrow staircase to the top if the building where our safe house is.

Upon arrival to the destination – and of course following the code – it is important to hold a meeting upon arrival between the person in charge and myself or my handlers, so that the transfer of documents and authority is done smoothly and with consent.

In other words, I'm expected to have a meeting with the Stratos' high commander. General Mason Griffith.

Something I'm not all that happy about. I have only met this mortal once when the king had called upon me to help resolve a somewhat *delicate* matter for him.

I didn't like him then and I don't like him now. I don't suspect that he will remember me, given the years between our unexpected meeting. But that may just be wishful thinking.

The short, stout man is overconfident and greedy. Without shame, he abuses the position that was gifted to him by the Director. With his lack of military background, beyond his father's service. Mason was unlikely to get the position he wanted, by the grace of the Director's abilities – and that alone – whispers were placed into the ears of those that mattered. Those with enough say in his majesty's court. General Griffith has been sitting on that overstuffed cushion of luxury ever since. That was nearly twenty years ago now and still, he himself, hasn't raised a finger during the ongoing war with Duranda.

"You couldn't have picked somewhere nicer?" Rich queries looking around at the apartments interior.

Declan grunts and shoves past him.

The apartment comes with one main room that's small in size, the sofa is pushed up against the wall, with one armchair with a tiny pine coffee table in the centre. The kitchen is visible from the door, with a miserable two-person table shoved into a corner. A corridor – if you can call it such a thing – leads off to three more doors, two tiny bedrooms all with slender beds and a shared bathroom, with a shower so small I begin to wonder how Declan is going to fit in there with all that packed on muscle.

The image is quite humorous, until it changes into something much more intense and immensely inappropriate.

My cheeks flush pink.

The colours on the walls are pale and tired, with no real shade left in them. Grime mars nearly every wall and light fixture. A scratchy feeling develops on the back of my neck and the overwhelming urge to sanitise this place from head to toe is becoming more of a necessity than a desire.

Walking back into the main area after dumping my things in my claimed room, I'm hesitant to touch anything beyond my own things for fear of catching some type of virus or bacterial infection.

Eyeing the sagging brown couch warily I stand and await my starting command.

Rich spins to see me eyeballing the place.

"See, even someone who doesn't have standards thinks this place is a hovel."

"Handler Kieta, just because I do what I do, does not mean I do not have standards," I scold plainly, looking at the curtain pole that's nearly black with mould.

"No, of course not. I didn't mean…"

"It is quite alright. But I must say this is certainly a step down from my last few assignments. But it will do."

Declan scoffs but doesn't try to defend his find.

"What's been the best then? Come on, tell us the best place you stayed."

I see the cockiness on Rich's face, he's teasing me, that much I can tell. The twinkle in his eyes is so innocent and unique that I almost don't want to diminish it. Something akin to giddiness bounces to the surface, quickly quelled by the serum still poisoning my veins.

Declan stands there with his arms over his chest, mirroring Rich's cocky expression, he too expects something low from me. He always has. Ever since he learned what I was. It wasn't long before he regretted his decision to save me from certain death. A year and a half has passed since our first meeting and yet so much has changed. All except for me.

I clear my throat and tell them; their faces fall almost immediately, and I step towards my bedroom. Ready to relieve myself of this bone-deep tiredness that has crept forth.

Not that this is a competition on who's had the best place to stay but still, I feel like I've won, even if it is a small victory. Stepping into my bedroom I stare at the lumpy bed before me wondering just how I ended up here.

It's certainly no fluffy mattress with duck-down pillows. The kind you'd find in the royal palace. I sigh at the thought of that soft comforter and cloud-like mattress enveloping me once more. What I'd do to stay there again.

CHAPTER SEVEN
ANSRUTAS THE UNIQUE

Morning comes with the sounds of horns blaring angrily through the thin single-paned window, pulling me from my, mercifully dreamless sleep. The obnoxious sound makes me instantly miss the howling of the icy wind as it batters the side of Chasin Mountain. The cold, not so much.

Rising slowly, I automatically begin my morning routine, brush, and tie my hair, wash my face and dress in my training gear.

Once dressed I step out of my small room into the narrow hallway. The door across from me opens in near-perfect synchronicity, to expose a tired-looking Rich. He smiles shallowly, which is followed up by a big yawn.

"Good morning," he grumbles, lumbering to the bathroom.

"Good morning, handler Keita." I bow my head, "permission to go on a run?"

His back straightens and his shoulders tense under his pale blue shirt. Without turning around, he replies, "Give me a few minutes and I'll come with you."

"As you wish."

He nods and closes the bathroom door.

"So how often do you train?" Rich ask between heavy pants, keeping perfect pace with me.

"Every day," I breathe.

"Oh right, that makes sense," he nods, trying to keep his breath under control.

"Do not keep your breath shallow if you need to take a break, we can," I say, watching him suck in a lungful of air.

"No. No, I'll be fine." The lie bitter on the tongue. "It's just I've not run this kind of distance for a long time."

"Then it is best to not overdo it," I explain, slowing gradually to a stop.

Leaning on his knees he breaths deep and often, sweat beading along his forehead. I guide him to a nearby step, at the front of someone's townhouse, he drops down like he can no longer hold his weight up, placing his head in his hands. His shoulders rise up and down rapidly while I stand like a sentry over him.

Movement from a nearby alley draws my attention, to a homeless man walking out looking cold and tired, his greying beard knotted and scraggly, his dirt ridden, colour-drained clothes have multiple of holes in them, and his beanie hat covers what I'm positive will be unclean hair.

Rich follows my gaze, "I didn't think Ansrutas had problems with having people sleeping rough."

"Every place, no matter the wealth of the country, will have this problem," I reply, turning back to him, making a point of making eye contact. "It is commonplace that even the friendliest and cleanest of places hide the darkest secrets. It's the same with most people, they, however, are far more complicated. It's those with the brightest smiles you have to watch out for, they are the ones who hide terrible pain." He looks up at me with an emotion I can't place. But his eyes have a strange fondness in them that makes me squirm under the intensity.

We don't speak further while we walk back to the safe house, Rich still struggling for breath, and I, thinking ahead to the meeting I will be having later today.

Declan is up and dressed by the time we walk back through the door, in a white dress shirt, sleeves rolled up to his elbows and black dress pants. My steps falter uncharacteristically when I look him up and down. My blood heats, flowing every which way through my veins, my cheeks begin to warm, and my hands become clammy, as though I have become sick. I touch my forehead, questioning this unfamiliar reaction.

"Something wrong, Siren?" Rich asks behind me, looking quizzical.

My attention cuts to him and my heartbeat slows back down at the sight of the concern written clear on his face. I'm very aware that Declan is also watching me, although he doesn't say a word. I nod to Rich and move to my bedroom to change my clothes.

Upon my return I see the duo staring angrily at each other. They haven't noticed I'm here yet, but I can only imagine what they are talking about.

"Declan, listen, you need to keep yourself calm, everything rides on this meeting, so it has to go smoothly despite your own issues."

"Griffith may be a bastard, but I know how to handle him."

"I'm not talking about Mason," Rich snapped, "you're evidently more pissed off with Aella than anything else. Just do your job and then come back home. Beyond that, you can go do what the fuck you want and leave her to me."

Declan grunts in response.

"You were a Lieutenant Colonel. You commanded a division of nearly six hundred men and women alike, surely you can do this." Rich places his hand on his friends' shoulders.

"You are terrible at a pep talk, you know that?" Declan mutters shaking off his friends' touch. The floorboards creak as he walks across the room.

Donning a long-sleeved shirt and breeches and tightly laced combat boots, I step further into the main room. Rich's expression softens as I enter the room once more, but Declan's attention turns elsewhere.

"You look like a damn shadow," he grumbles, sipping from a mug of coffee.

Looking down at myself I see exactly what he means, "I believe that was the desired effect upon designing the suit."

"Declan what did I just say?" Rich sighs ignoring my comment. Declan pours his coffee into a travel cup of sorts and holds up his hands.

"Fine. Fine," he relinquishes.

I pull out my mask and my numbered bulletproof vest from my bag.

"What are those for?" Declan growls, eyeing my mask with a hatred I'm all too familiar with.

"It is disrespectful for me to show my face to anyone in the king's court. As decreed by his majesty himself," I answer, fastening it to my face, "General Griffith is among his court."

Declan's jaw work, the muscle flexing and the vein along his temple makes itself known.

"Maybe I should just go, instead," Rich sighs, looking at his watch.

"We agreed I'd handle Griffith. It's fine. But after this, I'm done," Declan snaps, pulling on his lapelled jacket.

Neither of us speak once we are back in the vehicle, the tension palpable. I tighten my mask around my head and adjust the straps on my vest.

"Permission to speak..."

"What?" he snaps.

"Handler Angelos, I'm sure you are already aware, but you will be expected to refer to me by my number in General Griffith's presence."

He sighs, "Fine."

There's a swift beat of silence as I watch from the passenger side. His fingers grip the wheel tightly and his brows are lowered. Hie attention fixed completely on the road before us.

"You appear agitated," I observe as he pulls up alongside the monstrous building, the pale sandstone bricks shine in the mid-morning sun, while it sits prettily over the others in the area. The matching steps make the otherwise plain building all the more grandiose. "Maybe I should take this meeting alone?"

"No. Not a fucking chance am I going to leave you alone with that man," he snarls, turning the engine off. His aggression is something I have become accustomed to, yet I can't help but wonder if he's concerned for Griffith's wellbeing, or my own. When I look into his eyes, I find my answer.

Stratos officers stand guard at the large brass front doors that are nearly the same size as the building itself, they watch us closely as we walk up the many steps, their hands resting not far from the weapons strapped to their belts. Even more of them line the entrance hallway. The soft pale marble of the floor and ceiling reminds me of the guild only more decorative, with twirling pillars and several busts of those over the centuries who have made advancements to the world we now live in.

"Name?" A petite female guard asks of us, from behind what was once – I'm sure – a receptionist's desk.

"Declan Angelos. We have a meeting with General Griffith," Declan replies as I watch on.

"And your friend?"

"That's classified," he replies, not even finding a source of calm in himself long enough to flirt with her.

"She won't be allowed in if I don't have a name," she retorts. The other guards in the room move subtly towards us. I can smell their fear from here, and it is delicious.

He looks at me as if asking for permission, but I give nothing away.

"Her name is..."

"Let them through." A voice booms through the near-empty room echoing off the marble floor. At the top of the overwhelmingly large wooden staircase, a round mortal male stands, with greying hair. He is silhouetted by the light gushing through the two-story windows at his back.

"Yes, General Griffith," the female guard responds. "I'm going to need to take any weapons you have on your person before you step in here."

Three male guards' step towards me, sharing glances. The first reaches a hand towards me that I snatch out of the air, he strains to keep me from snapping it around. It's then I begin thinking about how I could make this morning all the more interesting, by cutting his hand off and starting a collection of limbs in jars. The thought has that wicked darkness within me lashing with delight.

"Siren!" Declan snaps. Those around pause, everyone turn to me their eyes wide and mouth slightly agape. I turn my glare on Declan, still holding the guy's hand; like we needed more attention.

"Are you deaf, girl? I said let them through," Griffith snarls interrupting, I promptly drop the male's hand. The collection will have to wait for another day.

I walk past the stunned males who watch me with barely contained hatred, Declan is quick to step up to my side while we climb the stairs to greet the wretch of a man.

"What the fuck was that?" he snarls as we reach the bottom step.

"I could ask you the same thing," I grit out, fighting back against the serum as it burns through me, forcing me to silence myself.

"I take it you're my *assistance*?" he hisses, clearly unhappy about us being here at all, despite being the one who called the Fort of Ajay for aid in the first place.

"Yes sir, we are," Declan replies, his demeanour changing dramatically before reaching out his hand to the man, "it's good to finally meet you, General." I can see the discomfort clearly coming from Declan and the way his posture is too stiff as they shake hands, their grips a little tighter than necessary.

"Yes, a pleasure to meet you, son. I've read your file; you have an exemplary record. A Lieutenant Colonel no less." Mason, still holding Declan's hand, smiles formally all the while. "If you'll both follow me, we can get you started on your investigation."

We follow him down a long, panelled corridor lined with oil-painted portraits of former mayors of the city, to what can only be assumed is his office. Each doorway houses an armed guard watching us just like the moving eyes of the portraits above us.

His office is an overly flamboyant room with dark wooden panelling and a bulky walnut-coloured desk right at the centre, framed by floor-to-ceiling arched windows. The walls are filled with medals and certificates and maps. We take a seat at the front of the desk opposite him while he makes his way around to sit in his overstuffed brown-leather wingback chair. He notes my curious browse of his belongings.

"It's nice, isn't it? It used to be the mayor's office, but that coward didn't have the stones to deal with these rebels. He has been relieved of his duties until further notice. I claimed this room the minute I arrived," he boasts puffing up his chest, proud of his meagre accomplishment. His grey-green military suit pulls around his middle so much I fear a button may pop off and catch me between the eyes. Medals – undeserved medals – decorate his breast pocket in every colour known to man, shine in the mid-morning sun.

He thinks gloating about this will surely impress me. Maybe he even believes that he will find an ally in myself, but he is sorely mistaken. The notion already becomes apparent when he quickly, and quite dramatically, physically deflates when I stay silent.

He clears his throat and changes the subject, turning back to Declan once more. "I have to say son, I thought they'd send more... *people*," Griffith says, gesturing with his hands as if that would make more people magically appear.

Declan side-eyes me, clasping his hands together as he leans back in his seat, "Being the General of the army of Anaphi, I'm certain you understand that sometimes less is more. Surely you have seen what only a few men can do in battle using stealth and wit, compared to having a whole battalion who have to take the fight head-on." Declan raises a brow in challenge, both of us know this man hasn't seen a real battle a day in his life. "And I have been led to believe that you, yourself, are aware of how the guild operates, so you should know the answer to your own question, therefore this investigation can be dealt with quietly with only a few operatives, compared to say a dozen Furies running around the city, plus the added bodies of their handlers?" He picks some lint off his coat, his muscles bulging deliciously under the fabric.

Griffith seems astounded as though he hadn't expected Declan to be so articulate, it takes him several moments to catch up while both of us stare at him. "Well of course. I am a close personal friend with the Director of the organisation." A poorly formed lie, setting aside my own issues with the Director, I know the pair do not get along. The relationship between Rueben and his majesty, Theodore, is already very strained. So, Mason's and Reuben's is most certainly fabricated.

I cock my head to the side, enjoying the sight of Griffith squirm under the intensity of my stare. But Mason doesn't take too kindly to the implied insult on his behalf, his bushy white eyebrows pull together, and he turns his focus to me. "And I am well aware of what I said. I'm just doubting that one of those *things*, can get the job done," he spits, throwing the insult my way, grinning when Declan's fist clenches on the arm of the chair. My eyes narrow and I watch as his expression shifts from smug to terrified within a second. That darkness comes to the surface, snarling and whipping under my skin desperate for its pound of flesh. His will do.

Griffith's breathing changes from slow and deep to shallow and rapid within a matter of moments, and an oddly enjoyable feeling wells in my chest.

"I apologise for being so forward, *General*. But we have travelled a long way for this, and we would appreciate a quick transfer of information. Everything that you have gathered so far so that we can determine where to begin with our own," Declan drawls, breaking our impromptu challenge.

"Ah yes," Griffith clears his throat, all too pleased for the distraction. The lack of colour in his cheeks is noticeable on his face and is a blatant comparison to the redness of his thick neck. He leans down to the drawer in his desk, eyeing me as he does, and pulls out a small beige folder, the contents of which hardly look worth the paper it's printed on.

"This is it?" Declan inquires, reaching across the desk to the flimsy file. A singular page and a set of pictures of what appears to be a year-old protest are stacked together.

"No. But it's a good start for you," Griffith insists, puffing out his chest once again like a mating toad.

Declan sighs and pinches his brow, clearly the agitation was never too far away, "We are going to need everything you have if you want this dealt with quickly."

Griffith starts to protest, "I simply cannot give away every scrap of information I have on a whim. My people have worked hard to garner what they can. I don't know you and I don't care who you claim to be. You'll work with what you're given until I see fit that you are competent. Do not forget who is in charge of this operation, boy." The redness on his neck intensifies.

"I understand you have reservations; like you say you don't know us. But need I remind you, *again,* that you asked for our help? You reached out to the Director; I'd hate to have to tell him how difficult you're making the proceedings. You're the one who needed us to deal with this business, so tell me, General, who is competent and who is not?" Declan argues, relaxing back in his chair again, still looking irritated yet perceptively smug.

General Griffith goes to argue again, I roll my eyes and stand. Both sets of eyes turn on me, observing closely.

"Three-Nought-Nought sit back down," Declan demands, I look at him and see that the demand is as fragile as the mortal man on the other side of this desk. In fact, I think he could be genuinely curious to see what I'll do.

I stalk around the other side of the table and throw open the drawer.

"What in the Hel do you think you're doing?" Griffith hollers, his sausage-like fingers reaching out to grab my wrist.

They don't make contact.

Quicker than a coiling snake, I reach for the blade sheathed at my thigh. The metal curved like a claw and sharp enough to pierce through flesh like its mere paper.

He throws himself back against his chair as the blade glints under the fluorescent lights; I press it deeper into his throat. The frame creaks loudly, and his terrified eyes look up at me as sweat starts to bead on his brow. I don't remove my knife from his now bobbing oesophagus while I reach into the drawer and pull out the rest of the files, throwing them to the other side of the desk.

Declan's face is a picture of shock and a small drop of something I don't recognise.

Re-sheathing my knife I move away from the General and back to Declan's side.

"Well, I think we can agree that that didn't need to happen. We'll be in touch, Griffith," Declan says to the room while standing and nods at me to follow him.

The air is stiflingly awkward when we climb back into the car minutes later. "I had that handled you know; the knife was a bit much." I can tell by the tone of his voice that he isn't particularly happy that I interfered, but there is a hint of something akin to admiration.

"My apologies, we were going around in circles, and he was never going to give it up willingly without some incentive. It is a torture technique. Give them something they cannot say no to."

His head tilts. "You torture people a lot?"

I cock my brow and turn to face him, "Probably more than you think."

He nods seemingly unfazed. Neither of us speak for a time, it's only when we stop at a series of lights does he clear his throat. "Will you receive punishment for that?"

I turn to him, "In the meeting?" He nods in answer. "It is likely yes. If he actually wants to admit that he is incapable of doing his job."

He snickers but catches himself quickly. Thinking that is the end of the conversation I look back out of the window. "How?" He asks.

Keeping my gaze on the street, "If I am lucky, it will be fifty or so lashes. Maybe more depending on who is doling the punishment out. It is likely to be either yourself or Rich, given the length of my stay here."

I think back to the 'lesson' I learned from Tuli. Eighty lashes later I was in a total daze barely clinging onto consciousness and she left me to hang out in the snow for the rest of the day, and well into the night. Wolves began howling at the moon before someone came to collect me. My blood had frozen to my back and my bare skin had turned blue. Madame Killick had a few choice words for me that night as she had Gregory carry me back to my room.

"Lashes? As in a whip?" His brows lower, casting terrifying shadows in those usually warm hazel eyes.

I nod.

He swallows, "Have you been whipped before?"

"Yes."

"What will happen if you aren't *lucky*?"

I'm not quite understanding this conversation. This is the most he has spoken to me in just over a year when the duo took me to Kos to get my wounds seen to by a professional. When Declan learnt of my profession, he was all too quick to leave. Claiming he couldn't be in the presence of such evil. We had been friends once and I never understood his sudden change. I clung to his words, lying awake at night trying to understand what I did wrong. I quickly concluded that it was because I was no better than a murderer. Someone who enjoys killing and making a game of it. Maybe he saw the darkness that resides within me and thought I was death incarnate.

"Does it matter?" I ask instead. He doesn't want to be here, there's no point in pretending to be more than acquaintances. People who hate each other. Enemies by right.

He scoffs, turning his attention back to the road, "No. I don't suppose it does."

Declan storms up the stairs, not bothering to slow down or wait for me, not that I would expect that from him. Nor would I welcome it. I'm a floor below when the apartment door ricochets off the wall.

"What the fuck is wrong with you?" Rich's startled screech hollers down the narrow stairwell, I snicker at the unusually high-pitched sound, "And where is she? Did you leave her?"

"No, I didn't leave her, she's..." The floorboards beneath Declan groan as he steps back into the hallway barely missing me as I turn to step inside, "there."

Rich is sitting on the couch, eating his way through lunch, the sauce from which dampens the collar of his shirt, presumably when he jumped from Declan's anger. "I take it the meeting didn't go so well then?" he asks.

"The meeting went fine, Handler Keita," I reply, closing the door, observing the dent in the wall from the handle. "Handler Angelos is distressed about another matter."

"What other matter?" He turns his attention back to Declan, boring a hole into the side of his face with his angry stare.

"Having spent time with me," I smile, taking my mask off, readjusting my hair. The heat from Declan's glare could warm this whole room, not just my face.

Rich lets out an annoyed grunt but doesn't push the matter, clearly knowing his friend too well.

"Now, if you will both excuse me. I will begin my work." I step toward Declan and hold out my hand. He drops his gaze, staring at it for a moment, wondering what it's doing getting closer to him. "The files if you will, handler Angelos," I urge. He passes them to me with such a force one would believe a fire has been lit beneath him, and then turns to the kitchen.

Rich follows me to my room and stands awkwardly in the doorway as I drop on the bed.

"Need help?" he asks timidly.

I look him up and down. He's feeling torn between wanting to help me and feeling remorse for whatever Declan is going through being here. That much I can read on his face. "I do not require it. But if you find yourself at a loss for something to do. You can read through that." I throw a file containing clippings from a multitude of different newspapers that have even a scrap of information about the connected attacks.

I tuck my feet up under me and he takes that as an invitation to join, sitting down next to me on the bed. I can hear Declan potter around in the kitchen for several minutes but put it to the back of my mind. Everything fades into the background when I open the files in front of me.

The Stratos has had such trouble pinning individuals down that they've put out a reward for any information from the public. Forcing terror into the hearts of the people by calling them terrorists.

Rich and I sit in companionable silence for a long time, just reading through our respective texts. "It seems here, the Stratos were making headway. Why call the guild in now?" He muses, breaking the silence.

"Ajay has resources like no other government on the globe. Nor any other guild. It makes sense that they would call us in. But I question why it took them so long," I answer in kind, placing one piece of text down only to pick up another.

Rich picks up the pictures while I keep reading.

"Roman... Garcia." My tone is thoughtful as I look over the file made for him, "he appears to be the main antagonist of '*Dawnya*'. They have a warrant out for his arrest." I picked out a picture from the file of a dark-haired fae both of his arms filled with eccentric and colourful tattoos, tall in stature with well-defined muscles.

"*Dawnya*?" Rich asks, tasting the word on his tongue.

"Yeah, apparently that's the name of the organisation they've created," I say absentmindedly. "Oh, but they do have a snapshot of some CCTV footage of another suspect, but no name." I pick it up and look at the pixelated image frowning, "there's no way you can make out anyone's features with that as a reference," I mumble.

A tingling on the back of my neck tells me someone is watching me; I look up to see Rich staring at me. "What?"

"Nothing. I've just never seen this side of you. You didn't exactly talk much when we picked you up and took you to Kos," he responds.

"You have a very calming presence, and when it comes to work, I tend to focus more on that than the code that force feed at the Fort," I reply.

"Is it voluntary?" he ponders.

"In a manner of speaking," I mumble, squinting at the CCTV image as if it will magically clear itself up so I can see something other than black and white fuzzy lines.

"I know someone that might be able to clear it up," Rich replies, taking the photograph from me.

CHAPTER EIGHT
THE CROWNS' WORD IS
LAW

"You're to see the king," Declan announces walking into my room sometime later, looking down at his phone.

"Well, isn't that a nice surprise" Rich mumbles next to me. Both of us haven't moved much in the hours that have passed. The only change, is now Rich has sprawled across the sheets, pulling them out from underneath the mattress.

"You seem... dare I say, calmer?" Rich preens, looking at Declan. "What time?"

"You know, I'm talking to A..." he cuts himself off.

"Yes. I am aware, thank you," Rich back chats, ignoring his fumbles.

"When has he requested a meeting, Handler Angelos?" I reply.

"Don't call me that," he snaps, "but, and I quote, at your earliest convenience, which really means right now," he says. I stand from my bed, without fuss or complaint, and reattach my mask to my face, before strapping my vest back around my chest.

"I'll come with you both," Rich groans standing when I do.

Declan opens his mouth to speak but closes again, nodding he turns away and leaves us to follow behind.

The drive to the next meeting is fairly quiet, the sound of the radio the only bridge between us and total silence.

Declan takes an unexpected turn onto a different road.

"Permission..."

"I thought you had permission to speak until told otherwise?" Rich's cheeky grin lightens some of the anxiety I'm feeling at this unexpected turn of events.

Otherwise ignoring the comment, I try again, "Are we not heading back to the City Hall?"

"No," Declan grunts, offering no further comment.

I turn my attention back to the road, watching the people on the streets and the cars merging into different lanes of traffic.

He sighs from the front seat, "We are heading to The Circle. The five towers we saw earlier, his Majesty arrived shortly after we did. He got here this morning, something that the General decided not to share with us. I believe the Director has been in contact with him, informing his majesty that he has sent someone to deal with the situation. I'm assuming he felt he needed to come down here himself to oversee your progress."

I nod my thanks and once again the vehicle falls quiet, our collective attention caught by the mass those towers make as they get larger and larger upon our approach, becoming looming pillars that look as though they hold up the sky itself.

The Circle is a mini, man-made, island designed with those towers in mind. They fit like the five points of a star, perfectly aligned; the island connects to the mainland by a series of intricate bridges and beautifully painted gondolas.

New checkpoints are stationed on each bridge with guards dressed in gleaming golden armour, checking people's identification. The King's

Guard, his elite soldiers who answer to his every whim.

Pulling up to the Northernmost tower, General Griffith stands in the entrance and a disturbing smile splits his face, reminding me of the creepy-looking jack-o-lanterns that are used for Samhain.

"Griffith," Declan grunts when we draw close enough.

"A pleasure to see you both again," Griffith replies, "and you." He turns to Rich, the wolfish grin still in place and deception laces his tone. Then he steps closer to me, "His majesty, for reasons that only he knows, wanted to meet with you. But he will not put up with your attitude girl, so watch your back in there. Someone may just put a knife in it."

Declan steps up to my side placing a tanned hand against Griffith's chest. His jaw and cheekbones have never been sharper than they are in this moment. His barely tempered anger rises, coupled with his disgust for the mortal in front of him.

"I suggest you take a step back, or her *attitude* will quickly become the least of your problems," he growls. His usually vibrant hazel eyes glow a bright shade of amber and his fangs appear longer, but that could be a trick of the light.

Griffith visibly swallows and steps back, "his majesty is waiting," he says gruffly.

Declan's jaw remains clenched as he watches the weak male shuffle away, now under the protection of two members of the king's guard that stand tall, waiting for us to proceed. All too suddenly I feel as though I've swallowed my tongue.

A royal servant greets us in the opulent lobby, a low-hanging crystal chandelier lights the white and cream circular room. The young dark-haired male is dressed in a rich, blood-red, velvet jacket, standing starkly in the middle of the room, adorned with gold thread on the cuffs and collar, with the royal crest on the left of his breast.

"Greetings, his majesty would like to thank you all for heeding his call on such short notice. If you follow me, I will lead you to him," the young man greets. Russ, a servant I met when I worked in the palace years ago. Undercover of course. Beneath this mask, he hopefully won't recognise me.

He turns to lead us to the elevators, a new invention, designed for these towers. With so many floors and stairs being the primary source of elevation, something else had to be thought of. A small box lifted by machines was what they invented.

The five of us plus two armoured guards, load into the small box, the servant pushes the button, and the doors close. The jolt of the mechanics has my anxiety flaring to life once more. I've never experienced an elevator before, and the current practice is none too pleasant when there are multiple males inside, all built like bulls taking up the majority of the space.

My heart beats so loudly I'm surprised no one can hear it and my palms begin to feel clammy, my breathing quickens. The elevator starts to feel too small for all of us to be in here, so I shut my eyes, willing the swiftly rising panic to calm, without success. My panting breaths beat back at me from my mask, the warmth of my breath heating my lips and cheeks until the air becomes stifling, and my panic surges higher.

Another jar and groan of the system jumps me.

Something warms my hand; I look down to see I've grabbed a hold of Declan's palm. My brain short-circuits and without releasing him, my eyes rise until I'm looking at his face, his eyebrow is quirked as he looks down to our entangled hands.

I let go, wiping my sweaty hand against my trousers. My panic swells more and more and my chest begins expanding painfully with the quickness of my breath. I can tell I'm moments away from collapsing, and yet I know that I need to be the picture of calm and collected. The thought helps me very little, instead, I try to focus on how the experience will be over soon.

I can feel Declan's eyes roving over the side of my face. I can practically see how he is trying to work out what made me react that way, trying to understand what it was that made me reach out to him.

He says nothing as he grabs my hand, intertwining our fingers, giving them a comforting, and reaffirming squeeze. The contact isn't something I'm used to, and yet it feels so natural. The racing of my heart slows down, the shaking of my hands too. The rapid rise and fall of my chest evens out, I turn and nod my thanks to him, squeezing his hand back.

I expect him to let go once I'm comfortable again. But he

doesn't. Instead, he seems to hold on a little tighter.

Russ pushes open the heavy wooden doors to the large meeting room that holds a dark mahogany table, the length of the room, reflecting the light beaming in through the floor-to-ceiling windows. The view is of the bustling and beautiful city below and is lined with matching chairs.

More servants stand proud in their white uniforms, with their arms behind their backs, parallel to the white painted walls, waiting patiently.

Two figures sit at the farthest end of this grand table still eating what remains of their dinner, through courtesy alone they give us their attention when the double doors groan loudly.

The servant announces our presence and proceeds to guide us up the length of the table where the king sits, now relaxed back, wiping his mouth with a white linen napkin. His son, the crown prince, sits to his left mimicking the action.

King Theodore sits there watching our approach, a look of bored satisfaction on his aged face. His green eyes hold malice, and a small predatory smirk tilts his lips up on one side. The golden crown upon his onyx-coloured head is made from antlers and forest vines, adorned with red rubies and diamonds.

The general takes a seat to the king's right, usually reserved for a close companion or a guest of his majesty's choosing. He eyes Griffith annoyed by the man's presence but does not tell him to move.

His majesty clicks his fingers, and the servants closest clear the plates from the table.

"Out!" he calls, and in perfect unison, they leave us alone in the room. The two guards from the elevator stand sentry on the doors, presiding over the meeting, their hands on the hilts of their golden swords.

The king's eyes find mine in an instant while I listen to the last of his servants leave the room and swiftly close the doors and the room descends into awkward silence.

"Your majesty, it's an honour," Rich says, bowing at the waist, his arms plastered to his sides.

"You bow like one of my knights, boy? Are you a part of my guard?" The deepness of the king's voice rumbles through the room.

"I'm from Sormbay, your majesty. I travelled across the Avak to aid in the war against Duranda."

"Past tense?" the king challenges.

"I was relived of my duty due to an injury," Rich responds.

"Ah." Is the king's only response, eyeing Rich like he doesn't quite believe him. He then turns his attention to Declan, who's a little more hesitant to bow before the king. But he does it all the same. If a bit woodenly.

"Three-Nought-Nought, a pleasure to see you once again," his majesty greets.

My knee hits the tiled floor and I drop into a low bow, it is only right to show the proper respect given who sits before me. A snicker comes from Griffith at his majesty's side.

"Rise," Theodore's voice rings out. He returns his gaze to the male next to me and plasters on a smile, unlike anything I've ever seen from him before. The hairs on the back of my neck rise while I fight the shiver trying to roll down my spine. Showing all of his teeth, he stands and holds his hand out in front of him for Declan to shake.

"Your majesty," he greets, holding the kings hand a little too tightly.

The red-faced general's mouth drops open clearly, he was not afforded the same courtesy. I see the prince smirking on the other side of the table, earning himself a scowl from his father when he sits back in his chair.

"Please, all of you take a seat and let's get this started." This extraordinarily kind persona his majesty has drudged up from the depths is entirely not himself and it's uncomfortably false. I don't even think that he believes he could be this polite and understanding.

After I spent some time behind the royal palace's walls, I know this man inside and out, and this version of him is one I haven't seen before.

I pull out a chair and cross one leg over the other, my hands clasped together in my lap.

"A good evening to you too, your highness," Rich greets, addressing the prince.

"Isn't it?" The prince replies smirking, he relaxes back in his chair, anticipating a thoroughly good show.

Prince Frederick is around the same age as I. He's the oldest of two and happens to look more like his mother than his father – lucky him – he got more fae genes than mortal.

Both he and his father share the similar trait of green eyes, and whilst the kings are still a deep forest green, they are nowhere near as bright as his son's.

Frederick, being only half fae doesn't have the classic flawless skin of his ancestors, the almost doe-like gracefulness, or the abnormally long life, but he still has the fangs and bright eyes, the pointed ears. He is stronger than the mortal guards that protect him and the natural swiftness his predecessors were known for. He will still have a longer life than the common mortal, but his full-blooded-fae mother will still likely outlive him.

My attention turns back to the king, who sits in front of me, his tall and broad frame drowns the chair behind him, yet he seems to sit comfortably with his fingers steepled. His tanned skin appears more aged and thinner than the last time I saw him. Not a single scar cuts through his skin.

"Your majesty," Rich begins, his jaw set as he stares at the king, "while it is an honour to be summoned, I have to wonder why you have. Like yourself, we have not long since arrived. We have not yet begun the investigation."

"Right, of course," he faces Rich, "I've heard from the Director, that General Griffith reached out to him a few weeks prior and asked for aid. Even after a request was put forth to his colleagues for assistance, that, should I remind everyone, was *denied*. I sent enough of a force here to deal with this. I am here now to ask you to fix this mess and keep our names out of it. I need the people's faith to be placed back in both, myself, and the Stratos. The fact that this cannot be dealt with by the military is no less than humiliating."

Griffith grumbles and looks as though he is about to say something, but Theodore raises his hand, stopping him without so much as batting an eye.

"I am not finished. I think a change of leadership may be in order, but that is another topic for another group of people." Griffith chokes on the air he's breathing.

"Sir, what is it you are trying to say exactly?" Declan asks, his brows creased. I can see he's fighting from downright punching the king in the face. Their history though is that of a mystery to me.

"I don't know how I could've spoken any plainer but, I am asking you to keep all of the noise quiet. I don't want any more news about the incompetence of my military and of me. Along with this problem, I don't want to see any more articles about it, and I don't want any more fuel added to the already stifling fire." He pulls at his shirt collar absentmindedly driving his point home.

Frederick's face drops from the cocky façade into an impassive mask, hiding his true emotions. Something he's no doubt picked up from his father's court. "Father," he says, "the guild has an exemplary record for a reason. They have sent their best to deal with your problem and we must now have every faith in their capabilities. I am positive this will be dealt with swiftly."

"Well, I don't know about their best but of course, you're right Frederick. they have been loyal all these years. Something that is fickle in the field they find themselves," Theodore replies, his tone harsher and more like the man that I know.

His Highness picks off some lint from his black tunic, lined with golden thread looking disinterested. I see something in his posture and note that his eyes keep flicking towards me. Before I can make anything of it, his attention is snapped away by movement from the general, who shifts his position awkwardly in his chair.

"In fact, this part is just for myself and Three-Nought-Nought, I would like to speak to her in private."

Declan tenses in his seat.

"Your majesty, my apologies but I don't think I can permit..." Rich begins.

"It wasn't a suggestion boy. Now out! All of you."

The others begin filing out, Rich eyes me as he passes but doesn't say anything further, even the guards leave us alone for this part of the conversation, I can't imagine this will be a good discussion.

"I suspect what I have to say, will stay between the two of us?" He quirks a brow letting me know he's serious in his assumption. I nod politely and he continues. "This problem is too close to home for both me and my family, although I doubt, they told you as much and I will not be enlightening you either, that is a private matter. But in recent months I have received several death threats, including a lovely gift which consisted of a pig's bloody heart in a box."

Shocker. He grinds his jaw no doubt reliving the memory.

"But I'm not stupid. I know the people's faith has been lost in me, due to the predicament we had with Tinos a few decades ago." His knuckles turn white with his grip. "You know I care not for you nor your *habits,*" he hisses. I know he isn't just talking about me. It's no secret the king, despite calling upon us time again, hates the Fort of Ajay and everything it stands for. It's not even what we do. He enjoys the torture and pain even from his own people. Until it calls his humanity into question. It's the fact that we are strictly women who are the perfect weapons.

Rueben had once told him the reason for it being women. *'They are less noticeable. They can slip into anywhere virtually undetected. No one would look twice at them'.* In the face of his example, I have to admit, I have walked into some classified places before now and have never been looked at twice.

I hate that he was right.

"I am also not so short-sighted that I don't know who I look at. I know why *you* are here. I know you are relentless and that you won't stop until the job is done. Just like you helped my Iris all those years ago with her problem. Not even a whisper in the wind was heard about her addiction. That is why you are here and that is why I know you will not let me down."

A strange untrustworthy warmth creeps up inside of me at the acknowledgement of my skill, and the previous job I did for their family. But I know I cannot trust him. The time spent in his palace taught me that.

"But heed this, *Siren.* Should you fail me, it will be the very last thing that you do. This needs to be wiped from all our histories, is that understood."

I nod my head in compliance wondering what this personal matter could really mean should it get out.

He takes his time looking over the half-visible portion of my face. I'm unsure if he dislikes what he sees in me or if he hates what I represent in himself. His eyes then darken in disgust. If he's figured it out, he doesn't share it with me.

"What is your primary objective?" he asks, after a few quiet moments, leaning forward on the table, he rests on his elbows, looking me straight in the eye.

"Find and eliminate the target, sir." He nods sharply, seemingly satisfied with my answer.

"Out," he snaps, gesturing to the door. I stand and bow again to him leaving him alone in the room.

I take several deep breaths when I eventually step out into the hallway. Even with the stifling air that lingers.

General Griffith stands off to one side, his gaze far away and his face devoid of colour. Declan has his arms crossed, leaning against the wall next to the elevator, watching the door to the meeting room. We lock eyes when I step out of the room.

Prince Frederick stands talking with his short, red-headed male servant, Elijah. I recognise him instantly from the time I spent at the palace. He was more than helpful to me during that assignment.

Rich looks me up and down, checking I'm alright and once he's satisfied, he nods to the elevator, where Declan stands, arms folded waiting on us. I step forward but I'm promptly cut off by the crown prince.

"A..." he cuts himself off, "Three-Nought-Nought, a word if you please." He clears his throat and adjusts his posture. Becoming more like his father by the day and not the young carefree prince I've come to know. Declan too comes over standing in between us. Frederick, although has initial shock, doesn't seem overly surprised to see him.

"Mr Angelos, Mr Keita a pleasure to meet you both. I read the files *Mr* Griffith gave us, they show two rather impressive military records." He compliments, "Your father climbed the ranks almost as fast as you did. Being a military man must run in the family." He turns to Declan as he speaks, holding out his hand for the shifter to shake, smiling brightly with a dimple on each cheek, fangs on full display.

"It sure does, your highness." Declan answers with an unusual tightness to his voice, "I would like to stay and chat but unfortunately, we must be getting back," he evades, shaking Frederick's hand all the same.

"I promise I won't take much of your time, I would actually like a quick word with this beautiful woman next to you."

One of Declan's eyebrows rises, and his jaw locks, that pesky muscle flexing once again.

"One minute, tops," Frederick places his hand on his heart, tilting his head and his chocolate locks fall to the side.

"One minute," Declan concedes, unhappily. The pair step away but keep a close eye on us.

Frederick grins broader and leads me away from the guards, down the hallway away from prying ears.

"Now I know I won't be able to get much out of you, peaches. But I could really do with a private meeting of our own – and no not the fun kind, before you pinch me," he grins, knowing me too well. I was in fact moving my hand to pinch his arm. "It's about my father's problem, I don't know if you're aware of a certain hiccup with the whole thing. But I feel like you would tell me now if you were." He places his hands on my upper arms, gently holding me still, before looking deep into my eyes searching for something. Anything that tells him I understand.

His mouth tugs down with a frown when he doesn't find what he's looking for. "I thought as much," he sighs. "Ok, I can send a car to you. Tell me where you are…" He stops abruptly when the dining room doors open and his father steps into the white and grey hallway. He eyes the closeness of me and his son, and he glares at Frederick. Within a matter of seconds, the prince released his hold on me, staring back at his father.

His Majesty shoves the door open wider, clearly irritated. I can't tell whether it's at his son or the stout man sitting on the only bench in the corridor with a face as white as snow.

"Mason, if you please. The others will be arriving shortly. It is time to talk about your future."

CHAPTER NINE
THE WAR

In the days after the war first began the earth was still ablaze. The screams of the innocent still ringing in the air, swallowed by the wind along with the ashes and the uncontainable grief.

A war with nothing to be gained.

The day Duranda landed on these shores neither country was prepared for the devastation they would bring. Tinos had been hit first. Even given their best efforts, Duranda's forces were far more savage than any they had come across before. Mounted on desert-steady horses with sickle blades and hatchets, Duranda burnt a whole village to the ground within a matter of hours. The residents had been sleeping and weren't able to defend themselves. But it wasn't until a village in Anaphi received the same treatment that the king had his army step in.

It had taken days for the armies to reach what they now call the scarred lands and even then Duranda had set up camps to keep them at bay.

To this day, Duranda still holds those lands, even in the face of the two nations calling a tense truce to remove them from the shores.

The border has become impossible to cross, through fear of being murdered by the - what they call themselves - 'dragon's sons.' A legend of the eight brothers, with dragons for mounts, is a story that has lasted through the ages. But it's slowly becoming more myth than legend.

It is said they protected the Southern Colonies from foreign invaders. The battle lasted for three days without reprieve, and as a reward for their bravery and commitment to their countries, each brother was gifted with an island of their own to rule and protect.

One day, one of the eight became restless wanting more than what he received as payment. Five of the brothers tried to satiate his growing discomfort. Whereas the other two pushed him into doing something foolish. He mounted his dragon, intending to take his eldest brother's kingdom. The one who ruled over Sormbay. Before he made it to the capital, his brother met him in the air astride his own dragon, a creature far greater than his own. It was said they fought for hours until eventually, the eldest defeated his crazed sibling. But at great cost, his dragon was injured and was unlikely to fly again. But he had saved his kingdom. His brother, with his dragon, fell from the sky in a blazing fireball.

To this day people believe his island makes even the sanest person disoriented with a manic fever. Aptly named 'The Wilds' only animals roam the lands now. No human, mortal or shifter has set foot there in the centuries since their rule.

Duranda, to this day, has kept to the old way. Still believing that one day the seven brothers and their dragons will rise again and continue their rule.

Two Years Ago

Those who survived long enough to be displaced by the 'sons' had either been moved to the capital, Larissa, or shipped to Ansrutas. The only two cities capable of holding and helping the mass of civilians forced to relocate.

Any injured on the frontline, myself included, have been transported across the country as of a few days ago, away from the border.

My leg bound tightly in a wooden splint which holds all of the bandages together, is propped up in front of me, as I sit in the wheelchair that Rich has thoroughly enjoyed pushing me around in.

Especially down ramps.

The city of Kos has opened its arms to those with injuries and its people opened up their own homes to those who needed one. The city isn't as big as Ansrutas, nor Larissa, but it is still doing its part to help those who need it most.

Kos is not only known for its spectacular wine but for its medicinal practices.

In spite of my own objections Rich and Declan had become my caregivers and while I'm tremendously grateful for their assistance, their constant fussing is driving me insane. I have told them countless times to relax and take care of themselves, but both have told me they are happy to do it. The medical professionals smile and laugh every time they ask a question about the medication I have been given, taking it all in stride.

The three of us, along with dozens of other injured soldiers, have been moved up to the highest part of the city.

One of the many vineyards – that this large town is made of - has an enormous empty estate, decorated with climbing vines and a few dozen water fountains.

The vineyard's owners, an elderly couple along with their family, graciously opened up the property for the medical teams to use as a makeshift infirmary, and nearly every room is in use.

The gardens surrounding the estate are like none I've ever seen before, neatly cut knee-high hedges border the entire area, and exotic blooming flowers in colours of delicate white, the softest purple, and the prettiest pink bring a rainbow of colours breaking up the shades of green. The scent of summer lingers in the humid air, and the pink and orange of the sunset sends a warm fuzzy feeling through my chest.

Kos stands proud across the many hills it has been built on. Buildings of white and cream catch and soak up the sun, accented in periwinkle blue and a soft sage green. Medicinal herbs grow in plant pots up and down the streets, and several terraces are canopied in hanging vines, with small flowering orange blossoms.

The only thing we can all be grateful for from the war is that it's not travelled this far east.

This wing of the estate seems deserted as we turn down yet another long, seemingly-never ending corridor. I sigh as we passed door after door, listening to new patients groan and grunt in pain, only to take a sharp turn where the warm breeze of the evening floats through the open doors before me, kissing my pale skin.

A mini square garden of sorts brings green to the terracotta tiled terrace, a wooden pergola draped in vines stands tall in one corner, with cushioned seats and several large settees in all imaginable colours and patterns. In the centre of it all, is a bubbling water fountain; the base of which is carved with stone fish and curling seaweed twisting up to the bowl.

Rich parks me under the pergola looking out over the colourful, vibrant city and to the grape vines scaling the adjacent hills and takes a seat next to me on one of the plush settees, legs crossed and smiling lazily.

He sits peacefully looking out at the view and I can't help but admire his side profile. At his plump lips and his black and silver eyes fringed by thick eyelashes, his groomed eyebrows, and his slightly crooked nose. I smile into the calmness, a small timid thing as I watch the sun bounce off his cheekbones and it's then that he smirks, revealing those shifter fangs.

"Would you like to take a picture?" he chuckles, turning to see me wide-eyed and red-faced.

My cheeks flush hot and I turn away looking back out at the view. Gnawing on my lip I feel his gaze on me and it's wholly uncomfortable.

Declan joins us a few minutes later, a tray of glasses with him, each filled with a different coloured liquid. One of which he gives to Rich and looking at its contents, it appears to be some bubbly, yellow drink smelling discreetly of lemon. He hands me a cold glass of water and he takes a seat on my other side.

"Thanks," I mumble, sharing a small smile with him. Taking a sip, I wince at the coolness running down my throat, before placing the glass on the ground. "You know, you didn't have to bring me here." I keep my attention on the tall cypress trees in the distance, swaying in the breeze.

"Sure we did, this place has the best healers in all of Anaphi... and the best wine," Declan replies, his eyebrows waggling up and down and I allow myself a small laugh.

"So, tell me was my assumption correct?" Rich asks after a quiet minute. I observe the colours of the sky, the dark blue creeping into the orange and pink of the sunset.

"About my profession? You never actually told me what you thought I was," I reply, taking a sip of my water. A sudden and profound sense of nervousness writhes awake within.

Rich chuckles placing his glass on the ground, "You're an assassin. From which guild I couldn't say but tell me, did I guess it right?"

I glance at him watching his smirk increase. "Unfortunately, you are correct."

Declan tenses beside me, his drink paused midway to his mouth.

"Why is it unfortunate?" Rich asks, smiling broadly.

"Because usually, I have to kill those who figure it out," I answer.

"But?" Rich drags the word out playfully.

"But you have helped me out, so I suppose I could go against protocol this one time."

Declan scoffs, catching Rich's attention. Rich's mouth tugs down in a frown and he shifts uncomfortably. I look between the two, still lost.

"Have you ever done that before?" Rich queries, his full attention on me.

"Done what?"

"Spared someone you shouldn't."

"Never."

"Of course not. Why would you?" Declan snarls. His sudden shift hits me like whiplash.

"Declan. Don't," Rich warns.

I turn to Declan to find he won't look at me, it doesn't take a genius to figure out why he has changed his attitude in such a short amount of time. Taking a shuddering breath I ask, "I killed someone close to you, didn't I?"

Both males turn to me in shock. The waver in my voice gives away an emotion that is foreign to me. I've never felt remorse or guilt for doing my job. But I suppose it's different when you meet someone who was affected by your actions. Someone who in spite of everything they have been through has come away with a heart of gold.

"It's not been confirmed," Rich's voice is quiet but firm and although the answer is for me, he speaks to Declan.

"The weapon used was unregistered and had no code on the bullet. How can it not have been them." His brows lower and his eyes darken anger swimming in those warm irises that I have come to know and love.

I watch two colourful bluebirds perch themselves on a high ledge before us, hopping up and down and chirping to one another, unable to see the heartbreak that is so clearly painted across his face. But it stains the air around, in a grey hue.

The two appear to have a silent argument for several moments before Declan stands and storms away.

I swallow as I watch his retreating back. My tongue feels as if it's turned to lead, even if I wanted to apologise to him, it wouldn't bring back who he lost. It wouldn't magically fix everything.

Rich clears his throat, "Don't mind him..."

"Don't downplay his emotion. He has every right to be angry and hurt." I rest my hand on his arm gently. "It may not have been me directly. But if what he says is true. It was likely one of my sisters and, in the face of pain, it doesn't matter who did it, only that it happened, and it can't be undone."

I rest my hands my lap, playing with my fingers. We sit in silence for so long the sun has closed the gap between it and the horizon.

"Aella," I squeak into the evening air. "The name the Fort gave me, other than my number, is Aella."

Rich turns to me with a tight-lipped smile, "It's beautiful."

"I wanted to say thank you for everything you've done for me, this past week and I don't have much else to offer."

Rich entwines our fingers together, squeezing my hand firmly.

"You don't owe us anything."

My heart has sunk so far in my chest that the smile I give him is forced. Even he can see it.

"He'll be fine," he mutters.

"No. He won't."

"Let's change the conversation. I don't want to spend the last few days moping."

"What did you have in mind?"

"I have like a million questions about what you do?" Rich tells me.

"Probably ones that I can't and won't answer." I turn to him grinning, watching his face fall.

"No! Come on, you can't do me like that," he whines.

"I can and I will."

"Just one," he begs.

"Make it a good one then and I'll see what I can share."

"Where do you report back to? Like which guild are you from?"

I blink at him, with my mouth open, "That's two," I point out grinning quickly, "but seriously? Out of all the questions you could've asked. That's the one you went with?"

"Why not? You've heard the stories of a particular type of assassin. The Furies -"

Dread curls in my stomach at the name. Something that's never happened before, it's an effort not to fidget as he continues speaking as if I'm not having an identity crisis over here.

"- But no one ever knows where they come from, it could be here, or it could be from somewhere far away, or it could be magic."

I snort into my glass, water coming out of my nostrils, as I laugh. His warm hand is on my back, rubbing circles in the centre while I regain my breathing. "No, actually I have not heard the stories, as you can imagine. I don't get out much."

Rich flinches, "Are you going to answer? Or are you going to make me feel terrible?" Then tenses turning to face me. "What do you mean you don't get out much?"

"I might make you feel a little worse. It seems kind of fun," I grin ignoring his comment and I wave off the giddiness I suddenly feel. "We do have a base of operations."

The stars in his eyes burned brightly with intrigue. "Where?"

"Here in the mortal realm. There is unfortunately nothing magical about us," I reply.

Realising my mistake, I roll my lips closed and hope to any gods that are listening he wasn't paying too close attention to me.

Peeking at him from the corner of my eye tells me I'm the most unfavoured of the gods children. He stares at me with wide eyes and an open mouth. "Us?" croaks out of his throat. "You're a fucking Fury!"

I wince at the volume of his voice. "Shush yourself," I panic, glancing around hoping no one else heard us. "It's not common knowledge and something I'm not supposed to talk about."

Rich hums letting me know he heard me sitting back in his chair, "I have to say though I thought you guys were a myth."

"You're being oddly calm about this." I turn, raising a brow at him.

"You play the cards you're dealt," he responds, as though this is the most natural conversation in the world and that he hasn't just found out that the female he has been caring for, over the course of the week, isn't a part of the world's most successful assassin's guild in history.

"When do you have to report back?" he asks, not looking at me, instead he looks down at the ground in front of him.

"I need to get in touch with them because I can't make my way back with a broken leg, they will have to come and collect me. But they are expecting to hear back from me by the end of the week."

"When do you guys head back to the Capital?" I ask, changing the subject.

"We aren't," he mumbles.

"What do you mean?"

"We are calling it quits, *liefling.*"

I raise an eyebrow at him, waiting for him to elaborate – at least on the nickname in his mother tongue but his only response is a wink and a cheeky grin.

"We knew at the end that we would, we've been there too long as it already is. Time to go home and live the rest of our lives."

I nod and we fall silent once more.

"Actually, you know what?" he starts again, doing a complete turn on our conversation. "You never explained how you heal so fast. I mean, I know you're not fully healed, but even a fae or shifter would still be bed bound, it's only been a couple of days," he asks, clearly trying to keep the conversation going.

"Honestly I don't even know myself; I've always been like this," I answer, taking the bait, not quite ready for the night to end just yet either.

"What do you mean?" Rich tries again, nudging against me.

"Well, I'm clearly neither shifter nor fae, as you've said," I gesture to my eyes and ears, "I look mortal; I age like a mortal; I feel mortal, but I don't heal like one."

Rich clears his throat, "Have you never been curious?" he takes another drink watching me closely.

"Of course I have been, but I do not know who my parents are, or if they're even still alive." Something cracks in my chest, something heavy and all-consuming. "They wipe our history the moment we walk through the doors. There is nothing about my past in my file. All I have is the guild. That is all I've ever known." I shrug.

He nods and we sit together in peace enjoying the final rays of the sun and the song of the grasshoppers in the distance. He squeezes my hand once again, "it's not anymore."

That night I lay in bed staring up at the ceiling twiddling my thumbs and listening to the crickets sing outside my window, harmonising with the trickling of the water fountain. The white chiffon curtains float eerily in the soft breeze and light up with the moonlight that filters into my room.

Despite the cool breeze, it's still too hot in here. The heat of the day has carried well into the night, and sweat has broken out on my skin. Throwing the covers off, I fumble around for the crutches that the healers have advised me to use.

Through Rich and Declan's meddling, I've managed to acquire a room all to myself, despite the rest of the injured being set up in one main room.

I hobble, not so gracefully, into the adjoining bathroom, where at the turn of a tap, water comes gushing into the glass bowl below. I splash my face with cool water, scooping up handful after handful. I place my cool wet hand on the skin of my neck, relishing in the droplets that race down my back.

Bracing my hands on the basin I look up into the mirror.

This is the first time I've seen myself all week. I'm almost afraid to look at the damage left behind.

Minor cuts and scratches slice through the skin across my nose and forehead, more creamy skin is married with a swollen mound on my cheekbone; my cut lip is almost healed along with the bruising around my eye - though still purple in the middle - has yellowed at the edges.

I sigh at the pitiful sight and take hold of the crutches once more and limp back to the bed, huffing loudly I throw the covers over my legs and lower body, the light cotton blanket feeling light as a feather as I continue to stare at the ceiling just as before.

"Three-Nought-Nought!" My name echoes off the walls of the large rectangular training room with its grey plaster exposed and a wall of glass overlooking the garages below, and the foam floor does nothing to keep any heat in the room.

The rest of the girls in Madame Killick's group turn their attention to me, whereas mine goes to the double set of glass doors where the female herself stands. I unfasten my training gloves from my hands and throw them into my bag, grasping the handles, I make my way across the room.

"The rest of you are to continue with your exercises, we will not be long," Madame calls to the room, my sister's collective attentions turn back to their training by the time I reach the doors.

Re-enacting the respectful bow, I come to a stop in front of Madame K, who seems impatient enough to wave off the motion and without words tells me to follow her. We walk in silence while she leads me up the many flights of stairs to the top floor. She stops outside the clean cream doors.

Dread curls in my stomach.

These rooms are off-limits to everyone except a select few. I am not part of the exception.

My mind begins running wild with all the possibilities as to why I have been summoned.

"Breathe," Madame murmurs, pushing open the doors, she gives me a small nod when I do just as instructed.

It's like a completely different building when stepping into these quarters. The rest of the Fort of Ajay is crisp and clean with whites and light greys on the floors and ceilings, black is the only other colour used and that's reserved for the lower levels.

With high ceilings and bare walls, it could be seen as quite a cold place, reflecting the harsh environment outside. But up here is designed more like that of a wealthy home. Silver-patterned tiles line the floor, glinting with flecks of quartz that are ingrained into each ceramic square. The walls are decorated in a pale cream colour bringing little warmth to the extensive floor.

Tall white pillars stand proud on either side of the room, outlining a large, white marble, round table in the centre, with a clear vase housing dried wild grasses. A plush cream rug hugs the floor, and a delicate crystal chandelier hangs from the middle of a substantially decorative ceiling rose.

A secretary's desk is nestled in one corner of the antechamber and a young fae female sitting behind it looks up as we enter.

"Good afternoon, ladies," she greets politely, "do you have an appointment?" Her pin-up is unmoving as she looks back to her computer screen searching through the calendar.

"Yes." Madame Killick sneers at the younger female, pretending – only to herself – that she is above her.

The fae picks up the phone and connects the line to the room behind her, "good afternoon, sir. I have Madame Killick and a project with her." A pause as she listens to his reply, "Yes sir I'll send them through." The phone hangs up and she once again directs her attention to us. "He is on another call at the moment, but he is expecting you." She gets up from her chair and opens the doors, letting them drift open wider.

Smirking Madame steps forward first, into the lavish office, clearly feeling as though she's won some sort of victory. The gaudy red-wood doors, carved with daggers and flowers – that flow perfectly with each *other – are what draws the eye the moment you step a foot onto this floor, they are the only thing in this chamber with any real colour.*

The carvings trigger a memory I have long since locked away.

A memory of his voice slithers into my ears.

One of his large hands cups my small cheek and his black eyes unblinking as he looks into mine.

His breath but a whisper on my lips.

'Even the most beautiful things can be deadly'.

Something I know about, all too well.

The dark wood floor shines under the artificial light and runs throughout the room, a couch and two chairs sit beside a glass coffee table, which make up a small seating area, in front of the limestone fireplace. Like the stone in the Nursery, this too has an almost mocking depiction of something that has no place in a setting such as this. Carved delicately into the stone is a depiction of most the Gods', sixteen statues in total with more than enough room for the others. Several of them remain faceless, while others look nothing like they have been described in ancient texts.

Madame K ushers me into the room and closes the door quietly behind us, I follow her towards an oversized black desk in the centre of the room that seems to swallow any light that touches it.

Behind it is where he sits.

Reuben Ostair.

A fae male with a ruthless tenacity to get what he wants. No matter the cost and no matter who gets in his way. He's lived for centuries. He's fought in countless wars following the orders of others who he deems lesser than him and now here he is. The Director of an assassin's guild. The one who pulls the strings. He built us from the ground up and spread us across the globe. We now, without question, follow his every order.

Endless black eyes follow our approach, all the while he talks into his phone in hushed tones, he holds up a finger stopping us just before the desk.

"Yes. Yes, the problem will be dealt with promptly. You have my full confidence, no one will know of your involvement. Yes, I'll be in touch with the progress of the situation. Goodbye Sir, we'll talk again soon," *he* finishes his call and looks up at us.

"Ladies, my apologies, just another government official having problems with his females," he rolls his eyes in an attempt to seem playful. "A pleasure to see you both as always. Thank you for coming on such short notice, shall we begin?" he throws a wolfish grin in our direction, nausea curls in my stomach and he motions to the two chairs in front of his desk.

"Thank you, Sir. It's an honour to be in your company," Madame Killick replies curtsying, his smile grows at the submission, and then he locks eyes with me. His head tilts as he looks at me, his gaze raking up and down my body, shifting his long black hair with it. I cross an arm over my chest and bow my head.

Madame takes the offered seat first, smiling all the while.

"Is this our chosen lady then?"

Madame K beams brighter, placing a hand on my forearm shining with pride and loving his attention. That might just unnerve me more than his unwavering awareness.

"Yes sir, I believe she has proven herself in these last few months to be competent enough to handle this mission," she replies.

His eyes drop down scanning every inch of me again and I fight the urge to fidget, a deep hum rumbles from his chest, showing his approval and he relaxes back into his chair.

"Well, I think you've chosen well Yvonne, her record is certainly glittering," he compliments grinning, and showing off his threatening fae fangs, and I watch as he closes a beige file that I didn't see previously on his desk, too distracted with the classically beautiful, yet extremely terrifying male in front of me. His already dark features seem to darken further when he catches me staring at his face and my throat goes dry.

Madame is practically glowing sunlight at the praise, it makes the nausea roll again, I try swallowing but the lump in my throat seems to expand as I do.

There's a beat of silence in the room while he thinks about what his next words will be. "The prince... I mean his highness has asked for aid in a... somewhat delicate matter." He speaks directly to me now and looks as though he is waiting for me to reply. I am, however, under strict orders not to speak a word to him, and that's just fine with me.

"All the more detailed information you'll be needing, will be delivered to your quarters and should we find out more in the meantime, which will be given to you on a need-to-know basis. We can't have such sensitive information falling into the wrong hands I'm afraid."

K glances at me, I can feel her eyes burning a hole into the side of my face. But I dare not look away from the real threat in front of me. He speaks again and a small grin pinches at his lips, tilting them up on one side, clearly savouring the experience.

"The princess, it seems, has obtained a rather unfavourable habit and before the public gets wind of it, it needs to be quashed."

I nod my head briefly showing my understanding.

"Your acting skills will come to fruition on this particular task. You'll be her personal handmaiden, doting on her every waking minute and when night falls, you'll be doing what you do best. You need to learn her habits and gain her trust. This mission will take time and we will not be able to monitor you on this or offer any outside aid, once you leave this building you are on your own.

I warn you now Siren, do not make a mockery of this establishment. Do your duty and when you have completed your mission you will return here." His stern stare is something I've been on the wrong end of before and it makes me quake with anxiety, his finger pointed at my face to emphasise his point. *"Frederick has also requested that his sister does not find out about his involvement."*

Yvonne shifts in her seat, practically beaming at me.

"You'll be working closely with the prince and his small entourage of courtiers, and they have been asked to provide any resource that they can, within reason of course, since we cannot." He sighs heavily as if this next sentence is too hard for him to say. *"Three-Nought-Nought, I do not want to hear rumours of you getting close with his highness, is that understood? I still have eyes and ears in that court, and they report directly to me. You are there to work, not to frolic."* His empty eyes shoot daggers at me, a not-so-subtle hidden meaning to his words. I nod my head slowly, *"lastly, you will keep in touch when you can. It will be difficult without giving away your real intentions. But if we do not hear from you, we will find you, there will be nowhere on this globe for you to hide."*

His gaze leaves absolutely no room for argument, so I nod my head again, still not looking away from his face. His eyes gleam with predatory intent, where I'm sure mine are open a little too wide, like a deer caught in headlights. I praise the gods' when Madame breaks the choking tension.

"Thank you, sir. You can rely on her to get the job done." She leans forward toward his desk, showing a little more cleavage than is necessary, trying to seek out his interest again and yet he does not give it.

"Out," he utters, his authority unyielding and when I go to stand, he stops me with his hand, "not you."

Madame K goes to protest but stops immediately when she's met with a deathly cold glare. She stands, curtseying again and hurries from the room.

The soft click of the door sets off my anxiety and my hands begin to shake. I curl my fingers into fists and try to calm the tremors.

"Aella," he drawls, closing his eyes and resting his head back against the chair smiling as if he's enjoying the sound of my name on his tongue. When he opens them again there's a fire in them, one that I've seen before. It makes me hold my breath and my whole body goes rigid as though someone has just thrown a bucket of ice-cold water over my head. I watch his every movement as he gets up from his chair and perches himself on top of his desk in front of me.

"Did you know that as a fae my senses are heightened? For example, I can hear every breath that you take. That your little heart has been racing since the moment you stepped foot in this room. That I can smell your fear."

Fuck.

"Hmm?" He seems to be genuinely waiting for an answer. Keeping quiet I observe. "Speak," he snaps.

Damn it. I clear my throat.

"I have heard some things about the fae that was one of them, yes."

"Why is that?" he asks, tucking a piece of my hair behind my ear gently. Too gently. It takes everything in me not to flinch away from his touch.

"I'm not sure, I have just been in the training room, which could have something to do with it?" I reason.

"No. No, I don't think that's it, and I know that you don't believe that either."

He talks down to me like a father would a child. I would prefer that. At least then I would be the deadliest thing in the room. But you can never tell when this particular viper will strike.

"You've built quite the reputation for yourself here, haven't you? My delectable little pet," he asks huskily, changing the topic, "although I always knew you would." He reaches over again, when his skin touches my own I want to gag, he softly brushes against my cheek before cupping it in his hand.

"What a fine young woman, you've turned out to be," he stills his now empty hand to allow his eyes to rove over my face analysing every angle, "my little whirlwind," he whispers. My hair falls from behind my ear once more, and I watch him pick up the strands. He seems fascinated as he plays with them letting them fall through his fingers. His eyes lock with mine once more and I tense further as he leans in closer to my face, my knuckles going white and my nails creating half-moons in my palm as I hold an impossible grip.

My anxiety spikes but I can do nothing but sit there while he gets closer and closer.

The Gods must have heard my internal screams for mercy.

A knock at the door cuts through the suspense drowning the room, and I don't have to make a decision that would likely have gotten me killed or worse.

He stares at my lips barely an inch away from my face for more than a few breaths, before he sighs and pulls away, the puff of air fanning across my face.

He calls out to the person on the other side of the door and his secretary walks in, stopping when she sees me still sitting in the chair.

We share an awkward few seconds and I rise quickly, taking that as my queue to leave.

I don't turn around.

I don't bow.

I simply reach for the door handle and pull.

"Don't be a stranger, pet," he calls out.

I don't reply. But I can practically hear the savage smile that splits his face in two, as he says the name.

I close the door gently and a full-body shiver racks itself through my bones. Madame K sits there in one of the plush armchairs, watching the door, a beige folder in hand.

She doesn't say anything, and I don't need her to. I nod, and she stands.

Neither of us wastes time, we hurry back down the stairwell. All I can think about is putting as much distance between myself and him as possible.

"Take this and go back to your quarters. Work this out in your head. I can't have you falling apart in front of the others." Madame demands, turning to me unexpectedly.

I don't nod, I just turn and leave and before I know it, I'm back in my room slamming the door closed behind me.

I want to scream out my anger, my frustration and helplessness, but I am forced into silence. I can't let them know. I can't let anyone know what's happening. I am reserved only to letting out the burning lungful of air that I didn't know I was holding.

My eyes burst open, and I suddenly find myself in a darkened room, moonlight gently seeping through the windows. I bolt upright in a ruffled bed and a sharp pain shoots up my leg at the movement. I pay no mind, instead my eyes dart around the room and my breathing increases rapidly, my limbs shake violently. The ringing in my ears is deafening, the darkness is suffocating me, and my pulse is racing faster than a hummingbird's wings. I begin breathing deeply, trying to stop the frantic anxiety fuelled shaking. When I finally begin to register the room around me. There are no threats.

I pull myself up to rest back against the headboard and close my eyes, letting my head fall back as I try to slow my racing heart.

Warmth clamps down on my arm and instinct takes over, grabbing for my knife under my pillow, I throw myself to the side, the blade across the attacker's throat.

My anger-filled eyes are met with fathomless black, and a snarl rips from my mouth.

"Woah, woah. Ella." The male's hands are raised.

One hand is pressed against his warm chest while the other presses my blade further into his oesophagus. My heart thuds wildly but my brain is slow to catch up, the black eyes are throwing me, and I can't help the adrenaline and raw emotion as it clouds all sense of reason.

He tentatively reaches out to me again and I shift the blade, a bead of blood dribbles down his dark skin. He lightly wraps his fingers around my wrist, his stare never once leaving my own and my breathing stutters, my grip tightening.

"Hey." His soft voice finally penetrates the fog in my mind, "I'm not going to hurt you." He tugs at my wrist, his other one reaching for the knife, prying it out of my hand. He goes to reach for me again and my eyes follow each movement of his hands, at the one that's placing my knife on the table next to the bed, and at the other that's reaching for my forearm.

He moves slowly and methodically, his breathing shallow when his fingertips brush my skin, he puffs out a lungful of air when I don't flinch away.

But the touch alone triggers the recognition.

"R...Rich," I croak, my cheeks damp and cold. I bring my hand up to my face to feel tears wetting the skin there. Strong arms wrap around me cradling me to a firm chest. He rocks us both back and forth, tucking my head under his chin.

We sit like that, in nothing but silence for far longer than I realise.

My heartbeat has slowed, as has my breathing.

"Do you want to talk about it?" he whispers into my hair, placing a kiss there and the shaking in my limbs has finally ceased.

"Not really," I whisper back.

"Ok," he replies. He doesn't stop rocking me, not even for a second. My fist is clenching around the blankets so tightly my knuckles have gone white, something he notices and begins to quietly unfurl each finger, one by one.

"How's your leg?" he murmurs and it's then that I realise I'm sitting in his lap, straddling him, and my leg is throbbing.

"It hurts like a son of a bitch," I chuckle, wiping my face with the back of my hand.

"Hey, hey." Rich stops me from violently pulling at my skin and begins wiping the tears with his thumb. He picks me up, tucking his forearm under my backside, and lays me back down gently, rearranging my leg onto a stack of pillows, covering me in the little cotton blanket. He flops down next to me pulling me back against his body, so his bare chest is pressed against my back with his arms bundling me closer.

I try to turn around and protest but my leg throbs harder, making me hiss. Rich squeezes my waist.

"Do you need more medication?"

"I should be fine."

His breath is warm against my nape, and I sink into him.

"I'm not going to push it but if you ever want to talk about it. I'm here." His sleepy grumble cuts through the still night.

I breathe deeply.

"Thank you, Rich." I squeeze his fingers that rest on my stomach and answer with a deeper snuggle.

Releasing a quivering huff of a laugh I shuffle closer desperate to steal his warmth.

"See isn't this nice?" he breathes in my ear. I twist quickly to poke him in the ribs, forcing an 'oof' sound to leave his lips and tuck myself back under his chin, smiling shallowly when he places a gentle kiss on the crown of my head, "Now try to go back to sleep."

CHAPTER TEN
LET THE GAMES BEGIN

Present Day

Just like the day before, Rich accompanied me on my morning run. He had anticipated my arrival in the main room, dressed and ready to go, looking far more energised than the day previous.

We ran around the first few blocks learning the streets. Jogging until our stomachs rumbled, and stopped at a lavender-painted bakery, the smell of fresh bread seeped into the morning air.

We each grab a pastry and a fresh box of doughnuts that Rich had insisted on taking back for Declan.

Climbing the stairs back up to the apartment Rich fills the time with idle chatter about his homeland, to which I smile and nod, juggling the three coffees.

"Where the Hel have you been?" Declan scolds, pulling the door open just as Rich reaches for the handle.

"Good morning, Declan. We rose early – something you should try – and went for a run. We were even so kind as to bring you breakfast."

A light sensation builds in my chest that makes me want to laugh. I kill it before anyone notices the slight curvature of my lips.

Declan closes the door quickly and turns to me eyeing the coffees in my hand with suspicion, before not so subtly taking in my outfit, his tongue darts out to wet his lips while his stare lingers a little too long on my legs.

Placing the coffees down, I grab the files and spread them out across the table with my laptop in the middle of the organised mess and take a seat on the floor to continue reading.

"What are you doing?" Rich asks, around a mouthful of doughnut.

"Breaking into the Ansrutas Police Department firewall," I reply, sipping from the steaming mug of goodness.

He blinks comically, sharing a look with Declan.

"You know that's a federal crime, right?" Declan states plainly.

I pause, my fingers hovering over the keys, the question stumping me for a moment, even Rich looks at his friend quizzically, "Really?" I ask, instead of rolling my eyes like a really want to.

"You feeling alright, Dec?" Rich asks, frowning but with genuine concern written there.

Declan *does* roll his eyes but says nothing more.

"What are you hoping to find?" Rich asks turning away from his friend to look over my shoulder, watching as I skim over the files and scroll through news feeds.

"I want to make sure that the information Griffith gave us is correct."

He hums in acceptance and moves to the bathroom, the sounds of running water from the shower become clear moments later.

The lid of my laptop slams shut, barely just missing my fingers and I'm met with fiery amber eyes.

"Just so we are clear, *Fury,*" he spits the word as if he's tasted something vile. "I'm not here to babysit you. I am here for Rich and him only. You *will not* put him in danger because of your *job.* If you jump into unnecessary danger, neither of us will be dragging you back out of it. So, think before you act." I nearly roll my eyes; he sounds exactly like Madame K. "I want nothing further to do with you. Do you understand?" His gaze is holding me captive, and I begin thinking of ways to get out of it.

I could punch him in the throat, which has always proven useful in the past. But attacking a handler is punishable by death, so unfortunately, it's not worth it.

At least, not just yet.

"Understood, *sir,*" I bite out the word. He smirks, and now I want to punch him even more. Of all the people in the whole wide world and I'm stuck with him.

After Rich had figured out what I was back in Kos. Declan had given me the cold shoulder. Spit hateful slurs at me wherever possible and even gone so far as to leave a room whenever I entered it. Each little thing has only built up our hatred for each other. He didn't even bother to say goodbye when I left to go back to the Fort. That hurt me the most. But I took that hurt and anger and made myself better, stronger. Made myself into the monster he truly things I am.

"If he so much as gets a sprained ankle. You *will* answer to me."

Grinning wildly I swallow watching the venom in his irises ebb and flow. Something wild stirs in me, greeting his own darkness.

"No harm will come to him. Because he is my handler, I have been taught to protect them at all costs. Even at the risk of my own life. He is forbidden to interfere in my affairs unless the investigation is in jeopardy."

He blinks slowly, and his jaw slackens. Surprise. He hadn't expected my response to be so clarifying and honest.

"Is there anything else, *sir*?"

"Yeah, stop calling me sir."

"What would you like me to call you then? Because I can think of a chosen few," I ask, removing his hand from the top of my laptop, trying to continue with my work.

"I don't want you to call me at all if we're being honest." He steps back but doesn't look away, he straightens. Standing impossibly taller, completely towering over me from my position on the floor.

"We are forced to be in each other's company for far longer than either of us would like. I must call you something, *sir,*" I grin at my screen, not making eye contact with him again. I can practically feel the eye roll from down here, but he says nothing. Moving away from me, he heads for his and Rich's shared bedroom.

"Why don't you think on it then?" I call after him. Chuckling quietly when his door slams shut.

The sun lowers in the sky by the time I finish correcting and updating all the files. Rich, claiming I needed to take a break from working, had suggested we all visit the bar down the street.

We perch ourselves on the stools up against the bar.

"So come on, where exactly is the Fort? Just give me a general direction."

My brow quirks at his persistence. The alcohol has warmed my blood and lowered my inhibitions. I should stop drinking before I regret it. But I am finding it hard to care about later, "given your best efforts to get me drunk enough to tell you, I am going to have to let you down. It's psychologically built into me. I cannot tell you. So, stop asking."

He pulls a face, "That place will never cease to confuse the fuck out of me." I nod in agreement, tipping my glass back and emptying it before signalling to the bartender for another.

"Ok, what can you tell me?" he tries again, making me sigh.

"Probably nothing, but I know that won't stop you so ask your questions."

Who knew alcohol could subdue the serum so much? I have not felt like this in such a long time. So long in fact, I can't seem to remember when my back wasn't as straight as a pencil, and I had loose enough lips in order to speak so casually.

"Why don't you start with what you can say?"

I swirl the ice in my glass, once, twice, thinking of something – anything – that I can say. "The stories you were told as a child. Not a word of them is true."

His mouth pops open comically wide.

"We aren't the *'wrath of the gods.'* I suppose you could say we are 'demons of the night.' But we don't swallow up misbehaving children. At least not *boys*. We are nothing more than girls stolen from our beds, our happy little lives, and turned into the ultimate killing machine." I raise my glass toasting to my pathetic little life.

If this had been any other handler, I'm sure I wouldn't have lived to see tomorrow, just for talking, let alone about the Fort and its projects. But Rich gives me a pitying look and despite not feeling comfortable with the emotion, I know he has good intentions and just his mere presence helps me feel at ease. I take another drink, turning away from him. "Gods I love this drink," I sigh, holding it in my mouth, savouring the taste of the clear liquid.

Rich wipes a hand down his face, "so what was it like living in the palace? Snooty and pompous? How long did you stay there?"

"You were part of the king's guard, you should know," I mumble.

He takes a swig from his beer bottle, "*I was never part of the king's guard. If you remember,*" he taps my forehead, "Declan was."

"Then ask him," I wave over in the general direction of where Declan is sitting in a darkened corner.

"I don't know if you've noticed, but he doesn't talk much and when he does it comes out more as grunts than anything else."

We share a boisterous laugh, catching the attention of said grumpy male, who upon arriving, split from us to find himself a bed partner for the night.

Rich stayed with me, chatting, at the bar all night and asking questions he knows I can't answer. But I take it all in stride. It's only natural to be curious about something no one truly knows anything about.

"So how is it you know the crown prince of Anaphi?" Rich asks seemingly out of nowhere.

My brow rises again at the topic change. "We have worked together in the past. Why do you ask?"

He shrugs, "I saw how cosy you got with him yesterday after the meeting. Until the king came out." He smiles, "an old flame perhaps?"

My cheeks flush crimson and I have to look away to stop my own bodily functions from giving away the answer. "It was never anything serious. We both knew that it would go no further than the physical attraction we had for each other. But that was years ago now. So, it's hardly relevant and will not disrupt the mission. If that is why you are truly asking."

Rich eyebrows pull together, "Not at all. I was merely making conversation." He seems to contemplate his next question, deep in thought, "How many times have you met the king?"

I pull a face, turning to him in surprise, "Several. Each time the Director needs a security detail. I am the Fury he takes and that is usually anytime he goes to the capital." Hoping that this is the end of the conversation, I take another drink.

"What's he like?"

My brow quirks and I see the genuine curiosity on his face, mixed with something else. Something I can't quite make sense of and it's gone before I can look into it further.

Looking around I make sure no one is listening in on our conversation, "the king is not a nice man. He seems benevolent to his people. But that is what he portrays to the media. Behind closed doors..." My attention drifts thinking back on a memory I'd rather forget. "I wonder if sometimes he is crueller than the Director." My voice is detached and hollow. Wiping the memory from the forefront of my mind, I turn back to him with a small smile. "But we needn't talk about him. Tell me more about your homeland."

I catch Rich's understanding eyes, but he too wipes the solemn mood away, and begins to weave another tale of the land where he grew up. Stories of his brothers and one sister and the torture they put each other through brings a glimmer to his eyes. He hasn't been back there since joining the war against Duranda, but the stories he tells bring happy memories and laughter forth.

Several drinks later, a darkened cloud looms over my shoulder, Rich greets it with a drunken smile, "Declan!" He opens his arms wide, narrowly missing his near-empty bottle. The vodka in my mouth sours a little at the sound of his name.

He sighs heavily, "alright that's enough from the both of you." He pulls on Rich's arm, who stumbles out of his seat onto unsteady feet, but at least he's upright. "You too," he snaps at me, turning away ready to guide Rich to the door.

"Prick," I mumble, tipping the last drop from my glass into my mouth.

A warm hand wraps around my upper arm, squeezing it just enough to let me know he won't ask again. "That wasn't a request, *princess*," he snarls, the heat of his anger further heating my already flushed cheeks.

I narrow my eyes at him, planting myself in my seat, "Why don't you go back to finding a 'fuckbuddy' we were doing just fine without you."

Rich snorts a laugh and I'm pulled impossibly closer to Declan.

With a voice as smooth as silk and devilishly dark, "Do me a favour, *Fury*. Stop with the jealousy. It doesn't suit you."

I scoff loudly, "We don't have any problems there, *Angelos*. You're not my type."

Rich hiccups from behind him, "No. Princes are more your thing." He giggles to himself while I watch Declan's eyes widen slightly, working his jaw. He releases me like I've burnt him and suddenly I wish I had the power to do just that. But another, quieter version of me, misses the contact.

"Get up," he snarls again, and I obey. Placing my feet on the floor I stand, and the world spins. I've had more to drink than I first realised. The world spins faster and faster and I feel myself falling until something solid comes up to meet me. It's firm and unmoving and I open my eyes to find my nose inches from... a back?

The cooling air from the outside envelopes me and a giggling Rich trails behind me.

"Put me down!" I yell, smacking Declan's back. The jostling makes my stomach roil violently.

"For an assassin, you don't know how to hold your liquor," he grunts.

I fall limp in his arms, crossing my arms over my chest. Rich pouts his lips, trying to make himself look sad, but his hazy eyes tell a different story.

"Sometimes it's nice to forget what I am, every now and then."

Declan's broad shoulder tenses beneath me but neither of us say anything more.

The morning brings with it a pounding headache and extreme dizziness. Declan had deposited me on my bed and closed the door on his way out, but I woke with a glass of water on the bedside and two white pills, with a note. *Take these.*

Perhaps I should've asked what they were, maybe I'm still slightly drunk and don't particularly care. But I took them quickly, sipping on the water lightly, hoping to not throw it back up.

The sun beams through the grimy window blinding me, and the heat of the room quickly becomes sticky and humid. My skin is clammy, my mouth is dry but all I want to do is sleep. Dropping my head back down on my pillow I close my eyes, placing an arm over them; when the door opens.

"Morning sunshine," Rich's too-cheery voice sings through the room. Cracking open an eye I see him standing there, coffee mug in hand, with a bright smile.

"How?" I croak.

"How what?"

"How are you not like me right now?"

He snorts a laugh. "Shifter, remember? We have a higher metabolism." He sits down on the side of the bed, setting the coffee cup down there, eyeing the water glass.

"What were those pills you gave me?"

"I'm assuming painkillers, but I didn't leave them. I've been making breakfast," he smiles.

"Declan?" He nods.

"He's not always a dick," he whispers.

"That remains to be seen," I mumble.

He snickers, "Speaking of. He mentioned something about you having made appointments today?"

It's then that reality hits, "what time is it?"

"A little after ten."

"Shit!" I jump out of bed, debating on whether to shower or just change. But the smell of alcohol clinging to my clothes chooses for me so I opt for the shower, cursing myself.

"Breakfast on the go then?" I hear Rich call after me.

We head out into the mid-morning sunshine. Declan, in spite of his *'I want nothing to do with you'* speech – and to *my* great annoyance – follows behind Rich. The pair seem deep in discussion until they reach me, waiting by the car. Handing Rich the two addresses for the two appointments I jump into the back seat.

Helena Sutton, a field reporter who has been present for every single one of their peaceful protests – until something changed and a riot broke out – and David McKay, who works for a local newspaper whose articles are controversially sympathetic towards 'Dawnya' and their cause.

I didn't have to search for long to find either of them. Both reporters have offices on the other side of the city.

From some of the photographs I have seen, I'm excited to see the west side. There are not many places in this world that I haven't been to, but Ansrutas is one of them, and the House of Asteria in particular, is an interesting sector of this ever-expanding city – named as such 'the house of the stars' – where music, fashion and art all come together in near divine creation.

Travelling through it is like I've stepped into a completely different city, from the east side, the colours and textures of the buildings are unique, and the way people express themselves through their clothing is extraordinary. At art decorating nearly every walkway, is like I've stepped into an artist's mind that they've made come to life. Even the foliage blooms in bright colours and follows unnatural lines.

Rich follows the slow-moving traffic until we pull up at a large, mostly glass, building that reaches up to the sky, 'The Ansrutas Post' sign hangs proudly over the main entrance.

"Did you *actually* make an appointment? You know now that we're here?" Rich asks, turning off the car and swivelling towards me, his black leather jacket creaking with the movement.

"Please," I drawl rolling my eyes, "do I look like a rookie to you?"

I hear him chuckle as I open the car door, walking towards the entrance of the building. Rich joins me not moments later, pushing open the glass door, allowing me to walk in before him. I nod as I pass and head straight up to the receptionist's desk.

The lobby is grand, made mostly of glass with a central natural stone wall, wet with trickling water that runs down its face; ferns have been placed to grow out of the cracks in the rock. Sat in front of it is one long grey receptionist's desk, with three people working away. Two females and a young male. One of the females looks up as we walk towards her. She scowls at me, similar to the frown Madame Campbell pulls at the sight of me – as though I'm but dirt on her shoe – her blonde hair is shoulder length and loosely curled around her face, which is made-up with simple, natural make-up. I open my mouth to speak and she cuts me off immediately.

"Appointment?" she asks, her irritable mood seeping in through her tone.

"Good morning, how are you?" I mock all too sweetly. I pause waiting for her to respond, she doesn't answer, but her kohl-lined eyes glare at me as though being polite is an inconvenience. "My name is Annie Munroe, and this is Zade Wilson, we have an appointment with David McKay at eleven."

Her face changes from that of a sulky teenager to a professional woman who is competent in her field, at the tone of my voice. I look over to Rich to see him biting his lip to keep from laughing.

"Er yes of course sorry Miss Munroe he did in fact mention that this morning." David has made a reputation for himself it would seem. Not even the too rude receptionist is willing to piss him off just to spite me.

Her eyes flick over the computer screen, "he's up on level twenty-five, take the first left and his office is at the end of the corridor."

"Thank you, Diana." I glance at her name tag and give her a small barely noticeable glare and walk towards the elevators pressing the floor number.

"What is it exactly they teach you at the guild?" Rich asks when the doors close, and the steel box starts ascending.

"Why?" My brows rise in surprise at the question.

"Because the fact that you can go from being an assassin you, to normal you, to whatever that was is quite terrifying."

"If you believe that to be scary, I'm afraid to tell you that we have barely scratched the surface of my skills," I reply regarding the doors with a renewed sense of interest.

"That's what I was afraid of," he mumbles beside me.

"How'd it go?" Declan asks although he doesn't look up from his phone.

"I would suggest neither of you come with me to the next one," I keep my tone calm despite the anger I feel.

"I feel like that's kind of rude but whatever," Rich mumbles, strapping himself in.

"That bad huh?" Declan utters, looking at Rich. More like scanning him from head to toe to see if he has acquired new injuries in the time that he hasn't been in his line of sight.

I roll my eyes. Something I seem to be doing a lot since Declan has been around. I'm afraid they may get stuck and never come down.

"I don't understand what you're so upset about, I was doing my job," Rich says. I can tell he's trying to lighten the mood with the teasing tone in his voice, but it's doing nothing more than pissing me off further.

"Handler Keita, impeding my work is not doing your job. You have cost me a very valuable lead, with your questions about how he sympathises with them. I could tell for a while he was getting annoyed with you."

"Then why didn't you stop me?"

"Quite frankly I thought you could see it too. He's not exactly an actor, who can hide those emotions, and typically I'm not allowed to speak out against my handlers."

"Then what are you doing now?" he counters.

I sigh through my nose and sit back in my seat. Rich turns around when I fall silent.

"The silent treatment?"

I stay quiet, looking out the window at the birds in the sky and the people walking along the street.

"Where's the next meeting?" Declan asks quietly, cutting Rich a disapproving glance. I lean forward to give him the address and the car is put into motion.

It's only a short distance to the next meeting point. A small park filled with statues, performers and artists drawing murals on every available surface.

Upon arriving I jump out of the car and walk away from the pair of them leaving Rich to call after me.

I walk around a small cluster of trees to see Helena, sitting on a bench in front of a water fountain, reading a thick book. I can't see the title of this far away, but she looks at peace here. As though she heard me, she looks up on my approach and offers me a bright smile. She can't be any older than me, maybe even younger. Her long blonde hair is up high in a ponytail, she wears natural make-up and gym wear, and her heart-shaped face makes her look as though she's barely out of her teen years.

"Good morning, Annie. I can call you Annie, right?" Her beaming smile falters slightly as she worries that she may have overstepped. Annie is the name I'd given to both her and David in the emails I'd sent them, asking them to meet with me.

"Of course. Good morning, Helena. Thank you for meeting me on such short notice," I say, shaking her hand when she stands to greet me properly.

"Can I ask what this meeting is for? I mean I know what it's for, but beyond that?" She seems timid, and it makes me wonder how she has become a field reporter with such a shy personality.

"I have been approached by a publishing company, whose name I cannot disclose as of yet, to write a book about the organisation, 'Dawnya'. About their struggles as a people and about their cause. It's neither supposed to be about gaining sympathy for them, nor spreading hatred. It's simply about telling their side of the story, and I wanted to start with scraping together some information from those who don't necessarily know them but have a connection nonetheless." An easy lie. One I made up on the car ride here. But one with enough substance that she won't look to hard into it.

"Well, I wouldn't say I have a connection. I just happen to be the one sent out when all of their rallies take place." She smiles distantly.

"Now, now give yourself more credit." I refuse, absolutely refuse, to let my eyes roll no matter how they are screaming at me. A part of me tells me to put my skills to the test and intimidate the information out of her. But that would only give away my true intentions.

"Oh, that's so good, have you got any more interviews lined up?" she asks, her keen eyes flicking from my face to the bubbles forming in the fountain in front of us.

"Not yet but that depends on what you can tell me about them today," I grin, trying to put her at ease.

"Oh, wow so no pressure then," she giggles. She sits in quiet contemplation, "what do you want to know?"

"How long have these protests been going on?"

"Not long, it's actually as though they popped up out of nowhere. But maybe somewhere close to a year ago, was the first."

Just as several officers and other personnel of the like begin deserting the front lines then.

"So, when exactly was it that the first riot broke out?" I begin scribbling things into a notebook, pretending to jot this down for later. When really, I have a recorder in my pocket that I switched on the moment I walked into the park.

"About six months later. As more and more civilians joined in on the protests, they grew frustrated with the lack of action from the crown, and they started going ballistic seemingly out of nowhere." Fear flashes behind her ocean-blue eyes, as she replays the scenes in her head. "I was reporting that day, it was all quiet and peaceful. They did the usual, sitting on the road outside of city hall. The police department had to block the road on either side for it, and then the next thing someone had thrown a brick through one of the windows of the mayor's office...and then it was nothing but carnage," she goes quiet, and huffs a tired chuckle, "the funny thing is that it wasn't even a member of 'Dawnya', it was just a regular civilian. But they took the fall for him anyway. That was the day the people turned against them and now look what's happened. They've taken the name 'criminal' and run with it. Blowing up buildings just so they'll be heard. As if Ansrutas hasn't been through enough this last fifty years."

I nod with her and go to ask another question but shut it quickly when she speaks again.

"Did you know I was born on the front lines? I wasn't actually planned." She huffs a little laugh, "But for the first few years, despite my mother's best efforts to take me to safety. That's all I'd ever known. People fighting and having to ration food." Her eyes glaze over. "I understand their cause, I really do. But they need to find another way to voice themselves. The people have been through enough. A bit of a warning... your book might not do too well in this city."

I laugh at her crassness, "Thank you for your honesty. It's rare to find these days." She smiles shallowly at me and sighs heavily.

"Is there anything else you wanted to ask?" I can see this has taken its toll and I pick my phone out of my pocket, looking at the time.

"Yes actually, the civilian. What was his name?"

"I don't know. No one does, he got into a black car not too far down the road and seemed to disappear into thin air. Not even the police managed to find him."

"Ok. Thank you for your time. Am I ok to contact you again if I have any further questions?"

"Of course," she smiles again, and I stand.

"It was a pleasure to meet up, Helena," I grin and shake her hand again.

"Yes, it was lovely to meet you too. I look forward to hearing from you and good luck with your book."

"Thank you," I reply and turn to walk away when I get a text from Rich. *We're bored, are you nearly done?*

I stuff it back in my pocket, he can suffer a little longer for messing up my talk with David. I take a lap of the park before finally heading back to the car.

"Got it?" he asks, as I fasten my safety belt around me.

"Yeah. As much as I can get."

"What did she tell you?" he questions, pulling away from the curb and merging with the traffic effortlessly.

"She helped to confirm the timeline of events for me. David was supposed to be a source of information." I look out the window watching as people and buildings whizz past.

"Sorry about that," Rich says, not even sounding remotely apologetic. "It is what it is, Handler Keita."

CHAPTER ELEVEN
THE MIDDLE OF THE
NIGHT

Back at the apartment sometime later I'm sitting on my bed sending the correct timeline of events back to Madame, eating a cookie that Rich bought me as an apology, when Declan comes storming in, with a face like thunder.

"Fury! Tell me what happened in that office. Rich won't talk about it." He stands in the doorway with his muscular arms crossed over one another. Completely blocking the threshold. "And I know you can't deny me."

"I can actually. You have stated yourself that you are not my handler. So, I don't have to tell you anything," I retort smugly. But when I look into those bright golden eyes that shoot daggers at me in the most delicious way, I cave. Cursing myself as it do. "Handler Keita asked some inappropriate questions; David McKay did not take it well."

"That's it?" he probes further. I nod my head finally clicking the send button.

"I already said I'm sorry!" Rich yells from the living room. Somehow, I knew he'd be able to hear me. Footsteps pad down the corridor, "And I bought you a cookie." His puppy eyes come out then and the pouty lip.

"He asked. I answered." I point to Declan and actively ignore them while I finish typing. When I spot something suspicious in one of the online articles. In the background of one of the televised reports, commentated by Helena, I see the same brunette male walking away from one of the riots pulling his hood up. The image is clearer than any of the others I've seen before now.

"You have done nothing but work since you got here," I hear Rich's voice cut through my focus. Declan has already departed from the room.

"Not true. We went to that bar last night. But work is what I am trained for, handler Keita."

"Do you ever take time for yourself?"

"I don't understand the question." I look up from the screen, Rich now leans against the doorframe.

"You seem different," he murmurs, looking me up and down.

"If you're wondering whether the vaccination is wearing. I still don't know if such a thing is possible. The serum doesn't stop me from talking, it reinforces compliance and the training I have gone through. But I have also been taught to adapt to each handler, to make their jobs easier. You in particular happen to enjoy talking, so I have adapted to respond more fluidly when you ask questions."

His mouth drops open, "are you saying I talk too much?"

"That's exactly what I'm saying," I answer, casually hacking into City Hall's security camera system.

"I feel like I should be offended," Rich remarks.

"That wasn't my intention, handler Keita. But most of my handlers prefer silence, most seem put off by my mere presence. I have never talked so much in such a short time; my voice is feeling hoarse and that is just from a matter of days of being in your charge."

Again, my observation is greeted with silence.

"Would you... do you want some water?" he snickers.

Rolling my eyes I shake my head and leave my laptop to download the files from the City Hall's mainframe.

"What are you doing now?" he asks, watching me stand.

"With your permission. I will be going for a run."

"I'll come with you." I nod and pull on my shoes.

The instant we step out onto the street, I take a deep inhale of the still-warm evening air, letting it fill my lungs to the point of bursting, the sun is just over the horizon and setting fast. The smell of salt heavy on the breeze makes me look towards the docks and as soon as I do, I feel that strange pull as if something is drawing my attention to them. Rich is beside me, tucking his phone away.

Neither of us speaks and he lets me dictate the pace and where we go. It's not long before clouds roll over and raindrops fall from the sky.

"Maybe we should turn back," Rich calls from behind me, wiping sweat and rain from his forehead.

I come to a stop in front of a tall chain-linked fence, when a feeling of contentment unexpectedly fills my bones, as though something is telling me I'm in the right place. For what, I can't discern. But I look around all the same while I try to catch my breath.

The main iron gate to the Stratos Dock stands before me, chained closed and steadily getting slick with rainwater. Rows upon rows of monstrously large, dark warehouses loom before me. The deafening sea crashes against the sea walls and the loading cranes creak with the movement of the growing wind.

Ducking away from the dim streetlights, I slink down the main street searching for a way in, moving only to get a better angle of the doors into the first warehouse, which is illuminated by a flickering security light.

"What are you doing?" Rich hisses.

I silence him with a glare, and he joins me in the shadows. Staying hidden for a while I search for any sign of life. Rich's quiet anticipation gnaws at me. I can tell he wants to ask questions, but I most definitely won't be answering them.

It doesn't take long for my patience to wear thin. Taking some tentative steps away from the fence into the empty road, I give myself a running start to jump the fence. My steps are wide before I jump grabbing the top while I haul myself over, the chain links rattling violently. I cringe at the noise it makes even after I've landed on the other side.

"Aella! Get back over here right now!" Rich whisper-yells at me, looking this way and that.

"You could do something useful and be the lookout," I whisper back, trying to redeem some form of stealth. I begin to quietly creep my way around the side of the first warehouse alone. Rich muttered a curse under his breath and slunk into an alleyway nearby to keep watch.

The concrete under my feet is covered with salty puddles that are only growing larger in the rain, making every step echo throughout the docks.

A scratching noise comes from nearby and a soaked brown rat bolts from under a stack of wooden boxes as I get closer. I watch it as it runs towards another dark alcove in yet another, adjacent, warehouse. But movement in the corner of my eye catches my attention and I see two shadows skulking around in the dark, their feet splashing in the shallow puddles.

Darting behind the boxes for cover I observe the pair, watching as they open a concealed side door into the next building over, they look around warily before slipping inside.

Bingo.

The breeze from the sea cools my sweat-soaked skin and I go to pull my hood up but remember that I'm only wearing my jogging gear.

Shit.

Deciding I should stick to the shadows, I slink through the door after them, cringing as it bangs closed loudly behind me, only to be greeted with a long and dark corridor; large crates of wheat and sacks of grain border the length of the passage, with nothing but a flickering blub above me providing very little light.

As I gradually inch my way through the room, I spot a sliver of light fracturing through the murkiness, and the faint sound of voices drawing me in closer. I reach for the handle but pause within a hair's breadth of it, the people inside are called to attention. I think better than to just walk into a room full of rebels and begin looking for another way in.

The outside door opens, and my heart stops dead. Scrambling away from the door I duck behind a large crate hoping it's dark enough that whoever this is doesn't see me.

A burly shadow marches towards me and stops just in front of the crate, I can hear the shift of their clothing as they look around, I peek around the corner to try and see their face, but they wear an oversized black leather cloak, all I can see is their tanned and heavily tattooed hand, with an ostentatious ring on each finger.

The door closes behind the figure, and I breathe a sigh of relief trying to gain back a steady heartbeat. I rest my head back against the box taking some fortifying breaths when a vent, just left of the door comes into view.

I grin and stand, moving to gently pop open the vent. With both feet under me and my hands guiding the way, I slowly begin ascending the vent. Another grate stops me. I push gently, and it gives way, catching it before it bangs against the balcony that overlooks the main floor. I place it down gently and crawl out, covered head to toe in dust. I lift myself up into the rafters and climb up perching myself in the middle. The lights hang low below me creating the perfect place to observe this unexpected meeting in the comfort of darkness.

A mortal male with long black hair tied into a bun stands on the makeshift stage giving a rousing speech about the oppressive Stratos Regime.

"Good evening, you all know by now why we are here. It's time the Stratos and the damn Crown start to take us seriously. They are all nothing but a scourge upon this once great land. Where every creature and being lived happily together, not divided. There was no such thing as war back then."

He pauses as the people surrounding him scream and holler their agreement.

"I look around and see too many faces that know all too well the pain it has caused." More yells and fists are raised in the air. The anger and distrust growing thick, I can feel it even from up here.

"The grief of losing family, homes, having to scrape together the bare necessities just to make it to the next day, while they sit lavishly on their thrones, not knowing what it's like to go to bed with empty stomachs." I search the crowd for the burly figure I saw earlier, but this only benefits me in gathering information about the people standing in the crowd. Most of these people are working-class citizens, who have given everything to the crown.

"They don't understand the pain of having to bury their sons and daughters in the ground before their time." His voice goes hoarse, clearly having had some personal experience with that kind of trauma, "or having to stand by and watch the only home you've ever known burn to the ground." In unison, they begin beating their fists against their chests, almost like a salute. "It is time those bastards out there heard what we have to say, and we have to do it in a way they can no longer ignore." He roars raising his fist, the people follow, the vibrations of such passion rumble against the walls. Each person here believes heavily in the cause. Some even begin stomping their feet on the ground.

With his palm out he hushes the rowdy crowd once more. "Melanie has come, she wishes to share with you, her plan."

I pull out my phone and discretely snap a few pictures of her as she steps up onto the makeshift stage. Her eyes glow like that of a shifter, her features are naturally feline, and she looks as though she belongs in an office and not in a decrepit warehouse.

She wears a silky dark green shirt tucked into black straight-legged pants, not even an inch of dirt on anything. Her mousy brown hair is in a messy bun at the nape of her neck, and her sun-tanned skin is littered with freckles. From the looks of her, you wouldn't think she would be the friendly type, yet she smiles at these people like they're her family.

She could be vital in finding Roman.

"Good evening, it's so good to see so many of you here," she sighs blissfully, "as Jacques has so graciously introduced, yes, I have come here tonight to discuss a new plan. I have been in talks with, well you know who." She grins and the people before her, shout, and howl in response. "We are all in agreement, which in itself is a miracle, and we think that this is the best course of action." She and the crowd chuckle and some of the angry tension seems to evaporate.

"In two weeks, the king is set to head back to the capital for the queen's birthday. Security will be more relaxed after the crown's departure, and that is when we will strike. An opportunity will arise when most of those who can, will storm the Rise around the city. It is a risk, but a risk that I think a lot of you are willing to take in order to achieve our goal. We will take our city back!"

The crowd cheer and clap loudly at her words.

Deciding to stay a little longer, I shift up on the iron rafter looking down, when a young male, no more than sixteen, bursts through the door.

"The Stratos are coming!" he yells.

The whole room pauses for a breath, as though time has stopped. Then it seems to hit them all at once, and chaos reigns.

Everyone scrambles towards every available exit, desperate to not get caught. I wonder how I'll be able to get myself out from up here. I don't move or panic. I watch them scramble like ants until a draft on my neck pulls my attention upwards. Moonlight shines brightly through one of the skylights, standing I reach for it, just as a group of guards come bursting through the doors. I open the hatch and climb up onto the warehouse's roof, the sounds of people being beaten and cuffed ringing in my ears. But it's only pity I feel for them. They should know better than to go up against the king.

The salty wind outside tugs and tears at my braid while I lift myself out of the warmth of the warehouse.

Now to look for a way down.

Both Rich and I sprint back through the city, my breath burns in my lungs but each step away buts us further and further away from discovery. We managed to make it back in half of the time it took for us to get there but at the cost of our bodies screaming for a reprieve. I all but leap across the road straight for the outside door, slamming into it so hard that it causes a dent in the wall behind it.

We charge up the stairs and panting hard as I look for my keys, before realising I don't actually have any. Rich comes up empty too.

"Shit," I curse quietly leaning against the door and sliding down it to the floor, my head in my hands as I try to catch my breath before thinking of another way in. Rich leans on his knees panting just as hard.

"You want to tell me what that was about?" He manages between breaths.

The door opens suddenly, and I fall onto my back, not expecting it, and look up to see a very pissed-off Declan, who stands there for a moment looking down at me with furrowed brows and rage in those beautiful amber eyes of his.

"Where the fuck have you been?" he yells, gripping the door frame, the wood groans under the strain while I stare up at him from the floor sheepishly.

"Ummmm."

Declan sits in the chocolate-coloured armchair, with his chin rested on his fist in nothing but black slacks, his tanned and scarred chest on full display. The muscles in his arm are flexed, his veins bulge under his skin. It takes all of my concentration to stay seated and not squirm uncomfortably, but as he looks directly at me, unblinking with unspoken barely concealed rage, I can't help but clear my throat looking at Rich.

Declan has at least allowed him to shower before he gets a scolding, as for me, I'm still in my wet jogging clothes sat on the couch like a child ready to get a talking to by their disappointed parents.

"Don't look at him," Declan snaps making me flinch a little. "What are you looking at him for? He won't help you,"

Goosebumps cover my flesh and I want nothing more than to jump in a hot shower and then go to bed, but I stand my ground – metaphorically at least while I sit opposite him on the sofa – I fold my arms over my chest to try and conserve some warmth within me.

"Declan, you can't be mad at her and not me," Rich begins. He's trying to help, but it won't work. I can tell by how Declan lowers his eyebrows, making his features appear darker and all the more menacing.

Declan ignores his friend altogether when he does eventually find words, "What did I say to you?" He asks.

Rich looks between us completely perplexed.

"If any harm comes to him, I will answer to you,"

"Right."

"Do you see an injury?" I challenge, "Because you won't find one. I went into that warehouse alone."

He grinds his teeth and his nostrils flare.

Rich steps in between us, "What the fuck is wrong with you?"

I look up, for a moment I think he's asking me, but I'm surprised to see him glaring at Declan. "You threatened her with *my* safety. Are you kidding me?" He's angry. I can feel it slowly seeping from him.

"Of course, I did. You know what she is. What she can do. It would not surprise me if she led you into that dangerous situation and left you there to die." Declan stands, from this angle he looks more muscular and taller. I'm not sure how when he is already much more attractive than some of the males I have come across in my life. But maybe it's that unspoken thing that makes him appear more divine. "I don't trust her and quite frankly, I'm questioning your sanity. You seemed to have bonded with her on these little runs of yours that you do in the mornings and if you remember that's not what we are here for."

Rich's fingers ball into fists at his sides mirroring Declan's.

"I remember just fine why we are here. I was there that night, same as you."

That piques my interest, but this is not my fight. Declan doesn't trust me and wouldn't tell me even if I asked, and I don't want Rich to feel like I'm prying too deeply.

"I'm not asking you to trust her. Hel, I'm not even asking you to like her. But make my job easier and stop staring at her like you want to snap her neck!"

It wouldn't be the first time someone thought that. I snort at my own intrusive thoughts and both heads whip around to look at me. It's then I realise I said that out loud. I roll my lips and sit back in the seat, wishing the couch would swallow me whole.

The pair quickly turn back to each other.

"Can we at least hear her out? I want to know what happened and why we were there in the first place." Rich tries to reason. Declan pauses still looking as though he throw me out of the window before listening to anything I have to say, but still, he nods.

Rich places a dry towel around my shoulders and I offer a small smile in thanks - hopefully the shivers will stop soon - before sitting down next to me.

"Where did you go, Siren?" Declan sighs, placing his chin back in his hand.

"We went out jogging and found ourselves at the gates to the dock." I roll my eyes thinking of how positively stupid this all sounds. I most definitely can't tell them that I felt a pull towards them as if some mystical tether had guided me there.

Surely, they'd think I was crazy.

Wouldn't they?

"Anyway, I found them. The rebels." I wave my hand through the air and look towards my bedroom door. I want nothing more than to be in a dry set of clothes.

"Excuse me what?" Rich sputters.

I turn back to them, intrigued to see even Declan's eyes wide in surprise.

"Yeah. They were having a meeting. Can I go change?" I ask, thoroughly uninterested in reviewing the night's events when I'm so uncomfortable.

"You can tell us what in the fuck you were thinking, is what you can do," Declan barks back.

"What if something had happened to you, in there? There's no guarantee I would've been able to pull you out." Rich scrambles to find the right words. Seemingly unable to comprehend the *danger* he thought I was in tonight.

"Clearly, that doesn't seem to be a problem." I eye Declan in the armchair, and he does the same back to me.

Rich snaps his mouth shut, "That's not funny."

"Was I making a joke?" I answer, allowing my voice to portray my disinterest. I squirm uncomfortably again and sigh.

"What was the meeting about?" Declan asks suddenly.

I swallow audibly and begin reciting everything I remember. It takes time to remember it almost word for word, even down to the details of the cloaked figure, but I manage to finally tell them everything.

"They can't be serious?" Rich asks, his mouth pursing slightly.

"As I understand it, they are."

He took a seat when I began my story, sitting on the edge of his seat, now, exasperated, he sits back wringing his hands through his hair, "Good gods, I don't believe it. They're going to get themselves killed."

Declan sits as still as a statue, unaffected entirely by the news, his chin still rests in his hand, but I can now see the tiredness pulling at him.

"What are we going to do? We can't let them get themselves killed," Rich stands and begins pacing back and forth along the room.

"If you wish to do something about it, handler Keita you can. But I cannot assist you. I am here on behalf of the Fort of Ajay." I stand and walk to the bathroom. "Maybe see if the personification of *emotional* over there can help you."

I don't wait to hear the response before I close the door shut.

The smell of food wafting under the crack of my door is what wakes me up in the late morning, or afternoon. I don't know. But the scent of it makes my mouth water. I groan loudly as I stretch out on my lumpy bed. The warmth of the sun invading my room is very much welcome after the rain from the night before.

I heave myself up and groggily pad my way to the kitchen where Declan is hunched over the stove.

"Good afternoon, liefling," Rich calls from the couch, who watches as I yawn and scratch at my head making my hair fluff up.

"Afternoon? You didn't wake me earlier?" I ask plopping myself down next to him.

He bumps his shoulder with mine, "I thought you'd need the sleep."

Declan places two bowls down in front of us and walks away. A rice dish slathered with a rich spicy sauce; it fills the apartment with a heavenly, exotic scent. My belly rumbles loudly.

"So, what's the plan?" Rich asks, digging into his food. Even though I'm hungry I can't be sure Declan hasn't poisoned my bowl so I'm much more hesitant to take that first bite.

So instead, I shrug, "I'm unsure yet. But I think it would be best to go and check out the warehouse again. To see if they left anything behind. I doubt it, but it's somewhere of interest."

"Are you ok with going out again?" Rich asks, looking a little uncertain. I nod in reply moving toward my room to get changed.

"You're going now?" Declan asks, eyeing the untouched bowl on the table.

"Is there a problem?" I counter. He doesn't reply. "Right then. Don't wait up."

"Wait!" Rich yells. I pause before walking into my room, "two rules. Rule number one, you are to check in every hour."

I quirk a brow.

"Agree or you don't go," he argues. I nod unable to oppose his worry, even if I can more than take care of myself.

"And rule two, do not die."

"Shouldn't that be rule one?" I tease, but not even the hint of a smile is present on his face.

"If you die," he continues, ignoring me, "not only will it be harder for us to complete this mission. But I'll bring you back just to kill you myself."

"You have such a way with words," I smile. The aura pouring off of him tells me he's clearly in no mood for jokes. "Every hour." I concede, nodding my head once to show him I understand. "And I will try my hardest to not die. Does that make you happy?"

"Nothing about you leaving to do this on your own makes me happy. I'm placing a lot of trust in you tonight. Do not mess this up," he scolds. His worry comes from a good place, but it is misguided if it is for me.

I change into my full combat gear, mask included, and shout a quick goodbye. Looking at my cloaked figure, I can't very well appear on the streets through a door, so I jimmy open the small window in my room and squeeze myself through the tiny frame. Standing on my tiptoes on the narrow ledge outside, I look to the neighbouring building, leaping towards the gutter and using the pipe to climb to the roof.

The air tonight still holds some of the heat from the day, having left early in the afternoon I make my way lazily back to the docks using the rooftops, familiarising myself with the views from up here. Listening to people stumble out of bars drunk and watch others loitering on corners waiting for a different type of company.

Upon entering the warehouse, I head straight for the main room being careful in case any of the dock workers that might still be working, even at this hour.

Coming in through the side door, the first thing that I see is that the area is now devoid of boxes and crates that were stacked in here only hours ago. Piles of sand, patchwork across the floor, an attempt at soaking up the blood that has been left behind from the brutal capture of the few unlucky rebels.

Taking the stairs up to the metal grated balcony, I push my way into the tiny office space, filled only with a tiny wooden desk, overflowing with files and papers and in each corner is a metal filing cabinet so old there's rust on each corner. The computer looks so ancient and boxy, and the stuffing is burst from the fabric on the swivel chair.

Stepping forward to the desk I begin looking through the paper, only to find that they are invoices and delivery information for various shipments. Nothing at all about the meeting from last night, I search for so long that I find nothing at all related to the rebels.

The side door creaks open before banging closed loudly. I duck swiftly into the shadows and peer around the thin wooden wall. It's so dark in here that I can barely make out the shape of the figure walking around on the lower level. The shadow pushes back its hood and hurriedly starts searching behind boxes and under shelving units.

His head is covered in dark, fluffy hair that shields his pointed fae ears, that much I can see. He searches behind empty shelving and behind the few boxes left behind, turning this way and that and I can see his brown eyes glowing dimly. The glowing eyes are a shifter trait, but the pointed ears of the fae? Unless the ears are fake? I have heard of this new technique of prosthetics. Where an artificial body part can be made for the wearer.

He growls kicking the box in front of him in annoyance.

I shift closer to the edge trying to get a closer look, his pale skin reflects the moonlight casting an ethereal glow on his flawless fae-like profile, and I can see his thick eyebrows are scrunched angrily.

As I take another silent step the metal under my feet groans under my weight and his body goes rigid. I physically cringe and sigh when his attention instantly snaps toward the sound.

"And just who, exactly, are you?" he asks into the shadows already on guard.

I think about it, I really think about replying, but I'm just not sure what it will accomplish.

He leans back against the box next to him, crossing his arms over his chest, "You can come out of the shadows, I can see you crouched down up there."

"Damn you fucking shifters," I curse, and he chuckles, having heard me even from so far away. I leap from the walkway and slam down onto a stack of boxes below and that is where I stay, not daring to get any closer.

"Hmm, that's better."

"Not really," I mutter back, thinking of all the ways Madame K would gut me if she ever found out I was seen so easily.

"First time spying?"

"You'd be surprised."

"Really? Then what are you doing here?" He asks leaning forward to get a better look at me.

"You probably don't want to know the answer, Roman Garcia," I reply, my gaze never leaving his face.

"Now I *am* intrigued." He grins showing two perfect little dimples, one on each cheek. His neck and hands are tattooed, I can see more travel up his arms underneath his sleeve, with a multitude of different designs, some in colour and some in black and white. A gaudy ring on each tattooed finger.

The figure from last night.

"I'm at a bit of a disadvantage now though. You know who I am, but I don't even know what you look like."

"And you will never get that privilege."

"Oh, come on, never say never." His grin widens.

"Gods, you're like a clique teenage boy with daddy issues."

"How'd you figure?" His bushy brows draw together, his chiselled jaw locks shut, all trace of humour gone in an instant.

Clearly, I've touched a nerve, instead of pushing it further I say instead, "Does it matter what I think of you?"

That pesky smirk is back on display, "Yes because this is by far the best conversation, I've had all week."

"And that includes the plan you made for Dawnya? Wow, aren't I special?"

His face blanches and his body language becomes guarded, "you're incredibly special if you already know about that." He tries to mask his surprise by putting on his cocky façade once again. He looks me up and down and licks his lips. "Come then. Tell me your thoughts on the idea."

I step down from the boxes, so we are now on the same level, "personally I think it's reckless and utterly stupid. You are going to get your followers killed and for what? What do you have against the king?"

His spine straightens and he pushes off from the crates behind him. He marches forwards until we are chest to chest. If I tilted my head up some more, he'd be able to see my eyes and I can't afford that to happen.

"What does it matter to you?" He grunts.

"Are we going to continue going in circles or are you going to answer my questions?"

"You're very demanding for someone I don't know the name of," he deflects, again.

I roll my eyes, and his breath stalls in his lungs.

"You have beautiful eyes," he smiles, and it's my turn to be stunned.

"Fucking shifters," I snarl. Grabbing the knife from my holster I slash it towards him.

He dodges the blow but doesn't fight back like I expected him to instead he begins backing away, "what did I do?" he screeches.

"Enough talking!" I hiss, waiting for him to bolt for the side door. He doesn't disappoint me. The bang of it is once again loud like thunder rolling through the room.

With a sadistic smirk across my face, I tuck my knife back into its holster and take off after him.

I barge through the door and listen to the splash of water as he runs through puddle after puddle.

Catching up to him is easy, but I'm silently impressed by his agility as he uses the wall to parkour over the linked fence landing beautifully on the balls of his feet. I'm quick to chase. Hopping over the fence after him, I land lightly spreading the impact up my legs keeping myself low to the floor as he tries to run away.

"Roman Garcia..." I yell, taking a step towards his retreating form right before a gunshot cracks through the air.

A gasp punches through my lips and I stop walking. Everything seems to happen in slow motion. I crease my brow as I watch Roman skid to a stop nearly falling to the floor with the motion. His hair whips upwards as he looks to the side, his eyes widening and then back to me. His eyes roving up and down my body in quick succession and his mouth pops open when he sees me clutching my stomach. I stumble back a few steps, my breaths coming out short and quick.

Three figures, all dressed in black their hoods covering their faces in shadow, come charging out of a nearby alleyway straight for him. With their weapons drawn, they are diligently pointing at me.

Another shot is taken and shreds through my thigh.

I cry out as I crumble to the floor.

Yells echo around me and two of the assailants pull Roman away by his arms. He tries to shake them off, but their grip is firm.

I'd been so focused on the hunt that I hadn't taken into account that he might not be alone. But even Roman seems to be in shock by their arrival.

The third hovers by me acting as a barrier between me and them, or rather me and Roman. I can feel by the build of them that it's a woman and that's even before her sweet scent blows through my nostrils on the salty breeze. She spits on the ground in front of me.

"You will not get another chance at him. This war will continue whether you're here to see it or not, bitch." She pulls the trigger again hitting me in the chest before taking off after the others, leaving me bleeding in the street.

I want to scream — I want to cry — instead, I stick with cursing.

"FUCK!" I yell out in pain, "FUCK, FUCK, FUCK!" I scream as I rifle through my pockets, searching for my phone only to find it has a bullet hole through it. Pieces of glass fall from the screen and whatever isn't broken is splattered in my blood.

I groan, "fucking shit." I slam the device into the concrete beneath me. Anger is as much of a motivator as any, finding my legs under me I begin trying to lift up from the ground. My thigh spurts blood and I can only hope they didn't hit the artery. But I need to get up before the shock sets in.

Despite the agony, I crawl across the road to the path and pull myself up into a seated position. Hissing and groaning all the while.

Pain and fear will cloud the mind, find something else to focus on, Madame K's words come rushing through me like a lifeline.

I stand — on shaky legs no less, but I stand. The motion is excruciatingly painful, but I am once again on my own two feet. Maybe Rich should've come with me. But then I think about what that would mean if it was him in the mess and think better of it. Declan would without hesitation kill me before I got a word out to explain.

I take in several deep breaths as I lean against the wall of a nearby building, with one arm over my stomach, and my other hand curled tightly into a fist.

Lifting my cloak to reveal my sleeve I pull out the knife from my boot, I start cutting at the fabric making makeshift bandages. I crumple one piece and stuff it into the bullet hole in my stomach, another I tie tightly around my thigh and lastly stuff another piece into my left breast.

"Bastard!" I hiss as the pain shoots through every nerve ending.

I grit my teeth as I force myself to take a step, and then another keeping my feet under me. Using the brick wall next to me as a makeshift crutch.

What I really want to do is break down and cry about my situation.

My blood starts to dribble down my skin and clothing, leaving little droplets in my wake. The fire in my veins is overwhelming, but all I can think about is how I will not die here. This will not be how it ends for me. It's not even a question. I know I need to keep going, because if I stop now my body will go into shock, and I will be as good as dead.

The sun is rising over the horizon by the time I make it back to the apartment. The torment of having to drag myself back is nightmarish.

Too many times I had to stop and catch my breath.

Too many times I thought about sitting down and closing my eyes.

But every time, something picked me back up and told me to keep going.

Relief floods me when our building comes into view. I stumble faster until I get to the door, slamming my hand on the glass to push it open. If I wasn't bleeding out, I'd feel bad for the person who has to wipe my smeared blood from it.

Knowing my left leg won't be of use climbing the stairs with a hole in it, I damn near crawl up the stairs to the apartment. It's humiliating and humbling at the same time to know that even if I feel invincible at times, I'm just as fragile as any mortal.

Reaching the door I finally let out a little sob and extended my hand to the handle. Only to miss it. I crumble to the floor, hitting the door on the way down. It rattles loudly on its hinges, but I don't care. I turn and rest against the dirty wooden entrance, and with what little strength I have left bang my head softly against it.

I look down at my body, at the blood soaking my clothes and drooling over my skin, staining everything in its path. I begin to apply pressure to my wounds, but my strength is nearly spent.

I 'knock' again but still get no answer. Sighing, I close my eyes.

I dab at the wounds with a blood-soaked gauze, before promptly giving up when I find it no use.

I feel so broken and tired, I can only imagine that I must exactly that. I scoff at the image compared to the strength I represent back at the Fort.

"This is not the coolest way to die," I mumble, my lips feeling to detached to say more, before I close my eyes.

CHAPTER TWELVE
PAIN & PENANCE

I wake to the trickling of water and soft warm grass beneath my palm.

The sun's rays are almost too bright for my eyes; the chirping of birds is joyful. Giggling comes from my left, like that of a mother and child chasing each other around. I open my eyes to a blue sky filled with clouds of all shapes and sizes that glide by silently. It's warm here, wherever here is.

The giggling grows distant as I move to sit up. This place is peaceful, almost heavenly.

Looking down at myself I'm in a white flowing gown, fitted delicately at the bodice, the skirt stitched beautifully with diamonds that spread throughout the light fabric.

A warm breeze wafts through my hair and I see a meadow stretching out before me, filled with wildflowers and a single oak tree, so tall it looks as though it's reaching for the sky. Putting my feet underneath me, I stand and take soft steps towards it. The giggling has once again increased. A little girl with white, blonde hair sits in the shade of the age-old tree weaving coloured thread together.

"Aella," she calls my name as I get closer, turning her young face to

me. Her voice seems to echo in my head. Her chubby cheeks are flushed a light pink, and her ash grey eyes glitter with joy, "come on sleepy head, wake up."

I sit down next to her laughing all the while, her tiny hands dropping the thread in her lap, her small, cold palms move to cover my cheeks. She can't be more than seven years old with the size of her, and the youthful elegance of her face.

"Good morning, to you too." I smile at her, the familiarity of this girl is unexpected and yet unsurprising, it's like I've known her my whole life.

"So silly." She grins, pinching my cheeks, her hair hangs in ringlets around her face, the look of pure innocence makes me feel like I should step away from her. That the blood on my hands shouldn't be anywhere near her.

The bright glow from the sun breaches through the branches above, lighting her up with an almost angelic and otherworldly shine.

Until her face drops.

"Aella, you have to wake up."

"What do you mean I'm already awake," I reply, placing my hands over hers on my face.

"Wake up!" she yells. Her hands tighten, frightening me.

"WAKE UP! WAKE UP! WAKE UP!"

My eyes burst open, and I take in an almighty gasp of air.

"She's awake!"

"Oh, thank the gods."

I'm lying on my back facing a ceiling, and for a few seconds, I'm confused as to why, when nothing but pain bursts through my body.

Air gets lodged in my throat, before a scream tears through with the first waves of pure agony, feeling as though every nerve ending has been set alight, and all I can do is burn with them. My vision is blurry, and wetness rolls down my cheeks.

"Deep breaths Elle, you're going to be ok." Rich is above me. "Declan get your arse in here now!"

I gain enough awareness to look around, seeing dirty cabinets under a fluorescent, yellow light. I try to sit up, but a hand on my shoulder pushes me back down.

"Easy, Elle. Lie back and breathe, this is going to hurt. Declan, get her something to bite down on." Rich's voice sounds distant and muffled.

A blurred figure comes steaming into the room in a flurry, taking something and folding it in half holding it to my mouth.

"Here," he pants, tapping my lips, they part seemingly on their own and he inserts something cold and leathery between my teeth. Instantly I bite down and then white blurs my vision. Something starts digging into my stomach and a raw scream rips through my throat.

Your pain will only make you stronger. Madame's voice echoes in my head. I'm panting so hard that I start to feel lightheaded.

My hand slams down against the countertop, I do it again and again to help distract myself from the tearing skin as Rich digs around into the wound again.

Black spots start to pop up in my vision and I start to feel faint, my eyes begin rolling in their sockets and tears subsequently run down the sides of my face wetting my hair.

"Easy," Declan's voice is right by my ear, softer now than I heard it at any point since meeting him. It reminds me of the last time I was in a state like this in front of these two males, back in Kos. He starts to smooth back the hair from my sweat-soaked face. "Everything's going to be ok."

The screaming starts to take its toll on my throat, and my jaw and teeth ache the harder I bite, my muscles hurt from the tension and all I want to do is sleep.

"Shouldn't we take her to a hospital?" I can hear Declan yelling at Rich.

"No!" I cry, but the sound is muffled by the leather in my mouth, I start shaking my head as they both turn to me.

"Almost there Elle," Rich assures me, I try to nod but a sob comes out instead; the pain is nothing short of excruciating.

Declan's eyes come into view; distress is clear on his face, but he offers me a smile all the same. I know he can see the suffering in my eyes by the pinching of his eyebrows. He sighs and places his forehead against mine, not once stopping his soothing strokes on my hair. The sweat on my skin runs in rivulets racing towards the countertop, I can feel it slide against my flushed cheeks.

"It's going to be ok, Elle. You're going to be ok," Declan whispers in my ear, telling himself that more than me. But I nod my head, all the same, letting him know I heard him.

The movement stops in my stomach, and I start taking deep breaths to calm my pounding heart. That is, until Rich starts pulling, and my screams renew. Try as I might, disassociating from myself right now is impossible, something that has proven useful in the past when I have been tortured, but now, when I can feel tissue and muscle tear continuously, there's no chance of a reprieve.

I shake off Declan's head and turn away looking at the dirty cabinets, praying for death. My eyes slam closed, and my voice starts cracking, the screams having destroyed my vocal cords.

"Got it!" Rich calls triumphantly, holding the blood-covered bullet up with a satisfied smile on his face. Declan blinks away his anguish and shoots him a scowl.

My eyes roll once again in their sockets, and I fight desperately to keep them open. Declan is over me in a second, crowding my space, his mouth opening and closing but I feel too far away to hear what he's saying.

"Come on, keep your eyes open."

I groan in response.

"Dec, give her some air," Rich replies, coming up on my other side.

My body is aching and exhausted, but I know that if I sleep now, there's a higher chance that I won't wake up again – but practice and theory are two very different scenarios.

I spit out the leather from my mouth, holding a flimsy thumbs up at them and sharing the weakest smile I've ever conjured up.

Declan lowers his head, not stopping until it thuds against the countertop. He doesn't say anything, but it's Rich who I turn to and despite his earlier pride in himself, he looks over my body taking everything in before finally settling on my face.

"I thought I told you not to die."

"I didn't. Clearly," I croak through my shredded throat.

"Your heart stopped," Declan mumbles, still resting his head against the countertop. "That counts as dying."

"I need to stitch you up; you might want to put that back in your mouth." Rich nods to the belt, ignoring Declan's comments. I go to reach for it, but Declan snatches it before I can move an inch and he holds it out for me once again.

"Looks like I owe you a new belt," I joke before I bite down again, and not a moment too soon as Rich starts stitching my wound closed making me wince.

Declan scoffs and rolls his eyes. Rich chuckles from over me but doesn't stop his work until all of my wounds are stitched back together.

"Please tell me you did the other two when I was unconscious," I groaned, handing the belt back to Declan.

"Yeah, you're all good. You're lucky they didn't hit anything major," Rich mumbles cleaning up his hands. "But you have lost a lot of blood. Hence the whole, heart stopping thing."

"You have such a wonderful bedside manner, Rich." I shift position wincing as I do so and thinking better of it. Wondering, instead, if I can just sleep on the countertop.

"Who did this to you?" Declan asks, his tone suggests there's no room for argument. I look up at Rich for help to see him smirking at me.

"Members of Dawnya shot me because I was chasing Roman," I grumbled.

"Roman? You found him?" Rich asks incredulously.

"More like he found me. I got inside to investigate, and in he walked, looking for something."

"Wait, you talked to Roman? About what," Rich questions, my blood still staining his hands.

"Can we talk about that later?" I pant trying to get up only to be pushed back down by Declan, "I tried to kill him, he ran, and I got shot three times."

"Four."

"What?"

"You got shot four times, there's four bullet holes in your clothes," Rich states. Pointing to each of them, one in my chest, one in my stomach and two in my leg.

"How did you not notice?"

"I'm sorry I was a little busy trying to make it back alive, to pay attention to how many times they shot me," I sass angrily, pushing myself back up again. "But if you must know, my phone is destroyed so I'm guessing it took the fourth bullet." Coughing violently when something tickles my throat I scramble for breath and wince at the rawness of my throat.

"I think the questions can wait for another time," Rich utters, watching my eyes flutter open and closed again, "get her washed up and then take her to bed, I'll clean up in here."

No other words are exchanged as I'm lifted into the air, my head spins rapidly from the loss of blood and nausea roils over my in a devastating wave. My hand flies to my mouth while I tuck my head into the warmth surrounding me. Breathing in the scent I quickly come to the realisation that Declan is holding me in his arms.

Intense sickness forgotten.

"Easy. I've got you," he whispers into my hair.

He carries me in silence, and I can't help the discomfort I feel in being in his arms. Like I don't belong there and yet... I do. Maybe it's because of his blatant disregard for me that makes me question his motive even now.

I knew Rich was a medic, but I never thought I'd actually have to see him in action. Looking at the blood soaking my clothes. I lift pieces up to see the delicate stitchwork Rich has sown for my skin to begin its healing.

"He trained hard in his field," Declan murmurs, his eyes trailing the pale and pink skin of my stomach, his intrigue scorches a path following in the wake of those fiery eyes. "He became a member of my team within the first few weeks of Sormbay joining the fight against Duranda."

"He could do with working on his extraction skills," I mutter still feeling the after-effects of that bullet tearing through my muscle. It was just as painful as when it tore its way in.

Declan surprises me by laughing.

The sound is deep and rumbly, and yet so melodic, and I can't help but stare at the creases next to his eyes and the way his mouth curves up perfectly into a devastating smile. A dimple appears on his left cheek. Just the one. A secret I'll take to the grave knowing I'll likely never see it again. Because he's just humouring me tonight. I got shot and he's playing nice because I am their way out. I have a job to do. That's the only reason I can think of for this oddly reversed behaviour.

"I heard that! And you're welcome!" Rich shouts from the kitchen, jumping me.

"How does he do that?"

"What?"

"Hear something like that from here?"

Declan seems to think something over for a second, "he's just got very good hearing."

I scoff.

"What?" he pries, humour still lighting his rugged face.

"That is a bullshit answer." He laughs again, jostling me in his arms.

My tongue starts to feel heavy, and my speech turns slow. The more I try to talk the more my words slur together, still try as I might I fight against the exhaustion. Everything aches when I'm placed down on the lid of the toilet under the bright spotlights in the tiny bathroom.

"Lift your arms." I can barely manage the movement, but Declan gently helps me lift the blood-soaked t-shirt above my head.

He runs the tap for a few moments testing the temperature of the water now and then, before wetting a towel and turning to me. "This may hurt a little, but I'll be as gentle as I can."

I nod in answer while he bends down in front of me and tenderly dabs at the two sets of stitches on my torso, I hiss at the discomfort it brings.

His thick brows furrow and I watch him scan every silver scar and blood-stained piece of skin on my torso. There are too many to count and too many to remember quite how I got them. Not all are from missions some are from my handlers or programme leaders. His thumb absentmindedly brushes over a few on my lower abdomen while he holds me in place.

"Sorry," he mumbles, not meeting my eyes and continues to clean me up. His familiar scowl back in place.

The tepid water burns against the newly torn flesh, it's an effort not to ask him to stop but even I know that these stitches are going to need cleaning before I can even think of sleeping again.

Declan helps me stand and assists in taking off my equally bloody pants. With my hands gripping tightly on the bowl of the sink as I step out of the pant leg. I turn to see Declan on his knees before me. He once again begins dabbing at my skin, this time on my upper thigh. I never thought I'd ever bear witness to Declan on his knees, let alone before me, helping me. My mouth dries and images flash across my eyes and I'm thanking the gods he can't read minds. Taking some deep breaths, I try to concrete on my balance instead of what our position conjures up within me.

Once he's finished, he tosses the towel and my clothes into the tiny bathtub. He picks me up once again, carrying me back to my room. I feel completely useless and coddled and utterly pathetic. I walked back from the docks with three bullet holes in me and I can't even walk ten feet to my bed, even if I understand that this is for the best. If I tried to clean myself up on my own there'd be no question that I would've ripped these stitches out.

He places me softly down on my lumpy bed and I notice a small pillow and a thin blanket have been placed on the floor. I quirk a brow at him, silently asking the question.

He places his arms over his chest. Stoic Declan is showing up again. "One of us is staying in here with you to keep an eye on you," he briefly glances at my near-naked form, "you need clothes."

"I'd say so," I croak again, looking down at the goosebumps covering my flesh. My unmentionables are covered only by a thin and damp layer of bloody cotton that I used to call underwear.

"Do you want help? Or..." Declan trails off, objectively looking me in the eyes.

I shoot him a plain look. "I can't stand by myself but yeah, I can get changed. What do you think, Declan?" He grins and when he doesn't move, I tilt my head to the side. "What?"

"You... er. You know what? Nothing," he chuckles, "you just have to say yes please."

Huffing and rolling my eyes I say, "Yes please Declan, will you help me change."

"You're very cocky for someone who just got shot, *Siren*." He jests as he kneels in front of my bed and begins to undress me. The lightness of our conversation comes so naturally that it doesn't seem real. Rich and I have spent more time conversing and I've come to understand more social cues than I ever have but even that wasn't as difficult to comprehend as the switch in Declan's attitude towards me has been.

Keeping his eyes to himself he stands before me once more. Being completely naked in front of another has never really bothered me before. My body has never truly been my own anyway. But a sudden feeling of self-consciousness washes over me now that the person before me looks as he does.

"I'll be back in just a second," he says, leaving the room. He comes back with a huge grey t-shirt, "Raise your arms."

Doing as he asks, it takes all my strength to comply, but he easily wraps me up in the fabric, the looseness freeing without being revealing. Tiredness washes over me in droves and all I can think about is falling back into the small single bed behind me, even if it's uncomfortable and cold.

He lays me down in bed, "anything else, dear?" he teases, tucking me in as though I am a child. I yawn and shake my head no, allowing my heavy eyes to finally shut.

"Thank you, Declan."

"You're welcome princess," he utters, "I'll be down here if you need me," he answers, and I hear him thud against the floor, into the makeshift bed.

Rich

Sitting in the corner of Aella's room on a rickety wooden stool with my knees nearly at my chest, I lean against the wall opposite from her with the lamp on, fully engrossed in reading one of the books I fished out from her bag - one of the many. I'm currently captivated by a rather steamy sex scene between the two main characters.

Chuckling at the still shivering female lying on the bed, next to me. *Of course, she'd read these kinds of books.* Her eyes flutter open and closed, dozing in and out of consciousness. She had woken when Declan and I had changed shifts. He had seemed reluctant to leave but I'd managed to convince him that he needed to get at least a little sleep. He had been watching over her all night and didn't seem to want to close his eyes.

The sky darkens further still outside, the patting rain against the window becoming louder in my ears, and the distant rumble of thunder sounds over the sea beyond the docks, which threatens to bring even more rain with it.

The pouring rain beats against the thin windowpane loudly, and flows in the rivulets down the surface, distracting me from the book in my hands for a moment.

"Rich?"

Her scratchy voice catches me by surprise, and I whip my head in her direction to see her fingers flexing. I watch as her eyelids open, and she tiredly looks about the room. I put the book down on her nightstand and kneel on the floor next to her immediately checking her temperature.

"Hey, sleepyhead." I smile, relief bouncing around my heart, "how are you feeling?"

"Rough," she croaks. I grab a glass of water from the bedside table and lift it to her lips, she takes a few long gulps before pulling away and inhales a few deep breaths.

"How long have I been out for?"

"A couple of hours," I reply quietly, brushing her sweat-riddled hair away from her forehead.

She huffs a breath of air and closes her eyelids again, before shifting to get comfortable.

"Still tired?"

She nods her head but opens her eyes again.

"What's your pain level?"

"Like a four," she groans.

"For the average person. Not a Fury."

"Oh, well probably like an eight then."

"Ok. I'll get you some more medication," I reply, resting my hand on her forehead and checking her temperature. A habit I've gotten myself into, with her blood loss, keeping her warm has been such a struggle.

"I think I might be hungry too," she mumbles.

"The only thing I can give you is water or ice."

"Mmm, frozen water." She tries chuckling but winces from the pain.

"You're chipper for someone who's just been shot."

"It's not my first time," she mutters back to me.

I can only blink in response to her words.

"Where's Declan?" She not so subtly changes the subject.

"I told him to get some rest. He was quite literally watching you sleep before. It was almost unsettling."

She flinches, "I wish you hadn't told me that."

I huffed a small laugh "Apologies, let me get you some ice." I stand and leave the room.

Turning the corner back to her room, I'm stunned to find her sitting up, looking down at the floor.

"What are you doing?" I snap, a little too harshly. "Sorry. But you should still be lying down."

"I know but I'm going to get bed sores soon." She smiles.

"No, you aren't," I replied rolling my eyes, "take these and then you're lying back down."

"Yes, nurse Keita." She salutes me, mockingly.

"It's... you know what nurses are just as good as a doctor, so I'll take it."

CHAPTER THIRTEEN
THE SIXTH SENSE

Aella

Having slept through the day and then again, all night, I lie in bed twiddling my thumbs. I've already finished the books Rich left with me and now all I have is to stare up at the grungy ceiling watching the early morning light filter across the flaking paint.

The songbirds sing in chorus outside the window happy that another day has begun.

Deciding I can't lie here for another minute, I throw the covers from my body, groaning at the pull on my stitches and the ache in my muscles. I shakily pull myself up into a sitting position, my fingers curling into the sheets, and I lift my legs over the side, the body lying on the floor is the only thing that makes me pause.

His soft snoring falters for a moment before shifting positions and dropping right back off again. They must've traded positions again after I'd fallen back asleep last night.

Declan looks so peaceful as he lies there, and I take this time to stare deeply at his features. At the stubble that is growing along his jaw and

Cupid's bow. At the scar through his left eyebrow and his thick lashes that brush against the tips of his cheeks, that twitch in his sleep.

Once unsteadily upright I quietly pull up my pants, tucking Declan's shirt into them, and walk to the kitchen making us all a fresh pot of coffee. My stitches are still tender, but I can already feel them healing. I've never understood how I can have such fast healing when I am a mortal. But it sure does come in handy.

I grab my laptop and place it on the coffee table in the tiny living area. Tentatively lowering myself to the floor, I spread out the files across the table and begin the long and arduous work of sifting through every camera file from the first protest to the present day. I can already get rid of nearly eighty per cent of the footage from certain dates where no active protest or riot takes place.

I check the dates for each event and press play on the first video sipping from my coffee.

Speeding up the video a little to make the process faster, I scan the moving images when the screen to my laptop shuts closed, and a pair of hazel eyes meet mine.

"You're supposed to be resting."

My mouth opens and closes like that of a blubbering fish gasping for air, unable to speak. His eyebrow rises and a flush begins heating my cheeks.

Those eyes are hard as stone with a stubbornness I've only ever seen in myself. But two can play that game.

"Y...yeah, I know." I stutter, flinching. Thinking I had more strength than I do. Rolling my lips, I fall quiet.

"Then why aren't you?" he asks, standing upright crossing his arms over his chest. His signature stance, I've come to recognise it well. He should look terrifying as he looks down at me from such a height. But instead, my blood warms and between my legs starts to tingle. My eyes flicker to the vein in his bicep - his bulging bicep - with healed scars decorating his tanned skin. My mind goes completely blank. "Are you going to answer, or did you hit your head when they got the drop on you?"

I scowl, snapping right out of my daze, "they didn't get the drop on me." Even the words on my tongue taste sour at the lie. They did, in fact, get one up on me, and if being petty was a competition, I can't let it slide.

He leans in again, closer this time so I can feel his breath fan across my cheek, "it sure seems like they did." His grin is malicious and oh-so-delicious. The defiance behind it has a strength that I can only admire. He is not willing to back down from it, nor is he willing to coddle me any longer. Last night was a one-off. I knew that even when it was happening but that doesn't mean I didn't enjoy it. But I am more grateful for this side of him. I don't need to be sidelined. Not when I still have a job to finish.

Placing a hand over his face I gently push him away, "I have work to do if you don't mind giving me some personal space." The grin I receive in response would have any woman weak in the knees. Luckily, I'm not just any woman.

He drops onto the lounge behind me, watching as I lift the laptop back up continuing the search through the City Hall database, he leans forward so his face is next to mine.

I can feel the heat coming from him. I shake the thought away and finish what I'm doing, praying he gets bored soon and leaves me in peace.

I have no such luck.

"What are you doing anyway?" he queries, his warm breath tickling my ear and a shiver runs down my spine.

"Morning," Rich yawns, mercifully interrupting my response, which no doubt wouldn't have come out as anything more than a whimper. *What is happening to me?* His bare feet pad past us heading straight for the kitchen. He appears once again beside us, dropping himself down in the armchair, coffee in hand, rubbing at his eyes. That is until he sees me. "What are you doing?" His voice quickly twists from sleepy morning softness to demanding.

"Working?" Declan replies for me, making it sound more like a question than an actual answer.

Rolling my eyes I turn back to the screen, "Just because I got injured doesn't mean there still aren't things to do."

"You should be resting," he retorts, sipping from his cup no longer looking at either of us.

"Yes, I have been told." I type louder in hopes that he'll leave me alone.

"Then get back to bed."

"No."

There's a heavy sigh and the clinking of a cup as it's placed down and then I'm lifted into the air.

"Put me down," I ask politely.

"No."

I sigh, folding my arms across my chest as I'm carried back to my bed. Rich says nothing as he puts me down.

"Can I at least have my laptop?"

Seething as Rich pulls out yet another book from my bag he leaves hastily, shutting the door behind him, locking it.

"Hey!" I yell, "You can't keep me in here!"

"Actually, yes I can," he calls back.

More days have passed by since the *minor* incident at the docks. Although my wounds have nearly completely healed, I'm still made to be on bed rest. I've never slept so much in my life and that's just because there's nothing else for me to do. I've already finished the selection of books I brought with me. I'll have to make a point of visiting the nearest bookstore soon to get some more. Madame won't be happy but she's never happy, so it won't make any difference really.

"Rich," I call, drawing out his name - for the umpteenth time - from behind my, once again, locked bedroom door.

I hear a heavy sigh and the creak of floorboards as soft footsteps pad over them. The lock clicks followed by the turn of the handle.

"What?" he asks, his beautiful face as bored as I've ever seen it. He stands there dressed head to toe in black, filling the door frame with his arms crossed. My blood heats at the sight, sending a delicious tingle throughout my body, I cough and look down hoping my cheeks aren't as pink as they feel.

"I'm bored," I whine, remembering why I called him in here. Throwing the scratchy covers off my body, I shift so my legs are draped over the side of the mattress, "let me go for a walk before I go insane."

"That is the seventh time you've asked me this morning and it's only eleven." His face remains emotionless, as he counts on his fingers trying to remember each of our encounters this morning, nodding when he knows he's got the number right. I would otherwise laugh at the humourless expression but I'm feeling too restless to risk being cooped back up in here.

"And it won't be the last," I tell him, standing up on wobbly legs.

"See this is why. You aren't ready, you can't even hold yourself up properly." He steps forward, his cool hands are around my waist in an instant.

"That's because I've been lying in bed for five days."

"It's been three."

"And you won't let me even walk around the damn living room."

"Because you got shot in the leg."

"Stop trying to make it sound better!" I snap.

"Clearly, I'm not."

I pout at him, and I know he can see the fire in my eyes. He looks down at me and I can tell he's not going to concede to me.

"Fine." I lift yet another one of Declan's shirts over my head. Rich's fingers flex against my skin, but not once does he look down at my completely bare chest.

"Why don't you just go with her if you're so worried Rich," Declan's voice reverberates from the kitchen.

A muscle ticks in his jaw, his dark eyes not leaving my own, "don't encourage her," he yells back.

"I knew I preferred Declan," I tell him quietly.

"You wound me," Rich drawls, not fazed by my untruthful words.

We stand there staring at each other for a few moments until he exhales heavily through his nose.

"Get dressed, we'll go round the block."

I grin so wide my jaw hurts from the action.

"The moment I feel like you can't take it, I'm bringing you back here and I refuse to carry you."

Rich walks silently next to me out in the blazing sun minutes later. His presence was near menacing to those around him. He walks with a sinister air; his posture shows his displeasure. Oh, and the scowl on his face.

He's annoyed that I got my way, but I think more annoyed that he was ganged up on by Declan agreeing with me.

Though my wounds are healed the pain is still with me and limping down the street trying to match his long strides is no easy feat. I'm out of breath before we turn the first corner.

The thunderstorm from a few days ago has already been long forgotten, the air seems cleared of all the humidity, the rain has washed away the uncomfortable heat along with the rolling thunder, and even the people seem rejuvenated.

Rich's upper arm brushes lightly against my shoulder, our height difference stark now that we are walking next to each other, he doesn't seem to want to stray too far from me. Nevertheless, I breathe in a lungful of the fresh salty air, with the scent of cooking bread not far behind.

We walk down the streets and up at the same little bakery that we stumbled upon last week, just around the corner from the safehouse, the feeling of the sun on my skin is something I didn't realise I would miss, but even at the Fort with the biting cold winds, the warmth seeps in minutely.

I can't help the feeling of contentment filling my chest as Rich and I continue to walk side by side. Even without talking, I feel the most at peace I've ever felt.

"Are you happier now?" Rich asks suddenly, his voice rough.

"I don't know if I understand the context of 'happier', but I do feel better. Thank you," I reply, looking up at him, shielding my eyes from the sun as my gaze travels higher and higher up the height of him.

Opening the door to the lavender-painted bakery we step inside, to the smell of freshly baked bread and dough with the bitter brew of coffee. We instantly stand in line, waiting to be served when a question comes to mind.

"Wait am I allowed coffee, on antibiotics?"

"No. I have begun to lessen your dosage, but you still can't have caffeine. If that's what you're asking. You can have the pink lemonade that they offer though." He points to the board behind the counter, displaying their stock.

I open my mouth to protest even though I know it's fruitless, when my skin prickles violently, the hairs on my arm standing on end. My spine goes taught and my arms hang loosely at my sides, my chin rises, and my breathing becomes shallow.

Rich's attention snaps to me in an instant, looking me up and down. He doesn't say anything, but I know he heard the change in my breath.

He leans in closer, "What's wrong?"

"We are being watched, sir," I reply, slipping back into protocol without even thinking about it. "Do not make a scene. Pretend like you are simply next in the queue. I'll find a way out." Scanning the tables at the front of the bakery-café, I determine that the person watching us is at least not among us. Meaning they have to be outside on the street.

The space is small and glass-fronted, so whoever is watching will know our exact movements. Off to one side, there's a pastel beaded threshold, with stairs that lead up to the stockroom – no guarantee of a way out up there. Or there's a door leading to a hallway that branches off to the toilets and the kitchens at the back – one of the doors will surely lead to an alleyway beyond.

Without wasting another second, I grab onto Rich's hand and tug him up to the counter.

"Hi sorry. We can't wait, are we ok to use your restrooms?"

"Only paying customers can use them," the caramel-skinned waitress behind the counter replies.

"I know, I read the sign, but like a said, we can't wait." I dance on the spot to emphasise my point. She sighs and nods allowing us through.

Rich follows dutifully behind and once we are out of view from the windows, the daunting feeling evaporates. I push Rich through the door to the kitchen, palming my thigh to feel the weight of my blade resting there in its holster. He begins profusely apologising to the bakers as we sidestep past them aiming for the back door, smiling, and waving politely all the while. They gawp and holler all the same at the audacity, but we bolt for the door letting it slam behind us loudly and find ourselves back outside, facing a dank alleyway. Pride fills me, but caution is never far behind.

"We need to get out of here," I say looking at our options. Heading towards the street will only make us visible if there was more than one and they've split up. We could take a risk and hide behind the bins, even a shifter wouldn't check behind them with the smell. Or we could scale up the fire escape to the roof of the neighbouring apartment building.

"What do you want to do?" Rich asks. Without another thought I run and push off up the wall grabbing onto the ladder at the bottom of the fire escape, it reels down with an almighty grind.

"Up!" I drop down and give him a leg up, he's quick to climb up and I'm just as quick to follow. Rich starts to pull the ladder up while I'm still on it, as a cloaked figure charges through the bakery's back door. The yells of the bakers echo all the way up to us.

The hood of the cloak flicks this way and that, until they see us, wide-eyed watching them.

"Run," I murmur, scrambling higher.

The person following us bolts towards the ladder, as we run for the stairs. Pushing Rich in front of me, I urge him to climb the creaking metal staircase.

The unknown below us continues to jump for the ladder, the grunts from each attempt reverberate off the walls, as do the curses for each failure.

"Keep going," I pant. The wound in my leg begins burning from the exertion.

The rusty high-pitched grinding of the ladder wheeling down cuts through the air.

"Fuck," I spit, pulling out the knife from its sheath.

Our pursuer doesn't bother to be quiet as they ascend the stairs, every thump of their feet is like the beating of a war drum, loud and sinister and constant.

Reaching the top of the stair is another ladder, leading that little extra way to the roof.

"Climb," I yell at Rich, twirling the knife in my hand, covering his back.

His breath is coming out hard and fast, but he doesn't stop. Pulling me up with him we climb the ladder quickly until we are on the roof.

"Where to now genius?" he pants, keeling over with his hands on his knees.

"Ever jumped across rooftops?" I ask.

"Yeah. You know what in my younger years all the kids did it. NO! What kind of question is that?" he yells, his heavy breathing stalls, and he stands up to his full height, looking down at me when I do nothing but snicker. "You can't be serious?"

"Either that, or you get to witness me commit manslaughter?" I retort, allowing my face to tell him I've never been more serious in my life.

"I mean it would be murder, not manslaughter," he begins to reason.

"It wouldn't be murder it would be self-defence, resulting in the death of the attacker. Murder would be preordained and something I set out to do. That is not the case here, but I should mention that whilst we are discussing this, they are closing the lead we just made for ourselves."

His gaze hardens, "which way?"

I nod my head to the building across from us with the shortest distance. He begins bouncing on his toes and shaking his limbs, puffing sharp breaths out of his mouth.

"Keita, I don't mean to pressure you, but they are getting closer."

Sure enough, the pounding of their feet grows louder and louder.

Rich yells pushing himself forward, he runs the length of the roof, leaping over the edge, like an ungraceful gazelle. I'm both impressed and amused while he lands on the side, tucking and rolling unnecessarily.

The assailant begins to climb the ladder to the roof, right behind me. My attention peels from Rich to the sounds of them climbing, waiting for them to rise over the lip of the roof. I punch them square in the nose, the crunch is sickening and loud and so brutal they let go of the ladder to hold their nose. Squealing they pinwheel backwards, falling from the ladder onto the platform below. The thud makes even Rich wince from where he is.

"Still alive?" I call out over the roof.

A groan answers and for a moment I think that is all the confirmation I'll get.

"Yeah," a muffled reply comes from the guy writhing on the stairwell.

"Good, now give it up," I shout, turning away from the ladder.

Leaping the distance from building to building is more of a bunny hop than the life-changing, flailing jump that Rich will no doubt explain it to be.

"Come on, next one." I pat Rich on the arm guiding him to the next jump.

"How many exactly are we doing?"

"Just this next one, then I'll pick the lock, and we can use their stairwell to get us out onto the street. *Then* we can blend in."

The guy groans, still holding his bleeding face as he drops himself down on the roof.

"Come on," I urge Rich again. This jump is bigger, much bigger and yet he gives it less thought than the last. He jumps with better form and more confidence.

"This is kind of fun," he calls once he lands on the other side.

I step up to the ledge and look down. The salty breeze teasing through the loose strands of my hair tempts me. The icy breath of death tickles the back of my neck. I don't even know if I can make it, with my leg still so sore, and my breathing becoming ragged, my vision begins to blur the more I look down. Unsteadily I begin to gently sway from side to side.

"Elle." Rich's honeyed voice suffocates the rising panic, stifling it into nothing, when I meet his understanding eyes. "You've got this."

I don't break our connection as I step back, and tuck my knife back into its sheath, the male behind me completely forgotten as I give myself a running start. Rich nods encouragingly at me, bracing himself to catch me and I break out into a run. Stepping broadly, I don't give myself time to think about the height as I soar over the alley below. Stumbling as my feet touch the roof on the other side landing right in Rich's arms, knocking the air from his lungs as we tumble to the ground.

"Sorry Rich," I groan, pushing myself up.

"No, it's ok," he grumbles back, sounding winded.

"Thanks though," I chuckle into his shirt, "you're quite comfy. But we really should get going."

He clears his throat and nods, pulling us both to stand, "yeah. You pick the lock, I'll cover you."

Turning the corner, we at least get some cover from the male with the bleeding nose. He's no longer chasing us, but his phone is to his ear and his gaze has not left us once.

Someone's laundry hangs on strings up here, floating eerily in the breeze, giving us more cover as I bend down to pick the lock, jimmying the picks left and right in the hole, listening intently for each pin to click into place. It doesn't take me long to have the door swinging open, a triumphant smirk on my face.

"We are going to have to be quick, he's called in backup," I say, limping forward, hissing at the tightness of my skin.

"And you can't walk," Rich sighs, "I knew this would happen."

"I'm fine. If it comes to it, you leave me behind and I'll do what is required," I reply, hopping down the narrow stairwell.

"What is required?"

"That is a conversation for another time," I answer, wincing. My legs go from underneath me, and I'm lifted into his arms held tightly against his chest.

"This is not going to be good if we have to run again," I grumble.

"I quite frankly couldn't give a shit right now. I need to get you home."

Rich's breath had barely become uneven after carrying me back, I'd been our eyes behind whilst he had charged through the crowds garnering strange looks from passers-by.

"We need to find a new apartment. Now." His voice is commanding as he steps through the door into our now not-so-safehouse, with me still in his arms.

"What? Why?" Declan asked his brows creasing as he takes us in.

"We've just been chased through the streets, by what I'm assuming are Roman's associates."

His jaw flaxes and he looks at me. His eyes darken, silently threatening me. He looks over Rich quickly, as the latter places me down on the lounge.

"We're fine by the way," Rich answers the unspoken question.

"I'll make some calls," Declan grunts turning away from us.

"Aella! Your lack of concentration is infuriating me! We have been at this for hours. Now FOCUS! Or it'll be the whip for you for the second time this week." She sighs heavily. "AGAIN!"

I roll my shoulders at the reminder of the pain she put me through for talking back to one of the guards harassing me. I put him in his place, and I was proud of it to. Until he went running to Madame, who had no choice but to take a whip in hand and teach me better.

The blindfold over my eyes is damp with sweat and the moisture stings my eyes. The cold stone room falls deathly quiet once more.

I hear a soft inhale behind me and the brush of a boot against the concrete floor to my right. While I try to orientate myself in the room, I begin to feel the loss of my eyes. I miss the sound of a harsh exhale, before feeling the harsh contact of a boot connecting with my lower back, sending me careening across the room, all the air stalls in my lungs and I bounce off the cold unforgiving floor.

My face ricochets off the ground and warmth begins pouring from both my mouth and nose. I spit out a mouthful of my own blood, wheezing and fighting for breath.

Pushing myself up to standing, still completely blind with my hands once again raised, I step gingerly back into, what I assume, is the middle of the room.

A niggling sensation of exhaustion winds its way into my mind, spreading throughout my body. But I know all too well that this exercise will not end until I complete it. I shake the thought from my mind and take a deep breath, in through my nose and out through my mouth, refocusing myself.

A scuffling sound rustles from my left and I suddenly feel the air change as they charge at me. I duck low swinging my leg out as I do, snagging a heavy weight with the movement. A surprised yelp rings through the space and the thud of a body hitting the ground is gratifying.

I finish the manoeuvre by twirling myself back up hands raised again in a guard in front of my face, the coppery tang of blood swallows my senses of smell and taste, taunting my concentration.

An electric charge crackles through the air, followed by the sound of violent zapping.

The bastards got a taser baton.

I relax my hands from a fist to an open palm, fingers flexing. The other two attackers charge towards me at the same time, the one trying to jump me from behind reaches me first - the one with the baton. I duck away as he raises his weapon and I grip his arm, twisting it around his back, making him drop the baton and cry out in pain. Reflectively, I catch the baton and shove it in his neck, the charge forcing his body to convulse aggressively, and he crumbles to the floor.

The smell of burnt hair permeates through the air and I clutch onto the baton harder, twirling it in my hand preparing for the final attack.

Rather than making it easy for myself by electrocuting the third male, I take my time dancing around him, making him second guess his own movements, before catching him off guard as he lunges at me. He goes low thinking I won't be able to tell. I instead, crack him around the head, hard, with the metal pole in my hand and his body collapses onto the floor. While he lies on the floor, I electrocute him. Just for the satisfaction, and I can finally yank off my blindfold.

Madame K cuts the light on then, blinding me and marches over to where I stand.

"Get better," she sneers, looking over my blood-covered face with disgust, "and do it quickly." She looks over at the males sprawled across the floor, something akin to pride flashes across her eyes so quickly that I believe I made it up.

She leaves me alone in the room to find someone to clean up the unconscious bodies lying around us. But as I stand here completely unsupervised in the room with three males, who are slowly coming around, my mind begins to play through little scenarios, none of which are leaving me feeling comforted. So, I follow after Madame K, through the metal door and out into the too-bright, white hallway beyond.

I close the door with a soft click and turn, running straight into a wall of muscle. My breath dispels from my lungs, for the second time today –

both for totally different reasons - the scent of this male is all too familiar, and not in a friendly way. Looking up quickly, desperate to apologise only to find my throat has dried up.

Reuben Ostair stands there looking down at me, his face is emotionless and his black eyes fathomless. He seems so much taller than me, my eyes travel so far upward that I have to take a step away just to see him in full, hitting the door at my back.

From the few records the Fort has on me, I've just passed my seventh birthday and even with my advancing skill set, he still poses quite the intimidating figure.

No matter the room.

No matter the situation.

He claims everyone's attention wherever he goes. Whether they want to give it or not. His presence is magnifying.

He crouches down, now just lower than my eyeline, and his palms move slowly until he cups my chubby cheeks in his hands. The tips of his fingers brush against my sweaty hairline. Tutting as he observes my face.

"Little Ella, what happened to you, my sweetling?" he coos in a way that makes my skin crawl, and the hairs on my arms stand on end.

I don't reply frozen with fear, I can only stare at him.

"Never mind that anyway, let's get you cleaned up." He smiles, taking my hand and leading me away from the room that I'd now wish I'd never left. My already pounding heart now races faster and stronger, it beats sporadically in my chest until tingles begin spreading through my arms and legs making them feel as heavy as lead. My vision starts to blur and the breath in my chest begins to increase in speed, the need to pass out takes hold and I don't understand why, what is this feeling?

"How are you enjoying your studies, you've moved into the advanced classes already haven't you?" Reuben asks, the question slithering like smoke over my skin, making me shiver.

"They are more challenging than I previously thought. But I am managing it." The voice that comes from me is steadier than I feel. I'm not sure where in myself it came from, but my confidence seems to please him.

"Good. It pleases me to see you thriving here," he replies, grinning at *me. His hand squeezes my own, keeping me close to his side.*

The sound of heels clicking against the shining stone floor sounds down the hallway, walking quickly and Madame K appears, turning the corner, she nearly runs right into Reuben.

"Director! Sir, may I help you?" she asks flustered, her hand flying up to her chest in shock. She steps back and finally sees me, she begins eyeing our joined hands, before finally looking back to Reuben.

"No not at all, I was just going to help our little prodigy clean her face," he answers, smiling down at me like a proud father would.

"Oh, you needn't waste such time on the little brat, I can take care of her." If I didn't know better, I would say K seems nervous because I can hear a slight tremor in her voice.

His expression changes from his normal relaxed, almost bored expression, to one of uncontrollable anger in the blink of an eye. My doe-eyed expression flickers between Madame K and Reuben, his hand squeezing impossibly tighter around my small fingers. A whimper crawls up my throat, but I catch it before it can give birth to noise. His pale skin tightens, and the edges of his face seem sharp to the touch, his long black hair whips around his head as his attention drifts between me and Madame K. It's clear she's about to be reprimanded, her chin rises preparing herself.

Bootsteps squeak across the floor, and the Captain turns the corner.

"Ah Director, I've been looking for you," he smiles, painfully unaware of the growing tension, his dark hair wet, evidently having just got out of the shower.

I imagine the torture session he has just come from was a brutal one.

"What is it, Cornelius?" Reuben demands, not taking his angered attention from Madame.

"It is a matter to be spoken of in private I'm afraid. About our upcoming event," he states.

"What of our guest?" Ostair asks casually as if the murderous glare on his brow is a common occurrence.

"He is part of our discussion. He has given us fuel for the fire, as it were."

Reuben nods in understanding, glaring at both of the adults, until they step away from us. He kneels down to my level once again and cups my face.

"Stay strong my beautiful resilient warrior. Stay strong and you will become the deadliest of us all," he grins, showing his fangs. Avoiding my nose, he leans in and places a soft kiss on my cheek, breathing in the scent of my hair.

Pulling away he waves over Madame K. "Take her to the infirmary, her nose is broken." He places another lingering kiss on my forehead and stands to leave, hesitantly letting go of my hand.

I hurry over to Madame K, shaking out the pain from my fingers, which have turned to a raging red. I turn to see him looking from me to his own hand, seeing how he curls his fingers into a fist.

While I know K is no safer than he is, I still feel calmer next to her than I ever will with him.

Especially after what he did.

She gently puts a hand on the back of my head and guides me away from the two dominating males, and I can feel Reuben's stare on my back the entire way.

That was the first time I felt the prickling sensation of being watched and it's not a feeling I'll likely forget anytime soon.

CHAPTER FOURTEEN
HELLO THERE

We walk quietly over the threshold of the off-white double doors of the new safe house. It's airy, it's spacious, it's light and most importantly... I'm claiming the biggest room.

Upon stepping inside, it is definitely more inviting than the beaten-down hovel we were holed up in before. The soft pastel colours on the walls bring in a calmer and fresher feel to each room, ranging from an almond-tinted cream to a seafoam green and a misty blue.

The windows house a small protruding railing, creating a minute balcony that overhangs the river – that splits the city in two - two stories below, where rowboats bob with the waves and gondolas glide across the glassy surface. The occasional motorised boat speeds past, sloshing water up the sides of the buildings.

"Why have you been holding out on this place, Angelos?" I wonder, eyeing everything in sight.

The decorative panelling adds texture and depth to the tall walls, and the high ceilings play host to a series of intricate ceiling roses, some large enough to cover the entire room's width.

"Because it's not on the safehouse list, this is a recently vacated apartment, the people who lived here only moved last week," he replies, huffing under the weight of the many bags.

I spot the room I want and charge through the doors, throwing myself down on the bed.

"We've got the bags," he grunts, dropping them on the floor.

"I was told not to strain myself by Nurse Keita," I say back, leaning on my elbows to watch them both struggle.

"No matter what I say, it doesn't stop you from running and jumping though, does it?" he counters.

Rich drops onto the bed next to me after collecting the rest of the bags from downstairs, "how are you feeling?"

"Better," I look at him to see him already staring at me and give him a soft smile, "ready to move about more."

"You look excited," he grins.

"Have you seen the size of this room," I beam, "the other one was like a broom closet compared to this one."

He laughs at my enthusiasm, "I think Declan is also excited to have his own room." His demeanour sinks, looking a little sulky making me chuckle.

"Aw poor baby, do you need big brave Declan to protect you," I tease, and he looks up at me, his lip stuck out with wide doe-like eyes to match, nodding at me.

I mock him by sticking out my own bottom lip, "You can always stay in here with me." I cuddle into his side, he stops me by wrapping his arms around my chest, flipping me onto my back, careful not to put his weight fully on me as he hovers over me. The broad smile on his face shows off his fangs and the unadulterated amusement in his black and silver eyes.

"Oh yeah? Anytime?"

I roll my eyes at him and slap the side of his arm, "not like that idiot. Now get off me you cheeky bastard."

His chest rumbles with laughter as he flops back down to my side, bouncing us both with his weight. We both lie there in silence for so long my eyes start to close and my breathing gets deeper when Rich softly clears his throat.

"What is it?" I ask, a little groggily.

"Ermm... I... er... I don't really know how to ask it." He sounds uncertain, my eyes fly open, and I roll onto my side facing him.

"Why don't you just come out and say it." I grin at him and it's his turn to roll his eyes. He doesn't make eye contact with me again.

"What will happen to you if we fail this mission?" he mumbles so quietly I almost miss it, and it's my turn to feel uncomfortable.

"Oh, erm... I'm not sure exactly," I replied, my brow scrunched.

"That's helpful," he huffs.

"But it's the truth, I don't know. But you don't have to worry about that. I'll handle it." I try to reassure him by squeezing his arm. He looks at me and I can't understand the emotion in his eyes.

"I know you can, but it won't stop me from worrying. I mean I'm sure you've heard the stories, how no one knows where you come from, that you just appear as if by magic, and kill anything and anyone in your path."

My heart clenches.

That's not what you think of me is it?

I want to ask, but I also know I'm not ready for the answer.

Instead, I say, "I wouldn't know about these stories. I don't get to leave the Fort that often, only for missions and even then, I don't get to interact with anyone. Not how you can freely do so." That seems to shock him, but it soon slips into curiosity.

"Doesn't that bother you?"

"I'm not sure I understand."

"That you don't get to do, you know, normal things?" He seems both curious and cautious, as though he's scared to ask the real questions.

"I've never been allowed to think like that. To think for myself is to go against the Fort and their teachings. The only time I can think freely is when it comes to killing a target. But it would appear I am in a talkative mood. So, if you want answers, Rich. Now is the time to ask the real questions."

That makes him grin and I can tell he's a little giddy with excitement, and he rolls over to his side so that we are face to face.

"Ok, first one. Are you really a punishment from the gods, like do you descend from the otherworld to punish those who displease the gods? I mean I know you all reside in the Fort but are you born by the blessings of the gods and sent here? Is, I guess, what I mean."

I grin and try to hold in my laughter, "I never took you for the religious type, Kieta."

"I'm not above praying to a higher power if I think it'll help my loved ones. But I'm not really asking for me, Declan's mother is a big-time devotee, and I thought I'd ask to see if her faith is placed righteously." He breezes over waiting for my answer.

"No, we are not 'the wrath of the gods', although I do like that. It at least sounds cooler than the truth."

"Ok, then what is the truth?" This one stumps me, there are some things that I can tell him and a lot that I cannot. I chew on my lip trying to find the right wording.

"We are a group of highly trained assassins and spies who get deployed when and where we are needed."

"Who's we? How many of you are there?"

Declan comes in and stands in the doorway, his arms across his chest. I smile at him and pat the bed; he doesn't return it but comes over anyway and sits propped up against the headboard.

"I don't know the exact numbers, but more than a few thousand spread across the globe."

His jaw drops open, "there's... what?" He seems too flabbergasted to form a coherent sentence. "Just a few thousand. Like that's normal." He shrugs looking at Declan, who in turn interrupts with a quiet question of his own. Given the topic of conversation, I'm surprised he is still in the room. He's not exactly been a fan of talking about what I am and what I do in the past. "Ok, so how long have you been doing what you do?"

"Since birth."

He tilts his head to the side. That's all he does to show me he heard but is waiting for me to elaborate further.

"I was raised at the Fort and from the moment I could walk, they put me into training." But he still looks as though he's waiting for me to continue.

I try to explain further, "right ok," I sigh, "how do I start? I have never known who my parents were, and I've been told so many different stories about how I ended up at the Fort, that I don't think any of them are the truth. The one I got told the most was that they died during the war, and I was found by a Fury on duty and taken. Another was that they didn't want me, so they left me there. That one was used to break my spirit when I was a kid." I grin at the memories of Madame Campbell going red in the face from screaming at me, and at how Madame K had punched her so hard in the face, she lost a tooth.

The pair have never gotten on.

Rich seems genuinely shocked, "who told you those things?"

"My programme leaders and I had no reason to question it. I learnt early on that there was only one way to escape and before long I didn't want to. I studied hard and understood that I was good at what I was training for. So, I had no reason to leave. It's given me stability and a skill set most don't possess. I know multiple languages and have travelled the world; I have seen things most would only hope to." When I finish, quiet fills the room. Not the uncomfortable kind, just the kind that is filled with understanding and maybe a hint of pity.

"Damn," he whispers.

"And even if my parents were alive, they likely wouldn't recognise me now anyway. So, I wouldn't have them even if they lived and breathed. Which is unlikely. The Fort ties off its loose ends."

The pitiful air is stifling now. I've never once felt sorry for myself. I have only ever pushed through and done the duty I was created for. Others have had traumas in their life and yet I don't even feel like mine would be classed as that. It was just simply how I was raised. The fact that they pity me is more of an annoyance than a comfort. I did not tell them the story to gain such emotion I was merely answering their questions.

"What's the next step in the plan then?" Declan asks. He's become uncomfortable. I can tell by how he's shifting around.

"She's still on bed rest," Rich cuts in.

"I actually have a friend I need to see," I reply.

"A friend? You?" Declan mocks.

"I do know some people, thank you," I snap back.

Rich rolls off the bed, mumbling something about tension and leaves the room.

"I thought you said Furies couldn't have attachments?"

"Oh, so you have been paying attention then?"

"Barely," he corrects.

I smirk leaning in, "Is that jealousy I detect Angelos?"

"You wish," he hisses back.

I bite my lip and look down at his mouth. Psychological warfare is always the most fun. I hum. A gentle thing. Something that could be mistaken for a purr. I lick the corner of my mouth. "Interesting," I murmur.

"What is?" His eyes track the movement of my tongue and he's decidedly stuck between which to follow more my tongue or my continuation of closing the gap between us.

"The game you're playing," I murmur softly.

"And what game is that?" he questions, his eyes on my lips. His breath quickens as the gap becomes non-existent. His nose brushes against the skin of my cheek and I chuckle seeing his eyes flutter.

Leaning in further until my lips brush his ear, and my breasts are all but in his face. "If you haven't figured it out by now. You will... one day," I place a kiss on the shell of his ear and pull away. Relishing in the blush that reddens his cheeks.

He clears his throat and gets up from the bed, subtly adjusts his pants and leaves without another word. I chuckle to myself and get ready to have a shower.

The salty air whips around my hood and seeps through my mask as I stand on the dark tiled hipped roof a few stories up from our vintage apartment below.

The gentle push and pull of the river below me is barely heard over the rumble of engines darting through the streets.

I look up to the enormous five identical spires that are now just blocks away since we've moved closer to The Circle — at the centre of the city — the island where the five towers are built upon. Their towering size is much more intimidating the closer you get to them, but the lights from multiple floors twinkle like stars in the night.

Several bridges of varying sizes and designs arch across the water connecting the towers to the rest of the city, each blocked off with small stations for guards – who seem to be checking the identification of those who wish to cross over.

I swiftly check the boats tied to the small docks, every single one under watch by armed guards. I look across the water to check the small island and see dozens of guards, all armed to the teeth and patrolling the grounds.

Great.

With the boats all tied up and the bridges locked down, I have one of two options; jump into the frigid river and swim for it.

My least favourite option.

Or try to jump the width of the water.

All except for the streetlamps, it's nearly pitch black out tonight due to the heavy cloud cover. I'll have to remember to give thanks to the goddess of storms later. But for right now all I can do is wait for the guards to circulate their patrols.

Taking a couple of steps back from the river's edge I steady my breath, steeling my nerves before sprinting forward, my strides long and strong. Advancing on the edge of the wall all I can think is how stupid this idea truly is but before I know it, I've leapt into the air.

The wind whispers harshly in my ears. My hood flies back and the strands of my hair come loose from the braid I hastily wrapped up before I left.

I shift my body so I'm feet first, preparing to land on the other side - that's looking just a little too far away. I start descending and I close my eyes waiting for the impact of the water, instead, my boots connect with the concrete. It's a jolt and my eyes burst open, I quickly tuck and roll across the ground evening out the impact, coming to an instant stop on my knees. I look back at the distance as I stand and can't help the little well of smugness at having made it. My still healing wounds blaze like a burning fire as the skin is pulled around, but that doesn't stop my burst of pride.

The brief pause doesn't last long for me to catch my breath because I hear the footsteps of approaching guards. I duck behind one of the neatly cut, hip-height bushes, using the shadows as cover and watch as they breeze past me, none the wiser.

It doesn't take me long to figure out which spire my target is in. With extra guards standing at every entrance, the northern spire can be the only viable option.

"Now just to make it across the courtyard," I whisper to myself.

Once again using the shadows as my blanket, I creep across the stoned courtyard slowly, hiding in the shrubbery when the guards get too close.

Every floor of this magnificent building houses a balcony, making it look like it has a very difficult outside staircase, just ready to be climbed. I pull out my retractable grappling hook, from my backpack and throw it high, arching it through the air until it clunks against the metal railing of a balcony several stories up. I assess the strength before tying the rope around my waist.

"Not your brightest idea, Elle," I puff out a slightly nervous chuckle before beginning my climb.

Well over an hour later I've finally reached the top of the northernmost spire, the wind whipping through my hair that has all but unwound itself from the braid, reminding me of the time I climbed that cliff face, only this time I get to enjoy the view.

Even if I'm hanging from a balcony.

Voices sound from above me, guards who are finishing up their nightly sweep through the top rooms and hallways. Readjusting my grip, I watch their flashlights dance around the room while they move, searching every corner both inside the room and even out on the balcony itself. All the while I'm trying not to look down.

The soft click of the glass patio doors is heard and the muffled conversation between the residence and the guards follow.

With what's left of my upper body strength, I pull myself up and over the glass railing, dropping down into a crouch on the other side, the white tiles cooling the skin of my knee as I wait for the patrol to leave the room completely.

The main suite door opens and closes quickly, leaving nothing but silence on the other side of these glass doors. I untie the rope from my waist just as the bathroom light clicks on, and roll the rope into a neat, untangled coil.

Unlatching the balcony door, I let myself in. The spray of water from the shower starts up as I push open the door, the plush white carpet is thick and bouncy under my boot quashing any sound I would've made if it were wood or tile.

Closing the door behind me, I readjust the light curtains that become misshapen with the wind blowing through them, before flopping down heavily on the white, leather-bound armchair.

The room is cast in darkness, and I wait for my target to appear.

But even despite the darkness, white is the chosen colour for the room, glass too. White walls and carpets, with matching doors. White lounges bound in leather and white fur rugs lay across the floor. I scowl as I look around, it reminds me of a hospital. The only spot of colour is in the furnishings, grey cushions.

Dried grasses in beige vases dot various side tables and coffee tables. Small house plants are the only other accessory that brings colour, but even they are not bright enough to cut through the overwhelming amount of white that has been splashed throughout the apartment.

Throwing myself down in the nearest armchair I wait for my target, my body feels exhausted and achy it's obvious I've not fully recovered from my injuries.

After what feels like an eternity the water cuts off and I shift sitting with my back straight and both of my arms resting on the arms of the chair. I pull my hood up quickly, grinning from under the shadow of it.

Then a certain brunette prince comes sauntering out of the bathroom, wearing nothing but a white fluffy towel around his waist. Beads of water run down his lean torso and across his muscles, looking ethereal with the light of the bathroom at his back. He flicks the switch on, lighting the main room and stumbles back a few steps when the light illuminates my imposing figure, almost dropping his towel in the process.

"You fucking freak! Why are you sitting in the dark?" he whisper-yells, looking at the front door. "With your bloody hood up!"

"For the drama obviously," I reply, rolling my eyes playfully as I pull my hood down. "Nice look by the way, you should wear this more often. You look hot."

He blushes slightly and clears his throat awkwardly, I plaster on a wolfish grin, which of course he can't see due to the damned mask I'm made to wear.

He wanders across the room pulling the curtains closed harshly, "Are you trying to get caught in here?"

"You're the one who wanted to see me and how would I get caught anyway? We are nearly eighty stories high." Referring to the windows that no one can see into.

"Actually, how *did* you get up here?"

"Magic," I tease, wiggling my hands around.

"My mother would be disappointed with that joke." He retorts dryly, but he smirks all the same.

"How is she doing? I miss her."

"Let me go change, and we can talk properly," he walks towards his bedroom, without another word.

"Don't feel like you have to get dressed on my account. I'm rather enjoying the view," I chuckle, pouting when he walks past me anyway, rolling his eyes, he shakes his head when he sees me blatantly checking him out.

He comes back a few minutes later, now dressed in grey slacks and a white tee, the sight is nearly as enticing as the teeny tiny towel. He looks considerably less princely here than I've ever seen him.

Still incredibly hot though.

I shake the impure thoughts from my head and focus on why I'm here.

"Your Highness, it's good to see you and to see so much of you," I wink at him, and he sits down on the couch, arms comfortably spread wide almost like a welcoming embrace with one arm lying across the back of the couch and the other draped along the arm, with one of his legs crossed over the other.

"What's with the formality, Siren?" He cocks his head to the side putting emphasis on my name. "And what's with this?" He points to his own face, asking me about the mask. "We have worked closely together in the past. *Very closely*. I think the time for titles and protocol has passed us by, wouldn't you agree?"

"What exactly is it you wanted to see me for?" I breeze past his comments, he knows exactly why I have the formalities in place.

"Your mission. What exactly does this one entail?" he questions plainly, picking off some fluff from his t-shirt.

When I don't reply he locks eyes with me once again. The brightness of the green swirl together as if his eyes are enticing me to step forward and drown in the depths of green like they're a secret tunnel that only I'm allowed to know about. "Are you here to kill him? Roman I mean."

I shake off the tingling sensation that has created goosebumps on my skin long enough to reply. "Given my history, in which you are well versed, you know what I'm capable of. But you also know that any information that I have received is classified. Even to you, *your Highness*." My tone is boringly flat.

He pauses watching me carefully before continuing, "Right, ok I'll just get to the point then. I don't exactly know what you know about the situation and I'm aware you can't tell me, but I can offer you protection if you can do me a favour..."

"No." The word is muffled by the mask, but I know he hears it as clearly as if I'd whispered it in his ear. *Damn fae ears.*

He pauses. "Excuse me. You haven't even heard..."

"No, you can't. You can't offer me anything because you hold no power," I interrupt, stunning him. "At least not over them. Not that I need you to. I've survived this long on my own, I don't need your protection, nor do I want it."

His eyes ignite in anger, "So, what? You're going to kill your way around Ansrutas until you find him? That's a high body count even for you Siren. But I don't suppose that will be much of a problem for you, will it?"

"Excuse me, your royal assness, but you didn't seem to have a problem with my skills when I dug your sister out of that drug scandal a few years back. Or is that it, huh? As long as it benefits you, you're ok with the killing. You know if I had my eyes closed, you'd sound just like *him*."

"I am nothing like my father!" he growls automatically, pointing a slender finger at me. It's clear this isn't the first time he's been accused of such.

"Really? Then tell me what's actually going on. Why are you both here and what does it have to do with my target?" I push, observing his demeanour and how it changes with each question.

"That's something I can't tell you."

"Then why am I here?"

"Can't I just see an old friend?" My eyebrow quirks of its own accord as I stare him down. "My father has been intolerable since you've been called in. He blames the Stratos of course. Cursing General Griffith for his incompetence, he's been hereby suspended from his duties, they are bringing someone in as his temporary replacement." He pauses looking at me. "He wants people to believe in him again, in the Stratos, but I think there's another motive. I believe he wants to prove to himself that he doesn't need to rely on the guild. You know how he feels about you all."

"I think his first words to me went something like, 'those vile whores'." I chuckle at the memory and Frederick laughs with me.

With the tension eased and both of us smiling again, we continue our previous discussion.

"Given our history and his own fragile ego, my father has forbidden me from seeking you out, even on business terms." He winks at me, "he's had me under guard since I stepped into this city and he's cracking down hard on the Stratos. You'll likely see more of them patrolling the streets by the end of the week. He has called for more soldiers to transfer from Larissa."

"Oh, so the fun is on the way then," I respond humourlessly.

His eyebrows pinch, "you need to get out more if you think that it will be fun."

I drop my facial expressions and stare at him, watching as the wheels turn in his head until it finally clicks.

"Oh, yeah. Right." He smiles nodding, looking down with a blush on his cheeks. He shifts bringing his arms behind his head, so he can lean against them and regards me for a moment. "You know, not being able to help with your predicament is the worst possible pain."

This stuns me, I hadn't expected something so heartfelt to fall from his lips. I can tell he means every word just by looking into those endless green irises.

"Clearly you've never been tortured." He chokes on a laugh.

"Fuck, Elle. You can't say shit like that," he scolds, even as he grins from ear to ear.

I can see where this conversation is headed, "Frederick, my well-being isn't something you should concern yourself with."

The humour drains from his eyes, "It is something that I should concern myself with Elle..."

"No. What you should be worried about is how to remove my target from the equation, before I find him." I give him a pointed stare trying to relay a hidden message.

He nods understanding, and I exhale in relief.

"Because if I do. There's only one way to stop me, which is something you will also need to consider."

"Absolutely not," he snaps, barely letting me finish my sentence, pretending only to himself that my death isn't even an option.

"What does he mean to you?" I ask softly. He sits there silently looking down at the floor, the fur rug tangled between his toes. Stress lines frame his face, and he looks as though the weight of the world rests on his shoulders.

I nod my head and get up. I walk towards him and crouch down holding one of his warm hands in my own.

"I cannot make you any promises. I will do what I can, but do not let me catch him first unless you are willing to do what is necessary."

"I will never be willing to do that," he whispers back, holding my gaze.

"Then you need to be quick and efficient," I relay the urgency, "if he truly means that much to you. You will need to have a way out for both you and him. Leave everything else behind. Because it won't be me who comes after you should either of us fail."

I get up then, his utter confusion sets my nerves ablaze. He too gets up and keeps pace with me, looking bewildered. "Ella, tell me you will be ok."

"Am I not always?" I grin, hoping the humour lightens his darkening thoughts. I bend down to pick up the neatly coiled rope and tie it around my waist once again.

"No fucking way, did you grapple up here?" I turn to see him leaning against the door frame, his arms crossed over his chest and his face portraying scepticism.

"I'll have you know it took me nearly two hours to climb this fucking building, and now I have to rappel down it."

"Two hours? What did you crawl?"

Tightening the knot, I turn and punch his arm, "I'd like to see you try it, Fritz."

He blinks at me and narrows his eyes in mock annoyance. "Only my mother calls me that."

His hand comes up and brushes some hair away from my face gently caressing the side of my head, before pulling my hood up, looking deep into my eyes.

"It's good to see you, Elle." He leans down and presses a gentle kiss to my cheek, pulling away only to rest his forehead against mine. "Give 'em Hel."

"Only because you asked so nicely." I pull away, turn around, and jump over the railing casting out into the night.

CHAPTER FIFTEEN
COMMUNICATION IS KEY

The atmosphere is tense and heavily charged in the apartment when I eventually slip back through the open window into the living room. Declan's bedroom door is closed, and a grumpy-looking Rich sits frowning at the television screen, watching some sports game with fifteen a side and an oval-shaped ball. I pay no mind to the idle commentary much, like Rich it seems, as I take a step towards him. I appear to have caught him by surprise by the way he jumps out of his skin. Raising my hands in a friendly gesture, I slowly lower my hood.

"Everything ok?" I question quietly, nodding towards Declan's door.

"Fantastic." With the amount of sarcasm dripping from that one word, I'm almost offended.

"What's happened?" I try again, slipping off my mask and throwing it down on the kitchen counter, I grab myself a glass of clear distilled liquid and move back to sit with Rich on the plush fabric couch.

When I get no reply, I try a different tactic. "It's late, how come you're still up?"

He sighs heavily, "I couldn't sleep, and I was waiting for you. To make sure you came back in one piece this time." He takes a mouthful of beer while watching the screen in front of him.

I hum a thank you back to him and take a sip from my own drink, hissing at the satisfying sting as it glides down my throat.

"Where were you anyway?" he grunts.

"Oh, I went to see Prince Frederick. He had asked me to meet with him and asked me a bunch of questions. I told him what I could," I answer in hopes that he'll grant me the same respect and answer my own questions, only to have silence greet me instead. The only sound is the commentary from the game.

"Are you going to tell me or are you going to be cagey about it?" he snaps suddenly.

A flash of anger suddenly flares to life in my chest.

"To put it simply, he doesn't want me to kill Roman."

"Wait what?" His voice changes, showing genuine surprise, and he turns his body fully to face me.

"I told him that I couldn't make any promises." Sipping from my glass I watch as the males on the screen pass the ball to each other and begin running up field.

"And?" he pushes.

"*And...* I told him to find him first."

His eyebrows lower and the silver in his eyes seems to glow brighter, he looks furious and it's pissing me off.

"What?" I snap.

To which he scoffs, "What do you want me to say? That I agree with him and don't think you should do it. That Roman's an innocent man, doing what he feels is right. Is that it? Is that what you want to hear?"

I furrow my brows angrily watching him release his own frustrations while he stands up throwing his arms in the air, he starts to pace in front of me yelling all the while.

"Do you sympathise with the rebels, *handler* Keita?" I tilt my head to the side, watching him like an eagle would a mouse.

Rich's eyes widen, and his mouth slams shut.

"What are you not telling me?"

"I shouldn't be surprised you always do what you're told. Ever the good lapdog for the guild, aren't you? The perfect weapon. That's all you're good for, isn't it?" he deflects, letting his anger shine back through. But that suspicion still remains.

He rages for a while rambling on and on about nothing and everything all at once. His anger is not directed at me, but I am a good outlet for it. Or so my other handlers have told me. But nevertheless, I still wonder what has happened tonight for this to be occurring right now.

I sit there unmoving, taking in his wrath and letting it wash over me. I watch him pace back and forth. Staying silent all the while, listening to him. That was how I was trained after all.

When he finally turns back to me his words fall flat on his tongue. My eyes are so focused on him, trying to understand where this outburst has come from, that I must look like I'm about to suck out his soul.

"Elle…" He tries, wafting a hand past my face.

"I suggest you sleep off the alcohol, handler Kieta. That is my only solution for the current episode you are going through." I rise myself and walk past him, taking my drink with me.

Declan comes out of his room his face dark with annoyance, "what the fuck is going on in here?"

"Why did we disturb your beauty sleep?" I ask from the kitchen, pouring myself another drink.

"Funny," Declan drawls. I smirk and rove my eyes over his very naked torso, making sure he sees every movement. I scoff when I come to the waistband of his sweats that cover those thick thighs.

"So, I've been told," I sneer, taking a drink.

"Is anyone going to answer me?" he tries again.

"I suggest you ask your partner. He's the one with the problem." My stare is pointed while I look at Rich. He's become calmer under Declan's command. Clearly showing the Lieutenant Colonel and Field Medic dynamic that they are so used too.

Declan turns to his friend and we both wait for Rich's answer, I send him a look that says, 'I won't tell if you won't.'

"Nothing Dec, just a misunderstanding."

I smirk and take another mouthful of my drink. Declan snaps his attention to me when I place the empty glass back onto the counter.

"Where have you been?" he snarls.

"To see a prince."

The muscle in his jaw flexes, and I watch it with wild fascination. "Care to elaborate?"

Reluctantly pulling my interest from his jaw to his angry eyes, I sigh, "Perhaps in the morning. I'm tired." I move to my room, swaying my hips a little too much, just because I know they're both watching.

Declan growls and I close the door to my room, chuckling to myself. Two can play the game of seduction but only one will come out on top.

The next day passes in a blur of viewing the CCTV footage I stole from the Ansrutas Police Department.

I'd left early the next morning before either had woken up, taking my laptop with me. I heard them having a heated discussion after I departed for my room last night, but the words were muted behind the walls.

This morning however, I found myself in a coffee shop down the road and set up camp at a table in the window watching the people pass by, sipping on a sweet and syrupy coffee.

In the late morning, I sent off my second week's mission report directly to Madame K and proceeded to sift through more and more of those grainy videos.

The one I'm currently watching is from a few months ago, around the same time Helena had told me about that mysterious male that climbed into a darkened vehicle to get away from the crowds. After a particularly brutal riot, one he had started by throwing a brick at one of City Hall's two-story windows, he simply walks down the street and climbs into the car leaving everyone else to either run or be caught. The police weren't kind to those who captured them. I've seen many a person tortured in my life. But watching these people be beaten and handcuffed turned my stomach into knots. But this at least confirmed what she had told me.

Pausing the image, I immediately start enlarging it in hope that I can see the licence plate of the vehicle. The image only further pixelates the more I enlarge it, huffing out a frustrated sigh I hack back into the

Ansrutas PD database and upload it into their software and begin clearing it up. An extra trick I have recently picked up from being bedridden for days.

"Nothing's ever easy," I mutter to myself taking a sip of my deliciously warm coffee.

Once cleared, I run it through another algorithm in search of the car's owner. Within a matter of minutes, I find a match and my eyebrows pinch at the result. A Mr Edward Lincoln.

Otherwise known as Eddie 'Black Foot' Lincoln, one of the two mafia bosses in Ansrutas. A lynx shifter, who's bought out half of Ansrutas PD, and has been known to disembowel his victims leaving their bodies smeared across the streets. His mug shot is just as terrifying as his reputation. His eyes are empty, they don't even seem to have the familiar glow that a shifter should have; and his smile, his cunning, petrifying smile is framed by several deep and jagged scars. He is definitely someone I don't want to cross paths with, but I have a mission to do, and a ruthless mob boss will be the least of my problems if I don't complete it.

I've already heard from whispers on the street that Lincoln's domain 'The Black Pines' is the one place in the city that is completely lawless. No police nor civilian dares to step foot across his border.

Now that I have my next target, I have a side quest to complete. Get a new phone, something I really don't want to do, but something that is necessary.

The evening comes around quickly. Soft rain starts to fall through the city, and I tighten my cloak around myself, I stand at the water's edge staring ahead across the bay and directly at The Black Pines, with my hands deep in my pockets trying to keep them warm.

As expected, my phone vibrates in my pocket. I haven't been back to the apartment all day and I've had countless messages from both of them wondering when I'll be back. With my target in sight, I ignore it and start thinking of a way to slip under the radar into Eddie's territory.

Of Fire and Shadow

All around me are the white-collar housing estates with small black-iron fencing and all with a minute patch of grass out front, separating the houses from the street.

Some of the wealthier families who have built up reputations on scandal, murder and organised crime live there and it's all controlled by the two mob families. The Lincolns and the Adlers and no one and nothing comes or goes without them knowing.

Those same families have lived by their own rules, yet also by religion. Decades ago, they had built their own temples in their respective territories, where everyone can celebrate their health and good fortune to the God, Abizer, The Father of Wealth and Merchants.

I use the shadows cast by the buildings to slither my way through the quiet streets until I come to a small limestone temple, low burning candles flicker in the arched stained-glass windows, depicting Abizer in rooms filled with gold.

Above the door is the Lincoln family crest and a fraction of dread slithers into my heart, I shake it off and rush to the wooden front door pushing it open with a slight creak, right into the antechamber of the luxurious red, white, and black sanctuary, adorned with golden furniture.

The space is quiet this late at night, but soft words can be heard in the main hall that catches my attention, they echo gently off the stone walls, under flickering candlelight.

I skulk up to the door peeping through the small crack, seeing only one person in there. I push it open slightly and squeeze into the room to see a young female knelt down in front of the flower and wine-filled altar, the clicking of golden coins hitting an impressively large golden plate on the floor by her knees as she rocks tenderly is the only other sound beyond her mumbled prayers.

I glide into the last row of pews at the back of the room, taking a seat to observe the room as a whole.

Decorative stone arches line the room and hold up the overhanging balcony that shapes three sides of the chamber, that last holds a floor to ceiling stain glass mural of Abizer counting and weighting out his gold.

Vases and religious symbols made of solid gold shine brightly in the low light of the candles, that flicker in their golden stands and illuminate the female's rich brunette hair that hangs down to her waist. For several minutes we stay this way and I listen to her quiet prayers taking the time to really look at her, at her bowed head sending stray hairs flowing over her shoulders into her face; her shoeless feet, crossed over one another; her shaking form, covered only in a silk white nighty that's speckled with rain drops.

Her head rises and she kisses an amulet that she had been praying into, shuffling to put her soft pink suede pumps back on. I instantly recognised this woman upon seeing her face, she was there the night of the meeting at the docks. She was the one standing up on the terribly makeshift stage, talking to the rebels. Melanie.

She gracefully sweeps down the steps that lead up to the altar and begins to make her way back down the aisle, she seems to be muttering to herself, it's then she finally looks up and her eyes connect with my own, not that she can actually see them because of my hood but she freezes anyway.

Her breath quickens, and I pick up on the way her chest starts to rise and fall rapidly. She really is beautiful, her slender cheeks frame her soft yet feminine face, her rich sun-kissed skin carries no scars or blemishes, and her golden eyes glow bright.

Her animal is lying in wait to pounce, yet even from here I can see the unshed tears shimmering as she trembles where she stands.

The hairs rise on her arms, and I can see the goosebumps forming, but she doesn't try to move any further up the aisle. Instead, I watch her claws extend from her fingers, her once pink nails turning black around tufts of grey fur that slowly cover her hand.

I sigh and stand shuffling out from in between the pews, not really in the mood for a fight, but I'll be damned if she gets the upper hand before it's even begun.

Her fangs elongate and her face scrunches in anger forcing herself to shift.

"I'm not here for a fight," I say, she pauses and looks at me stunned, but doesn't put her claws away.

"You're a woman?" she hisses, looking genuinely confused.

With my hands raised I look down out myself and then back to her, "err… yeah?"

"Huh." Is all she answers in reply.

Confused by the question I continue, "I would like for us to talk. Just talk." Stepping forward I keep my hands raised to show I'm not a threat to her. Of course, that's a lie I am a threat to her, but I don't need to prove that it's a lie.

"I'm sorry but I don't talk to strangers who creep up on me in my own temple, in my own territory!"

She's still fearful. Good she needs to be.

"Black Foot's daughter."

She rolls her lips realising her mistake.

"It's about Roman." Her spine straightens so fast it clicks with the movement. So, she does know him then. "Where is he?"

"And why would you think that I would tell you?"

"Because otherwise, I could send 'daddy' pictures and videos of your unsavoury company. I know he doesn't like the rebels and their cause because it affects his business, doesn't it? I'd bet he'd also be loathed to know that his precious daughter's been shacking up with the leader of the organisation when she is due to be wed in four months." I clasp my hands in front of me shunning away the smug feeling that threatens to bubble over as I look at her.

Her lips have thinned and her golden eyes spew so much hatred in my direction, a fight is imminent if I don't watch what I say now.

"That's right, Melanie Lincoln. I know who you are. But I'm not here to air your dirty laundry. I just want an answer to my question. Where is Roman?"

She relaxes and plasters a lazy grin on her face and shrugs, "I don't know a Roman."

I sigh and roll my eyes, "don't make me ask again."

"Then don't!" she growls, charging towards me.

I duck under her arm as she sweeps it at me, aiming for my throat, and twist, using my leg to kick hers out from under her; she thuds loudly against the floor in a tangle of limbs.

"Trust me when I say, you don't want to start something you aren't willing to finish," I warn her, observing as she stands listening to the defiant growl as it rips through her throat.

I can't let her turn, or she'll rip me to shreds.

I let my fist fly, cracking her straight in the nose.

"Sorry, love," I tell her before getting her in a chokehold, her back pressed up against my chest.

I tighten my arm around her throat, cutting off her air, but she's too quick. Her claws dig into my leather cloak, through my cotton t-shirt underneath, and tear right into my skin.

I hiss as she punctures through my muscles, until she drags them down, slashing everything as she goes. I scream and let go giving her the advantage, she twirls and rakes her claws through the air, barely missing my eye.

I grunt as she catches my cheek and pull out my knife.

"You want to play dirty? Then we will, just don't cry when I win," I hiss, through gritted teeth. I twirl my knife, readjusting it in my grip and her eyes widen at the size of it.

With the width of her, it would likely pierce her skin and come out the other side, fully impaling her. She turns to run up the aisle back towards the altar, but I quickly give chase. She makes it back to the steps before I trip her, her head bounces off the stone floor, and blood instantly pours from her nose.

"Is it really worth dying for Melanie Lincoln?" I hiss, stalking towards her, the blade in my hand glinting reflecting the candles. The ebony handle is a stark contrast to the soft feathered wing embossed in the metal. My thumb automatically runs over those words on the cross guard.

She spits in my direction, blood, and spittle landing on my boot. I grin and watch with delight as the colour drains from her face.

She pulls herself up into another guarded fighting stance, but the anger has fled her body and fear has taken its place. I can tell by how she's hopping from foot to foot, it's shaky and uncoordinated.

Melanie's fist comes fast, intended for my face again but this time her claws have been retracted, and I slap it away as if a child had just tried to punch me. She is panting hard, clearly able to defend herself, but not used to the physical strain of doing so.

Pulling my leg up I kick her square in the stomach, and she stumbles backwards into the alter. I move forward relishing in the way she scrambles to pull herself back up.

She starts to drag herself to the side door – that no doubt leads to the priory – her belly scraping against the gold carpet, now stained with my blood as it drips from my arm. I drop all of my weight on her, stopping her from going any further and flip her around underneath me. She flails, slapping and scratching at me until I press the knife to her throat.

"Stop it. You're just pissing me off," I snap, my voice deep like thunder.

All of her fight seems to leave her when she finally realises that she's not getting out of this.

"Now. You can either start talking or I can start cutting. What's it going to be?"

Soft whimpers are coming from her throat with each pant of air she takes, but she doesn't start talking like I thought she would.

"Ok. Which one?" My eyes bore into her own.

"Which one, what?" she sobs, her lip wobbling.

"Which finger am I cutting off first?"

She whimpers again, louder this time, and the tears start falling but she still doesn't talk. I snatch her right hand and bring my blade to her smallest finger. She struggles and fights me, screaming at me to stop.

"Then tell me what I want to know!" I growl.

Yet she still doesn't give it up. She's strong. I'll give her that. My blade touches her skin, and she starts singing the words I want to hear.

"HE'S IN SALACIA! THE SEA QUEEN OFFERED HIM PARDON IN EXCHANGE FOR HIS HELP!"

I grin at the little bird.

"That wasn't so hard Melanie Lincoln, was it?"

"Stop saying my whole name. I get it, you're a big bad assassin who knows everything about me!"

"Just making sure the point got across. Now tell me, what does she want with our little Roman?"

She grits her teeth, "he's not yours."

"No, of course not. But he is my target. Now what does the queen want with him?"

"I don't know." I pick up her hand again and watch her writhe as I bring the knife back up to her finger. "I SWEAR I DON'T!" she screams.

"Ok, another question. Who is this man?" I pull out my phone showing the image of the brunette male climbing into her father's car.

"I don't know," she sobs, shaking her head.

"Somehow, I don't believe you." Pressing the knife back into her finger she squeals again.

"What my father does in his spare time is up to him," she replies, gritting her teeth. Her animal is back waiting just underneath the surface, her eyes glow brighter in response.

"See now I know you're lying to me, Melanie Lincoln. That may be your father's car, but that can't be your father in the seat across, because that male, is a member of Dawnya. Just. Like. You." I tap my blade against her bottom lip, emphasising each word.

Her eyes widen when the penny drops. She's caught in a trap with no way out, yet she doesn't want to betray her companions.

I lean down to whisper in her ear, "I admire your courage little lynx, but are they worth dying for? Where are they now when you are in trouble?"

She closes her eyes and cries, the sight reminding me of a child who's scared and without help.

A personal memory depicting the very same thing cuts my heart in two.

"Alex," she whispers, pressing her face into the carpet desperate to hide away from her shame. "Alexander Nephus."

I pause, watching her for a moment. "I believe you." I drop her hand and rise from the floor climbing off of her finally.

Taking the steps back down to the aisle I turned to see her on her elbows watching me with wide eyes.

I drop into a bow, "thank you for your cooperation, Melanie Lincoln," I drawl, grinning as I right myself.

She groans and drops back onto the floor, the blood from her nose pouring freely into her hair and saturating the carpet beneath.

Climbing to the roof of the temple I watch her storm from the sanctuary, her head whips this way and that looking for me before she begins furiously wiping at her blood-covered face cursing my very existence.

Using the rooftops to move further away from the Lincoln territory I mull over this new information so many questions spin around and around in my head making me feel like I'm going insane.

Why is Roman so important? Enough for the Queen of the Sea to want his council. Why is she protecting him? Who is Alexander Nephus? And what does he have to do with this whole thing?

I wander the streets for around two hours and note the amount of Stratos guards walking around, there aren't even close to this many on the other side of the city, they must be watching over the mob families. But I know that even at this hour, I have no doubt that if they catch me, they'll arrest me, so I keep to the rooftops and the shadows and continue moving away from The Black Pines.

Knowing that I can't continue with my investigation tonight, I begin heading back to the safe house for some rest, just as the rain beats down heavier.

In the twilight hours of the morning, I take my time walking back to the safe house and watch as the downpour of droplets flood the streets and run-in currents along the roads, puddles gather around drains along the walkways, and I listen to it gurgle down guttering pipes.

I'm soaked through and the throbbing in my arm hasn't lessened even slightly, blood is still pouring from the wound now diluted with rainwater.

"That needs wrapping," I groan looking at the ruined flesh. It needs more than wrapping if I'm truly honest, but it will have to do for now.

For now, I rip a gauze from my shirt and tie it tightly to stem the bleeding.

Looking up I find that I've wandered into The House of Asteria sector, and my breath catches in my throat. The last time I was here was in the daylight about to meet Helena. Somehow, it's even more beautiful at night. With its muted colours and obscure shadows, I take in the splashes of bright colours and exotic patterns that brighten the walls of each building, at the cleanliness of the streets, the plants and trees grow wild here, and each available space is covered in murals that are now being washed away in the downpour. Each space will be ready again in the morning for the next set of artists to express their inner passions.

The House of Asterias' Museum lies in front of me, the building is so grand is almost looks out of place in such a colour-filled portion of the city, but the residents have blended the old and the new so seamlessly, that it's hard to tell it was built centuries before all the clothing stores and skate parks.

I could really see myself exploring this sector more when the day comes. I'd love to see the colours radiate under the light of the sun and see people living so free and happy.

Stop it.

Something hisses in the back of my mind, the voice sounds reminiscent of Madame K. I shake the thoughts from my head and make it my mission to get back to the apartment while I can still feel my arm.

Back at the apartment, I waste no time heading for the quaint pink bathroom that's attached to my room. I fling my cloak off and let it drop to the floor as I pass my bed. I cut the sleeve off my shirt and pulled the gauze out of the wound, hissing at the pain. Blood spurts and oozes from the wound. *She must have hit a vein.* I'm surprised I'm still standing if that's the case.

I sneak into the kitchen and dig out the emergency kit, and a needle and thread from one of the drawers. Trying not to wake either of them, I bite down on my blood-soaked shirt to muffle my groaning while I clean and sanitise the wound and swiftly begin digging around inside to make sure she didn't actually catch a vein. She missed it by centimetres, my eyes widened briefly before I began stitching the skin back together.

The sun is rising by the time I've finished, I walk to the patio doors securing the bandage on my arm and listen to the bird's chirp upon waking.

I flex my fingers testing my mobility and then pick out a fresh t-shirt and pants, I swing my cloak back around my neck looking down at the ruined arm. "Damn, I'll have to get that fixed."

Testing out the strength of my arm I climb back up the wet guttering to the moss-covered roof. The rain had stopped shortly after I arrived back last night, put everything everywhere is still covered with water. I pull out my new phone bringing up the maps.

"Where's the damn library?" I mutter under my breath; I turn this way and that, trying not to slip off the roof when I find it. A few streets down from City Hall. "Perfect."

I jump to the adjacent roof loving the feeling of the air whipping through my hair as I move.

I leave the coffee shop – hot, delicious coffee acquired – and turn in the direction of the library. The early morning sun warms the skin of my face beating away the cold of last night's rain when my phone vibrates in my pocket. I snatch it and answer without looking at the name.

"Hello?" I chirp.

"AELLA!" His voice booms down the receiver and I physically jump earning funny looks from passersby.

"Good morning, Rich," I greet too sweetly, "what is it you want?"

"What do I want!" He yells, "I want to know where the fuck you are and if you're alright and *why* there's blood all over your bathroom sink."

"You went in my bedroom?"

"Where. Are. You?"

"I'm out," I reply, sipping from my drink.

"Oh, you're out. Hey Declan! She's out. Like we didn't think to check there!" His sarcasm is very nearly funny. Nearly. "Where are you? I'm coming to get you."

"Hmm, you don't need to." But even so, I can hear the distinct sounds of him shuffling around and the unmistakable jangle of keys. "I don't need you to come and get me. I have a job to do, or did you forget that that's all I'm good for?" It's a low blow but there isn't any malice in my comment.

In fact, he made me realise that I've wasted enough time these past two weeks and I need to get my head back in the game.

He starts talking again but I cut him off, "Rich I can't talk right now. I'm busy."

I end the call and pick up my pace.

Marching up the steps to the library I comprehend the scale of the building, with over one hundred and fifty thousand tomes covering their seemingly never-ending shelves, with doors just as gaudy as City Hall's – made of embossed bronze – this place looks like it was made for giants, or gods.

I laugh to myself and step inside.

The large glass dome ceiling is the first thing that I notice, the sky has never looked clearer and the clouds never so fluffy. The abundance of light it casts throughout the colossal chamber help to illuminate the beautifully carved darkened wooden bookshelves that stretch up to the second story.

Little nooks hug the walls each with their own lamps and tables, and a grand walnut wood staircase sweeps up connecting the two floors. The upper-level houses even more shelves and extra private seating areas.

A silver-haired librarian sits behind the front desk and looks up at me through her half-moon glasses, with a look of utter disdain. Her rounded mortal ears are tucked under her grey hair, that's pinned back in a delicate twisted bun, I offer her a smile – one that she doesn't return. The urge to piss her off further and show her the dried blood on the sleeve of my cloak is brewing.

Instead, I keep my sadistic thoughts to myself and give her a polite nod as I walk by. Her blue eyes burn holes in my back until I duck into one of the aisles and out of sight.

It's quiet here, only the shuffling of other librarians, the flipping of pages and hushed voices as people discuss topics amongst themselves. Meandering up and down a multitude of aisles I pull book after book from the shelves, anything that I think might have any relation to the history of Ansrutas.

I take a seat at one of the nooks in the very far corner of the great space, furthest away from the old librarian at the front and set my great stack of books down on the tiny side table, before ridding myself of my ruined cloak, draping it across the back of the raggedy navy armchair.

Hours pass by and I've had several texts and missed calls from Rich. Not to mention the several nasty glares I've received from the greying mortal female, and some of the other librarians, probably because I dared to enter with a hot coffee. I've winked at her each time, much to her surprise, and I chuckle as she shuffles off quickly after every encounter.

Turning over another page I sigh deeply, the information I've gathered so far is both unhelpful and frustratingly irrelevant. I rub my forehead again and continue reading more useless scripture when the snuffling of a nose interrupts my focus. A rough wet nose suddenly rubs against my fingers, startling me. I slam the large leather-bound book shut, only to be met with deep brown glowing eyes and the large spotted head of a snow leopard.

I put the book back down on the ever-growing pile, and the leopard grunts at me rubbing its head against my thigh.

"Yes, hello to you too, Declan," I say, scratching behind his ear. His eyes close and he purrs loudly, pushing his head against my hand.

He jumps up, pinning me to the seat and stares into my eyes. "Um excuse you. Down." I point to the floor.

He blinks once slowly as if to say '*Really?*'

"If you would like to talk, a conversation would be easier in your human form." I try to stand my ground, but I can't help but melt when he butts his head with mine. "Ok, I concede. You are a Hel of a lot cuter like this," I gush, scratching under his chin, and he begins to purr, clearly enjoying the sensation.

As if he's just remembered something he backs away and looks me over quickly before his sharp eyes zero in on my arm. He sniffs the air and I know he can smell the blood.

"Oh yeah." I put my hand over the bandage as if that will hide it from view. He growls, loud and fierce. "I'm fine."

His eyes lock with mine again, and I can see the anger in them, but I'm too mesmerised by the glowing amber leaking through the hazel. He mews getting my attention once again.

"I'm not telling you who it was because I handled it." He chuffs and gnashes his teeth in my face, letting me know he's annoyed. I scratch behind his ear distracting him and watch his eyes drift close and he leans his head further into my hand purring again, louder this time.

Declan and his animal form is like having two completely different twin brothers. It's giving me whiplash just trying to think how Declan acts compared to this sweet snow-coloured creature in front of me.

Rich comes round the corner then, dressed exquisitely in a white dress shirt and grey pants looking noticeably angry.

"Where the Hel have you been?" he seethes, storming up to us.

"You're looking very formal, Richie boy. What's going on with you?" I tease, ignoring his temper.

Declan meows again and I realise I've stopped scratching his ears, I chuckle and resume rubbing his head, he backs up from the chair and sits down at my side leaning his full body weight against my legs.

"You don't get to brush this off, Aella. You scared the crap out of both of us."

"I doubt that very much," I reply, nodding in Declan's direction.

Declan – or rather his animal – rests his head on my lap looking sullen, his eyes wide as he looks up at me. I rub between his ears, soothing him.

"I was working, ok? If you're still having an attitude over, only the gods know what, then you can leave. I still have a job to do after all."

The glare he gives me could turn fire to ice within a matter of seconds before he says, "Working how? And you know what? What's with the blood in your bathroom? What happened?" He scans me from head to toe as well.

"I got in a fight, and I handled it but if you must know I was retrieving information."

"Stop being cagey and tell us the whole story!" Rich asks incredulously, but his features soften slightly.

"Stop being arsy and dramatic, and maybe I will," I glare at him, and we come to an impasse, one I know for damn sure I'll win. I always do. Although I'm not sure if that's a good thing or not.

From the corner of my eye, I see the librarian has poked her head around the bookshelf again. I send her another wink and her cheeks go pink and she scurries off. "How did you find me anyway?"

Rich nods down towards Declan, "We used his nose to follow the scent of your blood, not hard to acquire since it's smeared all over your bathroom which is something that I still do not have an answer to."

"That's both impressive and a little creepy."

Declan nods at my statement making me laugh.

Rich sighs dramatically crossing his arms and begins rubbing his forehead with his slender fingers barely containing his annoyance.

"Sit. Take a load off," I tease, pushing him a little further, grinning when he stops and glares at me.

"Just answer my question," he huffs, plopping down in the dust-ridden chair opposite mine, reclining back.

"I found out where Roman is hiding." Both shifters' eyes widened in surprise, "and I found out who our mystery man is as well."

Rich is stunned into silence, his lips part slightly and I can tell he's impressed but doesn't really know what to say. "Wow, you really have been busy. So why are you in the library?"

"Looking for information on the Salacian palace. Although these books are so far useless." I wave my hand to the large stack of books sitting on the small, now bowing, table next to me.

"The two relate, how?"

"Well, Melanie told me that Roman is hiding out there, but no one knows the exact location of Queen Cordelia's Palace."

"Wait, Melanie? Who's Melanie?"

"Melanie Lincoln, keep up Rich, so she told me..."

"You threatened Melanie Lincoln? The daughter of the most notorious mob boss of the South, Eddie 'Black Foot' Lincoln?"

"Yeah, so?"

Declan chuffs, his leopard's way of laughing, I guess.

"So? What if he comes after you?" He practically screeches, looking around quickly as if someone could be hiding amongst the bookshelves.

"Then... I'll kill him," I reply, making it sound like a question, but it's more of a statement.

His eyes are blown wide as if I've just said the most ridiculous thing in the world and throws his hands up, his mouth agape, "You're not indestructible, Aella. You have no idea who you are messing with."

"Then you clearly have no idea what I'm capable of if you think a small-time lynx shifter can kill me."

I picked up yet another book, this one is bigger, older, and covered in dust. I have high hopes that this one will prove more fruitful.

Rich seems to understand this conversation is over, at least for the time being, and begrudgingly picks up a book to help in the search, while Declan rests his large head in my lap closing his eyes and continues to purr gently as I scratch between his ears once again.

CHAPTER SIXTEEN
TRESPASSING & ESPIONAGE

Hours later the three of us make the trek back to the apartment, the mid-morning sun warming me from the outside and reaching something dark and cold within.

Declan trots happily beside us still in his animal form. With most of the population of Anaphi being mortals, it is certainly uncommon to see a shifter in their animal form. They are usually kept secret so as to not draw attention. Felines are the rarest. Having been hunted to near extinction over a century ago. Their unpredictability made them far too dangerous to mingle with mortals. Only the strongest bloodlines have survived. So, seeing people actually cross the road because of him is disheartening. Not that he seems to notice.

I checked out the old tome to read in my own time, having barely scratched the surface of it before Declan's stomach growled loudly.

That's how we are here, with a spotted feline holding a paper bag full of food in his mouth trotting joyfully down the street, leading us back to the safe house.

Rich slows his pace to match mine, "Hey."

I nod in acknowledgement. "Rich, please don't apologise. There's really no need. There are going to be times when we don't get along and they will happen more frequently the longer we stay together. But you did help me to understand that I need to shift my focus back onto the mission. I have already delayed more than I should've."

"Wait what?"

"Oh, also do you happen to know a tailor in the area. I need my cloak fixed. That little lynx has got some claws." I lift up my arm showing him the tears and the dried blood.

"Er, yeah, I do. I can take it for you if you want?" he says, still looking a little confused.

Rich turns the key in the lock, and I hear something drop from beyond the door placing my hand on his arm, I stop him from pushing the door open.

"Give me a weapon," he whispers, having heard it too.

"I only have my knife. My guns are in there." I whisper back, nodding to the door.

"Fantastic," he mumbles.

I put my finger to my lips and pull out my knife from my thigh holster, pushing the door open.

"What are you doing?" He goes to grab my arm but thinks better of it when he sees my bandage. Even Declan lets me know of his discomfort by butting his head against my leg.

Much to their displeasure, which I'm sure I'll hear about later, I Ignore them both and take the first step inside, over the threshold and begin instantly scanning the kitchen and living room.

With the main living area being an open-plan design there really aren't many places that I can hide should I need to, so I keep myself low and vigilant, with my knife in front of me while I start my search.

The delicate, white patio doors in my rooms are flung wide open and the sheer curtains flap soundlessly in the breeze.

I tighten the grip on my knife, my palms already starting to feel clammy.

Taking tentative steps around I'm careful not to step on any of the creaky floorboards and plan to start clearing out the bedrooms.

Declan's is first since his room is closer to the front door. His door creaks open and the place is in tatters, his sheets have not been touched but two boxes have been tossed around his bed, their lids are discarded across the floor with their papers scattered on the sheets. I haven't seen these before but now is not the time to investigate them. The drawers to his cabinets are pulled open with his clothes hanging out and the doors to his wardrobe hang limply.

Rich's room seems untouched, except for some of his clothing hanging from his drawers much like Declan's. It would seem whatever they were looking for they found in Declan's room.

But still, I keep searching.

A floorboard creaks behind me and I whip around keeping my knife parallel to my forearm, only to be met with Rich's panicked face.

Panicked only because he wants me to remain quiet, his finger is pushed to his lips.

Declan, still in his animal form, is stalking towards my bedroom. Each of his steps is slow and calculated, the bag of food sits on the floor by the door behind him, long forgotten.

I sheath my knife back into its holster, understanding that whoever broke in is now long gone. They likely left when the key went into the lock.

Still, I want to check in every nook and cranny, so I move to do a sweep of my room all the same. Which has strangely been left untouched. Not even my weapons back has been moved.

"Nothing's been taken in here," I yell, across the apartment, "how is it looking on your end boys?"

"Same here, surprisingly!" Rich replies.

I turn to see Declan – back in his human form – working his jaw, looking around his room turned upside-down.

Whatever they were looking for they clearly didn't find. *But what?*

I take a step towards the doorway, the open plan living area allowing me to see both of their rooms at once.

"You want some..." My words die on my tongue, my throat dries up, and my heartbeat flutters as I appreciate the sight before me.

There he stands angrily looking about his room, holding a tiny towel around his waist. I sigh and lean against the doorframe greedily drinking in his well-toned physique and note each white scar that decorates his olive skin.

The dark swirling tattoos across his shoulders and chest, are carefully placed and written in a language I – so suddenly and very desperately – want to learn.

"Living the dream Elle?" My eyes snap over to Rich, glaring at him to be quiet. "Oh, and yes he probably does," he snips again, winking at me.

"What?" I croak.

"Want some... That's what you asked right? So I'm answering. Yes, he probably does."

My mouth snaps shut and my cheeks flush hot, that only makes his cocky grin widen further, which in turn succeeds in angering me more.

Declan is either ignoring us on purpose or is so busy trying to gather up his stuff that he doesn't hear us at all.

Honestly, I'm hoping for the latter.

It's less embarrassing that way.

The following day I wake to the sound of a deafening snore in my ear and the charming melody of a passing gondolier. The sun beams through the doors as if it's pleased to see me.

A weight is draped across my ribs, suffocating me slowly and I look down to see Rich's arm curled around my body, the pressure of it resting there is still better than listening to Declan snore.

After the incident yesterday both of them had stayed in my room until the twilight hours of the morning. We had begun talking about possible leads and the next steps that would lead to the end goal. That was until Declan had fallen asleep on my pillow, so instead we'd all settled in for the night huddling close.

My current situation is something that only my subconscious had ever dreamt of, being in between these two magnificent males, but the reality of that is substantially less enticing. The heat that is radiating off both of them has my hair glued to my forehead from sweat. I feel like I've crawled into an oven and begun cooking myself slowly. That, coupled with the sun's heat coming through the curtains, I might as well have woken up in the middle of the desert, with no water.

Without wanting to wake the pair up I try to wiggle my way down the bed in an attempt to get away from the unbearable heat.

Unexpectedly Rich's arm tightens around my waist, pulling me back against his blisteringly hot chest. I freeze, worried I've woken him up with my movements, but when he doesn't speak, I try again, prying his arm away and lifting it off me gently.

"Stop squirming," he grumbles into the pillow without opening his eyes.

I freeze again, "well I wouldn't have to if it wasn't like sleeping in a volcano between you two."

He opens his eyes to look me dead in the face. "Most females would kill for this opportunity. Only a few have had the privilege," he smirks, winks, and closes his eyes again, snuggling back down.

I huff not caring if I wake them anymore and proceed to bounce down the length of the bed.

The first thing I do with my freedom is search the apartment, just in case our friend came back in the night. I check all the doors and windows for any sign of forced entry and once I'm satisfied that there's not so much as a scratch on any of the window frames, I decide to make coffee for the three of us.

Minutes later Declan stumbles from the room first, yawning loudly with his hair in disarray. Rich is quick to follow, looking decidedly more awake than his counterpart.

"Morning boys," I sing, earning a glare from Declan.

"I smell coffee," Rich sniffs the air heavily. I push two mugs towards them and take a sip of my own.

"What's the plan for today?" Rich asks over the lip of his cup.

"I don't know about you two, but I have a possible lead that could help with the investigation. I do think it would be useful though, to figure out who broke in."

"I'll take care of that," Rich chimes in, "you get on with what you need to do."

We both turn to Declan who's managed to stay quiet this entire time and looking at him now, I see why.

He looks exhausted as if he's been up all night.

"You want to take him, or should I?" Rich asks.

"I will. I'm doing some reconnaissance, so it won't be too taxing for him."

Day turns to night bringing with it a cool wind blowing in from the sea. It's then that I release the tension from my stiff and aching muscles but at least I got what I came for, the daytime routine of the guards and their changes. Every hour on the hour.

Princess Iris had shown up a little after the sun had reached its apex in the sky, bringing with her a veritable trove of guards along for the journey. I'm sure her brother will be pleased to know of her arrival.

Declan grumbled up until around midday, just after she arrived. It had gotten so bad and distracting that I snapped at him to go back to the safehouse and leave me to get on with what I came here to do. Considering he doesn't like me nor what I do, he didn't put up a fight about how I talked to him. He glared angrily and left without a word of protest.

The king and his spoilt princess left the building hours ago, Iris talking animated – probably about the latest fashion trends, while Theodore smiles like she's truly a marvel of this world – taking with them the half a dozen armoured vehicles, which had arrived along with Iris, and drove back in the direction of The Circle; most of the guards left with them and it's now that I'll seize my opportunity.

The back of the building, which faces out towards the bay of Ansrutas, has been left nearly completely unsupervised; only a few guards actually police the grounds, but the back of the hall faces the sea and is ablaze with the dusky sun rays that are setting over the horizon.

Knowing that I'll have to wait until it's completely dark before I attempt anything, makes me feel itchy with impatience.

Once the sun has finally set, I climb down the rusted ladder and creep around the desolate streets to the back of City Hall and jump, up and over, the iron fencing ducking into the evergreen bushes that hug the wall and watch the, too few guards that walk the grounds from between the branches.

My eyes rove over the three-story building in search of an open window and find nothing.

The old-fashioned way then, breaking and entering; and praying I don't get caught.

When the last of them turn the corner, I dash from the evergreen bushes straight to the sun-bleached wall, careful to stay out of the camera's sight. My heart thumps wildly under my breast, the anticipation making me feel alive. I draw a small throwing knife from my sheath and jimmy it under the window's seal and drag it towards the lock, trying to pop it open.

With a click and a squeak, I open the window it's only small so that'll be a trial climbing through unseen. I puff out a steadying breath and cock my head to the side analysing the gap. I crouch down, jump up clasping the frame as I do so. My boots squeak against the glass trying to find purchase and when I'm steady enough I push myself up, wiggling my body through the window. Landing lightly on the other side.

I crouch listening and waiting to see if anyone has heard me.

Upon closer inspection the room, from what I can see in the darkness, looks like registration's office. Five desks line the entranceway, each with a pair of chairs placed in front, and the rest of the room is made up of shelving units and filing cabinets, piled high with boxes and countless official papers for all manner of things.

The air here is stale and smells of old paper making it hard to breathe almost suffocating; it's clear the windows are never opened.

I creep over to the door, careful of the flickering torch light coming from the hallway and the soft murmuring of voices from the guards as they talk amongst themselves.

The room I need to get to – the archives – is downstairs and I need to get there without being seen, but that requires me to walk through the lobby, right where the voices are coming from.

Turning the handle of the door I'm overly cautious about making no noise, and I cringe when the hinges creak loudly, the sound echoes down the marble-floored corridor effectively silencing their conversations.

The building grows so quiet you could probably hear a pin drop from the upper level, and I wait with bated breath to see what they will do; my heart pounds so furiously I can feel it in my throat.

The sound of footsteps approaching snaps me out of my frozen state, and I quietly fumble to find a hiding spot feeling almost giddy with anticipation.

The door opens further, and a blinding light comes through the gap first searching around the room, before a tall, dark figure enters followed closely by another.

"You see anything?" One of them asks, a cautious waver in his voice. I watch them stealthy move about the room, fighting to keep my breath shallow and silent. I see they've traded their usual golden armour and swords in for bulletproof vests and black tactical gear paired with rifles with lasers and torches.

I wonder what they've got in here that would need these guards.

"I've just stepped in the room, what do you think?" The other snaps back. A grin spreads on my face, the pair reminding me of Declan and Rich.

Then a scary thought pop into my mind. What if Rich and Declan know these two guards. Declan was at least part of the Stratos at one time. Going so far in his career that he became a part of the King's Guard.

The duo spread themselves out, one checks under each desk and the other starts searching through the rows and rows of shelves; the things that I am currently hiding behind.

The torchlight from his rifle advances closer and closer to my aisle and I palm the handle of the blade at my thigh enjoying feeling the weight of it, my blood runs hot as my heart beats faster and faster.

"Come on man there's nothing in here, it must have just been a draft," the second guard moans from across the room, pointing to the open window.

The male closest to me stops just before my aisle and I hold my breath, my fingers curling around the handle.

"Alright, come on," he replies and turns back to the door. I keep my breath locked in my lungs until the door clicks behind them.

I release the breath – and my knife – and run to the door, pressing my ear up against it. I listen to their retreating footsteps and for any others that might be in the hallway. Using the echo of the boots I pull open the door again and slip through, jumping into the shadows to use them as cover. When they reach the lobby, they turn and head for the exit leaving the inside free.

I listen to the guards making their rounds on the upper levels to make sure none of them are going to descend down the marble stairs. Being in here at night compared to the daytime is strange, seeing the moonlight pour in from the windows gives this already ominous place a more eerie aura. I can practically see General Griffith standing proudly on those stairs just like the day I met him. Only he isn't there and isn't likely still in the city if he has been suspended from his position like Frederick had mentioned.

I take in a deep breath and hold it before I make a run for it across the foyer, my cloak whispers behind me, my footsteps light and quick. Using the light as my guide, being that of a dull orange glow from the streetlamps outside. I fly past the curving receptionist's desk trying not to slip on the freshly waxed floor and skid to a halt outside a set of double doors, those of which lead to a stairwell, which in turn lead to the basement, where the archives is located.

The staircase echoes with voices and my breath shutters in my breast, yet I feel no terror, in fact, I'm blossoming under the pressure.

Whipping my head from side to side I open the closest door and slip inside just as they open the stairwell door. I look around to see buckets, brooms, and chemicals.

A broom closet, how cliché.

The buzz of my phone vibrates in my pocket, and I pray they haven't heard it as the patrol passes me by and I curse myself for not having turned the damn thing off before starting this crusade. I'm quick to pull it out of my pocket and see Rich's name at the top of the screen. I slide my finger across it and press it to my ear.

"I can't talk right now," I whisper, still listening to the patrols that crawl like ants all over this building.

"Why?" he whispers back, before realising he doesn't need to, "what are you doing?"

"Currently? I'm hiding in a broom closet," I reply, hearing Declan mumble some slur in the background, "am I on speaker?"

"You are now. What's going on?"

"Shh."

The guards' voices quieten, and I feel like they know where I am, my hand drops back down to my thigh, to the knife that's strapped there, the hunk of metal feeling perfectly weighted in my palm.

"I'm telling you, man. I think she's hot!" One of them says breaking the deafening silence.

"Nah she's too spoiled, did you not hear her when she got out of the car, she literally screamed 'Daddy!' not to mention that she's too inaccessible."

"Maybe, but I bet she's a great in other departments." They both laugh agreeing with each other. I scowl knowing they're talking about the princess. They don't even hear me as I slip by them and into the stairwell.

"And now I'm running down the stairs," I whisper into the phone, my eyes wide scanning the dark.

"Where the fuck are you?" Rich asks, sounding genuinely curious I can almost hear the smile on his face.

"Can you just trust me a little please," I huff.

He sighs down the line and I know he won't ask again but flying off the handle.

"City Hall," I reply, reaching the final step while checking the corridor and then checking it again. I creep down trying the handle on each door as I pass.

"Tell me you're joking?" he groans. I can almost picture him rubbing his thumb and forefinger over his eyebrows. I pass several brown unmarked locked doors until I finally find the archives.

"Would you believe me if I tell you I was?" I try, and I tuck the phone in between my ear and shoulder as I kneel down, pulling out a wrapped suede pouch from my pocket filled with lock picks. I pick out two and begin the long process of unlocking the door.

"You sound very convincing," he drawls, his words all but dripping in sarcasm.

"So no, then."

"How did you get in?"

"Oh, only a little thing called breaking and entering, Mr Keita." He snickers down the receiver.

"Do you need any help?" Declan asks. His voice surprises me, especially because he's being nice and offering help instead on an insult. It take my brain a minute to catch up in order to form a proper response.

"No, because I'll probably be done by the time you get here, but thanks," I whisper back. The latch clicks and the door pops open. "I should go, I've reached the target."

There's hesitation down the line and I can tell the pair of them are exchanging glances.

"Alright. Be careful," Declan finally says.

"Will do, boss man," I answer, hanging up. I enter the archives swiftly, closing the door behind me. The room has a lingering musky aroma in the air, mixed with the near-intoxicating scent of books and paper. It's pitch black in this room except for a slither of moonlight coming in through the half windows up by the ceiling. The archives are in, what is essentially, the basement of the public building, so each room down here only has half windows that sit up high.

In front of me is a large circular wooden desk with a dusty old computer perched in the middle, every inch of it is covered in documents and scraps of paper, with a small, unwatered plant off to one side. Behind that are rows and rows of shelving that are stacked with boxes and climb upwards brushing the soft tiles of the ceiling.

"Fantastic," I groan, looking at the huge room filled with filing cabinets on one side and boxes upon boxes on the other.

I look at the time on my phone and set a fifteen-minute timer, which should alert me of the next incoming patrol and set to work. I pick a filing cabinet and turn the light on, on my phone and I instantly start flicking through the A-B section hoping there's anything linking Anaphi to Salacia.

On cue, my timer goes off exactly fifteen minutes later and I hear the doors to the stairwell open and bang closed, I feel the vibration of it even down here. No voices accompany the solid footsteps, but I still hastily turn the light off and duck behind one of the shelving units, using the shadows at the back of the room to keep myself hidden, instantly feeling at home in the darkness.

Their torchlights ominously flicker along the beige hallway walls, and I can hear them jiggling each door handle that they pass by. My pulse quickens knowing I haven't locked the door behind me.

The outline of a head pokes in through the window in the door, I hold my breath when I feel their eyes burning into my own, the handle jiggles but the door does not open.

The shadows seem to surround me, as though they're my protectors, and that whoever this guard is can't see me, but that doesn't stop me from pulling out my knife and rolling the familiar weight over and over in my palm.

"Clear in here," the guard says, in a deep growling voice, one that is distantly familiar, like I've heard it before – in a dream perhaps – before he moves away proceeding with his other checks down the corridor.

I stay hidden and listen intently as they continue to sweep up and down the hall and it's not until I see them pass by the door again that I continue on searching. I wait patiently counting their steps back up the stairs, and for the tell-tale sign of the doors banging closed, when I pull out another drawer in the cabinet labelled with S-T, praying that it will prove more fruitful.

I shine the light inside looking for the name Salacia and see it written in cursive on at least three different documents, and I waste no time in pulling them from the drawer and drop to sit on the floor, crossed-legged, spreading the documents out in front of me.

Another half an hour ticks by and it's nearing midnight by the time I've finished flicking through the first file. Two more patrols have come around since and disturbed my peace, and I decide that now is the time to leave. My luck will only stretch so far. I've already taken pictures of everything by now and I'm pushing the drawer closed when the door handle turns and the hinges creak with the movement of the door opening.

Of Fire and Shadow

Without wasting any time, I drop to the floor, the action so quick it makes me dizzy. I begin crawling along the old, rough carpet, my skin acquiring new scratches as I duck into the closest corner filled with shadow.

"Fury?" A rough voice calls from the doorway and my heart stills in my chest.

"Angelos?" I reply, with nothing but the purest form of confusion in my voice.

"Obviously. Where are you?"

I roll my eyes and move quietly to the door. Sure enough, my eyes land on his hulking form crouched low trying, and failing, to make himself look smaller. "Could you not wait a little bit longer, I'm literally about to leave now."

"Rich was worried and wouldn't stop pestering me," he grumbles, taking a step towards me, then I hear Rich's muffled reply.

"Do you have an earpiece in?" I ask incredulously.

He side-eyes me, "Yes."

"Where is he?"

His lips thin and he stares through me seemingly reluctant to answer but I don't waver, instead I cross my arms over my chest and calmly wait for him to answer, "he's waiting for us... outside."

"Gods above." I roll my eyes shoving him out of the way and walk past him into the hallway. He scrambles to get up off the floor to follow. Neither of us speaks as we ascend the stairs back to the main floor. Declan keeps close as I push open the double doors.

Two guards silently cross the lobby; the squeak of their boots on the polished floor is the only sound, both using their torches to light the way up the main staircase. I slip through the tiny gap I've made not wanting the hinges to grind and give away our position and stalk out into the dark corridor, listening intently for anyone else, only to hear the retreating footsteps ascending the stairs.

We make a run for it across the grand foyer and into the opposite corridor, heading back to the registration room. The door clicks closed behind us; I breathe out a sigh of relief.

"How did you even get in?" I ask finally.

"The front door..." he answers, jutting his thumb over his shoulder and looking confused as if it was obvious.

"Where? There is a crap tonne of cameras and security guards," I question, tilting my head to the side, my eyebrows pinching harshly.

"There wasn't anyone outside when I got here."

I shake my head, "bullshit! They're crawling like insects all over this place and those cameras pick up on more than you know."

He puts his hand to his ear as if he is listening to something, "Rich is already altering the security footage as we speak but better yet, how did you get in?"

I cross my arms over each other and jut out my hip, pointing with my thumb over my shoulder, mimicking Declan's earlier action, to the small window at the back of the room. It's still hanging wide open and chilling the room with the salty breeze drifting in.

His face drops and he scoffs, "There's no way I'm fitting through there."

"Maybe not, but that's the way we are leaving because the guards outside are about to patrol past those windows, probably seeing that left open, and then they're going to head back inside and search the room. So it's now or never, big guy." He steps forward angrily so we are chest to chest.

"You don't get to call the shots here, *Siren*. You got us into this mess and now I'm going to fix it," he snarls.

"You can't fix your own attitude. So why would I trust you to fix this and if you remember correctly, I didn't get you into anything, but I'll refresh your memory just in case, Rich is the one who coerced you. That's not *my* fault, so step back."

"Or what?" he glowers, she very little humour in my challenge.

"Or I'll make you," I snarl back.

The tension is palpable. It's flowing around us in waves as we stand staring at each other. Challenging the other and neither willing to back down. My fingers twitch to grip the knife at my hip and it takes everything in me to not reach for it.

"Step back, *Fury*." His face darkens and the humour my challenge brought has changed, becoming something more akin to rage. I feel its force rolling from him like clouds before a thunderstorm and I loving the way it's electrifying the air around us. Relishing in the way it makes me feel more alive than ever. It's heavy and twisted and utterly delightful. My own darkness comes up to greet his and they seem to be evenly matched.

"Or what?" I mock, with a devilish grin.

Heavy footsteps from outside round the corner. I look to see the guards' shadows wander past the windows trampling the grass. Neither seems to notice that the window is open at all, and they pass by without a proper interruption.

Turning back to Declan I see him staring at me, murderously. Seeming completely unfazed by the guard's surrounding us. Rich's muffled voice comes through his earpiece again, I can't quite make out the words, but Declan grabs my arm and drags me towards the window.

"You want a hand up?" I tease.

He grunts in response, lifting me up to the window. "Go," he mutters. It's as if I weigh nothing to him the way he manoeuvres his hand under me. I reach for the window and his hand lands on my rear.

He coughs uncomfortably, "Sorry." I hear him mumble and I bite my lip to keep from laughing before hauling myself through the window.

Dropping down quietly in the bushes outside, I crouch down and await Declan's arrival. I don't have to wait long but he's less than graceful on his touchdown. The bush almost completely crumbles under his weight, but he's somehow managed to close the window on his way down.

I nod at him when our eyes meet and go to leave across the lawn when large hands circle around my hips pulling my back until my back against a warm, hard chest.

"Rich is overriding the camera, just wait here for a second," Declan whispers in my ear. His hot breath warms my cheeks as he holds me still; his anger and embarrassment already forgotten.

I nod my head, soaking in his warmth. I hadn't realised how cold I actually was until he drowned me in his heat.

He tucks his head in closer to mine, trying to keep us concealed in the shadows, and my head leans to the side giving him better access while I press back further into his touch. Closing my eyes, I bite back a moan when it seems like he tucks in further, almost as though he's breathing me in.

The firm form of his front is pressed entirely up to my back and the feeling of his fingers tightening their hold on my hips, makes me dizzy with anticipation. The heat of the moment quickly fizzles away when Rich's muffled voice sounds in Declan's ear, and he pulls away, almost too quickly, as though I'm made of fire, and he'll be burned if he holds on.

I instantly miss his warmth as he steps away from me, the fresh air revitalising my senses in a way that makes me feel like a bucket of ice has been poured over my head.

"We're...err...good to go," he says, not meeting my eye, I nod and move towards the evergreen bushes not waiting to see if he follows feeling both equally embarrassed and turned on. My body feels alight with electricity, and instead of doing what I actually want to, like climb Delcan like a tree, I channel it into climbing over the brick wall, back out onto the street.

Declan drops down swiftly beside me a moment later and starts walking away without saying a word, I follow behind him silently, keeping to the shadows.

Rich joins us shortly after with a laptop in hand, my laptop in fact. I eye him suspiciously and he offers me a shrug, "yours was the only one available."

I don't say anything about it, but I do know that I'll have to change my security features in the future, not only does it have private information on there, but it also has data on each and every mission I've ever done, all of the gory details and even some private information on the clients that have hired me in the past.

No one speaks as we walk back to the apartment, it almost makes me feel uncomfortable but I'm more confused about the feelings that seem to flurry around when I'm alone with Declan. I don't understand what is happening. I feel so free and at peace when he's with me, something that is forbidden to me, I'm an assassin, no more than a weapon. I'm not allowed to form bonds with anyone let alone something I don't deserve.

I've killed people.

I've *enjoyed* killing people.

That's what I'm trained for.

What I was born for.

It's likely what I'll die doing.

I need to complete this mission quickly and get back to what I do best.

I'm not here for anything else, I don't deserve anything more.

Aria

"I have eyes on the target," I speak into the phone Madame gifted me before leaving the Fort.

"What do you see?" Her voice hisses through the receiver.

"They're just leaving the City Hall basements and are now travelling East, presumably back to their safe house."

"City Hall?" she questions, mulling it over in silence for a heartbeat. "Fury Three-Five-Nine you are to keep eyes on target as your primary mission but watch out for her handlers. Something is going on and I want to know what. Find out what they know and do not get caught."

"Yes, Madame."

"Remember do not contact me. Wait for me to reach out to you, this is strictly off the books."

I hang up the phone looking down at the street below me. Three-Nought-Nought has changed since I last saw her, and the thought disgusts me.

Traitor. The conniving little voice hisses in the depths of my own mind and I wholeheartedly agree.

Being careful not to be seen, I move stealthily across the rooftops following at a distance, stalking them all the way back to their haven.

CHAPTER SEVENTEEN
A ROYAL DROP IN

I wake the next morning to a tingle on my neck, the hairs on my arms rise and dread curls in my lower belly.

I'm being watched.

I don't know where from, but the feeling is unmistakable.

My fingers curl around the handle of the blade under my pillow, lying face down doesn't give me an advantage in this situation but it does give me time to pull a knife on whoever is in here with me. My muscles tense like a snake coiling in on itself ready to strike out at a threat. My eyes pop open and I fling myself around the blade cutting through the air without so much as a whisper. Stopping dead when I meet a pair of bright green eyes filled with unadulterated humour.

"Well good morning to you too, love."

"How did you get in here?" I groan, eyeing him as he's sitting in my burgundy winged-backed armchair in the corner of my room, perfectly relaxed, before flopping back down against my pillow.

"Your delightful friends let me in, and I must say this is a much better upgrade from your last place, this is much more you," he chuckles, looking around the room.

"How would you know what's me?"

"Ouch, Peaches. Come on, don't cut me so deep. I know you better than those two out there, that are listening in on this conversation."

Sure enough, I hear Rich and Declan fumbling away from the door, and I laugh lightly. "What do you want, Frederick?"

"I want a lot of things from you, love, but for right now I would like to extend to you, an invitation."

I sit up then and rest back against the headboard in nothing but a sheer white cotton tank top, fully aware that he can see through it.

"An invitation to what?" I ask drawing his attention back up to my face, now I'm not the only one caught off guard.

"A... um. A ball that my father is hosting." The groan that comes out of my mouth is most unladylike, but Frederick laughs all the same.

"I know you don't like him..."

"It's not just him that I don't like. It's people as a whole, Freddy, I kill them for a reason."

His face drops but the glimmer of mischief never leaves his eyes, "you kill people because you don't have a choice, love. Something I intend to fix one of these days. But I need a date, and if I don't find someone I can tolerate, then my father will pick a noble lady. One that will no doubt be dreadfully boring and will only be after one thing." He throws me a wink coupled with a wicked grin, showing his shorter fae fangs.

"Thank you so much, for thinking of me first," I drawl rubbing my hands over my face, wiping away the sleep.

"Of course, I want someone that I can bitch to about those noble ladies," he replies grinning, yet it falls just as quickly as it appeared, and an awkward silence delicately descends on the room. "What have you found?"

"He's in Salacia," I reply understanding what he's asking, "Anything on your end?"

"What do you mean?"

"You mean to tell me that you haven't got something set up for him if you find him first, no transport to somewhere else or a safe house?"

"Would it matter? You can find anything and anyone, given the right resources."

"But it would give him, and you, a head start."

"And it would get you killed."

I don't blink at his words, my death has never meant anything to me but another step that one must take, "if he means as much to you as your eyes reveal. Would it not be better that way?" I'd never usually consider trading my life for a target, but I've always had a soft spot for Freddy, and I can tell Roman means more to him than he's telling me. My life means very little in the grand scheme of things, even to the Fort. They'd replace me soon enough and I'd be nothing more than a forgotten whisper in the circle of life.

Anger splices in his eyes, darkening the glowing green and he runs his hands through his chocolate-coloured hair pulling at the strands.

He looks down at the floor in front of his polished boots, it's then that I note his appearance. Hiding beneath the grey tunic and black pants are muscles that weren't there when I last saw him.

He's been taking his training seriously then.

His father has been demanding he take it seriously since his eighteenth birthday, knowing one day Frederick would take the crown, Theodore had claimed that the people wouldn't follow him if he was a scrawny bookworm who spent all of his time studying. Frederick had spat back that the people wouldn't follow an uneducated King either.

Despite the flaws his father claimed he had; Frederick was still handsome even before he packed on the muscle. Noble ladies chased him down the corridors and his confidence never wavered. He looks much more like the man his father wishes for him to be. One that the country can lean on should they need.

But looking before me now, I see a boy. A boy who's caught between his head and his heart, wanting everything but in danger of losing it all the same.

"I don't want to choose," he whispers, his head resting in his hands, his elbows on his knees. I get out of bed throwing the cover violently across it and slowly walk over to him. I crouch down in front of the chair rubbing my hands along the sides of his thighs in an attempt to soothe him.

"Freddy, the time might come when you have to." His head sweeps up abruptly trying to cut me off, but I hold my hand up stopping him. "It might seem like the most difficult decision of your life. But remember in the face of adversity choose what is right for your people."

He stares at me for a moment, and I have a hard time trying to read him.

"Did you just quote my mother to me?" He groans. I smirk at him, just glad that he understood.

"Yes. Yes, I did." He shoves my face away from him.

"You're so lame," he laughs, and I join him, glad to see the pressure eased from his shoulders at least for a little while.

I stand and move to root through my bag looking for fresh clothes, a black shirt, and pants. "I miss her. Tell her I'm thinking of her. Oh, wait, is she coming to the ball?" He sees me light up at the prospect and gives me a small smile.

"No. She and Dad are not on great terms again at the moment."

"Are they ever?" I ask genuinely curious.

"Ha! You have a point there." He smiles brightly.

"Are you staying for breakfast?" I ask.

"Yeah sure," he smiles getting up, "as much as I'd like to see you in nothing but your underwear and a tank top, get dressed, love. I don't think the cat would approve of my perusal."

I tilt my head in confusion, "what?"

He pats my cheek as a mother would to a child, "Still so much to learn." He turns and vacates my room, leaving me dumbfounded.

A few minutes later I come out of my room to a very charged energy, Declan is glaring at Frederick and Frederick is sitting there smirking back at him. Elijah, the red-headed manservant to his Royal Highness, is looking between the two, looking as though he's ready to jump in should a fight break out. He visibly relaxes when he spots me.

"Aella!" he chirps. He's just younger than Frederick and I, yet still has a more level head than either of us.

"Elijah! How are you?" I beam, moving to hug him, something he gladly receives.

"I'm currently thanking the gods you're here," he whispers in my ear, much to Rich's delight, who is standing over the stove grinning from ear to ear, looking wolfish.

I pull away from Elijah and look back between the two.

"Breakfast anyone?" Rich singsongs cheerfully, making Elijah wince.

"I'd love some," Frederick replies, emphasising his enthusiasm and getting up to move over to the dining table.

Rich can barely contain his excitement and it's quite contagious. I smile along with him as Declan glares at Frederick with deadly intent, his eyes following the half-fae around the room.

"Angelos? You want some breakfast?" I ask sweetly, trying to not set him off. I'm not sure what has been said between them, but he doesn't look happy.

When he turns to face me, his face softens slightly but he doesn't answer. He simply gets up and moves to the table, sitting down on one side, facing Frederick, his eyebrows pinch again and his mass of muscle tenses up.

Rich's face must be hurting, he's not stopped grinning since I came out of my room, clearly enjoying whatever show it was that I missed.

Elijah looks at me, his eyes begging me to do something, but I don't even know what this is about, so I shrug and help Rich plate up the food.

"What's going on?" I whisper to him.

"I am not the person who will help you in this situation." He laughs full and hearty and it's a beautiful thing.

I roll my eyes and take Declan's food over and sit down in the seat next to him, he seems to relax a bit but there's still a thick tension lingering in the air.

"So, this ball, Fred. When is it?"

"At the week's end," he states, only taking his eyes from Declan to meet mine, enjoying Declan's annoyance almost as much as Rich is.

I take a bite of my food and nearly melt at the flavour. "What's it for?" I ask after swallowing.

"It's to celebrate his daughter, of course. What else is there?" He rolls his eyes, fed up with his father's favouritism.

"Ha! Then I'm definitely not going." Declan scoffs beside me, clearly happy with my answer.

Rich brings everyone else's food and sits down.

"Princess Iris is here?" he asks.

"Yes. Do you know her?" Her older brother questions sounding defensive.

Just because his father is biased towards her doesn't mean there's any love lost between the siblings. He wouldn't have bothered to ask me for help all those years ago otherwise.

"Only of her." Rich chooses not to say more but I know what he's thinking as he rolls his lips together.

"Come on, Elle. She's not mad at you anymore. In fact, she told me she'd like to thank you," Fred pleads.

"Frederick, she tried to have me killed. She may have forgiven and forgotten. But that doesn't mean that I have." He gives me his 'puppy dog eyes' thinking I'll break; he only lasts a few seconds before conceding.

"I'll buy you a new dress?" he bribes. That gets my attention and I regard his stance, sitting back in the chair. I cross my arms over my chest giving him a challenging look, something he rises to, and he matches my pose.

"Black."

"Navy."

"Black."

"Blood red."

"Oh." My lips purse and my interest has peaked, I'm very aware that I'm being watched by everyone at this table. "Done."

"Yes!" He punches the air, grinning. From the corner of my eye, I see Rich looks over to Declan before continuing to eat his food, saying nothing.

Hours later I'm sitting on my bed typing up another mission report. This one won't be as informative as the first two because nothing much has happened this week. Declan comes in and throws a box down on my bed, I watch it bounce on the mattress as he walks away without saying a word.

"Hey!" I yell. He stops dead in the doorway and visibly takes a deep breath. "What's your problem?"

"Nothing," he snaps over his shoulder and walks away.

I narrow my eyes at his retreating form, shaking my head when my phone buzzes next to me on my bed.

"Hello?" I greet placing the phone in the crook of my shoulder and ear.

"Three-Nought-Nought." Her voice slithers through the receiver like smoke across the surface of a lake, my spine is straightening and my eyes dart around the room looking to see if she's in here with me.

"Madame," I reply, being courteous but still obedient.

"I'm just checking in. I've read through your mission reports and sent them forward to Logan." She tells me that I need to know what's happening, whilst I'm away. "I'd like to think your third is coming along nicely?"

"Yes Madame, just typing it up now in fact." Rich appears in my doorway, the sleeves of his black shirt rolled to his elbows as he leans against the doorframe, his black dress pants are fitted to his form finished off with a black leather belt. The male is drool-worthy in his finery, but his scowl tells me he knows exactly who is on the phone.

"As expected, the Director has asked me to check up on you. I know we spoke of little to no communication, but I would've thought you'd have replied by now, considering I asked your handler to tell you that I'd called nearly a week ago."

"My apologies Madame, he did tell me. I've been busy following a lead." Rich's eyebrows shoot up, clearly not knowing that Declan has had a missed call from K.

"Three-Nought-Nought, I expect better from you. I didn't raise you to be insolent. Do better."

"Madame before you go. I have some questions." She sighs and Rich stands tall looking antsy.

"Talk," she commands.

"What was it you wanted to talk to me about? Do you remember, before I left? I think it might help me understand some things."

"What kinds of things?"

I think about it, trying to understand why the leads are falling through or why they aren't being tied up in a neat little bow like they usually are. In fact, I don't seem to have gotten anywhere in the time I've been here. I stand up and walk to the patio doors overlooking the river. "Some things aren't adding up like they should be. I'm just curious to see if your information may help me progress quicker."

"The line is not as secure as I'd like for this kind of conversation, Aella. If I can get it to you. I will."

"Thank you, Madame."

"Only the strong survive," she recites the mantra and hangs up.

I sigh looking at the blank screen. As strange as it is to say. I miss her. She has been my mentor from the beginning. Pulling me up when I've fallen despite not being allowed. She has protected as best as she can in a place where quite literally only the strong survive. I think I may be the only person alive that has seen her smile. When she became drunk one night, and I had taken her back to her room. She let slip that if she were to have had a daughter, she would have liked for her to turn out like me. That was the only time I saw her so open. It's not happened since. It's a bittersweet memory for me. I finally saw the real Yvonne Killick. But that night Reuben Ostair showed me his real villainous face for the first time.

"Why'd you lie for him?" Rich asks softly, pulling me from my memories.

I turn and smile softly at him, "I would lie for either of you. But I did it because neither of you needs to get into trouble with the Fort because of me."

"I would take their wrath over you being dead any day of the week," Rich states walking forward until he's by my side looking out the window too.

I don't answer. I've never really thought of myself as worthy of such gentleness. Of such care and affection. But that's what Rich does. He cares. Maybe too much. He wants to prove that everyone deserves a second chance no matter who they are or what they've done.

"What's with the wistful face anyway?" he asks, nudging me with his shoulder.

"I'm just thinking how much has changed I suppose and yet, in the same breath, nothing all at once."

He moves to sit down on the bed, patting the space next to him, "care to elaborate?"

I nod and sit next to him. "I suppose I mean that I've never been myself for long enough for it to matter. But this is the freest I've ever felt. Like I can make my own decisions for the first time in my life. I don't have someone breathing down my neck, correcting every little thing I do. But when it's all said and done, I'm still an assassin and I'll be doing this until I inevitably die on a job." I pause, taking a deep breath. He doesn't rush me. Doesn't put pressure on me to continue and that's why I find talking to him comforting. "I'm sorry, I'm rambling." I wave feeling embarrassed by where my own thoughts have taken me.

"Expressing your thoughts is never wrong, Aella. I think I'm just lucky enough to be the one you've finally opened up to." He smiles and pulls me to his side, tucking me under his arm, squeezing me tight. "Thank you for telling me. I know it must be hard for you to trust people." He places a soft kiss on my hair.

Tears come to my eyes. I begin to wonder which God it was that blessed me with such a loving companion. I clear my throat hiding the growing lump in my throat. "Where are you going all fancy anyway?" I tease, pulling away and waving my hand up and down.

He looks down at himself, "Oh, an old friend is in town and I'm going to meet them for dinner."

"A lady friend?" I tease further.

He chuckles, "Maybe."

We share a secret smile, and he gets up, "Well, have fun at your 'dinner.'" I wink watching as the silver in his gorgeous black eyes blazes bright like the stars in the sky.

"Thank you." He gives me a small smile and grabs his jacket. He pauses at the door to my room, "I will never push you to talk. But if you ever need an ear, *Aella.* I will be there."

My heart skips a beat in its cage. I nod in answer, not trusting my voice and he leaves. I sit back against the headboard and curl my arms around myself.

A sadness swallows me up.

My chest feels heavy and yet empty at the same time. I can't find the energy to do anything, except for crying. I've never been sad about my life before. I've never been able to see how I've been dealt the worst hand imaginable. I've always felt unstoppable. But if these past weeks have taught me anything, it is that I am most certainly not unstoppable. In fact, I think I might be more fragile than I realise. If it weren't for both Declan and Rich, I would already be just another number to replace. Another corpse in an unmarked grave, with no one to grieve me.

That makes me think of my parents. How they are likely in an unmarked grave. Though I suppose, for a time, there was at least someone to grieve them. Family and friends. But I have been raised alone, despite being constantly surrounded by people.

I will be replaced and life on the planet with resume, like I was never there to begin with.

Wiping my silent tears, I turn to the box at the end of my bed. I know what it contains. It's the dress Frederick has bought me for this ball he wants me to attend. I can tell by the white envelope resting on top with my name written in cursive.

Aella,

I'd like to formally invite you to be my plus one, to the ball that will celebrate the miracle that is my little sister, Iris.

Yours always,
Frederick

P.S. Given your task, your companions are also invited to join us.

I can feel his eyes roll as he writes the words, and the thought makes me let out a little watery giggle. Setting the letter aside, I open the box. The blood red, satin dress, as promised, shimmers deliciously in the dusky evening light shining through the windows, the style is designed to hug each curve of my body with thin straps at the top, and a slit at the bottom that would reach up to my hip. Simple yet elegant.

"Huh, maybe you do know after all Freddy," I mutter.

I hang up the dress somewhere it won't get creased and set my laptop on my work to begin working when Declan comes into my room once again, this time calmer and carrying two bowls of food, the aroma of which, fills the space with spice.

"I made venison stew," he grunts, placing the white bowl down on the side table before taking a seat resting against the headboard.

"Thank you," I answered, eyeing the steaming bowl.

"I haven't poisoned it, Fury. If I wanted you dead, there are so many more creative ways to do it. Poison is the least fun."

"Good to know. Thanks." I scoop up the bowl and we sit in silence. The only sound for many minute is spoons clinking against the ceramic bowls. He doesn't even seem bothered that we are silent. But it's unnerving me. I have been trained to withstand torture from the most creative of captures. But this, here and now, is truly unbearable. The silence is so loud, until I break it.

"Why don't you want me dead?"

His spoon pauses halfway to his mouth, "what would be the point in killing you now?"

"Oh, well thank you for being so gracious," I snap back. My appetite leaves me. I put the bowl back on the table only half eaten.

He sighs, "Eat. You need your strength."

I ignore him and instead say, "Why are you in here anyway? Or did you forget you hate me?"

He rolls his eyes and sighs deeper, placing his bowl down he turns to me, "What makes you think I hate you?"

I laugh. I can't help it, "what doesn't?"

His head tilts to the side but his eyes harden. When I don't answer his question, he turns back to his owl and continues eating.

I watch him for several minutes, he doesn't even seem remotely self-conscious that I'm observing everything he's doing. How his holds the spoon to how his throat works and how the muscles of his shoulders are bunched while he's hunched over the small bowl as he tries not to spill the stew down himself.

I'm very conscious that my own food is getting colder the longer I watch him, but my suspicion is far too high to care too much for that.

"The day you answered Rich's questions. The day we moved in here. Is the day I realised that you're not... all terrible," he speaks finally.

I raise an eyebrow my mouth in a tight line, "what do you want?"

His eyes roll again, much more dramatically, "right now. For you to drop the cautious act and eat the damn food."

"Sorry for thinking there is something weird about this considering we have never done this before. You can barely stand to be in the same room and me for longer than about five minutes."

"Eat." The look in his eyes tells me he won't tell me again. So, I pick up the bowl and continue eating. Our eyes don't leave each other until I've finished the bowl.

"Well, that's probably the most uncomfortable meal I've ever had," I mutter wiping my mouth with the back of my hand handing the bowl back to Declan who places it down next to his on the bedside.

"I lost my father." The sentence is so quiet I almost miss it. "He was a major-general in the Stratos. He was on his way to the capital when he was shot in the head." He swallows, lost in his memories, "The bullet had no marks. Nothing on it that could be traced, by any number of people. It was dubbed a freak accident. But I knew different.

When I joined the military, I looked into it myself. I knew from my training that it was an assassin. But I couldn't prove it. No matter how I tried I couldn't prove how I knew. Everyone else knew. But without tracing the bullet there was no way to find his killer. I don't know why he was killed. I don't know what he had on his person that made him the most valuable target that day. But I vowed to myself that as long as I had breath, I would find his killer."

The darkness in his eyes is different from before.

It's not rage.

It's not sick and twisted.

It's horror.

It's sadness and it's grief.

"When... When did it happen?" I ask quietly. Oh, so quietly I almost don't recognise the voice as mine. I need to make sure beyond any reason or doubt that it wasn't me. I can't have been me. The void in my chest, where my darkness usually resides, opens wider. Empty of everything I thought I knew. I rack through my memories and pray to whatever gods are listening that it wasn't me.

"About eighteen years ago."

It shouldn't relax me. The male in front of me has lost someone close to him and it was likely because of one of my own. But it does. It can't have been me.

I don't know what to say. I've never been good at talking, especially about emotions, and I most certainly have never felt guilty about what I do. But now everything is new, and I don't know how to navigate these uncharted territories.

"I'm so sorry Declan. I know that cannot bring you peace, nor will it bring him back. But truly I am."

His eyes widen, and his jaw slacks a little. I think I can see the silver lining his eyes, but he turns before I can be sure.

He clears his throat and stands, "Right well. Good night, Siren." With that, he leaves the room and I'm once again, alone.

The rising dawn sun warms me and my already flushed skin, but it's not able to take the chill off the cool misty air, not quite. Jogging in such a cool foggy morning reminds me of the Northern mountains, running through the snow and ice, I can't quite see my breath like I can when running through the snow but still it drifts upward with each pant and evaporates quickly behind me.

It's still too early, most people haven't even risen from their beds yet, and there's next to no one walking the pavement, but I run through the streets, my heart pounding, thoroughly enjoying the stress melting from my body.

Rich had come home a little after midnight last night and had woken me up. I was instantly on alert thinking the – still unknown – intruder had returned, afterwards I'd struggled to get back off to sleep as I began replaying Declan's conversation over and over. So, I'd left before the sun had risen over the city, wanting to clear my head, something isn't settling right, and my gut is telling me there is more to this than I know.

I know Madame said she would send her information in one form or another, but for her not to just tell me over the phone, it's clearly classified and she's worried about it being overheard by others. So, it's not common knowledge.

Sweat drips from my brow and trickles down my face to collect at my chin as I push myself further and faster. I don't stop until I'm red in the face and nothing else matters but the breath in my lungs, and the fuzziness in my brain has ebbed.

The information Melanie gave me has proven fruitful, I've managed to track down Alexander Nephus to an architectural firm in the Trades Centre named for himself, of course, Nephus Designs. I didn't exactly come out this morning with this in mind but I'm here. So, I might as well check in on him.

Stepping into what can only be described as a village at the side of the city, the buildings look like an engineer's nightmare but an architect's dream. Layers upon layers of brick, mortar, concrete, and wood mesh together to create a stunning masterpiece. Bringing nature and metropolitan life together in sinful unity.

Before I know it, I'm across the street from Nephus Designs, looking at the beautifully complex structure with awe, with sweat dripping from my forehead and just about everywhere else.

I'm standing in a square of sorts. A place where all the buildings face each other with a small decorative park in the middle, I take a perch on one of the benches, panting hard, wiping my sleeve along the skin of my face.

I sit there for mere minutes when I spot him running down the road, a briefcase in hand and a cup of to-go coffee in the other, looking dishevelled and panicked. I have to admit despite his flustered hair and face, he's a handsome male. His beard has grown in some, since the security footage I've been analysing, and his hair has grown longer and darker.

It's almost a shame I'll have to kill him.

I hum out loud in response to the thought and catch myself when a lone passer-by gives me a wary look.

A Royal Drop In

He charges through the glass door to his office without slowing down and disappears from view.

I could stay out here all day and watch his movements to see where he goes, but I've not come equipped for that and someone sitting in a park this small, surrounded by shops would look far too suspicious.

Seeing cameras on every corner I use my phone to hack into the security feed of the tailors across the square from Alex's office, that in turn links me to the others in the area, giving me a clear view from every angle; surprising even myself at how easy it was.

I get up, groaning at the ache in my muscles – even down to my bones – and head back to the apartment, eager to hear about Rich's date.

CHAPTER EIGHTEEN
DEATH & DEFIANCE

I decided to make a slight detour on my way back to Rich and Declan. Mostly because the streets are still so quiet, I can't help but take advantage of the cooler morning.

Whilst sitting in the park a sudden compulsion drove me to want to visit our old apartment. I know I'll likely find nothing of note there, but I'm curious. After being followed by Dawnya all the way home, it's made me intrigued to see if they've utilised the building or if it's been left bare by the landlord.

So, it's there that I stand. Outside the old sandstone building looking up at the small windows on the top floor where we stayed. I can't help the sense of foreboding that creeps up behind me, flashes of the night I was shot come trampling their way into the forefront of my mind.

A bloody handprint smeared down the wall as I hauled myself up step after step. The stumble I'd taken and the slicing pain I'd felt from when I had to crawl up the last few steps.

On the landing outside of the old apartment, I see the carpet in the hall is still ruined with the remnants of my blood. I can tell that time and again they have tried to clean it, but a dark patch still remains.

The door is slightly ajar when I finally look up from the floor and it makes no sound when I push it open and tiptoe inside.

To uncover nothing.

Absolutely nothing.

The entire place has been cleared out.

No furniture has been left behind, what stands before me is an apartment completely void of everything. No curtains hang from the wooden poles either, the light of the day blazes through the grimy windows.

The only thing that is in here is a small wooden box. Black in colour with a diamond pattern carved into the wood and finished with a delicate, swirling, golden lock.

I stand in the middle of the old living room, taking in the cleanliness of the place. I suppose that might be a strong word for what is around me, but it at least feels a lot cleaner than when we first walked in.

My footsteps are light as I cross the wooden floor, my pulse is quick, and the silence of the room is sinister as though someone is listening to every sound made.

I step into the kitchen and snatch up the heavy box and leave without looking back.

Rich is the first of the pair I see when I walk back into the apartment sometime later. He looks annoyed, a face I've become accustomed to over the course of our time together. Both of them have looked at me the same way on multiple times.

"Where the Hel have you been?" he snaps, placing his mug down with a little more force than I think even he meant to use.

"For a run. I run every day, Rich. You know that."

"Why didn't you wait for me?"

"Because you were asleep and I wanted to go," I spell it out for him as if he should already know this.

He grunts back clearly dissatisfied. "What's that?" he asks instead, picking his mug back up and it's then I realise he's in nothing but his black slacks, his toned chest completely bare.

"A box, Richie boy," I murmur back, watching the muscles of his arm work as he brings the mug to his lips, grinning when I see him roll his eyes.

"Ok. Let's try again, where did it come from?"

"It was at the old apartment."

"Why were you there?" he asks, placing his drink down, taking the box from me.

I shrug not really understanding the logic behind what drove me there either. "Just checking on things, I guess."

He eyes me suspiciously and I can see he wants to press the matter, more because I went without him, I think, but he also doesn't push the issue any further. He sets the box down on the kitchen counter and tries to open the lid only to find it locked.

Declan comes out of his room then, mercifully fully dressed, I don't know how I'd cope if both of them were in a state of undress right now. Especially not after what happened yesterday at City Hall.

The lock is easy for me to pick, and I begin slowly push the lid up.

"They wouldn't put a bomb in such a pretty box, would they?" I whisper rhetorically, but Rich's mouth pops open hysterically, that I chuckle, and he takes a small step back. Declan eyes us both from afar choosing to steer clear of the box entirely.

"I wouldn't if I were you," he murmurs.

"Why?" I pause something glints within the boxes' inside, but it's still not fully open enough to see.

"The box... it smells... off."

"What does that mean?" I snap, slightly anxious now that I have it half open and he's only just telling me something is wrong.

"Whatever is inside. Do not touch it," he takes only one step forward.

Tired of the run around I open it. Inside laying on green silk, is a small and slender obsidian dagger about the same size as a throwing knife.

"Phew," I audibly sigh.

"Erm, that's not something you should be so relaxed about," Rich warns, moving closer to get a better look. "I've heard about these before and they're not good news."

The word *'Fury'* is inscribed into the stone of the blade.

"Why? It's so pretty," I reply, reaching out to pick it up.

"Don't!" Declan growls snatching at my hand, he scowls at me and grabs the envelope stuck to the inside of the lid. He reads the note aloud.

Fury,
Whoever you are. Whatever you are.
*When I find you and I **will** find you.*
I will kill you.
Slowly, painfully.
No one and I mean no one touches my daughter and gets away with it.
My people are looking for you. So, it won't be long before you and I can play.

See you very soon,
Eddie Lincoln

Rich's face drops. I've never seen such a conflicted emotion across someone's face before. He doesn't know whether to be angry or horrified. He finally settles on the former.

"Are you crazy? Why? Why would you go after that family? As if we didn't already have enough to worry about and now the fucking mafia is after us."

"Me. They are after me," I utter, completely mesmerised by the black stone in the sharp of a dagger, just lying there. Made entirely of obsidian. Declan, surprisingly still holding my hand pulls me away from the box.

"Hide that from her. She's going to get herself killed,"

"What do you mean?" I mumble staring at the box until Rich slams the lid down.

"There's some sort of spell on that," Declan informs the room as if he's not just openly talked about magic.

I scoff, "excuse me."

"You cannot tell me little miss 'I've travelled the world' has never come across magic."

"Magic isn't real, Angelos,"

"Believe what you want. Just don't touch that 'gift'." He finally drops me hand and takes the box from Rich, to hide.

I watch him take the box and Rich clears his throat, "Are you even listening?"

"Yeah. You're upset that I went after Melanie, and now her 'daddy-dearest' has sent a gorgeous obsidian dagger to me, threatening me with the information that there's now a price on my head. So not only are the Stratos keeping tabs on me, but so are the mob. Does that roughly sum up the lecture?" I ask sweetly, peering around Declan's door to see where he's hiding the box, only for Rich to slam the door closed.

"I suppose so, yes," he answers in a grunt. He shifts uncomfortably but still holds a scowl on his face.

"Good," I smile back.

I choose not to give too much information about where I'm heading tonight, maybe because of what I am about to do isn't strictly safe – or legal. So, dressed in my full gear, right down to the bullet-proof vest and military-grade combat boots, and my cloak tied tightly around my neck I head to my next destination.

The night brings with it a drizzly rain and a bitterly cold breeze, something that is hard to forget as I charge across the rooftops and jump the gaps between buildings. My limbs are cold, but my blood is hot in my veins, and the contrast is making each stride increasingly more difficult.

It doesn't take me long to reach my target. Crouching down on the adjacent building and begin inspecting the darkened windows. The people on the street below are loud, threatening to pull my focus. Lights flicker on in other apartments but before me is Alexander Nephus' apartment.

Shortly after I made it back from my run this morning, death threat in tow, my phone buzzed with a notification, an alert of movement from his studio.

Pulling up the footage immediately I watched him leave, no longer looking flustered from his lateness, as I'd previously witnessed, but instead looking troubled, like something was gnawing away at him.

I used those same cameras to follow him home and there's where I am now, perched on the adjacent building watching his windows.

The lights are off.

"Curious." I pull out my phone, checking the cameras. Since his arrival I haven't seen him leave. But still, I scroll through the videos, finding nothing.

I tuck the device away and make to jump the short distance from the rooftop to the fire escape. Descending down the ladder takes all of five seconds. The window isn't hard to open either, it's as if the whole place is inviting me in.

Something isn't right.

I pause just before I enter. Listening. Waiting for any sound or sign that he is still awake and in the building.

My foot brushes the floor of what appears to be his office and I land without so much as a thud; pausing to see if he might be hiding in the dark. The immediate feeling of dread that I get from the room has every hair on my body standing to attention and every nerve ending lights with electricity.

His walls are painted a light brown with bookshelves lining nearly every available space, every shelf is filled with texts and volumes too big for anyone to read. Wherever there's available space whether that be on the floor or any spare space on his desk there are even more books; client files lay scattered on the overflowing desk. With deft fingers I move a few skimming over any details that may help me.

"How can one work in such a state?" I ask in a whisper but find nothing of use.

The door silently swings open when I move on from his office and tiptoe out into the hallway, careful of the old squeaking floorboards. The walls are filled with artwork mostly of buildings and pieces of unique architecture.

"Talk about bringing work home with you," I mutter.

Unlike his office, the rest of his house is meticulously clean and organised. Everything has a place, and everything has been dusted to within an inch of its life. His living room is cosy and filled with multiple pieces of unique antique furniture.

A large fireplace takes up one portion of the wall and part of the rug that might as well be carpet it's so large. Another bookcase sits in one corner, this one considerably neater than those in his study. Plants fill any empty spaces on the windowsills and side tables and several photographs are hung about the walls, each with different people but all smiling brightly at the camera.

Earthy tones bring comfort into the large space, with a decorated archway on one side leading to the impressive modern kitchen, a contrast to his almost cottage-style living room.

A small side lamp clicks on, revealing Alexander Nephus himself, sitting in a brown leather armchair, one leg crossed over the other.

"I should at least thank you for not trashing the place, I suppose."

"You're welcome, Alexander Nephus," I reply, my voice dropping a few octaves. I'm not surprised in the least to see him. I could hear him breathing the instant I stepped into the room.

"Although the water dripping from your cloak, I could do without." There is a brief pause as he takes me in, his eyes taking in every inch of my haunting figure.

"Well, I can only imagine what you're here for, given the phone call I received from Melanie just a few days ago."

"She already told me about Roman."

"Of that I am aware. So then, why are you here?"

"And give the game away?" When he simply stares at me, I continue, "I have reason to believe that you're a high-ranking member of Dawnya. I'm just here for proof."

"The truth? How refreshing," he mumbles, "you might as well sit I have a feeling we'll be here for a while. You want a drink?"

Not heeding his request, I stayed standing in the middle of his living room. "No."

"You know I can't tell you anything right?" he says.

"I am very aware that you can't, but that doesn't mean that you won't," I grin.

"What? You plan to torture it out of me?" He doesn't seem the least bit fazed by the notion, he in fact relaxes back further into his chair.

"How un-original." I shake my head and he chuckles.

"My apologies for appearing so dull."

The air is charged with inescapable tension for a brief few moments, the only sound is our combined inhales and exhales. Posturing and sizing up my opponent is not something foreign to me, but each is different. It takes me mere seconds to take in everything he has to offer. His eyes don't leave my hooded silhouette, but mine take in every scrap of information that I can.

The books on his bookcases, the titles of each are mostly related to art and architecture, the bindings of which are mostly leather. *Old tomes then.* The newspaper on the table next to him, with today's date; at the half filled in crossword and the leaking pen sitting on top of it.

The wooden fireplace with yesterday's logs still lying-in ashes at the bottom, at the slither of burnt paper mingled with those ashes.

"Find anything interesting?" he asks, finally breaking the growing tension.

"I always do. The paper in the fireplace, what did it contain?"

"A manifest." *The truth.*

"And what did this manifest encompass?" I counter.

"A shipment of logs from the North mountains. The wood is strong and is easily an architect's favourite to use." *A lie. But still a good one.*

I cross my arms over my chest. He simply stares at the black mass around my head.

"You seem to be tense," he challenges.

"I just don't appreciate being lied to."

"Then why did you ask if you already knew the answer?" he opposes.

"I want to see what kind of male you really are. Or man," I answer, noting his rounded mortal ears.

"And your assessment?"

"You're loyal. Maybe too much and possibly for the wrong cause. A terrible liar. Artistic, open-minded yet arrogant and clearly seem to be someone who is lonely, given the pictures of friends and the lack of a family in your home. Tell me, am I getting warmer?" I grin leaning forward.

He grinds his teeth together but doesn't reply.

"Just from the look in your eyes, I can tell that that manifest contained something other than the Northern pine logs you just lied about," I sneer, his eyes have in fact darted back and forth to the fireplace, not leaving me for too long.

He waves a hand to me, prompting me to weave my tale.

"It was about a ship, the name of which is most certainly peculiar *'The Revenge'* as if it was designed to get a certain someone's attention. That ship was sailing out to sea, its destination was to the Southern Continent carrying nothing more than its Captain and his supplies."

He doesn't reply, so I continue.

"It's the headline from today's news about how the one-man craft took to the open water about a week ago and never made it to his 'supposed' destination. Isn't that correct?" Although he can't see my eyes I stare straight into his own.

The deepness of the blue there looks like the darkest of oceans. Still, he chooses to remain tight-lipped.

"My theory is that Roman took this boat, claiming he was traversing across the sea to other shores further South of here. But found his destination sooner than everybody else thought." I pause for breath, "So, somewhere over the Avak is where he will have met his transport detail into Salacia and I'm willing to bet that that manifest contained the coordinates he needed to find their location. But I'm also assuming that you didn't look at those coordinates for this particular reason, as to not allow somebody to chase after him. Somebody like me. But Roman knew. I suppose I did give away my intention the night you had your people shoot me, but for all he knew, I was supposed to be dead. So how did he know someone was still hunting him? And why did the mighty leader land his own people in the shit, just to save his own skin?"

He claps slowly, each sound calculated. It's grating.

"Well, you are certainly worth every penny aren't you."

I scoff. "Don't patronise me."

"I'm not actually. I'm genuinely impressed. Not many people would've been able to put that together in such a short amount of time."

I grin at that; he's just confirmed my suspicions and fell into my trap without me even trying. Exactly as I wanted. I turn and walk back to his office; he hurries to follow.

"Where are you going?"

"It's been a pleasure Alex, but I have a newspaper to buy," I tell him before hopping back out the window and onto the fire escape, he watches as if in shock that I left him unscathed.

But he's not my real target.

At least not tonight anyway.

I sit on my bed and read the article over and over until the sun rises and I curse myself for losing yet another night's sleep.

A local fisherman from Lefki had found the sailing boat in a nearby cove, bobbing to and fro, without an anchor to stop it from drifting. He'd boarded the boat only to find it empty.

"We need to go to Lefki," I announced to the two males talking in the kitchen, after deciding that we need to find this unnamed fisherman.

"And why is that?" Rich asks back.

"Because I'm following another thread, and it leads me to Lefki."

"It's like four hours away," Rich groans, only because he knows, out of the two of us, he'll be the one driving.

"And it's barely even seven in the morning," Declan adds in a grumble. He had let his guard down when I'd been shot. Built his walls back and then tore them back down when I stayed out all night, and now seems to be back to being sour all over again. I've never met a male who is so hot and cold. I'm not sure which side of him I prefer. The stoic brooding side, or the caring and sweet. I do wish he would pick one though and stick to it. It's making for some very crazy dreams when I do finally find time to sleep in the evening.

"I didn't ask for you to come and I don't see the problem here. Will you take me or not?"

They both glance at each.

"Yeah, but we have a few things to do today. Can it wait until later?"

Narrowing my eyes at the both of them I'm tempted to ask them just exactly what they are doing. The story Rich weaved about his 'date' didn't add up. But when I tried digging in further the details became more and more clouded, like he didn't even know them himself. Ever since I've been picking up on the little things. Like the glances between each other and the hushed conversations. "Fine. I could do with some sleep anyway."

"Elle. Where did you go last night?" Rich asks. Pausing, I turn back to face him.

"I was following up on a lead."

He doesn't believe me. I can see it plainly on his face. It's like he can see right through me. "And?" he questions.

"And it turned out to be a dead end," I lie, testing the waters. I want to see where they go with this. Wanting to see their reactions. It's clear that the trust between us is weakening.

"Then why the rush to get to Lefki?" Declan adds. I stifle the smirk threatening to give my intentions away. Glancing between them, they both watch me with a matching predatory expression, eyebrows down, eyes hardening, lips pressed into firm lines. It's very reminiscent of Reuben Ostair. The straightening of my spine gives way to my training. I almost cave and tell them the truth. Instead, I bit my tongue.

"What's with the third degree?" Both sets of eyebrows rise. "I am just trying to do my job, there will be a lot of failures and only some success, but it will work out in the end. Or did you both forget?" I challenge, clasping my hands behind my back. Watching them flounder for excuses is far more entertaining than I first thought and its more of a test to not laugh at their expressions. But that same glimmer of suspicion from earlier, flares back to life within me.

When they don't answer me, I give them my best smile and retreat back to my room. Questioning everything that they have ever said and done.

The drive out to Lefki is beautiful to say the least. Lush green fields border the car nearly the entire way, and it's not long before we find that cove where *'The Revenge'* was found. A sister river to the one flowing through Ansrutas cascades over the rocky cliffs, down into the cove meeting the waves below.

I had asked Rich to stop the car so I can have a look around, but from this high up all I can see is the tide crashing against the cliff face, and the miles upon miles of ocean.

"So, this is where they found it?" Rich yells, over the sounds of the wind and sea.

"Yeah." I point to the area having another quick look. "Come on, let's go talk to that fisherman."

The closer we draw to the town the louder the gulls caw from the cliffs and Lefki's docks. Salty air washes in from across the sea and the scent of fish is heavy, the odour lingering on the bobbing boats tied to the docks.

Lefki gets its trade from the major cities nearby, Larissa – the capital – and Ansrutas and although it offers the country fifty per cent of what it catches the village is in a total state of decay. The sea spray slowly chips away at the stone of the walkways and buildings built in, and around, the natural cliffs.

"So, what does this fisherman look like?" Rich asks, looking around at the people passing us by, on the cobbled and damp streets. Declan hasn't said much since we left Ansrutas, and when he does, it's strictly kept between Rich and himself.

"I don't know, it's not like there was a picture of him in the paper," I replied, marching further South closer to the docks, desperate for the walk. The car drive was torturous. Not only for the lack of talking and obvious tension but I didn't exactly have a lot of leg room sitting in the back as I was.

"So, we are going to be here all day?" Declan snaps.

Biting my tongue, I hold in my snappy reply and glare at him instead, "I can and will do this on my own since the two of you clearly don't want to be here. Don't wait up." I turn to walk away.

Footstep hurry to catch up to me. I turn to see Declan keeping pace with me.

"What are you doing?"

"If you think I'm going to let you loose on these underserving people then you have another thing coming."

"I'm not here to hurt anyone. Although for you I might just make the exception," I growl at him.

"Ok, well you two go and find him and I'll go find somewhere for us to sleep tonight," Rich calls after us.

"It's not going to take…" I begin, turning around to face him but he's already gone. Twirling in circles I looked everywhere, and he's nowhere to be found.

"How did he do that?" I breathe.

"Magic," Declan drawls without a trace of humour, my own expression matches his. Once again, we seemed to have slotted back into despising each other. I roll my eyes and begin walking away, not caring if he keeps pace with me. The silence between us is tense, but I pay it no mind as I begin glancing down alleys and baron streets feeling a sense of foreboding caress my senses. The hairs on my arm stand on end. We are being watched.

"Are we going to keep creeping around in the shadows or are we going to actually do something?" Declan grumbles, jumping me.

"Why don't you go and find Rich and leave me to do this by myself? Because I have better things to do than suffer through your emotional constipation. I understand you hate me Declan. You're not the first and you won't be the last. But right now, I have a job to do and you lingering in the background like a grumpy darkening cloud is not helping, so either shut up or leave." His eyes widened for a spell. He may be my handler, but I have enough free speech now to tell him to do one if I think he is bringing the investigation down.

"You're just pissed because I actually thought of a better idea than walking through the streets all night," he sneers stepping up into my face.

"Just lead the way then, sniffer hound," I bite back.

He doesn't take kindly to the nickname that much is evident by the anger on his face but uses his nose exactly as I thought he would, stopping outside of a rundown pub. I side-eye him but choose not to comment when he waves towards the door. The noise of the patrons can be heard from down the street and the dimly glowing lights are welcoming. Pushing the wooden door aside I step into the overwhelming warmth of the little pub.

Any and all conversation has died on the tongue, and everyone stops to look at the door. I pull my hood back and soften my face, Declan stands close to my back as I do. When a voice calls out to us.

"Aella! Declan!" Rich yells from the furthest corner, a cup of ale in his hand; drunk off his arse.

Conversations pick back up once more, and I gain enough confidence to step further into the room. Keeping my eyes locked on Rich as swigs from his glass.

"Is he joking?" I grumble on my approach.

"What the fuck are you doing?" Declan snarls, leaning in so they are practically nose to nose. I know those on the tables closest have stopped their own conversations once again to listen into ours, I can see the way they stiffen and lean towards our table.

"I found us all a room and then I came down for a drink," he smiles sweetly.

My brows rise as I take in the state of the place. Sticky tables and even stickier floors. The walls look just as tired as the waitress behind the bar and surely the windows are more for decoration than anything else given that one cannot even see the street beyond them.

"And was it necessary for you to have so many?" Declan asks, eyeing the multiple glasses.

With Rich's drunkenness and Declan's anger, I manage to creep away from the pair of them and out the doors back onto the street. The stale, alcohol-filled air had become too stifling and sickly, and my own anger threatened to spill over at the idiocy of the situation.

Declan comes out moments later with Rich slung over his shoulder, nodding towards the building next to us.

"Come on, let's get you to bed," he grunts.

"I appreciate the offer my man, but you're not my type." Rich's eyes meet mine, the silver in them shining so bright they nearly swallow the black. "Now you!" He points at me, "I wouldn't mind!" He giggles.

"Rich," Declan growls in a warning.

"What? Just because you won't doesn't mean I can't try." He winks at me, swaying gently with Declan's movements.

"Enough!" Declan warns again.

Stopping outside the door to the house next to the pub Declan jostles Rich in an attempt to hear the keys in his pocket.

"Is that my arse?" Rich hiccups, slapping what is in fact not his arse, but Declan's.

"I am *this* close to dropping you on the floor," he growls again, and I can't help the silent laughter that follows.

After fishing the key from Rich's pocket — which was no easy task with him flung over Declan's shoulder — we finally enter the darkened room. Draughty and cold with a similar style to those we used in Ellwey all those weeks ago, wooden floor covered in dust and a dark navy rug, too thin curtains that drift noiselessly — no doubt from the wind seeping in from the windows — wooden furnishings and ... one bed.

"He really is having a laugh now," I snarl, "did he even ask for a room for all three of us?"

"No!" Rich yells wiggling on Declan's shoulder, who doesn't hesitate to drop him on the mattress.

"Fantastic," he drawls.

Walking around the room doesn't take very long. Although we are in a house, I assume the upstairs is another apartment, he probably should've booked that one too.

"Wait, wait, wait..." Rich sits up, slurring his words, "People talk."

"Well spotted," I quip.

"People talk about Albert, you big nasty," he slurs.

I fold my arms over each other and take a steading breath reciting to myself how it is forbidden to physically assault a handler no matter how much I want to punch him in the face for putting my mission at risk once again.

Declan kneels down talking slowly, listening to Rich's explanation about how the people he was sitting with downstairs were talking about the article written in the paper.

Before he became too inebriated, he was actually quite useful.

Albert's house is situated at the far end of the town, a little white cottage on the outskirts of the woods.

"Thank you, Rich," Declan answers, patting his head.

"Stay here I will go. If too many of us go he may flee," I mutter heading for the door. He doesn't stop me. Nor does he argue which surprises me most. He's probably just thankful we no longer have to be in the others' presence. I take the walk up there to sort through my feelings. Something I've never had much of. But being with both of them for so long has made my humanity surface and it will likely get me killed if I don't get them under control soon. I need to place that black veil of control over myself once more before it's too late.

The sky is orange and red with the setting sun as the waves crash against the sea wall, but the streets are devoid of people, only the gulls make noise. The feeling of the salt air blowing through my hair is calming and I take some time to admire the sunset. It's warming and the quaint town behind me is cosy, something that is still so strange for me to wrap my head around.

I have only ever known the Fort and its harshness. Yes, we have been taught how others live their lives and we've seen it first-hand when we are sent out into the world. But there has always been something to pull us back to the Fort. Our handlers have been that solidifying force. Encouraging the ways and disciplines that we have been taught. Rich and Declan don't seem to be inclined to do so and my mission is suffering because of it. The lack of discipline has me slacking and yet it doesn't feel wrong.

I focus once more on the waves in the distance and on the setting sun just before it kisses the horizon. Understanding that this is what life is supposed to be like. These little moments build up into memories and it's better to do them with the people you love.

But I don't have any and I don't have the luxury to make those memories for myself. When this is all said and done, I will go back to the Fort and live out my days doing what I do best. At what I thought I enjoyed.

The stench of salt and fish mingles together pulling me back from the deepest corners of my mind.

'It's time to put the mask back on.' That sinister little voice hisses at me. I understand which one it means, and I begin the practice of shutting out my emotions all over again. It's harder this time. Images of black and silver and even fiery hazel eyes come forth. As if trying to block me from doing it. But I push through. I have to. Until all I feel is dark. A void without end. My senses sharpen once more. Back to the deadly assassin I was born to be.

A startling scent of iron joins the scent of fish and salt first. Enormous amounts of it flood my nostrils. Blood.

I pick up the pace pushing myself into a slight jog following the scent as best I can, allowing it to lead me to a small, secluded cottage on the outskirts of the main village. Exactly where the patrons said it would be.

The white painted walls are dirty with lack of care, window boxes overflowing with flowers that blow in the soft breeze and a wild garden with a small fish-filled pond.

There are obvious signs of a break-in, the door has been shattered, the wood has been split in half and hangs loosely from the hinges. The smell of blood is thick in the air here.

Pulling my gun from its holster on my thigh I begin to take tentative steps up to the little stone path to the door. The fishing gnomes seem to watch my every step as though they know what I'm walking into.

The smell is overwhelming, I have to breathe through my mouth just so I can concentrate on something else.

The hall is covered in blood, most of it is on the stairs where it looks as though someone was trying to get away from an assailant only to be dragged back down, the trail of blood leads towards the back of the house.

I do a quick check of the rooms to my left, away from the blood. Just in case whoever broke in is still here rummaging through his things. When I'm satisfied, I head to the right side of the cottage. My steps are silent, and my breath is perfectly even. Not even my heart has changed its beat. The true test that my humanity is back in its box.

The first room on the right is the dining room, the blood trail is thick in here as if the victim had been lying on the floor for some time before being dragged further into the back of the cottage. The cream carpet is overflowing with the thick, sticky liquid, it bubbles under my boot as I try to step around it.

He may already be dead at this point. I assess the situation around me. *And if he isn't, he will be soon.*

Still taking my time I continue on pushing through the broken wooden doors, leading right into the kitchen. The tile here too is drowning in blood, it thickens towards the back of the room.

It's then I hear a gurgling groan from behind the kitchen counter.

Spying the broken back door, I conclude that whoever wanted this man dead is long gone. The temperature of the room is cold enough to say it's been open for hours.

The old fisherman sits on the cold tiled floor, leaning against the counter with his blood pouring from his torso. A hole has been gouged into the centre of his chest so deep his slow-beating heart is just visible under the shredded skin. His ribs protrude through his flesh and blood covers every inch of his face and beard. Bits of tissue and muscle scatter the floor around him.

This may be the most brutal death I've witnessed to date.

I crouch down to his level, watching him wheeze and spurt out more blood. He doesn't seem to notice I'm there at all. He's too far, too lost in his own pain to register anything anymore. It would be a mercy to put him out of his misery.

"Whatever you know. Someone wanted to keep it a secret," I mutter, using a rag to cover my nose from the stench, looking up and down his body for any sign of who or rather what did this to him.

He speaks in a tongue I've never heard. But it's the last thing he ever does say. His diming eyes focused on one point on the floor before him. The man's attention glazes over and his open chest rattles one last time.

His visible heart stutters its last beat before deflating for the final time.

"Brother Damien, see his soul to the Golden Fields," I mutter a prayer, closing his eyes.

Standing up I look around the small kitchen, ignoring the body now lying before me. The attack can only have happened tonight, but with his injury, there's no way he could've survived more than an hour, two at the most. The draft wafting in from the back door pulls me to the shattered, wooden threshold. Bloody-clawed footprints lead into the woods beyond the grounds of the house. I can smell each one.

I make for the door, careful to step over the glass. Just because the prints lead into the forest it doesn't mean it's gone far.

The forest is too quiet when I enter, as though it is devoid of life, completely silent even the night insects don't dare to chirp, and I can't shake the feeling as though I'm being watched through the dense, moist foliage.

Whatever this thing is, it's heavy, each paw print is deeper than any animal I've ever seen before.

Keeping my steps light and even I advance quickly over the mossy, spongy ground following the scent of blood, through the trees right to the sound of running water.

The air is frigid and the sound of hooves running takes my attention. No paws follow, whatever this creature is, it has had its fill for the night if it's not hunting. Unless it has its eyes on another target. Every few steps there's a sound. The breaking of a twig. The skittering of rocks.

I'm being hunted.

I don't know which direction to look, so I keep moving. My heart now beating furiously. The hunter and hunted instinct is kicking in.

It's not long before I reach a large clearing, bathed in the purest moonlight, which is reflected in the lake's rippling water. Mossy rocks and ferns surround the water's edge and fireflies dance around in the air seemingly content with the lack of other animals. A large natural waterfall tumbles into the lake at one side and is clearly the running water I followed to get here, the foam and bubbles it creates in the dark water flow quickly downstream, before disappearing into the trees.

The calm of the water and the quiet of the trees make me quickly forget about the eerie sensation I had when walking over here. A cooling breeze wafts between the trunks rustling the leaves, and the sky darkens further above me. Clouds roll in, foreboding, signalling a storm is on its way.

Scanning the treeline, it's not hard to see why this is the perfect little oasis. That is until I get to the flatter part of the shoreline.

A beast the same size as a small bear stands lurking on the shoreline. Its black skin is covered in tiny tufts of black and brown fur, and small trusses of fluff peek out around its upright ears and long snout, much like that of a wolf's face. Its tail is no more than a stub. Its snout wrinkles into a snarl.

Water and blood drip from its maw and its yellow eyes glow brightly in the dark mimicking the fireflies.

And they're looking right at me.

CHAPTER NINETEEN
PLAYTIME

My spine straightens and my muscles tense.

Frozen in fear.

I've never seen anything like this before. It doesn't look natural. The scars across its back are deep and white. Healed over but they look years old, and I begin to wonder where it has come from.

Those golden eyes flicker from my face to the weapon in my hand and it snarls again showing those sets of deadly flesh-ripping teeth.

My heart jumps into my throat.

I take one slow step back. I don't exactly know what will set this creature off, but I also know that I cannot lead it back to the village. Especially if I want to prove Declan right when I said I wasn't here to hurt anyone.

It watches my retreat with a fixed interest and the muscles in its shoulder twitch. It's holding itself back from pouncing for what reason I can't fathom. Any other animal would have attacked or retreated by now. This thing, whatever it is, is different. It seems to be weighing out its options before acting. But from here it's too far away to catch me without a lengthy chase.

All I can think about right now is how I can't take my eyes off it.

Playtime

A breeze comes from around the trees howling around the trunks forcing me to close my eyes as it carries pine needles and leaves with it. I cover my face with my arm struggling to keep my breath as the storm strengthens. Little drops of rain fall from the cloud filled sky with coverage so thick it's as though the stars don't want to witness my demise.

When I can see again, I turn back to the shore, but the beast is gone. All that remains are its paw prints scored deep in the damp soil. The rustling of the wind through the trees makes it near impossible to hear if it is approaching me through the brush or not. But still, I whirl turning my back on the lake instead of the dark forest.

This creature is unlike any I've seen before. I could tell by its paw prints; I knew that it would be different from a bear. Built to be just as heavy but the paws are much more like a wolfs', only larger. Its eyes glowed yellow like a shifter's but there was something off about them. Something is missing.

The wind whispers through the trees again, softer this time, while I scan the brush. Ferns blow this way and that, but there's still no sign of the creature.

Straining my ears, I hear the buzzing wings of insects and the near-silent flapping of birds retreating further into the trees, none of them are what I need. The gushing of the waterfall covers all other sounds making it near impossible to find the patter of paws, but the vibrations are there, thudding across the soft ground.

"I know you're stalking me," I whisper into the air, slowly reaching for the blade in my boot. "Come, show me those unearthly eyes."

My fingers curl around the handle. The thunder of paws charges and a shadow rushes through the underbrush. The flash of yellow is the only thing I see as it pounces from the trees. Releasing the breath from my lungs I tuck and roll out of its way. It lands with a thud, skidding through the mud, and its claws dig through the ground, pulling up clumps as it tries to steady itself.

I know I won't be able to take this beast one to one. But that doesn't mean I can't damage it enough so I can escape.

With my heart in my throat and that instinct telling me to run like Death is chasing me, I raise my gun to its head. Just as I tense my finger to pull the trigger it jumps again taking me down to the ground with it.

I should've run when I had the chance, is all I can't think as the air is knocked out of me, and I'm tossed from side to side. Its jaw lock around my forearm tearing through the flesh. My scream is bloodcurdling, something I've never even heard from myself before, but it's all forgotten as I begin to feel a fire scorching through my veins.

My gun is tossed to one side in the dirt.

Bringing my leg up I kick it in the stomach. It does nothing but make it bite down harder. I can feel its teeth scraping against the bone of my forearm. The agonising scream that tears through my throat no doubt will echo for miles.

Gripping the blade tight I plunge it into the creature's shoulder, listening to it howl out in pain.

I take the distraction and kick my knee into its stomach again, pushing it off me. It lands with a growl on its side, scrambling to stand, my knife still sticking out from its shoulder. The blade stand proud sitting deep in the muscle with blood gushing from the wound.

My own arm shakes with the shock, the very same one Melanie had opened not a few days ago. With my limbs shaking it's difficult to keep my breathing steady enough to keep a clear head. I eye my knife, if I could just distract it for long enough, I could pull it out and then I'd at least be armed.

It takes one step forward, then two, stalking me, toying with me. It's gaze never wavers even as it lowers to the ground ready to pounce on me once again.

I mirror it, taking a step back, prolonging my life for a few more seconds. My stomach roils knowing I'll be lost in this forest as nothing more than a meal for this hellhound.

"I'm so dead," I groan. Snatching my much smaller curved knife from my belt. It won't do much to this bulky beast but it's better than nothing it all.

It growls at me, but something else growls louder. I turn to the side and something fast and white blurs past my vision, hitting the creature in the shoulder and it goes toppling towards the water of the lake and my knife comes free. I dive for it, holding it with a shaky hand.

I turn to see a snow leopard of the most brilliant white crouching there snarling at the beast.

"Declan," I breathe. He's placed himself in between the creature and I, with his hackles raised and snout wrinkled in snarl. The flick of his fluffy ear is the only indicator that he has heard me. He backs up one step, his heavy tail just brushes across my knees. "We need to go now." I urge, watching the creature stand and turn back to us.

Declan doesn't move.

"Declan," I try again, but the beats pounces, swiping violently towards Declan's face.

With him being so broad and tall in his human form it gives Declan's animal a bigger stature than that of a normal snow leopard, but he's still not big enough to fight this mammoth creature. Not on his own.

Declan dodges and jumps on the things back.

I take the distraction to find my gun. Partially buried under the mud I snatch it up and aim for the beast's head. Declan is thrown from its back, and it once again turns to me. I don't hesitate, I shoot the first bullet it hit directly between its eyes, and then just falls to the dirt.

Declan eyes me and I can practically hear his thoughts.

"Shit," I hiss, stepping back, keeping my gun raised I fire again and again and again, but the bullets don't penetrate the creature's skin.

"Run!" I call out, turning towards the trees, Declan fumbles to follow.

In my panic I've forgotten the way back. I can only hope that the way becomes clear, and I can lead us back to the cottage. As unethical as it is, we can use the corpse there as a distraction.

We push past ferns and rotting stumps from fallen beech trees. Declan keeps pace with me, despite being much faster.

The sound of thundering paw prints follows behind us, growing louder and louder the closer it gets. Before long the beast is upon us.

I jump into a roll avoiding the creature as it goes sailing over my head. I hit the ground so hard it knocks the air from my lungs but when the world is the right way up again, I continue charging away from the creature in such a desperate attempt to keep my pathetic life going,

Running up a sodden embankment it's no surprise when I lose my footing on the wet moss. "Fuck," I yell as my head bounces off tree roots and I tumble in a tangle of limbs down a muddy hill, blood dripples from my temple. Declan is hot on my heels, growling, urging me to keep going.

The beast, slipping and falling too, crashes into a boulder at the bottom of the hill, grunting and panting as it stands, its blood smearing over the rock, before launching itself at Declan. Its teeth sink into his shoulder, and he roars out in pain.

The beast tugs at his fur, thrashing on his back.

Adrenaline and anxiety course through me. Looking around on the forest floor I search for something, anything that I can use as a weapon.

Declan manages to throw it off and turns to face it head-on.

"Declan move!" I yell and swing a heavy branch, cracking the beast in the jaw. "Run!" I turn and begin running back up the embankment.

Disorientated, the wolf stumbles around, giving us time to get away.

"I'm so going to die of infection," I pant looking at my arm, now covered in mud along with its spittle and my blood.

The look Declan gives me says it all. *'Now is not the time.'* Though he does eye my wound like it personally offends him.

"We can't outrun it!" I yell, "well you can." I turn to him slowing down a little. He growls and nips at my legs telling me to keep going. "If I can distract it, that will give you enough time to get away and get help."

He snarls and gives me a look that says, *'Don't even think about it.'*

Once again, he snaps at my legs keeping me running.

"Ok, new plan." I think for a moment my mind is racing with adrenaline and yet seemingly blank of ideas, all I can seem to focus on is the sound of the creature's ginormous paws tearing up the ground, gaining on us once again. "The lake," I pant. "We need to get back to the lake."

Digging his paws harder into the ground he picks up his pace and the beast hunts again, throwing itself at him.

"WATCH OUT!" I scream shoving into him, he stumbles over a tree root while I receive a slash on my upper arm. I scream as I stumble down to the forest floor.

The beast prowls behind us snarling, growing more and more ferocious and agitated. Saliva and some sort of black substance drip from its jowls. The hound's muscles flex and retract, shimming its shoulders like a cat waiting for an opening to pounce. Its eyes filled with malice.

"That's not a normal animal," I whisper, completely astounded and utterly terrified looking into those eyes. They glow like shifters' eyes, but there is not an ounce of humanity behind them. I shuffle back until my back hits a tree and the beasts step forward its jowls snapping in my face. I can't take my eyes off of those killer teeth and whisper when it step closer still.

It howls pierce my ears at Declan rips into its neck. His claws dig into its shoulders keeping him steady as he begins pulling its flesh. Despite the pain and blood loss I push myself back up, panting heavily, I run in the opposite direction to the two fighting animals.

Another snarl tears through the air. The fear of being torn apart is steadily rising the longer the animal chases us.

Declan is by my side within seconds. Both of us burn with the strain of the air heaving through our lungs. The trees whizzed by us in nothing more than a blur of green and brown. Tree roots and rock splinter through our path making the ascent more difficult, the moonlight guides our way.

"Keep going, Fury!" Declan snarls, gripping my hand. He's shifted mid-run. But I can't think about it now as the gushing of the waterfall appears in front of us. The running water is the loudest I've ever heard.

My steps falter as yet another root appears in my path. The agony and the blood loss makes my stomach roil as they fight with my adrenaline. "Declan!" I whine through my teeth. Heights have never bothered me but suddenly the thought of jumping over such a large waterfall has my head spinning.

"No! The waterfall is up ahead, we can make it." His face is full of determination and his brows furrow further together.

Roots and small trees snap and crack as they are forced apart by the beast behind us. The terrain changes from wet dirt and uneven ground to slippery mossy rock, as we break the treeline at the top of the waterfall.

A roar vibrates through the air, sounding slightly more distant now.

"JUMP!" Our feet leave the ground as we soar over the deafening waterfall, without even thinking about the height. A silent scream bubbles up inside as we drop. We each take a deep breath as we descend. The height has my heart stuttering, and we hurtle straight down towards the water.

Declan's hand never once leaves mine.

I shut my eyes feeling weightless and sickened by this experience before I'm plunged into darkness and shockingly cold temperatures of the darkened water.

Opening my eyes all I see is black and my immediate reaction is to surface and take in air. Something wraps around my waist pulling me down further and I panic. My breath burns in my lungs, and I start kicking frantically. First, a wild beast on land tries to kill me, now an unknown water being is.

I look down to Declan's urgent gaze, he's shaking his head 'No' and I allow him to continue pulling me down, surprised when he wraps his arms around me holding me in place. He points to the surface, and I can see the rippling figure of the creature looking down at the water scanning the depths to find us. Bits of rock and grass hit the water's surface, pulled up from the ground as it skidded to a stop. I turn and nod my head, even though my lungs are screaming.

It takes so long for the creature to give up. Blackness has started to seep into my vision and my lungs beg for air. We watch as it finally turns away and when I try to pull out of his hold to swim to the surface, he tightens his grip still shaking his head no. My eyes roll in their sockets and my heart flutters as though it's ready to take its final beat and yet I can't seem to tell him otherwise. I follow my instinct to trust him and take his hand, allowing him to guide me closer to the waterfall. We surface under its unforgiving spray, gasping for breath, receiving mouths full of water in return.

"Are you trying to drown me?" I sputter, before his tanned hand covers my mouth, silencing me.

"Don't tempt me," he whispers, so close to my face his breath warms my shivering skin.

He leads me beyond the fall into a small cavern hidden behind it where a tiny ledge made entirely from rock protrudes from the rest of the wall, not exactly designed for anyone to sit on, but nevertheless, he lifts me up and places me down. Panting hard I rest my head back against the rock, the pain in my body all but forgotten in the face of nearly drowning.

Through my wet eyelashes, I see that he's able to stand up fully under here and he's completely naked, and bleeding.

"Declan you're bleeding," I yelp, pulling his shoulder towards me. Once again that tanned hand is over my mouth silencing me.

His head is tucked into my shoulder as he tries to catch his breath and I watch in fascination as his broad back expands up and down. Gently I gather water in one hand and run it along the teeth marks on his shoulder. He shivers at the drops but doesn't stop me as I continue cleaning his skin. Neither of us speaks for a long while until he pulls at the ruined sleeve of my cloak, ripping the entire sleeve off in one fluid motion, revealing my wounds that are still gushing with blood.

Declan leans down close to my face; our noses nearly brush together; his eyes find the cut on my temple and my breathing stalls again. "We need to get these cleaned because it will follow the scent of blood if we don't," he whispers, his breath tickles my ear and cheek and warms the soft skin on my neck, his thumb swipes gently at the blood on my face.

Not trusting my voice, I can only nod in response and watch as he tears at the fabric to make a few gauzes. The simple action alone has my blood warming and forgetting that I'm currently soaking wet and shivering.

"Elle, you need to be as quiet as you can. This is probably going to hurt a lot," he breathes again, pressing a whisper of a kiss on my cheek before dunking my arm under the waterfall.

He used my name.

A roaring in my ears drowns out everything else he said. The sound of it rolling off his tongue was as divine as wine made by the gods themselves.

"Bastard!" I hissed as he plunges my arm back into the cold water. He shushes me chuckling a little, resting his other hand on my cheek, guiding my head down to his shoulder.

"Keep quiet," he chuckles in my ear, "it's going to be ok." The stubble on his jaw scrapes harshly against my cheek and yet I can't think of a better sensation.

"It's hard to do that when I want to rip my arm off and punch you with it," I grit through the pain. Vividly picturing it.

His chest rumbles with a silent laugh, scooping up some water in his large hand and splashing it across my upper arm at a claw mark I hadn't even realised was there. Pain lashes up my arm once again.

"Now I really want to punch you," I groan, gripping his other arm, digging my fingers into his skin.

"Easy," he murmurs softly, the rumble in his forgiving voice is soothing me much better than the water cleaning my wounds and running down my skin. "Just one more." He splashes my arm once again and picks up some of the makeshift gauzes. He dunks them into the water washing off the blood and saliva and begins binding my wounds together, tying them off tightly.

"Better?" he asks again. I pull away to look at the patched-up job he's done. "They might scar…" he trails off, gently running his fingertips down the rest of the exposed and untainted skin on my arm, leaving goosebumps in their wake.

"Considering he bit down to my bone I'd say it's more than likely, yes," I breathe. He winces at my words, and I accept his closeness when he presses his cheek against my own, wrapping his arms around me in a tight hug. His body radiates a warmth similar to that when you sit idle under the sun, something I'm all too greedy to steal from him. You know, just to stop my teeth from chattering.

"I'm sorry," he whispers.

"What for?" I ask, pulling away to look into his eyes, only to find them downcast.

"Not pulling you out of the way." He looks at the cut on my upper arm and my mind goes blank. If he hadn't been here at all I would've been in the belly of that beast.

"Declan, you saved me. Without you following me I would have been carrion. I'm grateful you showed up when you did."

He winces, "You heard me?"

I smile devilishly, "of course I did. The beast was by the lake, but I knew something was stalking me."

"I wasn't stalking you," he scowls.

I pull him closer and wrap my legs around his waist, he doesn't fight me, instead, he rests one hand on my thigh squeezing it softly. The cold of the water and the rock wall behind me is bone-chilling, I've already lost enough blood to make me feel cold as it is. But the look in his eyes might just be worse than being chased through the woods by that monster.

"Do not apologise for something that wasn't your fault," I reassured him.

Declan's warmth wraps around me and stops me from shaking quite as much, he doesn't seem to be affected by the chill even as he stands hip deep in the ripples, bubbles froth and foam from the fall behind him.

He huffs out a heavy sigh and I can tell he's beating himself up and there's nothing I can say at this moment that will make him understand that even if that vengeful beast hadn't been chasing me, I would've fought to my last breath to keep him safe.

My breathing hitches at my unspoken, unthinkable epiphany.

"What is it?"

"Nothing. I just... Do you think it's gone?" I whisper against his lips which lay just a hair's breadth away from mine. As if on cue a howl bursts through the night, echoing into the distance. The creature is most definitely circling the shoreline searching for us.

"No," Declan grins, sliding his hands up to my waist, pressing himself against me.

My chattering teeth were quiet enough for me to ask. "What did it look like to you?"

He pulls away slightly to look at me, he scans my face before answering. "Honestly, like a hellhound. As big as a bear with a boxy head and no tail, like something out of a nightmare." He rubs his nose against mine. My heart beats impossibly fast, eyes splaying wide. "I mean I've heard the tales about the God of Death and his prophecy, how when the time comes, he will unleash the wrath of his domain upon this land and that will be the end of life as we know it. But seeing that kind of creature here is surely too coincidental."

"Prophecy? Really?" I giggle, "But yeah, that's what I thought it looked like too. Should we maybe call Rich?"

"You got your phone? Mine's back at the lodge that Rich snapped up for us." He's too close for me to be able to see the eye roll that I know he's just done.

"Well, shit. No, I don't. Mine's in my bag."

"Not that he would be much help in his drunken state," he reminds me.

"Gods' I forgot about that, seems like a lifetime ago when we tucked him into bed," I reply, sighing. He chuckles, his smile lighting up his tired and stressed face.

"Looks like we'll be here for a while," he sighs.

"Looks like it," I chuckle. My eyes betray my rational mind and flicker down his torso, skimming over his very wet chest. Keeping my eyes strictly above his abdomen I skim over his tattoos that look like they shimmer even in the low light. It's an effort not to trace the swirls and patterns with my fingertips.

Clearing my throat, I open my mouth to ask what language they're written in but as I look up, our eyes connect. My mouth goes dry at the boyish gleam in his eyes.

"What?"

"Your cheeks are red."

"Excuse me?"

"Don't play coy. You were shamelessly checking me out."

"I was not!"

"Liar." That sexy, smug grin is plastered across his face. "Not to mention your legs are wrapped around my waist."

"I'm cold and if you'll remember I was fighting for breath not ten minutes ago."

"Hmm, are they your only reasons?"

"Yes."

"Liar."

I glare at him and unfasten my legs from his back, his hands are instantly there holding them in place.

"I didn't say you could remove them."

"Well, you're clearly uncomfortable."

"I didn't say that either."

My heart is pounding so hard I feel it in my throat and the echoes of it ring in my ears. He leans in, his nose brushing against mine, the contact sends sparks across my skin. His thick eyelashes brush the tops of his cheeks as his gaze wanders down my face to my lips, staying there. His tongue sweeps across his own so gently, but I track the movement like it's holy scripture. The cold is all but forgotten now.

My hand drifts up to his face and my thumb runs across his jaw. "Declan..." I breathe before his lips attach to mine.

The gentle caress of his mouth on mine is maddeningly not enough. Not nearly enough, to quell this ache, this fire that has been burning in me for longer than even I know. My hands wrap around the back of his head and tangle in his wet hair as I press him harder against me, craving more of his touch, his taste. His teeth graze my lip, nibbling the flesh and I moan in ecstasy, tugging his hair harshly, yet pulling him impossibly closer by his hips. The groan he realises has my eyes rolling back in my head, and he forces his tongue into my mouth deepening the kiss, claiming every inch of me. His fingers dig into my thigh with such force I know they'll bruise, but I don't care. I want to be marked. I want to be claimed by no one but this male. In every way possible and that might just be scarier than the beast lurking in the shadows. But for this moment, where no one is around, where no one is watching, I want to be devoured. To be shown what it is to love and to be loved in return, even if it is only a fleeting moment.

I nearly growl when he pulls away panting. I don't need breath; I need his lips on mine again.

"Feisty." He bites my bottom lip, his fangs cutting the flesh. "Breathe," he scolds, pulling away further when I try to reconnect our lips. My fingers play with the strands of his hair, I groan but rest my head on his shoulder.

"I have a question," he asks, sounding a little too smug.

"Really?" When he doesn't reply I sigh, "What?"

"Was that your first kiss?"

I pick my head up so fast I almost get whiplash, but when I look at his mischievous face, my own must look like the picture of scepticism.

"Why?"

"It's a valid question. Answer it."

"No, it wasn't." His eyes widen before he masks his surprise in a grin. "You're surprised. Why?"

"I'm not. With the way you kiss, I'm surprised someone hasn't already snatched you up."

"You know why someone hasn't snatched me up Declan. I'm not anyone's to claim."

His face falls and there is hurt in his eyes, something he covers up just as quickly as his surprise. "Aella, I didn't mean anything by that."

"I know you didn't Declan." I offer him a small smile and place my hand on his cheek. He leans into it, closes his eyes, and puts his hand over mine, placing a soft kiss against my palm.

Our eyes reconnect.

"Stop looking at me like that," he whispers.

"Like what?"

"Like you want to devour me."

I can't stop the grin that splits my face, making him groan. "Would that be so wrong?"

He snorts and leans forward, once again sealing his lips over mine. The touch is electrifying. Even my own darkness seems content to sit back and enjoy. Feeling a deeper connection to him than I think either of us realises. His hands hold tightly to me like he's scared I'll disappear.

I wonder what changed in him. He has despised me for so long. For what I am. For what I represent.

I reluctantly pull away, and it's his turn to whine. Pushing his lips towards me again, desperate for more. I hold my fingers between them. "What made you follow me tonight?" I can't help it. It's something I need to know.

"I felt this pull. Like you were walking into danger and I knew you had gone alone. I should've come with you when you left." He lifts my forearm up looking at the blood staining the cloth there.

"You couldn't have known. I didn't either."

"It's not the point Aella. I know you're strong and capable. Hel I'm in awe of your strength. But it doesn't make up for the fact that you shouldn't have to do everything alone." He rests his forehead against mine. Breathing each other in. "I feel like I've been drowning for so long, having you here – wrapped around me like a snake on a branch – is like taking the first breath of air after drowning." He murmurs against my lips.

We'd been quick to head back to the cottage. The old man's corpse is still lying in his kitchen, his chest wide open. It didn't take us long to find his journal, tucked away in his bedside drawer. Declan made me promise to alert the first person we saw to his corpse, so that he may be buried, and I made the point to say that anyone willing to do anything will most likely be in bed by this hour. But I still wrote a letter, using his stationary and once we got back to the bar, I would hand it over to whoever was at the counter.

Walking back into the main village is strange and yet peaceful. After the events of the last hour, one can't help but feel on edge, and this serine village at the sea's shore, illuminated by the gentle moonlight, is bizarrely eerie. The choppy waves crash against the sea wall, as Declan and I walk by. Neither one of us dared to breathe too loud, let alone talk about what happened.

I look at him watching his side profile as he leads us down the dark pathways. His eyebrows are pinched but his subtly glowing eyes are focused on the way. His damp t-shirt still clings to his muscles, showing every crevice and vein so well that it's hard not to stare. Clothes that I had to convince him to take. He'd been reluctant at first until I made the point that the old man won't exactly be needing them now. To which I received an unamused glare. I clench my fists tightly to avoid running my fingers over every inch of his skin.

He must sense my stare because his gaze snaps to mine and his eyes soften, his lips twitch up into a smile and I turn away, my cheeks warming. He grabs my hand, the red journal in the other, lacing our fingers together.

The pain in my arm is ever present, each stretch of skin sends fire through my veins and despite the cold and wet clothing I'm wearing, my body temperature is rising.

A sudden disorienting feeling washes over me, and I stumble down the curb, gasping as I fall to my knees, clutching at my arm, I groan at the pain throbbing up and down it.

"Hey, hey. You ok?" Declan's face wobbles in and out of focus as he kneels beside me, observing me for a moment. Whatever it is he sees, he's not happy about it. "Ok, you're not fine. Let me get you to Rich." He lifts me up and the world seems to spin faster and faster.

"Stop! Put me down," I moan holding my head. My feet touch the ground in an instant, but his hands never leave my sides while he holds me up, allowing me to lean against him. The feel of the ground stops my head from spinning, but nausea roils through me. I gag, dry heaving until I vomit on the curb. What little dinner I had comes up, mixed with blood.

"What the fuck?" I whisper tilting my head. I wipe my mouth with my uninjured sleeve. He's there instantly rubbing a hand in circles on my back.

I stand and turn, only to be hugged tightly to his chest. His fingers tangle in my hair pulling my head into his neck and suddenly all I can feel is him. Not the overwhelming dizziness, not the pain still plaguing my arm. Not the nausea. Just pure sandalwood and bergamot, classically Declan and a sense of calm washed over me.

We are moving again, quickly, I'm rocking from side to side. My eyes flutter again and again as I breathe in his unique scent that's keeping the pain away. Keeping everything away.

Voices come in and out, they speak but I don't understand. Another scent joins the first, another familiar one, one that also brings comfort and sweetness. It's not until my arm is pulled away from my waist that I register anything at all.

I whimper at the agony.

"Shh, it's ok," a familiar voice hushes in my ear, and I tuck myself deeper into the warmth.

Declan

She tucks herself back into my neck and my heart beats rapidly. Both from fear of her wound and the feelings that have been stirring around all night.

"I need to make a tourniquet," Rich mutters to himself as he assesses her arm, still half asleep and stinking of ale. "You've done well to stop the bleeding, but doing so has allowed the poison to spread."

"The poison?" I ask, finally looking up from Aella's sweaty, twitching face.

He holds up her arm for me to take a look. "Yeah, how did you not notice? Her veins are turning black."

"Oh gods," I remove my hand from her face and run it through my hair, panicking. The overwhelming feeling to gag hit me. *Poison?*

"It's ok, Declan..."

"No, it's not ok. All I did was clean the wound, I didn't even look at it properly."

"Declan, it's a slow-moving poison. One that I need to remove."

"How are you going to do that?" He gives me a level stare and I can tell he's getting annoyed with my panicked responses.

"Deep breaths, Declan. I need to remove the poison and I need to do it now, there's only one way I can do that without the proper tools at my disposal. I need to drain her blood."

"Absolutely not!" I hiss, jolting forward towards him, I stop short when Aella whimpers in her sleep. I'd almost forgotten she was on my lap.

"This needs to be done and it needs to be done now. If not, you risk her life."

"She could lose her arm!" I argue.

"Better than her life," he replies, taking off his belt. I forgot I didn't bother to change him before following Aella. As soon as she left, I felt this overwhelming sense that she was in danger. I'd ignored it for as long as I could. I know that she can handle herself. But my pulse spiked and I all but jumped up from the chair I was sitting in and ran from the room, stopping only to lock the door on an unconscious Rich.

"What in the fuck are you doing?"

"Making a tourniquet. I told you before. It'll stop the infected blood from going up her arm to her body, in turn saving her from bleeding out completely. The only thing I need to do after that is drain her arm."

"The only thing," I grumble, looking down at her sleeping form again. She's so small in my arms, so delicate and yet possibly the strongest person I've ever met.

"Declan, you've seen her get shot and bounce back in a week. She's like a damn god with how seemingly unkillable she is. She's got this. Trust her," Rich says, moving to the bathroom.

I stand up cradling her in my arms.

"You need to make it through this because we need to talk about what happened. Do you hear me?" I murmur against the skin of her forehead; I place a kiss there and follow behind Rich.

"Where do you want her?" I ask once I step into the tiny room.

"In the tub. I need her arm accessible," Rich answers, watching me place her down gently in the copper bathtub, the rest of the room is wooden like a hunting cabin out in the woods. Completely natural, except, of course, the porcelain toilet and copper sink bowl. I sit on the floor next to it, placing my hand under her head as it lulls to one side.

"Are you going to tell me or am I going to have to guess?" Rich questions while he wraps his belt around the top of her arm before pulling it tight to stop her circulation.

"What?" I answer.

He starts to rifle through his bag and pulls out a syringe with a bottle of clear liquid.

"What is that?"

"A sedative. It will help keep her out, whilst we do this. She won't feel a thing," he replies, filling the syringe. He searches her other arm for a few moments, struggling to find a good vein, but he manages to inject her all the same.

"There. Now, let's get started."

Rich picks out a small skinning knife from his bag, the very same his father gifted him before he joined the army and puts it to her skin. I want to say something, I want this to already be over. But I keep my mouth shut. If anyone can help, it's Rich. So instead, I watch, sitting there in uncomfortable silence and wince while he cuts into her skin, my face pales as more of her blood trickles down her arm and runs down the drain of the bathtub. It's a slow process, but it's not long before black sludge starts to dilute through the cut.

"Urgh, that is nasty!" Rich's disgust is clear on his face, and he grabs a hold of the shower head, turning the water on his begins washing away the poison, "What exactly was it that attacked her?"

"It's hard to explain. It was some sort of beast. Not a normal animal, it was the size of a bear with glowing yellow eyes." I shiver, reliving the minutes we were chased down by that hound. Aella's scream as its teeth tore through her skin.

"We could do with finding it again."

My body becomes as taut as a bow string at the words that leave his mouth and my gaze snaps from Aella's peaceful sleeping face to his concerned one, "Are you crazy?"

He looks at me completely innocently, "only to study it and take a sample of its venom. If there's more out there it would be useful to have a vaccine."

"You can go hunting for it, then. The bastard was bulletproof, I doubt you'll get a needle through its skin."

"Bulletproof? Now that is interesting," he muses.

We both refocus back on Aella, watching her bleed from her arm and clean away the poison. It takes just over an hour to clear her bloodstream, Rich stitches her cut back together along with her other bite marks and torn flesh. He wraps them in bandages and removes his belt from her arm, her fingers a deep shade of blue.

"Will she lose them?" I ask, holding onto her too-cold hand, using my own body heat to warm them back up.

"She shouldn't, just don't warm them too fast or she will. Make it gradual," Rich says, bringing some folded clothes for her. "You never did say what happened between you two."

I start to remove her clothes, the wet material clinging to her.

"Nothing happened. We got attacked and we barely escaped. Aella took the damage for me." I look at her still sleeping form, her face unnaturally devoid of colour, and my heart stammers in my chest.

I can tell Rich doesn't quite believe me, but that is not my concern right now. "Whenever you are ready to tell me the rest of it you can. I won't push you."

He turns and leaves the bathroom. Leaving me to change her in peace.

CHAPTER TWENTY
TORTUROUS TORMENT

Aella

The next morning brings with it grogginess, pain and just a little disorientation. I can practically hear Madame K's voice scolding me for getting myself into another mess.

Be better, she'd say. I huff away the thought.

My body is warm, too warm and a weight rests against me. A deep masculine scent swarms my senses, it's comforting and familiar, but the heat of the body lying next to me is too much, yet I'm too weak to move or even fully open my eyes.

"Declan?" I murmur, peeling my tongue from the roof of my dry mouth.

"Morning princess." His own still unused with sleep. His arm tightens around my waist and his head rests on my chest, his fluffy dark curls tickling my chin and he tucks himself in tighter to me, as if such a thing is possible when he's already practically lying on top of me.

The sun is barely above the horizon and the seagulls call loudly from the rooftops, the sloshing of the waves against the seawall tells me we are closer to the shore than I originally thought last night. A boat horn sounds in the distance, putting the cherry on the cake for this peaceful coastal experience. I smile to myself enjoying the moment for as long as I can. Which is very.

A cough from the doorway puts a stop to my moment.

"Sorry to interrupt." I can already hear the grin on his face without even seeing it. "But I need to check your arm." Rich's smooth accent murmurs through the room. Declan doesn't move, in fact, I can feel his breathing has deepened.

"Rich, come around I think he's fallen back asleep," I whisper, following the sound of his footsteps until he comes into view, showing me that merciless smile.

"How are you feeling?" he asks, after crouching down at the side of the bed, immediately he begins unravelling the bandages.

"Drained, tender, tired," I reply, running my other hand through Declan's hair, if for nothing more than to distract myself from the bandages pulling at my skin.

"That's because you were. I had to drain your arm to get the poison out."

"Poison?"

He rolls his eyes at me, "did either of you look at the wound properly?"

"There wasn't much time, we were kind of running for our lives."

"So, Declan said," he sighs, the skin around his mouth tightening as he pulls the last of the cloth away to show a light blue arm decorated in red splotches of dried blood. The wounds have expertly been stitched together, but even I can tell that they will scar.

"Hm... I should probably thank you for saving my life, again, shouldn't I?"

"You can thank me by living through the next forty-eight hours."

"That's not much of a thank you. I'll get you some flowers when we get back to the city."

"Flowers?" he queries, dabbing clean water across the stitching.

"Yeah, boys deserve flowers too," I state, hissing when water gets under the stitching.

"You staying alive, will do just fine." I hum in acknowledgement of his request, but I'll still be buying him flowers.

Neither of us talk further while he cleans the wound, except for the odd hiss from me accompanied by a quick sorry from him.

Declan stirs gently as Rich rings out the blood and water from the rag he's using, something in his chest hums quietly. My brow furrows as I try to figure it out.

"Is he... purring?" I ask Rich who laughs loudly, but even that doesn't seem to wake Declan up.

"Oh please let me tell him when he wakes up," he begs, all too giddy to bully his friend.

Circling my fingers around his soft hair once again I look down to see his thick lashes bushing the tops of his cheeks. His lips are parted slightly, and the thought that I know how they feel against my own shocks me suddenly. Everything from last night comes back to me in such great detail I become embarrassed like Rich can somehow read my mind and knows exactly what I'm thinking.

"Don't worry he didn't leave your side," Rich tells me, mistaking my embarrassment for awkwardness. Then I begin thinking about the fact that we have been tangled this way all night, Declan had fallen asleep on my chest despite everything that has happened with us before, it was running for our lives had changed everything for us. It's like emotional whiplash. I almost died again last night, but Declan was there to save me, more than once, despite his objections to do so only a few weeks prior. The confusion of my predicament must be evident on my face because Rich speaks up, destroying my train of thought.

"What?" Rich asks, he doesn't even look up from his work. But he must simply sense that I have questions. "It's true what Declan says. Without even having to look at you I can almost hear your thoughts running around your head. It's so loud how have you not gone insane?" he chuckles.

"I mean clearly, I am. I keep putting myself in dangerous situations without thinking of the consequences."

"True," he nods.

"Where did you sleep?"

Surprise at the change of conversation is clear on his face and one brow raises, "on the other side of Declan. Why do you think he's practically a human blanket on you?"

I fight the grin at his comment. He really was. Putting his body over mine like he's trying to be a human shield or something. The thought made me squirm. It does not sit well in my chest at all and I physically shiver with the need to move.

"Let me finish this and I'll help you up," Rich speaks quietly. Again it's like he can sense what I'm thinking before I've even registered the thought myself.

"Declan described it. This *monster* you ran into," he murmurs, his expression turning dark. Those black eyes bore deeply into my soul, the silver stars so distant, so dim, they could be passed as light reflections in a void. "What did it look like to you?" His voice was thick and smoky. Commanding in a way I've never heard from him before.

I sigh never once breaking our connection. "Like something from the Abaddon." The Abaddon was known to many as the place where unworthy souls go when they die. To be tormented for the rest of their existence. They will know nothing but darkness and cruelty. Treated in death as they behaved in life.

A place I have no doubt I will be joining one day.

"That's what he said. *Like something out of Hel.*"

Neither of us says anything further I watch him wrap my arm back up and true to his word he gently lifts Declan up so I can shimmy out from underneath him.

The information I gathered was less than helpful. I sighed for the umpteenth time as I, yet again, flipped through the pages of the old mortal's journal.

The old mortal saw nothing, no hint of the captain, no belongings left on board. All he found was an abandoned boat drifting on the waves, its name *The Revenge* — at least that's what his journal says — an almost word for word the article.

The drive back is nauseating, the blood loss is making me dizzy and cold, even bundled up in Rich's coat I'm shivering. Declan has scolded me several time about continuing work when I've just been attacked. But he counted that someone had died for this knowledge – or supposed knowledge – and that his death would be meaningless if I didn't catch whoever caused it.

That shut him up and made my moral compass spin around and around to no end. After that a tension lingered over all of us. Still reeling from the nights events Declan and I hadn't spoken much this morning. He wasn't quite as grumpy as normal which I think I would've preferred to the uncomfortable tension that has now settled between us; he can barely look me in the eye. At least when he was throwing insults and threats at me, he did so confidently. Now he's like a child that been scolded by their parent, withdrawn and timid.

He chose to sit in the back of the vehicle with me, scooping up my legs as he sat down allowing me to stretch them out over his lap. His large hands rest against my shins, the touch is gentle and absentminded as I read and reread through the journal for the final time.

His attention is watching through the window. The trees blur by impossibly fast that it is near impossible to see anything lurking in the shadows of the elm and ash trees.

Ansrutas' keep comes into view a few hours later and several miles before we join onto the main road; the traffic is herded into the city, passing through the open gates. The outpost still stands outside the sandstone walls and still holds us up far longer than necessary.

I watch the wall start to shrink behind us as we re-enter the city. Vehicles form an orderly line behind us. A fast-moving car catches my attention almost immediately, one for its lack of licence plate and two for how it cuts off the car behind us to takes its place. The male behind the wheel has bushy eyebrows and a smug grin plastered on his scarred face as he looks through the window staring directly at me. His passenger and younger male with curl golden locks is speaking hastily on the phone.

"Ermm guys..." I begin, turning around to face the front once more.

The car jerks to the side, and the crushing of metal against metal screams in my ears. A blinding light flashes in my eyes, and my breath leaves my lungs.

The glass shatters from the window frames spraying Declan's face. The force pulls on the safety belts, cutting into my neck until suddenly I feel weightless. There's nothing like the feeling of floating, it's both freeing and daunting, because you now that it won't last.

The world comes crashing back down as I'm slammed into the side of the car, now laying on its side. The window shatters in my face, and shards of glass fly everywhere, leaving little slashes across my skin as it explodes from the door.

I'm disorientated, struggling for breath and the car groans as it rocks back and forth, settling itself.

The screams of people outside can be heard but that's not my first concern, "Rich..." I croak, coughing violently as my body tries to drag air back into my lungs. My hair hangs across my face once again in a shamble of tangles and a deadly fire licks up and down my injured arm.

"I'm alright," he replies just as shaken and confused. "How's Declan?" I hear the sound of a blade cutting through fabric and suddenly he's free and his face is between the seats looking between us to see if we are alive. The car rocks with the quick movement and my heart lurches thinking we are going to flip over again.

I look up at Declan and see he's completely unconscious and bleeding from his right temple, hanging limply from his seat, his safety belt the only thing stopping him from landing on top of me.

"Be careful when you move, the car might flip onto its roof," I cautioned, panting, trying to grab the small blade tucked into my boot.

Rich checks on Declan first seeing that my eyes are still open, "he's unconscious... and bleeding," he assesses, nothing I didn't already know, but clearly, he is clarifying it for himself. Slotting himself back into the role of a medic something that appears to be a comfort to him as well as necessary, "We need to get out of here and get him to a hospital."

"HELP!" I yell. Putting more desperation into my voice. The shuffling of feet is heard, and someone's head pops up by the window looking scared but determined. The same curled haired man in the car that followed us. He looks terrified like he hadn't known this was going to happen. But it's another voice that speaks to us letting us know that help is on the way.

Rich's hand is bleeding, and his face and arms are decorated with little cuts from the glass, that much I can see while he reaches across to Declan to stop the bleeding from his head.

The crunching of glass grates behind me and the car gently sways as they enter through the broken back window. They look to me and reach out.

"No! Get him out first," I call to the person.

"Elle if they cut him free he'll drop on you. It's ok. Go, we won't be far behind," Rich reassures me, ripping part of his shirt as a gauze to wrap around the wound on Declan's arm that I didn't catch earlier.

The hand wraps around my arm and a male voice calls, "Come on, this way. We'll get you out."

"You need to call for the emergency services. My friend, he's badly hurt."

"They're already on their way. Now come on." The male's voice is urgent.

I finally reach for the small blade in my boot and begin cutting through the belt.

"Rich..."

"Elle, go. We'll be fine. We're right behind you I promise," he replies, still tending to Declan whilst ignoring his own wounds. I nod, turning to grasp the outstretched hand, allowing them to pull me from the sideways car. I don't even make it to the window when a piece of cloth is draped over my face. I try to bat it away, but it holds firm, I look to the male in front of me to see a hideous grin on his scarred face.

I attempt to call Rich, but my words are muffled by the cloth.

"Elle?" I hear him call but the sound is so distant, like a dream.

The sweet scent fills my nose and mouth, and my head begins to feel woozy. A second set of arms accompany the first and both lift me weightlessly out of the window and into a solid set of arms. My eyes grow heavy and my head lulls backwards, my neck too weak to hold the weight. My limbs become more liquid as I'm carried away from the crumbled car.

Voices chatter all around me but I can't hear a single word they say, soft mumbles and weak protests leave me, but no one seems to notice. I'm hoisted higher into the arms of my saviour, the world spinning with the jostling, and I try not to throw up.

I'm thrown down and land with a thump onto something soft and pillowy and another piece of cloth is placed over my face, sending me further into complete darkness.

When I wake again my mind is foggy and my eyes roll around in their sockets. My vision is cloudy, and my hearing is dulled like there's plugs in my ears stopping me from hearing everything clearly. I struggle to take a full breath with my chin laying on my chest, but I don't have enough strength to bring my head up fully, it rolls to the side the more lucid I become, groaning at the pain in my jaw, I peel my dry lips away from each other.

"Wakey, wakey sunshine!" An all too loud voice calls from in front of me, concealed in shadow. A single light bulb dangles above me, the too-bright light sparking pain through my still-waking eyes, giving me an instant migraine.

Attempting to shield myself from the invasive light to cover my eyes, I tug on my hands to find that they are bound together behind my back with a thin plastic tie.

So not somewhere safe then.

My already injured arm blazes with agony. Along with just about every inch of my left side.

"I'd say it is nice to see you Edward Lincoln but I'm afraid I'd be lying," I spit trying so hard to not let my true level of pain show. Nor my anger.

He laughs still shrouded in darkness. "I shouldn't be surprised that you knew yet still, there are some things one would take advantage of."

My eyes latch on to the silhouette sitting in a plush armchair, the light from his cigar burns bright when he takes a drag. I watch as the plume of smoke dances and swirls above his head before disappearing altogether.

"Why exactly am I here?"

"You know perfectly well why you are here, *Fury.*"

"Huh, who ruined the surprise? I was very much excited for our game of cat and mouse," I grin, truly disappointed that I didn't get the chance to knock him on his arse first.

"Cute." One of his fingers taps rapidly against the armrest, a tell-tale sign one is beginning to get irritated. "I will say though I do like this image. The scariest legend known to this world... tied to a kitchen chair." His head tilts to one side taking me in fully.

I relax back further into the chair smirking still. "That's high praise coming from Edward 'Blackfoot' Lincoln. The most ruthless mobster in the South. Didn't you...er...kill your daughter's last lover? Because he broke her heart, right?"

His finger stops tapping.

"Oh! She doesn't know. Oopsie. Let's hope she doesn't find out; I imagine that she would be far worse than heartbroken about that, especially knowing it was your own hands that took his life."

"ENOUGH!" He yells slamming his fist down on the arm of the chair.

"And I was just getting started," I smile slyly.

The silence that spreads between us is filled with tension, his breathing is heavy and slow. I look around the room, but I can only see outlines. Silhouettes of at least four of his own personal guards.

"You know for the entirety of my life; I've heard your stories. About the Furies, the goddesses of vengeance. I even prayed to you a couple of times." He raises his hands as if in prayer, talking directly to the gods above, before chuckling and dropping them back to the arms of his chair. Shaking his head, he takes another drag of his cigar. "I always wanted you to be real, I prayed that you would come and take care of my own revenge. Hurt the people that hurt me, be my protector." There is no doubt in his words. He has prayed. Multiple times by the way he shifts a little uncomfortably in his seat. I can all but see him wondering to himself why he's telling me this.

It brings me a little comfort to know that he genuinely believed we were the wrath of the gods. How many people believed this? Who started this story?

He takes another, longer drag, "but like I said you were nothing more a bedtime story that mothers used to tell their children to get them to behave." He takes a sip of something strong, the ice clinking against the glass, the drink in his other hand. "But looking at you now. It's all rather... disappointing." His posture deflates on a heavy sigh, and he stubs out his cigar. He gets up and advances towards me, and instinctively I pull away. "Well, they do say never meet your heroes, right?" His toothy grin is the first thing I see when he finally steps into the light before me; that and the forked scar cutting into the skin around his lip.

"You win that in a catfight?" I mock, my eyes scanning the mark before slowly ascending towards his eyes.

"Witty..." he returns, his tone colder than a corpse. His golden gaze roves over every inch of my sweating and probably bloody face.

"I try."

He scoffs, "Where did you get the bite marks?" He eyes my bandaged forearm.

"Playing with puppies." I hear the slapping sound before I feel the sting on my skin, my head whips to the side and my brain rattles around my skull.

"You are trying my patience, girl."

"Come on let's face it, this is the most interesting conversation you've had all week." Repeating Roman's words from what feel like months ago.

"You think highly of yourself." He's gruff and lean and if you squint really hard, ruggedly handsome. He smells of smoke and scotch, with days-old stubble in his jaw. His features are tired with age and no doubt the years of being a Don. The stress and ruthlessness looks to be catching up with him.

"Hardly. I just know the truth." I watch him from under my eyelashes, his face is stern and scarred, and his amber eyes flash with annoyance.

One of the silent silhouettes carries a metal tray and places it down gently on a table behind Eddie, all done in the shadows with the blaring light streaming down from above.

"Now for the fun," he grins smugly, turning around and waving the other figure off. Walking to the tray he picks something up. He looks back over his shoulder and picks up another item. He turns back towards me, the glint of a small blade catches my attention first, then tweezers.

"One fingernail for every scratch you gave my daughter, I think." He seems almost giddy now that he has some delightful torture devices in his hands.

"That seems fair," I nod my head mockingly, rolling my eyes.

"I would have to agree and then I think, it'll be the toenails for each bruise." He nods to someone at the side completely missing my sarcasm, and two people are instantly at my sides, their thick, scarred hands wrap around my upper arms. A spark of panic settles into my chest. I have my fingernails pulled at before when they teach you about what real pain feels like and I can tell you, it's not the most pleasant place to begin.

I wince at the pain flaring in my left arm where Eddie's brutes are clasping it tightly holding me down. The two males at my shoulders are easily double if not triple my own weight, there's no way I'll be able to overpower them, especially when I'm already injured, a third man steps forward with more ties in hand. He cuts through the one holding my hands behind my back and then positions them on the arms of the chair and secures them in place with more plastic ties.

"Hmm... comfy." I wiggle in the seat feigning relaxation to hide my rising panic.

The three of them pause looking at me for a moment, probably debating on whether or not I've gone mad but slink back into the darkness all without saying a word.

Eddie pulls a stool out from behind him and sits down clicking the tweezers together in one hand, he twirls the small blade in his other.

"Are we going to do this or are you going to put on a juggling show?" I drawl.

"I know what you're doing, Fury." He points that surgical blade at me.

"And what is that?"

"Using humour as a defensive mechanism." He leans in until his nose is to my ear, his breath on my neck, "I can smell your fear."

The black pit within me writhes, lashing out wanting its pound of flesh for the ridiculous notion.

"Let's hear those pretty screams, shall we?" He steps back, dropping quickly into his seat, taking my littlest finger in his hand.

My lips thin and my breathing becomes shallow as I begin to shut down from within. Finding that place between the conscious mind and the subconscious. A place where no pain can penetrate. This was what they were preparing me for, and I found that grey area faster than even I thought. I watch through deadened eyes as he begins pulling at the little appendage, looking for a reaction.

The door swings open pulling me back into my body, it slams loudly against the wall behind it, and a feminine voice rings from the threshold.

"DADDY! WHAT ARE YOU DOING?"

My attention snaps to the door, and I smile seeing a very familiar petite figure standing there dressed in a white silk shirt and baby pink pencil skirt with matching heels.

"Hi, Melanie Lincoln," I wave, well whatever movement I can make with my hands tied to the chair, she doesn't return the gesture, but her eyes widen slightly as she looks me over. She's connecting the dots

"Fury?" she whispers. I smile confirming her suspicions.

"What are you doing here Mela?" Eddie sighs, interrupting us.

Pain in my little finger awakens and although it's only a small nail it hurts like Hel. I wiggle it seeing blood seeping from the bed. "You actually managed to pull some of it out," I gasp, kind of impressed but more unsettled that my nail is now a few millimetres longer than it was at the start of the day. Night? I have no idea what time it actually is.

Eddie seems proud of the statement. Melanie however, well that's a different story. Her cheeks have paled, and she starts the look a little green around the gills.

"Well, I came to see you. Now I wish I hadn't." She stomps her foot, and I can't help the snicker that comes out of my mouth at the adorable reaction, earning myself another slap to the face.

"Oh, come on!" I growl, trying to stop the chair from toppling over with me in it.

Eddie says nothing as he throws his tools down and grabs his daughter by the arm dragging her out into the hallway.

"Stay with her," he snarls, slamming the door behind him.

All four of them stand in the corners of the room. Just out of the light from the singular hanging bulb that blinds me from above.

Dropping my head back looking up at that same light, sighing. "Any chance of a glass of water?" I ask into the room. When I receive nothing but silence, I drop my head to my chest.

Of Fire and Shadow

I listen for a few breaths only to hear the sound of the father and daughter having a heated argument, about how inappropriate it is to have a functioning torture room and to kidnap a Fury. I smirk when I think about how I would in fact also have a torture room if I could. But I can guarantee it would be far nicer than an abandoned butcher's hanging room. The tiles and the grates everywhere have seen years of blood and death. But this room wouldn't claim another. Least of all me.

With four sets of eyes upon me, I know breaking these cable ties won't be easy. "I call you forth," I whisper into the silence. Reaching for the darkness within myself, calling it forward.

"What did you say?" One of the faceless thugs' growls from the corner behind me.

"Just saying some prayers," I murmur back, watching as my fingers elongate, the joints popping as they turn black and lengthen, curling into claws. "Does anyone here believe in the gods? Or do you all believe them to be gone like much of the country?"

The question is a pointless one. *I* don't even believe in the gods. But I need something to distract from my claws cutting through the plastic ties. "Are you all silent? Do none of you have a voice?" The first is difficult but the satisfying snap as it breaks is worth the cramp that's now seizing my hand.

"Shut up, witch. We know what you are. We also know that you won't leave here alive."

The other takes mere seconds, the angry voices raise higher as I listen through the door. With the quartet of mutes in the room I can't cut my legs free not without giving myself up. So, for now my hands being free will have to do. My claws shrink back into pink fingers, but the darkness remains near the surface. It is power untold; unlike anything I've felt before. I'm not sure when this darkness came to me, or if I was born with it already embedded into my being. But its ruthless and cunning have gotten me out of more scraps than I can count. It's cold and calculated, a lethal calm that washes over me, it's a rush of power at my beck and call; and sometimes it terrifies the shit out of me.

The door reopens and Eddie comes storming back in.

"How's Melanie?" I ask sweetly, simply to rile him up. His eyes darken at the sound of her name on my lips. I expect a slap instead I get a punch. One that cuts my cheek, inside and out. The coppery tang of blood fills my mouth, and the scent fills the air as I feel it dribble down my skin. "Ouch." I lick my lips tasting the blood there, smiling viciously. I have always wanted to be captured like this. To have my training put to the test. The thought should be unnerving. Totally outlandish. But I couldn't be happier.

"I'm glad that hurt." He steps forward pointing a finger at my face. "You do not speak to my daughter. Or about her." His threat dies on his tongue as something else catches him off guard. He steps back inhaling sharply, "What's wrong with your eyes?"

I narrow them at him, thinking this is some ploy to catch me off guard. But his concern doesn't go away.

"Did any of you give her something?" he snaps to those silent silhouettes, who don't seem too silent now as a cacophony of 'No's' blend together.

We stare at each other for a moment. The tension thickens like the weight of a heavy cloud. "Did you tell her?"

His concern is forgotten by those four words. Anger flares and he pulls back his fist once more. I dodge it by leaning to the right and he hits thin air; he tries again, and I dodge a second time, leaning left. He steps forward once aiming again to connect his fist to my face.

I take his close proximity and use it to my advantage and claw him across his chest, my fingers blackened once more. He stumbles back in surprise, and I cut my legs free standing up tall.

Eddie pulls at his torn vest and shirt where only splatters of blood seep into the fabric. I kick him in his manhood before he realises, I'm standing, and he howls in pain. I shouldn't get so much pleasure from watching him double over in agony, but I can't help that swell of satisfaction bloom in my breast. I kick up my knee hitting him in the face; the crunch from his nose is beyond pleasing.

His men jump to action, yelling curses and profanities at me, and I use my standing momentum to launch the chair at one of the larger guys, watching it shatter into pieces as he continues to charge at me.

"Shit!" My petite stature allows me to dodge the devastating blows all three of them are throwing my way, but they'll tire my out before long. So, I snatch a small blade from the table, the two goliath-sized males charge me both at the same time, I throw the knife catching one in the eye. He crumbles, screaming in agony holding his face, blood paints his fingers and hands within seconds. The blade is not long enough to reach his brain, but I did take out his eye.

The other pauses to watch, horrified, before turning back to me.

"YOU BITCH!" he bellows, swinging at me. I feel a wisp of air brush my hair as I narrowly duck away from his fist. His stance is weak, he's angry — not thinking — I kick out his ankle and he stumbles forward, giving me the opening I was hoping for. I slam my foot into his lower back, grinning when he falls face-first into the wall; it disorientates him enough for me to turn to the final assailants.

The blonde's face is an equal measure of shock, concern, and anger yet he still raises his fists and the brunette, well, he looks like a bear on Mica Glitter. Wild and untameable. The savage gleam in his eyes will no doubt haunt me for a few weeks.

"What are you waiting for? Kill her!" Eddie screams from the floor, blood pouring from his nose. I smirk when I see him still cradling his jewels.

The blonde guy is inexperienced. I can tell by his shaking breath and his form. He pulls a switchblade from his pocket and puffs out his chest and arms trying to make himself look bigger than he is.

The brunette pulls out some brass knuckles and I quirk a brow, "Really?"

The blonde steps forward slashing at me, pushing me back while I dodge each attack. My back hits the wall and I watch as he advances, the grin on his face tells me he thinks he has me cornered, he couldn't be more wrong. His cockiness will be his downfall. He raises his hand again and I punch him in the throat, the jab takes him by surprise, and he drops the knife right into my awaiting hand. His own go right to his throat as he tries to suck in air through his mouth and nose.

The brunette charges me, slamming into my stomach. I'm folded over his shoulder, and he keeps running until my back is slammed against the wall, and the breath is knocked out of my lungs. My head hits the concrete with such a crack, white covers my vision for a few seconds. He steps back, dropping me to the floor. Holding my stomach, I watch him looking down at me.

"This is going to be fun." Those brass-covered knuckles rise above my head glinting in the low light of the room. Eddie struggles to stand in my peripheral vision and that door bursts open once again. A ball of silver fur rushes in spitting and hissing, jumping on the brunette. A flash of white sinks into his neck ripping his jugular from under his flesh. The guy drops, his hands flying to his neck and the little fluff ball hops off his shoulder. Not a fluff ball. A lynx.

"Melanie! What the fuck do you think you're doing?" Eddie shouts slumped down in the armchair, still obviously in pain.

The little lynx paces back and forth in front of me, hissing and spitting at her father, and although I'm grateful she's saved me, I'm more confused than ever as to why. Especially when I'm trying to kill her current lover. But I'm not one to look a gift horse in the mouth.

Using the wall as a crutch I stand on my own two feet.

"Thanks for the warm-up boys," I fight the groan as I stretch out my back.

"Fuck you!" Eddie spits, still unmoving.

"Don't be so mean Eddie. You're only still alive because I've allowed it." Stepping up to him I put my finger and thumb on his chin and lift his head up, so our eyes connect. "Don't feel too bad, but you never really stood a chance," I grin, letting go of him.

"I will kill you. Mark my words, girl. YOU'RE DEAD!"

"I look forward to another present from you, Eddie!" I step out the door. Melanie's little claws click behind me.

"FUCK YOU!" His screams echo as I close the door laughing.

The hallway is empty and grimy and the light bulbs flicker in their shades. The corridor is narrow and grimy, and the light green paint is flaking from the walls, white tiles are stained with a patchwork of red and brown. The stale air carries the overwhelming stench of bleach and iron. It's an assault to the senses and quite honestly, I can't wait to get out of here.

"You shouldn't have done that," I muttered to Melanie. She leads the way to the back of the building, stopping behind a room just before the exit. Using her nose, she pushes open the door, kicking it shut behind her. She comes out minutes later dressed and not an ounce of blood on her.

"Maybe not. But it's not the first time I've pissed my father off and it likely won't be the last."

The irritatingly yellow lights buzz all the way down the hall, to an emergency exit. What's more surprising is Eddie hasn't sent men after us. I push open the emergency exit door and step out into the night.

The cold air is like a refreshing ice bath, I inhale deeply and look around. I'm surrounded by abandoned buildings and empty streets, not even the rats squeak as they scurry by. We are clearly hidden deep within The Black Pines.

"You will have to put me up though. Not a cat in Hel's chance am I staying here tonight," she sasses.

I quirk a brow, but I don't talk back. She did just save my arse back there, "you sure you can trust sleeping in the same apartment as a Fury?"

"Well, I'd like to think my actions in there called for a sort of truce between us. Even given the fact that I wasn't the one who caused the issue last time." She takes the lead towards the darkened street.

"You're kidding right?" I'm flabbergasted. Had she just answered my question and not tried to cut my throat out with those claws we would've parted ways as unlikely acquaintances.

"Nope," she sasses, popping the p.

Instead of fighting her I huff a laugh and follow behind to the street, where her black SUV is parked at the side of the street. With her personalised plate.

"A bit flashy for you, isn't it?" I tease. She scoffs in response and climbs in. Once I join her, she locks the doors and turns to me, staying silent for a breath or two.

"Why have you locked us? Are you planning to murder me, little lynx? And just when I thought we were getting along."

She stays silent still for longer. Watching. Waiting for I don't know what.

"What are you going to do now?" she asks quietly. Folding her arms over her chest, she settles back in her leather seat.

"About?" I drawl, wanting nothing more than to simply go back to the apartment and wash the dried blood from me.

"Roman."

We lock eyes.

"You're not serious?"

Again, she stays quiet. Waiting.

"It's out of my control, furball. I have orders."

She scoffs and rolls her eyes, "they are not absolute. Plans can be changed."

I narrowed my eyes on her.

"Do you know anything about the Fort of Ajay? About how they operate?"

"No but I think that was intentional on their behalf," she scowls.

She's not wrong. The Director, upon building the organisation made sure that everything was acquired quietly. Our jobs are done from the shadows because that's where he wanted it. Some sick and twisted part of him wanted to be able to strike without the victims being aware until it was too late. Every order from his mouth must be obeyed. Not a single one of us is allowed a choice. That was stripped away from us the moment we graduated.

"Just know that I don't have a choice."

She scoffs, turning back to the front, she turns the key in the ignition and the vehicle roars to life.

"But I may know someone who can help you."

CHAPTER TWENTY-ONE
HAVING A BALL

Melanie stops outside the building to our apartment. The sky is greying with the first rays of light in the morning when we step through the door. The apartment is empty. Nothing but a cold breeze blowing through the window that had been left open.

"This is cosy," she utters, stepping further into the room, "where are the boys?" She turns to me.

Like the crack of a whip, the crash comes back to me, "gods." I pull out my phone, seeing countless phone calls and messages from Rich, asking where I am and if I'm safe.

Without hesitation, I called him back and begin pacing in front of the door like a caged wild cat, waiting for it to connect.

"Hello?" Comes a very groggy voice on the other side of the receiver.

"Rich!" I all but yell down the phone, "Oh gods. Where are you? Are you ok?"

"Aella? Where the fuck are you?" We speak at the same time neither stopping to actually answer the other's questions.

Melanie snatches the phone from my hand, "We are back at your apartment and she's fine. Now where are you?"

She pauses waiting for his response, "Melanie. Obviously." I snicker at the deadpan expression on her face, "Lincoln. Yes."

She hands the phone back to me tentatively and plops down on the lounge.

"Why is she in our apartment?" Rich's voice rumbles in my ear.

"Annoyingly she saved my life, so I owe her."

"Saved your life? From what."

"Rather who, but we can talk about that when your home. I take it you're at the hospital?"

"Yeah, Declan took a pretty bad hit. But he's going to be fine. We should be home by the end of the day."

They were not. Rich had already been discharged in the morning, but Declan was required to stay another night for observation.

Melanie had invited herself to stay another day. Whether she thought she was doing me a favour by keeping me company or herself so that she doesn't have to go back and face her father just yet, I don't know. But our morning consisted of going to see the boys and then drinking through the night. Cackling at each other's stories. Well, *her* stories. She quickly told me my stories were depressing and unfunny. To which I nodded, agreeing, and downed nearly a full bottle of my favourite vodka.

She was both impressed and a little intimidated.

Which is exactly why I am now waking up with a pounding headache and a front door that is shaking on its hinges.

Jumping out of bed quickly and quietly is difficult with Melanie lying next to me with her head buried in one of my pillow and bottles all over the floor. We have made a trepid sort of peace. One I knew likely wouldn't last but the night had been about forgetting our worries instead of dredging them back up.

"Gods," I groan, rubbing my head. stumbling over to the front door.

"AELLA!" I hear Rich growl from the other side of the door.

"Coming!" I yell back finding the key on the kitchen counter.

The door swings open moments later, and an irritated Rich stands there with an amused Declan at his side.

"Good night?" Declan asks, taking in my dishevelled hair. I smile at him. Despite the bruising on his arm and a few cuts on his cheek, he looks as he always does. Strong and handsome. Rushing forward I wrap my arms around him, smiling into his chest as his warmth and scent fully surround me.

"Hello to you too, princess," he chuckles. The breathy laugh ruffling a few strands of my hair.

"What no hug for me?"

I laugh, "If either of you tell anyone I've gone soft like this I will kill you." The warning doesn't really stop the rising panic that upon my return everything will be brought to light, and I won't be able to refute any of it.

"Yeah, yeah." I turn and latch onto Rich pulling him in tight. I hadn't realised just how worried I'd been for them. Nor how much I'd miss them.

They've wormed their way into my blackened heart, and I know it'll kill me when I leave. Because that will inevitably happen. I will go back to the Fort, and they will continue on in their own lives.

Rich says something and his chest bounces with laughter. I turn back to Declan to see him already looking at me. His face crinkled in laughter, the pain of the accident seemingly far from his mind. Each bruise and cut that marks with two, makes me want to inflict more and more pain upon Eddie.

Leading the way back into the apartment, Melanie comes out of my bedroom looking refreshed and put together. Declan eyes me warily. He'd been more shocked to see her walk in behind me yesterday and I knew he would have questions.

Shaking my head, I take hold of his unbandaged hand guiding him to the lounge, perching myself on the coffee table in front of him. "How are you feeling?" Despite my own lingering pain, I lean closer to him, resting my elbows on my knees. He sighs, heavily, the stress of the past few evenings blowing away with it, leaving behind the full-bodied exhaustion and his own aching pain.

"Sore and tired. But I'm alright."

"Do you remember anything?"

"Not really. Just something smacking into the side of us. Who was it? Are they ok?"

"They're fine," I reply, cutting Rich off. I had told him briefly at the hospital where I'd been all night and he'd flown off the handle. He had also asked me until Declan was better, that we keep it between us. He didn't want Declan to feel unnecessary worry. "Just someone who wasn't paying attention."

Declan nods, none the wiser. The cut on his temple cuts close to his eye, mirroring the years-old one through his eyebrow. Minor cuts and scrapes over his skin match mine and Rich's from the glass windows; his whole hand is bandaged, comically large, along with his forearm. *But he's alive.* That thought alone has me sighing just as heavily as Rich. The deep breath expands my chest so much that I wince at the pain, I have to turn away to cover it up.

Having taken a homemade tonic for the pain, I now sit in front of the mirror in nothing but a towel, with my hair still wet from the shower, facing the reality check of what Eddie has done to me.

Melanie would be joining us tonight. I had hoped to introduce her to Frederick. The two seemed to have a similar goal in mind, in trying to save Roman and two heads are always better than one.

She had headed home to find herself a dress and would meet us later at The Circle.

Bruises litter my skin both from the car crash and the fight with Eddie's men and they won't be easily covered. The bandage on my arm, from the bite marks I received needs to go but the wound is still raw and weeping.

"Rich?" I call and moments later I hear footsteps approaching.

"Yes, *liefling*?" He leans against the door frame, his arms crossed over his chest.

"Do you have something other than this big ugly bandage to cover my arm?" I lift my arm to showcase the bulky white bandage.

"I can't take that off, but I might have something to wrap around it, something that's more your skin colour if you want?"

"Please, the dress he's given me has no sleeves, and I don't have time to go and get another one."

"Yeah, no problem." He leaves and comes back minutes later with a different kind of wrap.

Once tightened, I begin applying makeup to my bruises.

"You want help with the ones on your back?" Rich mumbles, watching me dab at my purple skin.

"It's not your fault," I meet his eyes in the mirror.

"I was driving," he counters, his mouth pulling down in a frown.

"It's still not your fault."

He sighs but concedes. I know he still doesn't believe me. So instead, I hand him the sponge and the make-up to cover those bruises on my back. It took several minutes of guidance for him to finally press onto my skin. The touch was so light I knew we'd be here all night long trying to blend it in.

"Rich, harder," I scolded.

"I'm doing it as best as I can," he moans back.

"What in the Abaddon is going on in here?" Comes Declan's amused voice from the entrance to my bedroom. He's quick to appear in the threshold of the pink bathroom looking divinely handsome in his shirt and dress pants. He tightens the cuffs looking over us sceptically. "It certainly sounds interesting."

"If only," Rich mutters, focusing hard on the sponge connecting with the bruises.

"It doesn't hurt. Can you please just do it harder and quicker so we can both get dressed?"

Declan's eyebrows rise, "definitely interesting."

"Stop it!" I scold, pointing a finger at him through the mirror.

He raises his hands in defeat backing off.

Luckily Rich understood my tone was not one to mess with and he finished his job quicker than I thought. I'd checked it multiple times to make sure that it was a good job and I'm happy to say he could be an artist. My skin looks to have never changed a shade.

As I finish off the last of my makeup I stare at my reflection once again. The dark circles under my eyes have disappeared, and in their place is bright youthful skin. Kohl lines my lashes disguising the bruising around my eye, and I finally have some colour in my cheeks and lips. There's not a bruise in sight and my body is wrapped deliciously in the silky blood-red gown, with its delicate off-the-shoulder sleeves; the cloth cinches in at the waist and flows beautifully over my hips draping down elegantly to the floor, the slit in the skirt does in fact cut all the way up to my hip, as I thought when I first saw the gorgeous gown. I pair the dress with a matching pair of blood-red heels with gold detailing on the heel, and simple yet sophisticated gold jewellery.

My hair flows in curls down my back, pinned up at the sides with golden feathered-wing clips.

I give my reflection a weak smile and sigh turning away, heading for my bedroom door. I'm much too tired to talk to dreadfully dull politicians and shrill-looking noble ladies all night, but I promised Frederick we would be in attendance.

"Let's get this over with then," I announce to the room, rummaging through my matching silk clutch bag making sure I have everything I need.

Both Declan and Rich stand in the main room, Rich is adjusting Declan's tie and the two of them are dressed in near-matching tuxedos. Rich is in an all-black ensemble, with a silver pocket square and Declan wears a white shirt with an amber pocket square.

I stop my search when I'm greeted with silence, taking in both of them greedily.

"Hello?" I ask, confused when I finally reach their faces, to see their eyes wide, "is something wrong?"

Rich clears his throat, "nothing. You just look..."

"Amazing," Declan finishes.

"Yeah." Rich nods hastily.

"Oh." I blush looking down at myself, "I don't look too beaten up. I certainly feel it," I groan rolling my shoulders.

Declan wiggles his hands at me. "I have to wear gloves to hide the bandage on my hand."

"That such a good idea I should've thought of that," I grumble looking to my own arm.

He steps forward, offering his uninjured arm for me to take. "Shall we?" he asks, and I link arms with him, smiling. He leads me out into the hallway where we wait for Rich to lock the apartment door before descending the stairs out onto the street.

"I'm so not used to walking in heels," I mumble, holding my skirt as I take the last few steps.

Rich chuckles from behind me, "Tell me this is going to look like a deer on ice. Please, gods, let this be a deer on ice." He pleases looking up to the sky, laughing harder when he sees Declan glaring at him.

"Don't worry about it Dec, if I fall and break an ankle, he's the one who will be carrying me home," I pat him on the chest as I walk by.

The driver – sent by Frederick – stands with the door open, smiling softly. The wrinkles on his face are deep and his silver hair pops out from under the black cap he wears, decorated with the royal crest stitched in gold thread. I smile my thanks and with the help of Rich, slide into the back seat of the car.

Declan takes the seat to my left and Rich slides in on my right, squishing me between the two.

"He should've sent a bigger car," Declan grumbles, lifting his arm out in front of him to avoid it being squished in between us; pulling his blazer tight across his back.

"You're telling me," I reply, equally uncomfortable, my arms also pinched across my front pushing my breasts together. "You two need to lose some muscle."

Rich chuckles again, seeming to fit in comfortably as we pull away from the curb.

The drive is mercifully short with the three of us now only living a few blocks away from The Circle. We arrive at the bridges to the man-made island within a few minutes, guards swarm the perimeter like ants in a nest; every last one is dressed in black suits, no doubt concealing their weapons under their finery.

We're slow to pull up to the Northern spire, the cars coming and going hinder the speed of the others. The number of voices and ringing laughter that comes from within, only add to the over exuberant expectations of the evening. The all-consuming dread that this evening brings only intensifies when I see just how many people have been invited. That's even with his majesty's expansive court still in Larissa, having not been expected to make the journey for this one night. But the candlelight, glowing especially for the purpose of making the spires look magical and enchanting, draws you into an openly captivating sense of curiosity and comfort, accompanied by the soft and beguiling music drifting into the air.

The royal crested car pulls to a stop at the bottom of the steps, I look up to see Frederick, dressed in a beautifully fitted black tuxedo, with a red bowtie and matching pocket square, the colour an exact match to my dress. His deep brown hair is styled in his signature curls, brushing the tops of half-fae, half-human ears; he beams down at the car.

The two shifters open the doors simultaneously, and Rich offers me a hand, I take it with a smile and slide across the leather seats out, once again, into the warm spring night.

I thank him politely and lock eyes with Frederick, who strides down the steps towards us.

"Evening all," he greets happily, his arms open wide. He walks straight to me and takes my hand from Rich, who seems a little reluctant to let go.

Frederick hooks my hand under his arm and instantly I feel uneasy, while he smiles excitedly at me.

"Especially to you, my dear Elle." He leans in and kisses me on the cheek, a rough cough comes from behind us, and we both turn to see Declan's stern face frowning at us. Ignoring the potential security threat that is Declan and his temper, his highness leads me up the steps into the hall beyond. The pair keep a leisurely pace behind us close enough that I can hear them mumbling heatedly between themselves.

We enter the reception area of the building where we are greeted by a handful of guards and more servants than I can count, all doting on Frederick's every whim. Melanie as if appearing from smoke spots us and wanders over.

"I hope you don't mind. I added an extra guest last minute. I thought you ought to meet her." He casually looks over his shoulder at the woman clade in a navy blue, form fitted dress, hanging off Rich's arm and his lips thin.

"I've already had the pleasure. But yes, I suppose I could humour her," he drawls, seemingly unimpressed.

Surprise bursts through me, sharp like a raspberry tart. *How in the world would the two have met?*

The servants escort us all up the red-carpeted stairs where we come to the extravagant ballroom, not a single one strays too far from their prince, who doesn't even seem to notice, but to me, there is nothing worse than being followed by a posse.

The room is circular in shape; the glass windows reflect the party within just like the several-tiered chandelier that hangs high in the centre of the room. The base is encompassed in a delicate ceiling rose that spreads across the whole ceiling. The wooden chequered dance floor is polished beyond perfection, it too reflects the lights and couples dancing upon it.

Tables surround the dancefloor, leaving little space for the bar off to one side, which is already overflowing with people. The white, gold and silver, along with the natural wood colours blend together seamlessly. The dazzling colours of every dress and suit in the room are like a moving sea of flowers blowing in the breeze, each one unique and just as bright as the last.

My eyes wander over everything leaving no detail out, and it's not until one of Frederick's adoring servants calls attention to the room, that I realise we are standing at the top of the stairs, waiting for the crown prince to be announced to the guests.

"His Royal Highness, the Crown Prince of Anaphi. Prince Frederick." The room erupts into applause while Frederick gently guides me down the stairs with him and I've never been so uncomfortable in my life, and I literally murder people for a living.

All eyes are on both of us as we descend, and I try not to show the pain I'm feeling with each step-down. My bruises may not be visible but that doesn't mean I don't feel them just as fiercely as I did before I painted over them.

People mutter incoherently amongst themselves, yet Frederick doesn't seem to notice. I keep my head held high and ignore each one, they don't know me and that won't change by the end of tonight. I plaster an unfazed scowl upon my face and continue to be led by Frederick.

Frederick chuckles beside me.

"What?" I ask, not looking at him.

"The scowl on your face. See this is why I invited you. You'll scare everyone off for me and then I can enjoy the night."

"That's doubtful by the look on your father's face at our linked arms." Sure enough, Frederick looks over to his father, whose tanned face is made up into a murderous glare, the green in his eyes darkening as they flicker up and down between our faces and arms. The golden crown on his head glints in the chandelier light, making a halo made of antlers around his head. If he wasn't a vicious, self-serving prick, he would come across as classically handsome.

"I take it you didn't feel it was a requirement to tell him you invited me here?"

"Not particularly. But it's none of his concern who I bring to these kinds of events."

"I beg to differ. You are the future king; your choice of a partner reflects the kind of ruler you want to be. It would be wise next time to bring someone he approves of. Someone your people approve of."

"Quite frankly no one has a say in what I choose for myself but what makes you say this?"

"Because the look on his face, on everyone's in fact, suggests I might not make it through the night."

Frederick's servants lead us over to his table, opposite the king's.

Fantastic.

I sit as directed, next to the prince, watching him smile politely as he sits down, throwing out a few waves to those closest to us. A flurry of waiters descend upon the table, giving us each a glass of champagne and taking orders from others. Within minutes I have a glass of my favourite distilled vodka – on the rocks, of course – in my hands.

"I can't wait to introduce you to everyone," Frederick murmurs in my ear. I can feel Declan glaring at us both from across the table. Guilt swirls in my gut, but I smile brightly back at Frederick and gently lean away; I've got a part to play tonight, and I can have no distractions.

The feeling of being watched by several sets of eyes has the hairs on my neck rising. I shift to see King Theodore staring at me once again, I shoot him a wink and turn away, my attention latches on to Declan almost automatically, my smirk falls a little when I see the anger in his otherwise beautiful hazel eyes.

My lips tug down. We haven't spoken since we left the apartment, and I doubt I'll be able to talk with him for long without the vipers around us getting suspicious of our intentions. I convey my apologies through my eyes which he seems to pick up on, he shuffles in his seat and clears his throat, nodding slightly at me, all trace of his former anguish hidden away for now as if it was never there, to begin with.

"I have a rule tonight, Freddy," I drawl my hand drifting up his arm.

"And what is that, my dearest?" He leans in to hear me better over the sounds of conversation and music.

"No one is allowed to know my real name."

"Why is that?" I stare him down for a few seconds and smile at his bewildered look.

"I don't know, maybe it's something to do with who I am, outside of this dolled up façade?"

"But I know your name and those two do."

He turns away sheepishly at my stare. "And that wasn't my fault, was it? And they are my handlers that's different." He nods but doesn't answer me, so I try again. "Was it, Fritz?"

"No." He side-eyes me at the name.

"Remind me again whose it was." I sip from the champagne flute.

His reply is so quiet I miss it.

"Hmm?" I urged.

"Mine."

"Damn right, it was."

"What happened?" Rich asks from across the table, he leans forward resting his weight on his elbows with his fingers clasped together in front of him; fully invested in this story.

"Do you want to tell him or should I?" I grin from behind the glass, taking another sip.

"I will. Because you will only spin it into some twisted fable." Frederick straightens the lapels on his suit jacket and rests back against his seat. "I had hired someone to come in and acquire some information..."

"Steal my phone," I cut in.

"Yes. Steal her phone, I wanted to know who I was working with because she gave me a fake alias."

"That's the point of my job."

"When I found out who she was. I gave her a piece of my mind and the rest is history."

"You left out the part where I kicked your arse for threatening to expose me."

"Yes well, I like to keep that fond memory to myself."

Declan scoffs and takes a mouthful of his whiskey letting it fill his cheeks before swallowing it whole.

"But you hired her. Why would you expose the one person who could help you with, well... you know?" Rich's face lights up brighter the deeper he delves into our history.

"Because I hired *a* Fury, not *'the'* Fury."

"What does that mean?" Rich's eyebrows pinch looking between us.

"Come on! Don't tell me you don't know," Frederick grins sipping from his champagne flute. Rich's face is stoic and confused, "tell me you've heard the rumours about her." When Rich stays silent Frederick leans forward to analyse him closer, "How is that possible?"

"Are you going to share, or continue to hoard the information to yourself?" Declan grumbles, swirling the ice in his glass.

I chuckle quietly. Frederick opens his mouth.

"I do not think now is the time to discuss such topics," I cut him off. Both Rich and his highness look disappointed at the missed opportunity.

"Besides the point, I thought I'd invited a fox into the chicken coop. No. Not a fox. A fox is too tame. A wolf. I got scared and then I got desperate." Frederick looks at me. "She handled it like a champ though. Kicked my arse and then got on with her job as if nothing had happened."

"Your courtiers were feeding into your dramatics because it's what they thought you wanted to hear and I couldn't beat them up without consequences, so I went after you instead," I counter.

"And you didn't think about the consequences of attacking a prince?"

"Oh absolutely. You went through a bit of an ego boost and needed to be knocked down a peg or two. You wouldn't have dared tell anyone because it would've made you look weak." He gives me a small smile. "The fact that you enjoyed it is all on you." I take a drink and listen to both males laugh loudly; the joint sound makes me smile genuinely. That is until Declan gets up and leaves the table without excusing himself.

"What's up with him?" Frederick asks, I watch him retreat and then look to Rich to see understanding in his eyes.

"Excuse us, your highness." Rich stands, bows his head and follows Declan.

Declan

"The strongest thing you've got," I call to the bartender as I lean against the wood, seething.

"Make that two." His deep melodic voice says from next to me.

Two glasses are placed in front of us filled with an amber liquid. I drink mine in one and hail for another, Rich takes his time, hissing when it hits his throat.

"Shouldn't you be chaperoning the happy couple?"

"Don't grumble, it's not gentlemanly. But they can take care of themselves for a few minutes and besides, I don't drink champagne," he grins, watching me from the corner of his eye.

I grunt in response.

"Alright. If that's how you're going to play it, I'll lay it all on the table for you instead." I take a sip from the fresh drink, begrudgingly listening.

"She cares about you." My glass stalls inches from my mouth. "She won't admit it, because I don't even think that she knows yet, but I can see it in her eyes when she looks at you and you care for her. This, tonight, is an act that she is putting on for these fuckers." He leans in as he says it, waving his hand around the room. "So, stop pouting, she's got a job to do and it's ours to give her all the support we can. Tonight, she is surrounded by enemies and people that would gladly see her head on a stick as long as it meant that they get to live. We need to be here for assistance *and* her friends. I know it's probably difficult to see them together, but at the end of the night... she won't be going home with him." His dark eyes sparkle in the low light as he levels his stare at me, I nod in understanding feeling a weight lifted off of my shoulders and maybe just a little embarrassed.

A glimmer of something fizzles away deep in my heart, making me feel light and maybe just a little giddy.

We both move away from the bar when another servant calls the room to attention, his blue skin shimmers like none other I've ever seen, and his black hair hangs down to his waist. His armour gleams in the chandeliers' light, the silver reflecting it near perfectly, his webbed hands are crossed behind his back pushing his chest out like a crested bird. The coat of arms sits proudly across his torso; a leviathan charging up to the surface from the depths, jaw wide as it lunges at a passing ship.

"Her reigning Majesty of Salacia, Queen Cordelia Delmare, and her daughter the Crown Princess, her Highness, Princess Mala Delmare."

CHAPTER TWENTY-TWO
THE DISTRACTION TACTIC

Aella

My eyes widened at the two females before me, Queen Cordelia standing at the top of the stairs with her daughter to her left and a team of guards behind the both of them. Her dark skin shimmers, much like her servants. It's as though pearls have kissed her skin, partnered with her silver hair that flows down her back brushing against the top of her buttocks.

Her pastel blue dress falls elegantly down the length of her body, bunching in a knot at her waist, with a slit in the skirt up to her thigh, the delicate fabric is decorated with tiny shells and sea glass beads. A golden seaweed armband winds up her arm and a gold chain necklace that holds one pearl that only proves to help accentuate her already glowing skin.

Upon her moonlight silver head sits a golden crown, moulded from the sea's rarest corals, adorned with sapphires and emeralds that are near blinding as the glow under the lights.

She smiles from the top of the stairs arm in arm with her daughter, who is the near-perfect image of her mother. Her silk lilac dress is embellished with fish-like sequined scales, and a sea glass necklace hangs gracefully around her neck; her silver tiara matches her necklace.

Her black hair – just as long as her mother's – is braided close to her scalp at the sides and falls down her back like a dark and silky waterfall. Her dark skin too, shimmers from within, a distinct blue colour in the shape of thousands of scales.

They both smile broadly at the crowd, they grasp each other's hand and descend the stairs.

King Theodore marches to the bottom of the steps, glancing at Frederick harshly. Elijah – who I didn't see until now – leans forward whispering into his ear. Frederick sighs, turns to me with an apologetic look, and kisses my cheek before getting up and walking away, offering his hand to the sea princess, which she takes with a genuine smile.

Theodore in turn offers his hand out for the queen to take, helping her down the last few steps.

Elijah offers me an encouraging smile, before looking back to his prince, hand in hand on the dancefloor, with what can only be described as the most beautiful female in the world.

I sip from my champagne flute, watching on as Frederick works the room, greeting a multitude of different people and smiling brightly at everyone. It's been nearly an hour since his father had collected him for the dances and a handful of times, I have seen him trying to break away only to be sucked back in by a different group of guests.

Iris had arrived just after the sea queen and her daughter. Succeeding in appearing fashionably late to her own party. She does look stunning I must say, the intricate design on her silver dress catches the eye of everyone in the room. Either that or it's the plunging neckline that nearly reaches her belly button.

Melanie had disappeared shortly after arriving. To where no one knows, but I thought I saw her, not so discreetly, heading over to the bar.

The prince being distracted had worked out in my favour though, I plastered a bored expression upon my face, whilst being anything but, and watched her majesty's guards with my chin rested in my hand. They're a tightly knit group, rarely breaking their formation. It'll be difficult to get close to her. But not impossible if I play this right.

It's those silver-armoured males that I'm looking at when a small cough off to my side pulls me from my thoughts, and I turn to see a hand extended towards me.

My gaze trails up the branch-like arm to meet a pair of nervous hazel eyes and a lopsided grin.

I sit back in my chair and smile up at him.

"Are you asking me to dance, Mr Angelos?" Some ancient thing deep inside warms in my chest at the gesture. He's so nervous I can see it in his eyes. At the way they glisten in the chandelier lights, and again when he shifts his weight from foot to foot. It's strange to see him like this. He's never one for public displays. He's not even much for talking half of the time. So, to see this side of him is refreshing.

"Are you going to make me ask or am I standing here like an idiot for no reason?" My smile widens at the unease in his tone. Even after everything that happened in the woods, how he saved me, and everything under the waterfall, he still thinks that I'll reject him.

He sighs and is about to drop his hand when I lace my fingers through his, standing up as I do so. "It's never idiotic to ask a lady to dance, Declan," I whisper to him, my breath fanning across his face with our closeness, our chests brushing against each other.

I can see him shiver before he pulls out his cocky smirk showing those delicious-looking fangs that have me burning with desire. "Is that what you are?" he teases, before pulling me to the dance floor, my naughty thoughts chasing me as I look at the veins in his hands, and the muscles hidden beneath his too-tight dress shirt.

"Where are your gloves?" I whisper.

"I've taken them off for this," he mutters, looking down, a faint blush on his cheeks. He twirls me around when we enter the middle of the floor, my skirt lifting with the movement, before he pulls me tight to him. Resting one hand on the small of my back, the other holds my hand gently yet firm enough that I know he won't let me go.

The thought has me melting into him further, where we share breath. Standing taller, his eyes brighten with a smile and he asks, "Are you ready princess?"

The nickname has me preening and I want to kiss him again. All over, I can't seem to take my eyes off his lips. Not that that's a bad thing, not at all.

The brass band begins to play an upbeat rhythm, something uncommon for a setting like this, but that doesn't stop others from joining us on the dancefloor. Declan takes the first step guiding us both through a series of delicate steps before the music hits the chorus. A laugh burbles up from my chest as he lifts me, spinning us both around and around, not caring for anyone else in the room. Once my feet touch the ground again, I'm instantly pulled back against his chest.

"Gods' you look beautiful when you smile," he grins broadly, his eyes searching my face before he leads me into another twirl. I follow step by step and a blush warms my face.

We come together again, and he leans in closer, his breath on my cheek. "And you look downright adorable when you do that."

"Stop that," I whine, tucking my head under his chin, soaking in his rumbling chuckle, my blush worsens. He leans his head against mine as the song begins to slow leading into another one that is classically paced. The surrounding couples move closer and sway gently with the music.

My hand slides up from his shoulder to the nape of his neck and my fingers play with the ends of his hair. He sighs at the touch, the intimacy between us feels like electricity sparking along my skin.

"Thank you for asking me to dance," I mumble into his chest, allowing my eyes to drift closed.

"I'll ask you to dance anytime, princess." His voice rumbles in my ear. "You looked so nervous."

He sighs into my hair, and the warmth slides down my neck, "I thought you'd claim to be working. You looked awfully busy staring at those guards."

I snicker, "I was in fact." I pause, "But this is better."

We sway together, holding each other close not wanting the moment to end, he lifts my head gently to look into my eyes and the moment they connect it's like the whole room fades away, both of us wanting the same thing. Wanting more of that closeness. I'm not sure who leans in first but suddenly we are nose to nose.

A gentle cough interrupts us, and we jump apart, our moment shattering into pieces.

My eyes never leave his face, even as he looks over my shoulder to see who it is and his face falls. Declan quickly snaps an impassive mask into place and steps away from me still holding my hand, his eyes find mine again and he smiles politely before bowing low and kissing my hand.

"My lady." He rises and squeezes my fingers before he lets go, my hand drops to my side and he turns to walk away.

"Seems you two are comfortable," Frederick says from behind me, placing his hand on my waist and I have to stop the flinch I feel at his touch.

"It's not like that."

"Ah, so denial it is then," he mocks, smiling all the while.

"Excuse me..." I begin, my anger rising, before I suddenly remember where I am and decide to keep my mouth shut.

We watch Declan's retreating back as he navigates through the room, before Frederick and I make our way from the middle of the dancefloor into a shadowy alcove, away from prying eyes.

He watches me with amusement.

"Stop it. It was nothing," I grumble.

"You know the only reason I interrupted you both was because my father told me to, I was mesmerised by the pair of you before that, most people were."

"And why did your father feel inclined to ruin a perfectly fine dance?"

"Because you are *my* plus one. It wouldn't look good if you left with another male now, would it?"

I roll my eyes. "That will likely happen anyway. Your father would never allow you to leave with me and like you would really care about that anyway. Wasn't it you who said you don't care what people think of your partners?" I fire back, sounding like a scolded child.

"When they are with me and not with others that they shouldn't be. People will have their opinions and I can't change that. That is what I meant, and you know that that is what I meant. Besides you are very well aware of my feelings on the matter, Aella." His voice is stern, something that I've only heard once. I do know why he stopped us, it wasn't just his father, but I can't think about that right now. I've already been distracted enough tonight. I came here for information and so far all I've done is observe.

"And now you know mine," I utter so quietly I would think he'd have missed the comment.

"What's that supposed to mean?"

"Nothing." I shake my head and turn to face him, meeting his eyes once more I smile brightly. "Let's just enjoy the night. Shall we?" I nod over to the side of the room, where a group of courtiers are desperately trying to get the prince's attention.

The curious look on his face tells me he doesn't quite believe in my intentions, but walks with me anyway, plastering on a fake smile for those watching.

"I've never seen any water shifters before," Rich murmurs, his eyes roving over the queen's guard a few tables away.

"I don't think most people in this room have," Declan replies, looking at all of the other guests all seemingly in awe of the queen and the princess, I even see a few of the younger females eyeing up the guards in a very different way to what I'm doing.

Frederick, once again arm in arm with Princess Mala, seems happy to introduce her to everyone of importance in the surface world. He's been ignoring me ever since my dance with Declan. He hadn't said much to me and when I split to go get a drink, he all but disappeared into the crowd.

"We need to improvise a new plan."

"What why?" Rich asks bewildered.

"He was quite a big part of the first one and now he's not speaking to me. He won't even look this way." I nod in the direction of a sulky prince, with a winning smile lighting up his face.

"Right," Declan grins, evidently pleased with himself.

"What do you want to do?" Rich asks after slapping Declan on the shoulder.

"I don't know. Maybe I can just use him as a stepping stone." My eyes flicker all over the room trying to find inspiration, but they always go back to the young couple laughing and smiling while they work the room and then it hits me. "Oh gods'," I groan, rolling my eyes.

"What?" Rich asks, eyeing them as well.

I down the rest of my drink, gather my skirts and stand. I saunter across the room over to Frederick and Mala, a false playful expression resting on my face. I place my hand on his waist and step up to his side.

"Freddy. Are you going to introduce me to your new friend?" I reply, my voice like smoke and my lids drop down in a sultry manner.

He seems shocked to see me, let alone hear me using a pet name.

"Hello, my sweet," he replies, placing a kiss on my hair, gently prying Mala's arm from his. "Princess, this is my lovely date..." He stalls looking at me clearly remembering my request from earlier.

"Annie," I fill in with a sweet smile.

"Pleased to meet you, Annie, and please do call me Mala."

"As her highness wishes."

"How is it, you've come to know the prince? If you don't mind me prying."

"Not at all. We are a bit of an unusual couple. I'm something of a dancer. I work in the House of Asteria, on the stage. His Highness was present for a show of mine, and he wanted to meet the cast. The rest is history," I lie, squeezing Frederick's arm gently.

"How incredible. What discipline did you choose?"

"Ballet. It has been difficult, but it's so rewarding."

Her smile is bright and her eyes glow brightly. She nods along as I lie through my teeth about this supposed life that I have. Frederick says nothing. Just smiles and nods along with me.

One of the silver-plated guard's steps behind her, clears his throat and leans forward, whispering in her ear.

"Excuse me for one moment, my mother is asking for me." I curtsy and watch her leave with the tanned wall of muscle wrapped up in silver, like a delicious treat.

"What are you doing?" Frederick hisses, his grip on my arm tightening.

"Doing my duty as your date," I reply sweetly, smiling when Mala steps back up to us.

"My mother would like to meet you. She wants to get to know the woman who has made Frederick so enamoured," she grins, lighting up the space between us, her accent thick.

I stand tall and bow my head. "It would be an honour to meet your mother."

Frederick squeezes my arm again; I wince under the pressure of it. But he lets go when Mala offers her arm, this time towards me. I gratefully accepted, much to the dismay of Frederick and let her lead me towards her mother's table.

A quick glance at Rich and Declan and I see both surprised and shock expressions on their faces.

Her statuesque guards stand every which way next to the table watching everything and everyone with a high level of suspicion, and all of it is directed at me when we reach the table, after weaving through a throng of people to get here.

A guard steps forward to halt us, and Princess Mala pulls me in closer by my elbow, her chin rises, and her chest puffs out, standing tall waiting for him to begin.

"Name," he grunts, looking at me.

"She's with me," Mala defends, cutting me off just as I open my mouth the respond. Frederick steps up close behind me, his presence commanding, all though this guard doesn't seem to have caught onto that, or he doesn't care.

"With all due respect your highness…" he begins, only to be cut off by a voice behind him.

"Adrian, that is *not* how you greet his royal highness, Prince Frederick, let alone your own princess. He is heir to the throne of Anaphi and will one day become king and hopefully a trusted ally. Not that you should require a refresher. There is no threat to be had here, now let them through." Queen Cordelia's voice scolds. His ethereal features, or what I can see of them from under his helmet, soften at his queen's words, before stepping to the side to let us through.

"I never did like him," Mala whispers in my ear, guiding me to the chair closest to her mother.

"Thank you for that incredible introduction, your majesty. Should we talk treaties and trade contracts now?" Fred teases, trying to break through the otherwise thickening tension.

She graces him with a subtle smile. "Please sit," she gestures to the seats next to her, "and you can introduce me to your lovely date for this evening." The subtle insult is implied but left hanging in the air. I'm not the first and surely not the last.

Mala squeezes my arm slightly giving me a reassuring smile, before breaking away to take her own seat at the other side of the table. I curtsy and Fred instantly pulls out a chair for me to sit at and takes one himself on my left, putting a supportive hand on my crossed-over leg.

"Of course, your majesty. It's my pleasure to introduce you to my dear friend Annie," he smiles. It doesn't reach his eyes.

Her face screams beauty, from the small wrinkles around her stunning turquoise eyes, down to the shimmering scales under her smooth skin. Those same eyes scrutinise me now. From head to toe, she takes her time soaking in every inch of my being. To the point where I almost cave and tell her all of my secrets just to see her smile once more. I shake the thought away and regain my composure.

Madame K has scrutinised me in the same way many times, and I had to learn not to become so wrapped up in people's opinions, it has worked for the entirety of my adult life, but looking at Cordelia now all I seem to want is her approval and I don't know why.

I have clearly spent too much time around people with feelings, and it has finally begun to have a terrible impact on my training. I will have to submit myself for disciplinary action when I get back.

"What a lovely creature you are, a pity about your affliction however," she mutters finally, not breaking eye contact with me.

I relax back in my chair taking the pre-offered champagne flute with me. Frederick tenses at my side and shuffles around, giving away the game before it's even played.

"Your majesty, I'm not sure what you..." he tries, clearing his throat and readjusting his suit jacket.

"Do not play coy with me Frederick. Her penchant for lying is to what I am referring. I've been alive long enough to understand when I have been lied to. She does however seem to have a particular skill for it, and it intrigues me. Now your name, girl."

Frederick breathes out a heavy breath and relaxes back in his chair, even as he eyes the guards all around us. None appear to be listening, but this family is far too important to not have a few eavesdroppers amongst its ranks.

I open my mouth.

"Your real name, child."

My teeth clack together with how hard I shut it once more and analyse my options. I could lie again, better this time, it is my speciality. Something I was quite literally raised to do. But that could risk falling through again and having her as an alley would be more useful than not.

"Aella."

Dread and regret are the first things to fight in my chest for a long time. I've never taken as big of a risk in trusting someone ever in my life. No one has ever been trusted with my real name before. Someone with power. Frederick still wouldn't have known if he hadn't been crafty and gone behind my back. Declan and Rich are the only people I've ever trusted to tell. The Fort knows because that is the name that they gave me from birth.

"Hmm, that's more like it. What a beautiful name, where are you from, Aella?" Her gaze softens with the compliment, and a soft smile twitches on her full lips.

"She's from Anaphi, from the North beyond the mountains," Frederick says interrupting.

"Is she incapable of answering her own questions?" The turquoise-eyed goddess snaps, her gaze lingering a little too long and a little too violently on the prince.

"Mother!" Mala scolds.

"What? It is a valid question. She seems smart enough to be able to hold a conversation with me, but if there is something wrong, I would like to know now so I know not to waste my time. Or if this is a case of male pride, that is something that can easily be dealt with." This time her smile is strained, and she once again eyes me up and down. Seemingly content with her assessment, she moves on to Frederick to do the same.

I snicker at her reply. Both Mala and Frederick relax back into their chairs. Even the hard lines of his face soften at the light-heartedness.

He clears his throat, readjusts his suit jacket once again and meets her stare, "My apologies your majesty. Please continue as though I'm not here."

He takes a drink from his flute and turns away to observe the room. I reach out my hand to take his under the table, but he simply bats it away like a sulky child.

"Forgive me, child. My curiosity gets the better of me sometimes," she chuckles while taking another sip of champagne. "I would simply like to understand why it is that you have been watching my table from the moment I sat down."

I blink at her a few times; she reminds me of Madame K. I never could hide anything from her either. I know without a shadow of a doubt that I was being sneaky in my observation of her guards. Never once did she look my way.

"You are good, I will give you that," she muses once more, "but I have lived a life, my dear and I scan a room before I enter it, just the same as you do. You, in particular, caught my eye."

Still at a loss for words, I force something out of my mouth, so I don't actually sound as incapable of solid thought like she asked only moments before.

"I wouldn't have expected such a direct answer from someone so high up as you. How refreshing," I hum. "I'm here for information." Frederick's head snaps back in our direction so fast I fear he might've broken his own neck.

"Oh?" She sits back in her chair and crosses one leg over the other, the slit in her dress falling open, revealing the top of her thigh. "And what information is it that you think I have?"

"I have reason to believe that you are harbouring a class A criminal of Anaphi within your court."

The audible gasp from Frederick has guilt swarming in my gut. There's a small part of me, screaming to comfort him, but the other wins telling me to get the mission done with. I cannot afford to be there for him right now, not when I'm so close to getting the answers I need.

Our eye contact does not break even as she hums in interest.

"Where has this information come from?"

"Multiple sources, ones that I am not at liberty to disclose."

Her face is unreadable. I can't tell whether she is simply unhappy with my response if she's trying to figure out who told me or debating on whether I'm worth her time. Cordelia's slender fingers begin drumming on the table and I can see Mala looking in between both of us from the corner of my eye.

"What is this supposed criminal's name?"

"Roman Garcia."

"And his crime?"

"Being an active member, or rather, one of the leaders of the rebel group Dawnya; enabling riots; bodily harm upon member of the police department and the Stratos; fleeing from Ansrutas PD, when they tried to bring him to justice, and a sprinkle of active terrorism."

Her sombre expression tells me all I need to know. Roman is in fact in Salacia. Her eyes twitched around to her guards, the only ones allowed to listen to this conversation for a threat to life against her highness and her majesty.

I have noted the not-so-subtle step that those same guards have taken closing the distance between them and the table.

She sucks on her teeth, appearing to mull over her next words. "Hmm, I have heard of an investigation being held against him. So, what are you then? A detective or something?"

"Or something," I shrug, smirking when her eyes widen slightly.

"And what of these other leaders? Are you tracking them?"

"I have been, and I am close to finding them," I lie, hoping she doesn't notice.

"Are you here to kill him then?" Either she doesn't notice the lie, or I have truly gotten away with it. But I can see that her patience is wearing thin, the tone of her voice changes as she speaks to me. I can see it in the way her eyes are starting to wander into the crowd – mostly over to the king's table – probably to see if he's watching us.

"With all due respect to your majesty. What I am to do with this criminal is my own agenda and will be of no consequence to yourself or your kingdom, provided you hand him over without objection." I twirl my glass against the table, a nervous energy building in my chest, something I'm not accustomed to.

"I will say. This is not how I thought the evening would go." Her fingers stop drumming.

"You and me both," Frederick mutters beside me, gaining a laugh from the princess, Cordelia only gives him a tight-lipped smile.

"How do I know that this is not some sort of plot, to get me to reveal secrets only to screw me over later?"

"Mother!" Mala scolds once again.

"Oh, hush child." She waves her off without looking at her. Her mesmerising blue-green gaze never leaves my own.

"To put it simply. You don't. I think whatever this relationship turns out to be, will be a very strained and cautious connection. You will have to put faith in me, as I with you and if it turns out to be nothing then no harm, no foul," I shrug again.

"You speak plainly for someone who lies so beautifully." Her whole face lights up. She looks me up and down again but this time I don't feel as though the look is deliberately trying to make me feel uncomfortable, but instead it's an appreciative once-over. "I wish to continue this discussion in a more private environment." She tells me, looking the embodiment of relaxation as she sips from her own champagne glass. "I will be in touch, Aella."

My name rolls off her tongue sending shivers down my spine. I still don't know how to feel about that, but I've just bagged myself a private audience with the queen. So, if a small truth gets me that, what will a big secret get me?

"Thank you for your time, your majesty. I hope you enjoy the rest of your evening." I smile politely as I stand, curtsy, and walk away.

I don't make it far before a large, warm hand wraps around my forearm.

"What the fuck was that?" Frederick hisses in my ear.

"Something you wouldn't even do yourself clearly," I spit back.

He doesn't say anything more and that scares me more than the furious look on his face, his eyebrows are pinched and there's a devastating emerald fire in his usual calm green eyes. He guides me towards the outside balcony, decorated with fairy lights and candles. The cool breeze whips up my hair as I'm forced outside.

"LEAVE US!" Frederick snarls at anyone present. They scramble to get out of the way. His voice turning deeper and darker, it's not just his royal privilege coming through, but his fae heritage. Their commanding presence is unlike any other being. A few of the guests hesitate before leaving, it's only when Frederick stares them down do they leave us alone.

He paces back and forth in front of me, wringing his hands through his previously perfect hair. He begins mumbling to himself. I watch him all the while waiting for him to sort his thoughts out. What I did was necessary for the investigation. But that doesn't mean that I enjoyed keeping him in the dark about everything.

"I can't believe you!" he yells suddenly, making me jump. "I brought you here for you to enjoy yourself. For you to be able to relax and have an evening that doesn't consist of murder or lies, and this is how you repay me? By humiliating me and making a mockery of my generosity."

"Frederick..."

"Don't Frederick me." He points a finger in my face, anger radiates from him. I take a step back trying to put some distance between us.

"You lied to me. You manipulated me. Hel you haven't even spent time with me this evening." His yelling gets louder and louder, and the people closest to the balcony doors watch the scene unfold.

"And whose fault is that?" I challenge, "After my dance with Declan..."

He scoffs and turns away, those strong fingers run through his hair over and over again. "Don't get me started on that," he snarls.

Pressing my lips together in a tight line I stand there unmoving and watch him continue to pace backwards and forwards.

"I suppose I shouldn't be surprised, should I? It's always the mission with you, isn't it? You never actually care about the people you meet along the way, they're just another stepping stone on your way to the top of the pyramid, aren't they?" He stops moving and turns to me with gritted teeth and too-dark eyes. The male before me doesn't even look like the Frederick I met all those years ago. This is no longer the careless boy who had girls chasing him down the corridors or spent his time out in the sunshine reading everything he could get his hands on. No. This is an heir to the throne. This is a king staring back at me, a ferocious fae leader and the thought alone makes me both proud and terrified.

"Are you going to say anything?" he growls, stepping forward so close that we're nearly nose to nose. His fae fangs are on full display.

"Would anything I say actually make a difference?" I murmur, making his eyes widen slightly, catching him by surprise.

His fists clench and unclench by his sides, and I can see him warring within himself. Frederick doesn't get to make a decision before a hulking figure stands in front of me, blocking my view of the angry prince.

"Back up. Now." His voice is so low and gravelly it's almost unrecognisable as words, the sound becoming more animalistic. Rich is there pulling me back before putting himself in front of me also, like two protective barriers.

Rich's hand clasps mine and he leans forward to whisper something in Declan's ear, who nods, not taking his deathly stare from Frederick, who in turn, shows just as much hatred for the male in front of him. I'm guided by my hand from the balcony and back into the main ballroom, surrounded by tables and people smiling and laughing, enjoying themselves.

"Are you ok?" Rich asks, leaning down to talk into my ear.

"Yeah, fine," I smiled up at him.

"You look surprisingly calm," he notes, looking over my face again and again.

"I have to be. If I react the way I wanted I'd be the monster they all think I am," I reply, turning away to look back outside to see Declan and Frederick yelling at each other. "Are *they* going to be ok?"

Rich follows my gaze. "Yeah. I told Dec not to hit him, but we've been looking for you for a while and as soon as he saw you with Frederick so close, looking murderous, I honestly thought he was going to pick him up and throw him from the balcony. Now! Enough dwelling, let's go get drunk." He offers me his arm, "my lady." I let out a breathing laugh and took his arm.

Sat at the bar sometime later, both of us have taken several shots of whiskey – which have gone straight to my head – keeping an eye on the balcony doors. We both watch as Declan emerges first, his face still laced with anger but there's a hint of content hidden beneath. He reaches the bar quickly and it's then I see Frederick slinking back through the door before being lost in the crowd.

"All good?" Rich asks, over the rim of his glass before taking a sip.

"All good," Declan replies, ordering his own glass of amber liquid.

"Well, I suppose a thank you is in order," I reply, handing over some money to the bartender before Declan can.

"That's not necessary," Declan replies, shifting awkwardly, "the bastard is lucky he's a prince, or that would've gotten a Hel of a lot worse for him." His voice is like thunder, rumbling and dark and entirely too erotic.

Rich grins, raising his glass in the air like a salute "You're welcome, *liefling.*

"Ready to go?" I ask, placing my own finished drink back onto the bar.

They nod and down the rest of their drinks, following my lead.

"Hey, cutie." A too-sweet, too-high-pitched voice floats into my ears and a pale hand wraps around Rich's arm. My blood instantly boils at the scent that wafts over us, vanilla and rose. It makes me want to gag.

"Oh, and you're here too." Her voice drops a few octaves.

My attention flickers to her. Iris Haakon, shimmering in the chandelier light, dangling from Rich's arm as though she belongs there.

"Princess, so lovely to see you again." My posture is wooden, as is my voice, this is not something I had prepared myself for.

"Isn't it?" she replies, just as rigid.

Rich is shell-shocked when she flashes him a wolfish smile once again.

"Your Highness." He bows his head, subtly stepping backwards untangling their arms.

My fingers curl into fists at my side. "Are you having a nice time?" I ask through my teeth, drawing her attention back to me.

Her face drops when she once again meets my eyes. "I suppose."

The tension thickens in the air and warm fingers wrap around my fist, unfurling each finger one by one. Declan's warm hand winds around my own, drowning it with the size of his.

"Well, your Highness, this has been a fantastic evening, but we were just about to..."

"You can't leave!" she whines, grabbing Rich's hand and pulling him forward again. "We were just getting to know each other." The grin on her face is full of mischief and desire, I can almost smell the pheromones coming off of her.

"This is going to be difficult," Declan leans down to whisper in my ear. The sensation sends delicious shivers down my spine, leaving goosebumps in their wake.

"There you are. I've been looking for you all over!" Another softer feminine voice cuts through the growing awkwardness. I'm shocked to see Princess Mala approaching behind Rich and even more so seeing her thread her arm through his.

"Oh, Princess Mala. Hi," he stutters, looking more confused than ever.

"You've met Princess Iris, I see," Mala leans into him, heavily squeezing his arm in both of hers.

I grin wildly at the possessive display.

"We were just talking about..."

"Getting another drink," I interrupt, Rich's shoulders tense, but I can't take my eyes off Iris. Her face becomes more and more sour the longer Mala stays clutching to Rich. Something dark curls in delight, deep inside my chest.

Declan squeezes my hand, and I can tell by the bow of his head and the shake of his shoulders that he too is trying to keep his laugh to himself, at the princess's expense.

"Would you like to drink with us, princess?" I ask Iris, her face becoming flushed with anger and jealousy.

Rich and Mala lock their eyes and appear to have a silent conversation that finally pushes Iris over the edge. She scoffs, gathers her skirts and storms away, the black of her hair flowing delicately behind her.

"I must say. You have impeccable timing, your royal highness," I say to

Mala.

"That or I saw her eyeing him up all night and thought I'd save the poor soul," she replies, smiling brightly up at Rich, who still seems a little confused about the situation. She finally takes her hands from his arm.

"How about that drink?"

CHAPTER TWENTY-THREE
THE AFTERMATH

"So, if I get the laser from my gun and point it around the room would you chase it like a house cat?" I ask, barely containing my joy at the mental image of a larger than life snow leopard bounding around the room. Declan gives me a hearty, full laugh that rumbles even the bed beneath us.

We lay here, both still dressed in our formal attire after having stumbled back into the apartment after a very successful drinking session with Her Highness, talking aimlessly.

"What? It's a reasonable question. Would you, or wouldn't you?" I defend, feeling lightheaded.

"That's something that we would have to try out because I have no idea, but I hope to the gods that I don't. You two would never let me live it down," he grins, looking fully relaxed and filled to the brim with joy.

"Rich!" I yell laughing.

"Don't listen to her!" Declan yells over me, desperately trying to place his hand over my mouth to stop me from saying anything further.

"SHUT UP! I'M ON THE PHONE!" he shouts back. Declan and I pause before laughing harder. Rich's bedroom door slams shut, and I laugh until

I'm wheezing, and tears fall from my eyes.

When I've calmed down enough, I see Declan staring at me, a bright smile on his face and a knowing twinkle in his eye. The attention makes me feel suddenly self-conscious, something I've never felt before.

"So, tell me. What is your relationship with the king?" he asks suddenly.

"What do you mean?" My eyebrows pinch and surprise coverts my features, I'm sure of it.

"Looking at the two of you tonight seemed like you were both trying to win a mental chess match. Why is it that he hates you so much? What did you do to him?" he smiles. Probably at the thought that I'd disrespected him in some way.

"I didn't do anything to him." My joy from earlier has gone in such a flash it's almost dizzying. "It's simply because of what I am. Of what I represent in his own self that he doesn't like."

He listens so intently it's almost scary how he seems to hang onto my every word. "What do you mean, 'what you represent?'"

I sigh and sit up moving to lean back against the headboard, smoothing out my dress as I do. "He doesn't like having to rely on us because he doesn't want to be associated with *our kind,*" I gesture with my hands at the quote that came from the king himself. "He believes what you think. When you asked me whether or not we were the wrath of the gods. It's similar to that. Although he knows otherwise, he sees us as nothing more than creatures that belong in the Abaddon. So, he sees us as monsters. Something he himself is trying not to be."

Having rolled on his back he turns his gaze up to the ceiling listening to my explanation, "So it's not actually you, he hates. It's all of you. What you are, what you do."

"Exactly."

He sighs, "Have you ever thought about killing him?"

The question shocks me, more than the first that led to this topic, "unless he is a target set to be killed. I am not allowed to touch him."

"That doesn't really answer my question."

"Declan, you know I am not allowed to think for myself and especially never about killing the king." I pause when he makes eye contact with me, the usual soft hazel is lit with a fiery amber that holds a sense of anger or resentment in them. I'm almost lost in the heady feeling of such an emotion until he turns away. Once more looking at the ceiling. "It's also if you haven't figured it out yet, treason. Something that people can lose their lives over."

He doesn't reply, doesn't take the bait for a lighter topic change. I don't exactly know where these questions have come from, but I can say for sure they are making me uncomfortable.

"Where is the guild?" he asks quietly.

"I can't tell you that," I reply automatically.

He sighs.

Sock-covered feet pad through the apartment and Rich appears in the doorway pulling at his tie. "Well, that was more exciting than it was originally thought to be." He flops down on the bed next to us, bouncing us on the mattress.

"The phone call or the evening?" I ask, smiling broadly, thankful for the interruption.

He chuckles, blushing, "The evening." His eyes flutter closed, and I note his eyelashes are so long they brush against the tops of his cheeks.

"Yeah, and you didn't even try," Declan adds, propping himself up on his elbow. His increasingly sour demeanour fading into the air, "You had two princesses after you and all you did was walk around. TWO PRINCESSES!"

I playfully slap Declan on the arm with the back of my hand, his gaze lingers a little longer on the curve of my smile.

"Hardly, one wanted to bed me and the other wanted to one-up the other," Rich replies, staring intently at the ceiling.

I think back to how Mala had been after Iris had all but stormed away from us. She led us back to her mother's table and ordered that we have a constant supply of drinks for the table. The queen had departed shortly after we sat down to mingle with the other guests and spend some time with his majesty. The three of them had bonded over some life experiences, even if they hadn't met before. I had become more and more aware of the things that I had missed out on growing up. But the drinks went down so smoothly that I quickly forgot about all that and chose to enjoy the stories being told.

"I prefer the second one," I say resolutely.

"I was just going to say…" Declan agrees.

"Oh, for the love of the gods, you two…" he groans, and he gets up to leave.

"Which one of them was on the phone?" I yell, but he doesn't turn around, he just continues on his way. "Rich?" I ask, I only receive a grunt in response, and I turn to lie back down at Declan's side. Both of us turned up towards the ceiling. The lock to Rich's door clicks shut and Declan turns to me, standing from the bed.

"Well, I suppose we should get some rest as well." His voice is soft like warm honey dribbling across my skin. There's a rumble to it that has goosebumps rising.

"I suppose," I whisper in agreement, watching his throat bob under his dress shirt.

He leans down and places a firm yet gentle kiss on my lips. I breathe in his scent. It's all around me, guiding me, tempting me. I've missed this. I only had a taste under that waterfall in Lefki, and I've been craving more since. It's all I've been thinking about — it's been very inconvenient — but all I know is I need his lips on mine like I need air to breathe.

His large warm hand smooths across my stomach, the silk acts as a gentle, soft barrier between the heat of our bodies, a barrier I wish wasn't there. He moves higher, brushing up and over my breast, rolling my nipple through his fingers as he goes. Not stopping until it hardens, and I become breathless under his caress.

That same hand moves to my throat, giving it a little squeeze before gliding to my cheek cupping it and holding me close.

My heart flutters rapidly like a butterfly trapped in a jar, waiting to burst out. The heat from his kiss burns me to the point of torture and yet I can't get enough.

I want more. I crave it.

I moan shamelessly as his tongue slips through my lips exploring my mouth over again, claiming it for his own. My fingers tangle into his hair pulling him closer, the groan I receive in response makes my lower belly throb.

He pulls away, both of us panting for breath, and he rests his head on my own with his eyes closed, breathing hard. I whimper at the loss of contact and his breathing stills in his chest before his eyes burst open.

"Do that again." His voice comes out hoarse.

"What?" I whisper, unsure.

He kisses me hard again, before pulling back just as quickly and I whimper again, wanting more. I try to follow him trying to regain the connection.

"Fuck," he growls, pressing his body against mine as his nose goes to my neck breathing in deep. "What are you doing to me?"

My whole body feels as though it's on fire. His hand goes to the slit in my dress and the rough skin of his hand drags the material up my body, baring me to him. Pulling me to him I'm dragged down the bed as he looks me up and down, greedily taking his fill and I can't help but feel more turned on by allowing him to take his time.

"Fuck! No underwear?" I feel his erection growing hard against my leg, and moisture dampens my skin at the apex of my thighs.

"It would've ruined the streamline of the dress," I chuckle.

"And we can't have that can we?"

I coyly bite my lip shaking my head. Leaning over me, his lips meet mine in a demanding kiss, one full of desire and fire, and his tongue slides into my mouth again. One hand holds him above me as the other slides the silky red fabric up higher exposing my stomach.

Declan takes a deep inhale, "Aella!" he growls, his fist bunching up the material of my dress. With his heightened shifter senses, I know he can smell my arousal and not an ounce of shame creeps in. Not when I see the unadulterated want in his fiery amber eyes.

I can tell by the flex of his muscles, he's barely containing himself, moving at my pace. I glide my hands up and down his arms feeling the muscles shake with restraint and all the veins in his arms as they bulge under his scarred skin. He climbs over me, his knees on either side of me straddling my hips, the buttons of his shirt begin popping open in his haste to rid himself of the material.

I sit up and begin helping him, nearly ripping it apart. His abs are in front of my face within seconds, and without hesitation, my lips are pressed against the skin there, and my tongue darts out lapping at the grooves his muscles have made. My hands glide around to the curve of his lower back, pulling him closer as he fights with his tie and the rest of the buttons. Growling his annoyance and desperation.

"Fuck!" The snarl rips through him and I hear the tear of fabric once again. My hands climb higher on his back feeling the taut muscle under my fingertips. Years of training and discipline have built this physique and I now get to reap the benefits of his hard work.

I place a kiss on his chest, right over his heart and look up at him to see him already staring at me.

"Arms up," he murmurs. Within a matter of seconds, my dress is on the floor joining with his own clothes and I'm pushed back onto the bed. His pants are quick to join the growing pile.

He's hovering over me, placing kisses on my neck as one of those calloused hands rolls my nipple again and again. Toying with it. With me.

"Tell me to stop," he murmurs in my ear.

He pulls back to look over my naked body spread out before him. Ready and waiting for him to devour. He takes his time drinking in each freckle, every dip and curve. Every scar. His eyes are like a crazed fire. My hands start to move. Feeling too self-conscious to be so exposed. To cover up the many imperfections that I know ruin my pale skin.

I can't read his face and that makes my discomfort grow.

His deft fingers snatch my wrists, stopping them from reaching their targets.

"Don't." That's his only warning. "You wouldn't cover a masterpiece, would you?" He leans down until his lips brush over the scar on my belly. My graduation scar. Something he still doesn't understand. He moves slowly kissing and licking each one, spending time to show every imperfection love and gentleness.

My heart swells and beats out of time, when he looks at me again, longing has replaced his lust.

"You're beautiful, Aella. Like a god's damned work of art. You're strong, fierce. Damn, sexy." Each compliment is accentuated with a kiss. "You're much more powerful than I think you even realise." Another kiss. This time over my heart. He settles in between my thighs. "And you're all mine."

I giggle.

"What?" he grunts rubbing his nose against mine.

"So possessive."

He rumbles with a chuckle and moves to begin sucking on my neck.

Tangling my fingers in his hair I tuck harshly on the strands. I've missed these soft curls tickling my skin. I moan when he bites down on the juncture between my neck and shoulder.

"Shit," he groans again. If I could bottle the sound, I'd do everything in my power to make it happen. "Aella, tell me to stop," he begs, even as he continues to kiss down my chest.

I'm breathless and panting by the time he makes it to my breast, sucking my nipple into his mouth tasting and teasing the bud until it's standing at its peak.

"Don't stop," I whimper, closing my eyes, relishing in the moment. In the total sensation that is him. He gently bites the underside of my breast and moves further down, kissing and licking at my navel. Paving his way lower.

His throat rumbles with a growl, the sound makes my blood hotter, my skin more sensitive, makes me needier.

"Declan," I whine. Wanting more, wanting everything, but unable to tell him with words.

"Use your words, baby girl. What do you want from me?"

I shake my head.

"Open your eyes. I want them on me when I pleasure you. Now tell me what you want." He places a kiss so gently on the inside of my thigh. I open my eyes to see that devilish smirk looking back at me.

"There she is. Such a good girl." His fangs extend and he scraps them along my skin, still not doing what I want him to. But when he nips at the sensitive flesh there, all other sense of rational thought rushes out.

"Declan please," I breathe, tangling my fingers into his hair.

He chuckles, "I can't make you feel good if I don't know what you want, my love," he teases. His lips trail higher and I think he's finally going to listen to my silent plea, but he instead skims over where I need him most and he kisses my other thigh. Frustration builds and I place my legs over his shoulders. He huffs a laugh against my skin.

"I bet you sing beautifully when you come."

"How would you know you haven't touched me yet," I growl, using my legs to pull him forward.

He laughs. The bastard laughs. "You only had to ask sweetheart. You don't need to beg." The name rings through me uncomfortably. But then his fingers are on my clit and the discomfort fades into something blissful. Something totally divine.

"Fuck!" I scream, throwing my head back.

"Aella, you've made such a mess," he tsks, dipping the tip of his finger inside of me, "Fuck. You're so tight."

A loud moan purrs from within me as he pushes it in the rest of the way curling and hitting that spot inside.

"Gods."

"My name is Declan, princess. I'll want you only once. I don't share." I gasp loudly when a second finger joins the first, stretching me open. Rolling my hips I look desperately for more friction, anything, as the pressure begins to build.

"You're close, aren't you? I can feel you squeezing me, princess."

"Uhm hmm," I moan, nodding my head vigorously, squeaking when he picks up the pace. "Oh fuck, Declan!" I cry out, the sound cracking and white-hot pleasure consumes me. I keep grinding against his hand, shamelessly wanting more, until the sensation ebbs.

He removes his hand, bringing it up to his lips. Sucking one into his mouth his eyes close as he tastes me on his fingers. When they open again his pupils are blown wide with lust.

"I'd love to taste more of you than that, princess. But if I don't get inside of you right now. I might actually lose my mind." Sliding my legs off his shoulders he positions himself better in between them. He grips my hips, lifting them for a better angle, and the head of his cock rubs against my clit. I shiver with anticipation and molten want.

"Please," I beg again, wanting more.

His eyes lock with mine, and I can see the hunger. His wanton need for me swirling in his irises.

"What did I say?" His voice is but a rumble.

I reach between us and guide the head of his cock to my entrance. He hisses at the wetness coating the tip. But doesn't thrust forward. Instead, he holds himself there waiting for my answer.

"Answer me, princess."

"And if I don't?"

I gasp as his cock parts my folds and slides over my wetness coating himself but not quite pushing in.

"I do so love a challenge. But I asked you a question and I'm still waiting for your answer."

"Declan," I whine, desperate for more.

His fingers dig into the skin of my hips, and I know now they'll be bruised tomorrow. Not that I care. I want those marks. I want that claim.

"Princess," he sings back to me. "What did I say about you begging?"

I search my mind for the answer. For anything to end this torture. "That I didn't have to," I pant, thrusting my hips higher to no avail.

"Exactly. But now I think I've changed my mind. Because you sound so damned divine when you whimper my name." He slams into me, and I'm caught between a gasp and a moan as he stretches me. He moves so he's leaning over me, his lips a hair's breadth away from mine. The groan that comes from his throat and my mind racing at dizzying speeds. The sensations are too much, and yet not enough. Not nearly enough.

"Fuck you feel so good. So perfect," he utters against my skin. "You might just be the death of me, Aella." He kisses me hard as he thrusts in, swallowing my breathy gasps and deep sighs.

My hands move to his shoulders and my fingers stretch across the muscle, feeling how they move as he begins thrusting, slowly at first but he's quick to pick up the pace.

He's so deep inside of me, he's all I can feel. All I can see as he covers my body with his, drowning me in his essence, in his presence.

I wrap my legs around his hips, feeling the push and the drag of his cock, keeping him close to me.

"Shit, you're fucking perfect," he groans into my ear.

"Funny. I was just about to say the same," I moan back, meeting his powerful thrusts. With his face buried in my neck and his thrusts speeding up I can tell he's chasing that high.

"I am far from perfect princess. But what I am is selfish."

I place one hand above my head, trying to stop us from falling off the bed and he pounds into me harder and faster. His mouth finds my breast, sucking and biting at my nipple as he drives in impossibly deeper. My fingers find his hair again.

"Fuck Declan." His hot mouth moves from one nipple over to the other and the cold night air has both of the little buds standing to attention. The sensitivity has me spiralling into a state that is both pleasurable and supremely unbearable.

"Scream it. Scream my name, princess." He drives harder and his thrusts become more erratic. "I'm not going to last much longer. You're too good. Too fucking good"

He grinds into me, kissing me hard. His hips and his tongue work in unison.

Pleasure washes over me in waves. It's so powerful I feel it flowing throughout my entire body. Declan catches my hand, entwining our fingers helping me to ride it out and he continues to chase his own.

Coming down from my own high I watch him come undone, it's a beauty untold. His blissfulness is captivating, and I can't help but be in awe of his loss of control, and he continues to thrust into me as he comes down from his own euphoric high.

Both sweaty and spent, Declan rolls off to the side of me, pulling me close to his chest. We both pant with exhaustion but still, he turns to me, stealing another kiss from my undoubtedly swollen lips.

"Gods above. You're something else," he grins, tucking a piece of hair behind my ear.

I draw little symbols and pictures across his chest with my fingertips, "funny. I was about to say the same thing," I grin.

His fingers roam up and down my rib cage, while we both regain our breathing. My eyes begin drooping, feeling weighed down with sleep. He gets up suddenly and moves to my adjoining bathroom, coming back with a damp cloth, and placing a hand softly against my leg. "May I?"

I almost laugh, after what we've just done, that he would ask, but the vulnerability in his eyes only makes me smile and I lift my leg.

He disposes of the cloth and arranges us so we're both under the covers, before pulling me close. My back to his chest with his arm thrown over me. I entwine our fingers soaking up his warmth.

He places a soft kiss on my shoulder, "Sweet dreams, princess."

A loud obnoxious tapping on my window wakes me the next morning. It hadn't taken me all that long to fall asleep last night. Not with Declan wrapped around me like some sort of heated blanket. I turn on my pillow to see the reason I had the most blissful night's sleep for the first time in forever. With his hazel hair in disarray and his cheek mushed into the linen-covered cushion, he looks like the personification of peace.

Following his warmth, I tuck myself further under his arm, until that same tapping starts up again. Groaning, I turn over and peek through the sheer curtains.

A brightly coloured puffin sits on the iron railing just outside the door peering into the room, the bird squawks loudly when it sees I'm watching it. I lift Declan's arm from my middle, and I slowly leave the bed, careful not to wake him and pad over to the white patio doors. The little bird's wings flap in surprise as I pull them open, but it stays still long enough for me to unravel the note rolled around its stubby little leg.

Aella,

I took a deep interest in our conversation, and I would like to know your thoughts, if you would be so kind as to humour me by answering my questions. I have the afternoon free. Drop by after mid-day. We may be able to help each other.

Sincerely,

Queen Cordelia

The Aftermath

The letter is stamped with both the Salacia crest and the crest of the Delmare royal family. The little bird squawks again, flapping its wings impatiently.

"What in the Abaddon is that?" Declan's croaky voice comes from the bed. I turn to see him rolling on his back, his eyes aren't even open yet. I smile watching him throw his arm over his eyes.

I turn back to the little black and white bird. I've never seen one of these before, another species that is native to the southern coast. I pet its little head and it snaps its beak at me angrily.

"Alright, alright. Give me a minute." I throw on the nearest clothes, a white shirt that is too big and go to the kitchen to root out one of Rich's granola bars. I break some off and feed it to my feathered messenger, who chirps happily, bounces on the spot, and finally turns, taking flight. I watch it fly over the rooftops and reread the note memorising the information.

Warm hands wrap around my waist from behind and a solid chest encloses me in.

"Why is a little southern puffin getting more attention than me, this early in the morning?" he mumbles into my neck, kissing the skin under my ear.

I smile and place my hand on his cheek, "because he was obnoxious enough to wake me up with his tapping on the window."

He chuckles, "How would you like to be woken up next time, princess?"

"I think I'll leave that up to you and your wild imagination."

He groans, squeezing my sides.

"It was a letter from Queen Cordelia. She wants to meet me today."

Resting his head on my shoulder we both watch the river flow into the bay below us, "that was quick."

I hum in answer. He sighs.

"Back to it then."

"I'm afraid so." I turn in his arms. "But that doesn't mean we can't steal a few moments here and there," I utter against his lips, taking the bottom one between my teeth. His eyes blaze with the same fire I'd seen last night.

He bends, picking me up. On instinct, I wrap my legs around his hips, and he carries me back to bed.

"For the record, this is what I'd do to wake you up in the mornings." Within moments he buries his head between my thighs. Tasting me as he promised to do last night.

The sun of the day beats down on the concrete and bounces back up making me so sweaty that my sunglasses begin to slide down my face. Even with my hair up in a ponytail, the heat is near unbearable.

Finding the embassy is easier than I originally thought. I chose the streets closest to the bay and followed the sea around to the pale sandstone building with a blue, almost pearl-like roof. The dome shines brighter than any other and the vines crawling around the small spires show just how in touch with nature the embassy really is.

I look up to the arch windows to see servants and guards scuttling up and down the corridors. I walk around the corner to the main entrance; a golden set of embossed doors stand at about two stories of height; they glimmer in the sunlight like liquid sand.

Two guard's stand-alone outside. One on each side, dressed in silver armour with black leather accents. I cringe as the heat seems to intensify the closer, I get to the metal doors; the sandstone steps are just as hot, if not more so, than the concrete street. The twosome cross their spears in a practised stance across the door once I step close enough.

"What business do you have here?" The one on the left snaps. Wary of my presence.

"I'm here to see your queen." I hold up the paper between my fingers, the one to my right snatches it from me and reads the words. Upon seeing the two stamped crests, she nods to her partner, and both push open the doors, the metal churning and groaning with the weight of itself.

Two sentries stand in the ostentatious lobby filled with antique furniture in an array of soft greens, pastels blues, whites, and creams all contrasted with natural wood flooring.

A servant dressed in a loose-fitted white linen shirt and dark brown leather breeches, with knee-high boots steps forward.

No, not a servant.

A servant doesn't carry a sword on his hip.

Not to mention they would be in uniform.

It's then that I look at his face, his pale skin is without a single scar, his blue eyes shine brightly, and his golden wavy hair brushes down to his eyebrows.

"Good morning, Aella," he says smiling and steps forward, his hand raised for me to shake, "I'm Adrian."

"Good morning," I reply, a little breathless at the welcoming sparkle in his deep eyes, taking his hand.

"I'll take you to her," he grins, and my knees feel weak at the sight.

I smile and nod allowing him to lead me through the corridors all following the same colour scheme as the lobby. He takes me to a round room at the back of the building under a glass roof, with an entire wall dedicated to an aquarium filled with unique tropical fish.

The queen sits by the window, reading a heavy tome as the double doors swing open.

"Thank you, Adrian. You can leave us," she says, not looking up from the book in front of her. He bows and closes the door behind him, not without giving me a warning glance before he does so.

"The get-up is a bit much... *Siren*."

I scoff and take my sunglasses off my face, looking down at myself. I didn't even put my vest nor my mask on for this.

"What? Did you think that I wouldn't find out?" she asks, turning to look at me with a devious smirk on her face.

"You've been busy since, what? Ten hours ago?"

She laughs, the sound light and filled with promise. "Not me, Adrian. He doesn't seem to trust the assassin whose reputation precedes her."

"Hmm, that's a shame. He has a lovely smile," I nod towards the door. Where I know he stands listening in.

"I'm sure he'd be pleased to hear that."

"He already has." I turn back to her and grin. "But it does not matter to me whether or not you know, but I am quite surprised that despite knowing who I am. Or rather *what* I am. That you would be willing to be left alone with me."

It's her turn to give a scoff. "If you wanted to kill me, I'm sure you would've found a way to do so last night. I know you were watching the guards." She clasps her hands together, analysing me as she does.

"Hmm, true. But that would've been one messy cleanup," I agree, placing my hands behind my back, and smirk at her. She chuckles lowly.

I look around the room, the dark blue panelled walls and dark brown flooring contrast to the surrounding hallways and bring a darker, moodier feel to the room.

The multitude of oil paintings decorating the walls all depict the sea and the shoreline, or ships on choppy waves.

"At ease, soldier." She notes my posture and stands up. She moves towards the ornate beige couch in front of the even more impressive, carved marble fireplace, sea creatures of every kind hold the mantle up.

I relax but stay by the door, watching as she takes her seat, spreading her arms out wide across both the back of the chair and the arm. Her flowing soft peach dress blows gently on the breeze that forces its way through the open windows, the smell of sea salt heavy in the air. She breathes it in deep and smiles.

"I hope you don't mind but the scent of the sea helps me to feel at home, especially when I'm forced to be above ground."

"Not at all," I reply, still hovering by the door. She may not be my queen, but she still outranks me, and my conditioning – although more lax than it should be – still dictates my behaviour around royalty.

"Are you going to stand there all day or are you going to join me so that we may continue our conversation?"

I take a seat in a fabric-bound white armchair opposite her, resting my glasses on the coffee table that separates us.

"A genuine Fury, hey?" she asks, looking at my exposed wrist and the number that is tattooed there.

"Is that going to be a problem?"

"No, I don't think so."

"Good. Now can we get on with the meeting or would you like to continue the idle chatter?"

The Aftermath

She laughs and the double doors open, and a handful of servants walk in pushing a golden trolley, holding several silver cloches. They spread the dishes out across the table and set down teacups in front of both of us, pour out two cups of tea and leave again all without saying a single word.

The predatorily way she watches me as she sips, reminds me very much of Reuben, although Cordelia's eyes aren't quite so bottomless.

"So, Roman Garcia," she starts placing her teacup down on its saucer. "You want to know if he is in my court, and I want to know who your informant is."

"I'll tell you mine if you tell me yours," I drawl, picking lint off of my pants.

"Ha, I do enjoy talking with you. It's a refreshing change of pace from those who wish to suck up to me. But this conversation is of a dire topic and could – if proven true – land me in an awful lot of trouble."

"Then how do you suggest we go about it?"

"I would ask for your word, but I'm afraid the word of a Fury means nothing in the way of politics, no offence."

"None taken I would've said the same."

She thinks for a moment. "Ok, how about a secret for a secret?"

"What are we fifteen?"

"Do you have an alternative, if so, I'd like to hear it."

I stare her down, "I could sign a non-disclosure. Even at the guild, I would not be able to give away my source of information."

"That is not something that I have to hand, and would take at least a few days to wrangle together."

"Well, that is just poor planning, your majesty." My tone is deadened, not really wanting to indulge in this girlish game, yet it appears I have no other choice.

I sigh and flex my fingers, "at the guild where I was trained. Where I was raised, they have an event called the graduation ceremony. It is a milestone in a young Fury's early life before they become a fully-fledged Fury. The ceremony entails a test to determine whether you live or die and the outcome of the test, in turn, decides whether or not you proceed further. If you are chosen, you become part of the elite and they put you through a procedure, where they..." I pause for a breath, "sterilise you." I look up at her finally and watch as she shifts uncomfortably. "I had mine when I was nine."

The silence that follows is so loud and uncomfortable. Cordelia opens her mouth to say something.

"I don't want your pity, nor do I need it. I do, however, want your information."

Silver lines her eyes that she blinks away quickly and straightens herself up. "I was born a twin," she pauses dramatically. Clearly, this story is close to her heart. "We did everything together. When we came of age – and being part of the royal household – we were expected to marry to help carry on the bloodline. My father had found a match for my sister, Guinevere, first. Prince Malik. What our father didn't anticipate was that Guinevere didn't want to marry." She pauses again with a wistful smile on her face. "We had spent so much time, planning and arranging the wedding that when my sister didn't turn up for the ceremony, my mother had come up with a last-minute desperate plan, for me to masquerade as Guinevere and marry the prince in her place." She huffs a small laugh, "it all worked out in the end though, didn't it? Prince Malik wasn't fooled by my mother's plan but married me anyway. Turns out in the time he'd been forced to spend with my sister they'd talked about me mostly, and he'd fallen in love from afar." The heartbreak from losing her husband is still an open wound. Even if he had died before I was born, you never really get over losing your soulmate.

"My condolences for your loss."

She nods in thanks looking away, wiping at her cheeks. When she turns back to me, I see a fire simmering in her eyes. "Roman Garcia is in fact within my court. He is under the protection of the Delmare family and the Salacian Government. Unless he so wishes, he will not be permitted to leave, nor will you be allowed to visit if your intention is still to harm or even kill him."

I hide my shock at her admission by shifting in my chair. "My informant was Melanie Lincoln."

Her eyebrows shoot up. "You threatened, Black Foot's daughter?"

"Everybody seems to think that. I went to talk to her, and she attacked me. *Then* I threatened to take off her fingers. If she had just had a conversation with me, neither of us would've ended up with scars."

She seems genuinely entertained by my forwardness. Maybe being queen for so long has been more of a burden than she makes it seem.

"Isn't Roman in some sort of relationship with her?"

I shrug my shoulders, "It appears that there have been rendezvous, but nothing more serious than a hookup. I believe she is engaged to another."

"What?" Her shock is palpable. I'm not one for gossip. In fact, I'm not one for talking at all, mostly because it's always seen as disrespectful to my handlers and programme leaders. But I can see the appeal.

"Hmm, maybe you could be useful to me after all," she trails off, watching me closely.

"And what exactly will that entail?"

She shakes her head, gets up and fills a plate full of food. When she sits back down, she takes another drink of tea before picking at her plate. "May I give you some advice?"

"If you must."

"Be careful who you trust. This investigation of yours is more troublesome than it's worth."

My brows scrunch and my head tilts to the side of its own accord, reflecting the confusion within.

"You're smart Aella, look closer to home and you'll figure it out."

My eyes narrow before I clear away any uncertain thoughts, not liking the new direction of this conversation. I've confirmed my information, now it's time to leave and think of my next move.

Leaning forward I pick up my sunglasses and stand, moving to the door.

"I haven't dismissed you," Cordelia examines, sipping from her teacup.

"And yet I'm leaving," I shoot back.

"Are you always this disrespectful?"

"I suppose. But I wouldn't know."

"Good. You'll never get anywhere with the vipers in this world by giving pretty smiles and kind words. Be kind to those who deserve it and the Helfire to those who don't. It'll only hold you back."

I turn to watch her for a moment and do something I never thought I'd do. I bow to the queen of the sea. "Your Majesty."

She cackles, putting her teacup down, barely containing herself. "Did that pain you?"

"A little," I smile, feeling light as she laughs harder.

"I will be in touch, Aella. Your skills prove invaluable."

CHAPTER TWENTY-FOUR
TRUST ISSUES

The walk back to the apartment was more torturous than the walk there, the heat of the afternoon was much more intense than the morning. It feels as if the sun has fallen from the sky and is walking alongside me. It's most certainly not something I'm used to, having come from the mountains where there is barely even change in season.

Keeping my pace idle I take my time walking back to the safe house, thinking about last night. I had gotten exactly what I wanted from the ball. A private audience with the queen. But I gained something more. A sense of freedom. For the first time in my life, I got to choose something for myself. My heart flutters as images of mine and Declan's dance come back to me, and it pounds harder with images of later that night.

I'm almost back to the safehouse when a royal-crested car pulls up beside me and Elijah's joyful head pops out of the window.

"Hello, Miss... you know what, I don't know your second name."

"And you won't. Ever." I smile. Truth is, *I* don't even know my last name. "What is this about Elijah?" I asked, crossing my arms over my chest.

"Your presence is required at City Hall."

"If Frederick wants to speak to me, he can come and do it himself and not send you in his place."

"It's not his royal highness, ma'am." His eyes are downcast, and a pale blush dusts his cheeks.

"It's the king, isn't it?" I sigh as he nods in answer. Dread curls in my veins. It's unsurprising. There's no doubt in my mind that he will have seen me sitting with Her Majesty last night, but I still wonder what exactly it is that he thinks he saw. Problems with the king are never as straightforward as they seem. "Alright take me to him."

"How was your chat with Queen Cordelia last night?" he asks, sitting across from me, his green eyes boring into my own. His gaze is hawk-like, focusing solely on me. Watching every movement with years of precision. Reminding me of the Director. The two share the trait.

His Majesty King Theodore sits in the overstuffed leather armchair in the office of the old mayor of Ansrutas. The very same room I had my meeting with General Griffith, now former General; his son, Prince Frederick, lingers in the background never once meeting my gaze.

I lean back relaxing casually in the adjacent armchair, adjusting my tee-shirt for the umpteenth time. I don't like being put on the spot like this. Especially by him, but I've dealt with worse, so I breathe deep and cross one leg over the other, oozing a false confidence.

"Rather dull actually."

His lips thin the skin around his mouth pulled taut, "that's a shame I've heard she can make for quite the conversationalist."

"I must not have been that interesting to her," I shrug. The king is used to the much more complacent version of me. The one pumped full of drugs. Now I know not to step out of line. I still have the psychological training to fall back on, but my tongue is much looser than it has been in years. No thanks to Declan and Rich. I still need to remember to look at their history with the Fort.

"On the contrary, I think your history is most interesting. Provided, of course, you told her the truth." He grins. That same grin the Director grins. Dark, menacing, and full of deep-seated malice. It's the same look The Captain gets before being given flesh to carve into, in the name information.

"Not exactly, your majesty. I know I don't need to tell you that we are forbidden to tell anyone our profession who doesn't already know what it is." I think back to that time when I let slip to Rich what I was. It was careless and stupid. Granted I hadn't exactly made it hard for him to figure it out. But I still should've killed him once he knew.

"Pity. There's no doubt that she would've kept you. She has a habit of *collecting things* that aren't necessarily hers, to begin with."

I sit with that knowledge for a while wondering what it is that she's stolen. When he grins again, it sends a shiver down my spine.

"My son tells me that you and your handlers are close to ending my predicament."

I glance behind at Frederick. He stands tall with his hands clasped together behind his back looking out the window, still refusing to meet my stare. "I'm not sure about close, your majesty. I have a potential lead to his whereabouts. But I am yet to confirm whether or not it's true."

"Frederick's manservant said he picked you up on your way back from Salacia's embassy." One of those decadently dark eyebrows quirks up and he sits back in his armchair, settling himself in. "What were you doing in there?"

I curse in my head at Elijah. *He couldn't have just told a white lie.* "Princess Mala had requested to see me. Being Frederick's date last night proved fruitful in making a connection to the crown of the sea."

He turns in his chair to where his son is standing in the sunlight. Annoyance and a hint of anger move the sharp angles of his face, "Yes. We have had a talk about that." Turning back to me his face falls once again, "You are to have no further contact with my son. You did your duty all those years ago, and whilst I am grateful my daughter has snipped the filthy habit. My son doesn't seem to have snipped his." He gestures to me. It's an effort not to laugh. I see Frederick flinch in my peripheral.

"Of course, your majesty." With how he acted last night I have no problems ignoring Frederick. At least for a little while. Until he has learnt his lesson.

He seems pleased by my words, but only for a split second, "Where's your mask?" Frederick looked over at us then, for the first time.

I was wondering when that would come up.

"My apologies, your majesty. I was not expecting an audience. I do not have it with me."

"You met with the princess without your mask?"

"She does not yet know of my profession. It would be unwise to lose the fragile connection I've made so soon." I speak plainly and politely, but inside I'm screaming to leave. Avoiding rolling my eyes has never been a bigger challenge.

"Be better," he echoes the words Madame K has said to me so many times. I can see the self-satisfactory thrill rolling through him as the words leave his mouth. My hand curls in my lap.

"Of course, your majesty."

He waves me off and I take it as my cue to leave. *Fucking prick.*

Rich and Declan are out when I return, and the apartment is far too quiet without their usual chatter filling the rooms. Thankfully I still have a few hours to wrap my head around what just happened before I tell them.

Moving to my room I see the stack of documents I've collected on top of the antique chest of drawers with my laptop in one corner. *Not where I left them.* I scowl at the closed device and the papers. The box that I keep them in is open on the floor. Empty. *Now I know that wasn't there when I left this morning.* Unease spreads through my chest and I can't help questioning the oddity of it all.

Queen Cordelia's words ring in my head, like a gong. *'Look closer to home. Be careful who you trust.'*

My heart sinks like a stone. Clenching my jaw, I look over at the closed bedroom doors of my handlers, wondering how many times I've actually seen them be left open. Something akin to dread, mixed with splashes of guilt, simmer in my blood as my sock-covered feet pad across the wooden floor.

The questionable nature of the transfer to the Fort comes forth. They don't play by the same rules as the others. They do not carry out punishment the very idea of it is unmentionable. Their behaviour around the serum was so strange to me, they should've been well conditioned to it by that point if they had completed their training.

My fingers curl around the handle to Rich's door first.

The dark-coloured bedspread is a gaudy contrast to the soft pastel green on the walls. His room is immaculate. Not an item out of place, not even a wrinkle on his dark grey bed sheet. It is painfully obvious that he has come from a military background.

I begin the search by looking under his bed, finding a backpack, an empty backpack. I move on to his wardrobe. Flinging the doors open I begin moving his shoes around to find something. Anything that might quell my growing suspicion. When I come up with nothing, I quickly and carefully put everything back exactly how I found it.

Each creak of the wood and every pop in the old pipes has my nerves flaring, an experience that I'm not used to having whilst on a job. Keeping my stealth training at the forefront of my mind is much more difficult than I could've anticipated.

The thought that Cordelia is playing me, rattles around for a few minutes but doesn't seem to stick as anything tangible.

Nothing. I find nothing amongst his things. Nothing to satisfy my swirling, darkening thoughts. Standing in the middle of his room with my hands on my hips I pout at the lack of evidence to back up my gnawing accusations. The hole in my chest widens and a small voice in my head seems to say I told you so. Checking everything is back where I found it, I leave his room quicker than a cat chasing a mouse.

Annoyed, only at myself, I shake my head and look over to Declan's room wondering if I should also give it the once over. My heart screams to trust them. That they've given no reason to be untrustworthy and Cordelia is just trying to divide us. She trying to stop me from getting too Roman, but first she has to isolate me. She has to pull a part my support system. It's clever. It vindictive. It's something I would do

But my training wins out and I open his door.

Rich

Aella's door is shut when we make it back. Declan had found out she was onto another lead from the collection of papers in her bedroom and we took it upon ourselves to go and check it out. When — unfortunately for me — Declan had brought up the topic of the two princesses again. Well, rather one in particular.

"I'm telling you. You need to reach out and see where that could go," Declan tells me for the umpteenth time since leaving the apartment.

I raise my brow at him, "she lives underwater. Literally in another world. I don't think it would *go* anywhere."

"I'm just saying..." he tries again.

"Well don't just say." My patience has worn beyond thin, "she was saving us from Iris. It was nothing more than a friendly gesture and a win over her rival. Nothing more, now will you drop it?" I pause and watch him chew on the words. He opens his mouth to speak again but I cut him off. "Say another word and I will punch you in the face." The cloying scent of shame suddenly hits me. I take a deep breath in, and my animal stands to attention.

"What?" Declan asks, pulling off his jacket. The bastard has been unbearably smug all day. I know why. I smelt it on him the second the pair exited her room this morning. Nothing has been able to wipe the smile from his face. Until now.

"I'm not sure yet," I murmur back, confused, but I still follow the aroma to my own room.

Aella's scent is everywhere in here, I can practically taste the scents of annoyance, disgust, and sadness on my tongue. It's on the clothes in the drawers, on the rug on the floor, on the bookcase in the corner. Hel it's even on my sheets. Another more potent scent drowns the others out. The bitter scent of panic tingles along my tastebuds and I cringe as though

I've eaten a citrus fruit.

She had clearly been looking for something, the cold and heavy feeling of dread seizes my chest, and my eyes automatically go to her closed door.

"Shit!" I whisper to the room. Leaving my bedroom, I see Declan moving towards Elle's room, probably to let her know that we are home.

He knocks on the door to no reply, when he tries the handle, the door opens easily as if it was never on the latch. We step over the threshold to find her room empty, all papers and files she has gathered are nowhere to be seen and all of her gear is gone.

"What the fuck?" Declan breathes, his fingers flexing as he stares at her neatly made bed. He moves to her adjoining bathroom, again coming up empty. "What the fuck!" he repeats more desperate now. "Have you had a text from her?"

Coming up behind him, I check my phone and see that I've received nothing, I see the panic rapidly spreading through him, "We may have a slight problem."

"What do you mean?" he asks, with his hands on his hips, gripping his sides so hard his finger start to turn white.

I raise my brow at him, "Her scent is all over my room."

He looks dumbfounded and angry at the same time, "Excuse me?"

"Calm down. It's only happened since we left the apartment."

The colours drains from his face and his jaw clenches, making him look both menacing and terrified. Reminiscent of the Lieutenant Colonel I served under for all those years.

He sighs heavily. Seeing him shift back into his commanding stature is awe-inspiring. How he can keep himself calm and collected like the leader I know he can be.

"Well, shit." He grumbles, switching back in the Declan he's become since leaving the guard. The blend of both personalities brings forth a new male that I haven't seen before. He takes charge and marches to his own room, and begins scenting the air upon opening the door, "mine too." He winces when he, too, smells the tang of her panic. Nothing seems to be out of place in his room but it's clear she knows.

A heavy silence hovers between us. "Maybe we should just tell her?"

"It's likely she already knows. Should she come back we can, and pray to whatever gods are listening, that she doesn't kill us. But for now, it's for the best that we move whatever we have, somewhere safe."

"Where to?" I ask, trying hard to keep my cool. Lying to her these past few weeks has been torture. Unethical, given we have asked her to trust us in return.

"Alex is probably the only one who can hide it for us. Let's start packing it up. We'll move it tonight."

Aella

The ground under my feet feels as though it is falling away with each step I take, the more my mind whirls with possibilities the more my gut wants to uncover. Only, I don't exactly know what I'm going to find. I just have a suspicion that there's more to this mission than I was led to believe.

Shaking the all-consuming thoughts from my head, I push myself faster as I speed down the narrow alleys and quiet streets until I finally make it to my mark. The Trade Centre's streets are barren at this hour, the only sign of life is the low lights from the surrounding houses and apartments.

Finding files and folders on all the leaders of Dawyna in Declan's room shouldn't have been all that shocking. It wasn't. Until I started reading and found information that even I didn't know. Then I found files on Rich and Declan themselves. They had never been a part of the Fort. They never took the training. More surprising still was the file on Alexander Nephus. That's where I am now. Across the street from his studio, Nephus Designs.

The floor-to-ceiling glass window at the front brings a modern twist to the face, in keeping with the buildings around.

I push through the front door marked with the studios name and am greeted with a modern interior. White tiled flooring covers every inch of the space and glass walls make up individual offices, each with a glass desk and high-tech computers.

A white curved receptionist desk stands before me, and a fair, freckled head pops up from behind it, her brunette bun bobs with the movement.

The setting sun illuminates the studio in colours of orange and red. I fire off a quick text to Rich letting him know that I am alive, but I won't be back for a while. Keeping up the façade, even though I don't feel completely secure with either of my *handlers* at present. I look up in time to see the receptionist do the same. Both of us smile.

"Good evening, how can I help you?" she greets.

"Good evening, I have an appointment with Mr Nephus," I reply, putting on a fake, gentle voice in the face of my growing anxiety.

My phone pings with a reply, but I ignore it on the account of the young woman replying to me.

"Mr Nephus is just on a new building site, but he is on his way in. If you would just like to take a seat." She gestures to the seats behind me.

I'm not waiting long before, his wavy brunette hair bounces through the door, panting, with a to-go coffee in hand, looking very 'un-rebel-like' in his dark pants, white t-shirt and huddled under a dark brown leather jacket.

"Hi, Isabelle," he says, trying to catch his breath.

"Hey Alex," she smiles.

"She here yet?"

"She is." This Isabelle nods in my direction.

His attention snaps to me, his cheeks red and he pants hard. Walks over he shifts his bag into his coffee holding hand and reaches with his other. I take it and we shake; the connection feels easy and comforting. "My apologies Miss Munroe, if you give me a few more minutes, I'll be right with you."

The realisation, that I have been in this male's house – without him seeing my face of course – suddenly dawns on me. The information gives me the upper hand and yet troubles me. If he recognises my voice, I'll be in a whole heap of bother.

"Isabelle, can you send me the contract for the Cliffman house."

"Sure thing boss, is Mateo coming in?"

"No, he called to say he's going to work from home tonight." His voice rumbles deeply in my ears in a strangely soothing manner.

With his back turned towards his receptionist, I know he can sense me staring I can tell by the shift of his weight from foot to foot, and before long he looks back over his shoulder, smiling brightly when he catches my eye, his beard scratching with the movement.

He disappears after that, placing his items in his office at the back of the building before coming back out to wave me over.

"I'm Alexander Nephus, as I'm sure you know. I own this company and am its head architect here. What is it exactly that you're looking for Miss Munroe?" He properly introduces himself, reaching out his hand once again.

I smile and give it a quick shake. Both of our eyes widen at the spark that flows through us at the contact, the first had been calm, but that little jolt had wakened something within each of us. I don't know what, it was like there was a part of each of us that had been searching for a connection and had finally found what it was looking for after so long.

He chuckles, "Wow. That's not happened before." His grin is infectious I find myself beaming back at him. We pull away and both of us subtly look at our hands.

His work office is just like in his office at home., filled with books, sketches, and illustrations of buildings that he has built in the past. Only, neatly organised.

"Please take a seat and let's begin."

I play along with the theatre that I started, feeding lie after lie about a house in the country that I own, that doesn't exist. All the while studying his mannerisms and tone of voice, it's familiar but there seems to be a fog in my brain and just when I feel like I've figured it out, it's snatched away, cut off once more by that same mist.

"I'm sorry." He stops me mid-sentence, and I begin chewing on my lips thinking I've said the wrong thing and that he's seen right through my show. "I can't help but think I've met you before." My heart stutters and I begin to panic even more.

"I don't think we have, maybe in passing. But I can't think where we would meet." I deny it, praying he doesn't put two and two together.

"You just look and sound so familiar... You look..." He trails off looking at me in the eyes and begins trailing down to the shape of my cheeks and the lines of my lips; he trails back up stopping at the width of my nose and my breathing stops.

"Alexander, are you ok?" I ask, around the lump in my throat. He looks down as my fingers clench into fists at my sides, nails digging into my palm.

"You just look like someone I met a long time ago," He sighs, sounding wistful and full of sorrow.

Clearing his throat, he pulls out some plans from a building that he has recently designed, mercifully moving past the awkward moment we just shared. While he's distracted by them, I pull out a small black device. Peeling off the sticky back, before planting it on the underside of my chair, pressing it firmly onto the wood to activate it. This device, once switched on, will allow me to hear anything that goes on in this room, for a distance of up to five miles.

We talk for some time up until the sun has all but set on the horizon by the time we stand and begin to say our goodbyes.

"Well, your ideas for this house are certainly unique Annie, and if I'm honest, I'm excited to see how it turns out. Whether I am your chosen architect or not." He smiles warmly, the age lines on his face coming through along his nose and eyes.

"I think I would like that too." I give him my most brilliant smile, selling the lie even in its last moments.

He stands with me and holds out his hand once again, "I look forward to hearing from you."

I shake his hand and thank him for his time before seeing myself out.

Stepping back out onto the street, I breathe deep, loving the scent of the sea in the air, as it cools my throat and lungs.

My mind seems torn, I know that he is the third leader of the group, but at the same time, there's this denial that rings through me telling me that he couldn't possibly be. I turn off the main street into the alleyway next to me, where I stashed my backpack full of equipment, earlier. Pulling out my laptop I begin looking for the connection between it and the listening device I planted. Almost immediately I hear him talking. I plug in my headphones, to make the conversation private.

"Thanks, Isabelle," Alexander speaks.

"No problem boss, I'm going to head out." Her voice is a lot fainter than his.

"Yeah, no problem see you tomorrow," he calls back, *"have a good night."*

I hear the front door open and close, and see her walking past the alleyway moments later, as she makes her way home.

I hear Alex's phone rings seconds later and I dial back into the headphones.

"Hello? What have I said about contacting me on this line?" A pause as he listens to whoever is talking, *"She's what?"* Another pause I curse myself for not having thought to bug the phone as well. *"Then bring her back and keep her occupied. Rich, come on it's not that hard. You already have her trust."* My whole world freezes. Surely, he can't mean *my* Rich. Before I can spiral, I hear his next words loud and clear. *"Then burn whatever documents you have and pretend like nothing is wrong. Rich this has to go right. So, get that Fury under control or we will have a bigger problem on our hands than even you can fathom."*

I don't hear anything after that, his conversation fades into the background. A violent buzzing fills my ears, like bees in a hive. Instant rage fills my blood, and my limbs start to shake uncontrollably.

My intuition was right. Again. I shake my head angrily trying to stop the rising gut-wrenching pain of betrayal.

They've been using me. Something had always felt wrong. How they had suddenly become in charge of me even when they were 'new' to the guild. The reason Rich had been an inconvenience to my missions. It all fits into place like some messed-up jigsaw puzzle and I wasn't even the one playing.

Anxiety further fuels my rage and the twisted mixture, pulses within me, dark and strong. It writhes and flexes beneath my skin as I try to fight back the tears that threaten my eyes. Blinking quickly, I just barely keep them back long enough to close my laptop and stuff it back into the backpack. Between this and the papers that I found in Declan's room earlier tonight, which led me to leave so abruptly. This confirms for me that they have been lying for a long time. Declan had been lying to me. Something deadly cracks in my chest but the darkness that thrives within me fills it almost instantly.

My face scrunches and I sit back against the brick wall behind me, allowing just a few tears to fall. "If Madame could see me now," I groan, rolling my eyes at the stupidity of my situation. The thought of her ice-blue eyes sobers me up quicker than I had expected. I wipe my tears and push myself up to stand using the wall as my crutch. My phone rings almost immediately. Declan's name lights the screen and suddenly I feel nothing but pure unadulterated fury.

Taking a sobering breath, "Hey," I greet, keeping my tone level.

"Hey princess, where are you?" His voice is joyful like he's happy to hear from me. My jaw clenches at the use of that nickname.

"Just following up on a lead," I reply, zipping up the backpack before swinging it onto my back.

"Oh," His voice lowers as if the answer isn't what he wanted to hear. "Well, we bought food. Are you going to be home soon?" I can hear the slight quiver in his voice. I really deserve a medal for keeping my composure for this long. Even one not fully trained the way I've been, could tell that there was something wrong.

"Home..." The word leaves me before I even think about saying it.

He pauses, only his breath comes through the receiver for a moment until, "Is everything ok, princess?"

I clear my throat, "Yeah. I won't be long." A longing enters me, and the emotion makes me sick. So, I turn the switch. I become the Fury that everyone thinks of me. Of the heartless murderer I've been accused of for so many years.

"Elle, are you sure you're ok?" he asks, There's something in his voice that I can't quite place. It could be caution, it could be understanding. But it sounds more like suspicion.

"Of course, why do you ask?"

"You just seem quiet," he replies.

"Just tired is all, I'll be back soon."

"OK, I'll see you when you get back." Again, his voice is solemn and almost alien to the Declan I've grown to know. Or at least the Declan he has shown me.

"Yeah," I sigh, rubbing my thumb and forefinger across my brow before hanging up the phone.

The sound of gravel crunches on the roof of the neighbouring building draws my attention up above me. The fact that someone might have been listening in on my conversation annoys me more than it should. At least they can be dealt with quickly. I move to the ladder and climb up to the roof, the backpack bouncing against my lower back with each step.

I pull myself up onto the ledge. Before I stand up to my full height, I have to duck out of the way as a fist swings toward my face. I don't get time to recover before a boot connects with my chest throwing me to the gravel floor. I land heavily on my bag; I hear my laptop screen smash, and I growl in annoyance. Quick to stand, I swing my bag from my back, and I throw the whole thing at the assailant.

A feminine grunt sounds and I finally look at their face. Half of it is covered by a mask, the very same I have at the bottom of this bag.

"Wait! Aria?" She throws my bag down onto the gravel and her brown eyes bore holes into mine. Her deathly stare fills like a wildfire on my skin. She uses my distracted state to punch me in the face. Her sharp knuckle connects with my nose, breaking it.

"Motherfucker!" I yell, and my hands fly up automatically to cradle my face. Within seconds I feel my own blood wetting my hands.

Her eyes have that dead quality to them, the same each Fury gets upon having the injection. The face of compliance. Slack jaw muscles and eyes that should only belong to corpses.

She walks towards me, intent coveting her every step. She's here to kill me and quite honestly, I don't know if I have it in me to stop her.

"Fury Three-Five-Nine," I try. She doesn't stop her pursuit. She throws another punch to my face, one that I block, another to my ribs that I don't, a grunt is forced from my lips with the impact, but I continue to block her attacks.

She grabs my hair, yanking it backwards, I groan in discomfort until I see her pulling a knife from the holster on her thigh.

"Alright, I tried to be nice," I snarl. Using my free hand, I throw a punch to her face, she catches my fist mid-air, but I kick her knee out from under her and she lets go completely, stumbling backwards. I raise my fists in front of my face, ready for her next attack.

She twirls her blade around in her hand, and steps forward clenching her fists, my blood marring her knuckles. The blade swipes fast and wicked, cutting through the air with deadly accuracy. I dodge and weave each attack until she cuts my cheek. I hiss and pull out my gun, pointing it straight at her forehead. She stops everything, her pursuit, her slashing, and her breath.

I take this distraction and use it to the fullest. Gripping her wrist, I knock the knife from her hand, and flip my gun around, hitting her in the temple with the butt. She's on her knees before she can blink until I wrestle her to the ground.

With a vice grip on her legs and arms, I try and reach her again.

"Three-Five-Nine, that's enough, who sent you?"

She continues to fight me, spitting out blood and clawing at my skin. Ignoring me she wriggles and kicks at me, trying to pry me from her. I somehow keep my grip tightened for long enough that she can no longer move. Her strength is mind-blowing. She is stronger than me, her fae ears remind me that while I'm a mortal, and weaker, my training has clearly paid off enough that I can subdue her when needed.

I roll us over, so her back is to my front, her arms behind her stuck between us, and I begin wrapping myself around her like a snake strangling its prey.

"Three-Five-Nine. I am your superior, now tell me who sent you," I hiss in her ear. Grunting again when she tries wriggling out of my hold.

"Madame Killick," she bites out. Clearly unhappy that I pulled rank. I don't actually have authority over her, but over the years I have learnt a few things that she has not.

"Why?" I pant and begin wondering how much longer I can hold her down.

"To keep an eye on you, and search for proof." She manages to free one of her arms and elbows me in the ribs, air flushes from my lungs as we continue wrestling. She uses her hips to turn us over and I finally lose my grip.

On instinct, both of us are on our feet facing each other once again with our fists raised. I uncurl my fists, flat palms facing her. "Why?"

She ignores me, and jabs me in the ribs again, before punching the other side of my face, my jaw clicks from the contact.

Her hand furls around my throat and lifts me in the air, choking me with my own body weight. I try sucking air in, to no avail, whilst I scratch at her fingers with my nails. It's not long before my throat begins to collapse and black spots crowd my vision.

I gather enough awareness to use her position to my own advantage and kick her in the stomach, the instant she drops me, I turn the tables and hunt her instead. I punch her in the jaw and again above her cheek, her head snaps to the side and her mask becomes askew.

"She believes you've been compromised," she says answering my earlier question, "and if what I heard is correct. So is her assumption." She tears her mask from her face. We both stand there observing the other for a moment and it's as if I'm standing looking into a mirror. We both pull our handguns out at the same time, dropping into the natural stance.

"And what exactly did you hear?" I ask, quirking my brow, silently fighting back my nerves. She steps to the side and without saying a word we begin circling each other like wolves about to fight to the death.

"It's not what I heard. It's in your tone. You have forgotten your training. You have forsaken the guild." The glower in her eyes hardens even more.

"You are mistaken. The mission still stands. I would never abandon what I've always known." My thighs begin to burn with the crouched side-stepping motion. But I don't show that on my face.

"That is not the only thing I found." She smirks at me, and the sight makes my knees threaten to buckle under me. "Your handlers have other plans for you." The swallow I take is audible, and she steps forward snatching my gun from my hands, I do the same to her. Twirling I connect the butt of it to her temple, knocking her to the floor. She drops her own weapon, and it skids across the gravel.

With her gun, or rather *my* gun, discarded on the other side of the roof, I point mine down at her and take the time to get more answers.

"And what exactly do they have planned for me," I pant, the fading light illuminates the curves of her cheek and the straight line of her nose. I know they are using me. But for what, now that is something they didn't leave in their files.

Blood dribbles down her temple and she seems to be debating on whether or not I know about their plans. Still, she decides to humour me.

"They want to use you to kill the king."

CHAPTER TWENTY-FIVE
UNEXPECTED ASSISTANCE

The chilly evening breeze is soothing my sweaty skin, as I sit on the roof of an abandoned warehouse watching the moon stream across the star-filled night sky, with a dirty rag pressed to my nose.

Aria is still asleep downstairs in the decrepit office, slumped over in a chair on wheels. After her admission, I slammed the handle of the gun into the back of her head again to knock her out and my head has been swimming since. With nothing to remove the darkened cloud that fills my mind.

Declan has called and texted me since. Understandably worried since I told him I'd be back tonight. But the constant ringing drove me over the edge to the point where I switched the damn thing off just to get some peace.

I carried Aria's limp body South to one of the unused warehouses on the docks and used whatever I could to bind her to the dusty chair, both her hands and feet were tied with bits of tubing and some old wires.

Breathing the salty air in – through my mouth of course – I remove the rag finally. The bleeding has slowed but now the swelling and bruising will take place, especially if I don't set my nose right. Clasping it in my palms, I steady myself and force it back into its original position. The grinding of the bone makes bile rise up in my throat, and I use the rag to wipe away the rest of the blood.

Aria's breathing changes and her body shifts tiredly. Before she can fully come around, I hop down from the roof, through the open hatch, landing right in front of her.

The movement shocks her, she looks at me, and then down at her body and the bindings I made to hold her. Taking in her surroundings slowly, I say nothing, waiting patiently for her to understand what has happened and where she is. Her mesmerising chocolate brown eyes meet mine, shock, and desperation flash through them quickly. She tries to break from the ropes but quickly understands that unless I allow it, she will sit in the chair for as long as I need her to.

"Morning – or rather evening." I look up to the stars, through the hatch, and her own gaze follows. She doesn't stop her squirming and I have to listen to the creak of the tubes and the grinding of the wires as she pulls. Pulling my attention back to her, I begin my questioning.

"Aria, you told me Madame K sent you to watch me. What exactly did she want you to watch out for?" What I really want to know is what she's reported back, but we'll get to that.

"I told you she wanted proof."

"Yes, proof of my treachery." I wave my hand in the air as if it will bat away the repeated comment.

She suddenly squirms violently, the chair tipping from side to side, creaking loudly. I lower myself down on a rickety old stool I found hidden and fold my arms across my chest, watching on, thoroughly amused. She huffs her annoyance and stops, flicking her hair back over her shoulder.

"Done?"

Her gaze snaps to mine and an intense silence descends upon us. To anyone watching on the sidelines this impromptu staring contest would look childish and comical, this act, however, is a challenge. A challenge to see who will come out as *alpha*. The term sickens me. But when you're raised by animals it only stands to reason that you become them.

Aria concedes quicker than I had expected. She's always the last standing if she can do anything about it. She closes her eyes and takes a deep breath before opening them again, focusing solely on me.

"Three-Five-Nine..."

"Aria," she cuts in.

I pause, I haven't heard her say her name in a long time. I nod in understanding and continue, "What did you mean when you said they were using me?" My voice is quiet and timid, and I hate it. I cough to clear it up, but her eyes soften telling me she heard it anyway.

"Don't tell me you haven't figured it out yet?" she drawls.

"Humour me."

She looks at me trying to find a hidden meaning behind my words.

"Start from the beginning."

Madame Yvonne Killick

I watch as the blast doors close shut with a mountain rattling bang, not even able to get a glance at the vehicle as she leaves the Fort for the first time in years. Disappointment and dread fill my chest as the final lock clangs into place. Many things – important things – have been left unsaid.

Puffing up my chest I straighten my blazer and hold my chin high, her training will help her understand everything I could not say. Though she does not know what is to come, Three-Nought-Nought can handle it.

No.

Aella can handle it.

Just as I turn to leave something catches my eye pulling it upwards. A figure stands in a suit watching from the training room. I don't need the lights on to be able to tell who it is.

Reuben.

He's always had an unnatural obsession with the girl. One that I have tried to keep her from. I've tried to protect her in the past. At least from him, there was one time I was too late. Something I'll never forgive myself for.

I give him a small nod and take my leave, his deceptive eyes hounding my every step.

Unexpected Assistance

I receive word in the late afternoon of the following day, from Three-Nought-Nought, telling me she has arrived in the target city. I breathe a shallow sigh of relief, before pushing it to the back of my mind, refocusing on the Furies in front of me. The training room is nearly full of all of those under my care, and I can't help but feel pride about that. Being the most decorated Fury has finally paid off. My chest puffs out and my chin rises impossibly higher as I snap out new orders and watch as they all move as one.

The only other surviving member of my own group is Michelle Campbell, or as the girls call her, Madame C. The bitch has always been as sour as a citrus fruit. She was always the one who tried her hardest, to receive no reward. Some people are built for this life, and some aren't. Me? I bested her at every turn. The challenges during our service, admittedly were easier back then, the things these girls have to do now has always sent my stomach roiling. But I can't show that to the girls.

Michelle's bitterness has seeped into her later life too, taking out her own insecurities on my group. Especially Three-Nought-Nought. Aella rose quickly in the ranks and has been flying ever since. I couldn't be prouder of her.

But Michelle, well, she was lucky to be picked for whatever missions they gave her. The poor girl tried but didn't quite have the stomach for the job, nor the natural agility.

I look around the room expecting to see Aella's face in amongst the crowd and then remember she's not here. Having had her close to me for this last year has been both a blessing and a curse. I've grown a soft spot for her, and *he* has been lingering around more. But still, I have had someone to take care of.

When she came back with that broken leg, I was sure that would be the end of her career. With her being so young, there would've been only one outcome if she hadn't gotten better quickly, and I shudder at the thought, knowing it would've been me to put the bullet in her head makes me sick.

Just under two weeks have passed and the days and drifted by in a flurry of paperwork and training. I lost another girl to the mountain, and Michelle hasn't let me live it down, if it weren't against the rules, I'd break her nose again. Oh, the satisfying crunch it made when I did it the first time. They had to send her to a plastic surgeon in the capital to have it fixed. With the procedure being experimental, I was hoping it would be a botched job, but I never do get such joy.

I read through Three-Nought-Nought's second mission report, it doesn't quite go into the same depths as her first and mentions something about the mob being involved. My heart skips a beat, she shouldn't need to get involved with such things if it can be avoided. The minimal contact leads me to believe something has happened, but I can't fathom what.

The information she gathered at the start of her investigation has given her a strong start. But even I can tell by the second week she has lost interest in keeping us updated. The paperwork side of things has always been her downfall and Logan has been on my back about her, only because I know Reuben is on his, so I sent everything she's given me, in hopes that it quells his curiosity.

Sitting in my office late one night, I grew curious about Three-Nought-Nought's mission log. It has not been updated since the first two statements, and two names – her handlers – she has mentioned make my curiosity peek. I decided then to pull up each of their profiles.

Declan Angelos and Rich Keita, both of the names are foreign to me, and their faces are even more so. It is not commonplace to let any of the newbies take the lead on missions especially when in charge of a Fury. Not to mention, neither of these two have prior experience in how to handle one.

Nevertheless, I use the number this Declan gave and call him. Hoping he had more news for me than Three-Nought-Nought.

The conversation lasts less than a minute and I get minimal answers and snappy replies, making my temper bubble in my chest. I think to call him back and give him a piece of my mind but a scrap of information on his profile catches my eye.

Both of these handlers have been a part of the king's guard. Something that has never happened before.

Every member of the king's guard has a deep-rooted hatred for us. Each time his majesty has a problem, he calls on us. Even though he has a two-hundred-strong guard at his disposal.

A seed of doubt starts to bloom in my chest.

━━━━━━━━━━━━━━━━━━

The following morning, I call Three-Five-Nine into my office, she sits there staring at me with those deep brown dead eyes, the conditioning is in full effect in her mind. I have never had to feel its effects, and I never want to. The sombre way she looks makes whatever little piece of humanity I have left, scream out in anguish.

I swallow whatever feelings I have and, apply my metaphorical mask.

"As you are aware Three-Nought-Nought has been assigned a mission. She has been gone for nearly three weeks, and I have reason to believe she may have been compromised. I am aware this is asking more of you than I should, but I need you to travel South to Ansrutas and locate your sister. You will monitor the situation and report back to me, only to me. I have not been given authority for this, so it must stay between you and me. Do you understand?" She nods her head, and a fracture of my anxiety eases.

There's a niggling feeling in the back of my mind that knows these words aren't true. To trust that she can handle herself, but I am not confident enough on the matter, to not check in with her regardless of my own sentiments.

"I will be the one to contact you, do not reach out to me. With this mission being off of the books, I will not be able to help you while you are down South. The only thing I can do for you is arrange transport down the mountain."

I had contacted Warren over an hour ago, knowing he'd be able to help her, just like he did for Three-Nought-Nought, but whether he can keep it to himself is another matter entirely.

"Good. You leave tonight." I stand with her watching her walk to the door, "May the gods be with you and guide you to good fortune." I whisper as she opens the door, rubbing the charm on my silver necklace. She bows her head, her arm across her chest and leaves without another word.

I'm not one for religion, I think in my line of work you'd be a fool to believe, but my mother was, and the necklace around my neck is all I have left of her.

Aella

"So, she thinks I'm a deserter?" I pace backwards and forwards. Aria nods. I worry my teeth over my lip. I can't help the snicker that leaves my mouth at the stupidity of the accusation. "I was just doing my job..."

She eyes we warily and I can see the tiredness in them. "Obviously not very well."

I chuff, "thanks." We share a rare smile, something that neither of us has ever done with each other.

"When was the last time you slept?"

"Like two nights ago. I don't remember," she answers yawning.

"Wait if Madame told you not to be seen, why did you engage in that fight with me?"

"She told me to retrieve you. After I found the proof of you conspiring with the rebels, I took you for a deserter. So, I thought to capture you and take you back so you could face your judgment."

"Where exactly did you find this information?"

Aria opens her mouth to reply to me but snaps it shut when her phone rings. Loud and clear, echoing throughout the warehouse.

"Untie me. I have to answer that," she struggles against her bonds again.

My face falls into an — I'm not falling for that — expression and I begin rifling through her pockets to pull out her phone, Madame K's name lights the screen.

"Madame," I answer keeping my voice calm, despite the anguish I feel when I think about her accusing me of desertion.

Silence greets me.

"Fury Three-Nought-Nought. I wasn't expecting you, although I have been wondering what exactly you've been up to. Where is Three-Five-Nine?"

"Three-Five-Nine is right here in front of me. Tied to a chair," I inform her, "however I'd prefer you use our actual names if you want to start pitting us against each other."

Aria cringes in front of me and Madame clears her throat on the other end of the line.

"She was only meant to keep an eye on you and your handlers, she was never meant to get herself caught." Her voice rises at the end loud enough for Aria to hear and she flinches once again.

I scoffed down the phone.

"I understand your frustration, *Aella.* But you have to think these things through, I haven't heard from you in a weeks. I needed to report something back to Logan. You've been here long enough surely you understand."

Annoyingly I do. "Although I am glad I have you here. I never did get to tell you what I wanted to say..." Stern voices and muffled replies come across the line before I hear her voice again, "Let me finish up this call and I'll be right with you."

I hear the door to her office close, "Aella listen to me, carefully. You need to stay strong and stick together. That is the only way you will survive."

I don't get to reply before the line goes dead and I'm left in a daze. I stare at the blackened screen of Aria's phone for some long seconds after. It's only after Aria clears her throat do I come back to the present.

"How are you feeling?" I ask changing the subject. She quirks a brow at me, clearly confused. "Are you still feeling the effects? Or are you, you know, you?" I say gesturing at her, and then slide her phone back into her pocket.

She thinks for a moment, "I've been becoming more of myself each day. K told me that as soon as I found out the information I was to head back, and I would have another one."

Sighing heavily, I pinch the skin on the bridge of my nose, wincing at the tenderness there that I had already forgotten about. "Well, I can't leave you here. But I also can't take you back to the apartment." I pace back and forth in front of her thinking; I stop short when an idea hits me. "But I do know someone who might be able to help."

Taking each large marble step up to the glittering golden door adds more and more weight to my nerves. Even with Aria at my side my anxiety ripples, I don't actually know if this plan will work.

The silver armour that sits proudly on the chests of the two guards, glints brightly in the mid-morning sun and is nearly blinding when they step in front of us, stopping us short of the golden door to Salacia's embassy.

"State your business." The one to my left demands gruffly. His light green skin shimmers in the sunlight, and each of his scales cast light in a different direction and colour; they cover every inch of his body and contrast beautifully with his yellow eyes, that bore into my own.

"I apologise for the intrusion, but I need to speak with your queen."

His anger fades and in its place amusement, as though he can't believe I've asked such a ridiculous request, "Her majesty is not here, and I doubt very much that she would take an audience with the likes of you."

"That is interesting since she's already asked for me." I pull out the crimpled letter she sent me a few days ago, hoping he falls for it.

Snatching the letter from my hand, he takes his time in reading his queen's scrawl and grunts, "Like I said. Her majesty isn't here." He flicks the paper back at me. It flows away on the breeze.

"Fine. Is her Highness here?"

The guard to the right shifts his weight and draws the first guard's attention.

"Ah, so she is." I smile, "May I speak with her? Tell her I'm a friend of her mother."

"You are no friend to the queen, and Princess Mala is not taking unexpected guests," he grumbles back.

I scoff, "You're not even going to ask if she'll see us?" I shift my weight evenly placing my hands behind my back.

They both respond by standing taller and puffing out their chests.

"Aella!" Comes a voice from above us. With the sun brightening the front of the embassy, it's hard to see without squinting, but I look up and as my eyes adjust, I see Princess Mala hanging over the balcony showing us a brilliant smile.

"I was wondering what all the fuss was about, now I know." She grins, her dark braids twinkling with gold and silver beads.

"Princess! So nice to see you again. May we have an informal chat?"

"Of course, anything for a *friend*," she giggles, her joy is infectious as she enthusiastically waves us in.

I bow my head to her and watch as the two male guards in front of us step to the side. I try not to smirk at them, but there's only so much restraint I have.

"She knows your name?" Aria leans in close to my ear.

"Yes."

"So how exactly is it that you got in, with Salacia's royal family?" She continues.

The soft blues and greens calm the thoughts that have been swirling around all night. Princess Mala's handmaiden, a petite young girl with purple skin and hair, guides us up the marble staircase and through the soothing blue and cream halls.

"Honestly? I went to a ball and threatened the queen. She loved it and then I got drunk with the princess." Her eyes widen, and she huffs a disbelieving laugh.

"Only you," she mumbles.

We enter what looks like a sunroom, a glass ceiling curves into a full wall of windows, overlooking a small, neat garden with blooming flowers of white, pink, and yellow. Three walls to the room are panelled and painted a deep sapphire blue, a black painted bookcase takes up one side with a white rolling ladder resting in the middle. Tall, bushy plants decorate every available space, and at the centre of the room, a white fabric lounge curls around a small circular coffee table.

It's there that Princess Mala sits sipping from a delicate bone China teacup, her leg bouncing up and down clearly waiting for our arrival.

"Thank you, Tiana, if you would please give us the room," Mala says softly, sharing a similar air about her as her mother. The handmaiden bows deeply and slowly slinks out the door, eyeballing us as she goes. I'm surprised no guards are at the doors.

She jumps up and practically runs towards me wrapping me in a hug.

"Aella. Hello, to what do I owe this pleasure?" she squeals, squeezing me within an inch of my life. Unused to such affection, I awkwardly wrap my arms around her and pat her back. Aria snickers at me.

"I believe an introduction is in order." She pulls away and steps toward Aria, her hand outstretched, now it's Aria's time to look uncomfortable.

"Ah yes. Your Highness this is Aria, a close friend of mine. Aria this is her Highness, Princess Mala of Salacia."

Aria bows low, and Mala gives us her brightest smile.

"Please you don't have to bow," she speaks dropping her hand to her side. She turns and leads us back to the lounge, resuming her position, she prompts us to sit where two unused teacups sit, waiting for us. She watches both of us with interest as she continues to sip.

"Do you think me uneducated, Aella?" Her bright otherworldly turquoise eyes scan my entire face before finding mine. Her teacup clinks against its saucer as she places it down on the table in front of her, once again. Her almost whimsical air vanished without so much as me opening my mouth.

"Excuse me?" Her question catches me off guard.

"Do you think of me as being stupid?" she repeats slower this time.

"Of course not, Your Highness," I reply, bowing my head in compliance. My anxiety spikes again.

"Then why do you treat me as such?" My mouth opens and closes like a fish, Aria's wary gaze cuts to me, and I can tell she thinks the jig is up. And yet no words come from my mouth.

"Let us stop the pretences, I know why you are here."

I smile. Not even surprised she knows not really, "spies everywhere."

"Of course. It's also not too hard for people to report a woman carrying an unconscious body to the docks and for the authorities to hear about it. They have since left but they came her to warn us," she smirks, enjoying the game just as much as me.

I can't help it, but a laugh bursts forth. The simple image of someone witnessing me carrying Aria has me cackling so hard. The emotion making me forget my problems if even for a moment.

When I've finally calmed down, I see both Mala and Aria looking at me with curious expressions.

"So, what exactly is it you wanted to talk to my mother about?"

"I thought you already knew?" I challenge.

"I do. But I want to hear you say it," she answers.

"Just like your mother. I need to give Aria a place to stay, and I was wondering if you would be able to help me out?"

"And what would I get in exchange for my help?"

I think for a moment unsure what to offer.

"An I.O.U?" I chuckle, only half meaning it.

But Mala stays silent, her turquoise eyes, the same as her mother's, scan me thoroughly, as though she's actually considering it.

"I'll take it," she agrees after several long moments, taking me completely by surprise. My mouth pops open.

"Seriously?" My brow quirks as I look at her as if she's gone mad.

"A favour from a Fury at the time of my choosing, tell me, what could I possibly want more than that? Aria you can be the witness for this occasion."

"You do understand I might not be able to actually come at your beck and call?"

"I'll figure something out with your guild. I am a princess after all."

Aria is stunned, much like me neither of us speaks, we only sit there trying not to let our mouths hang wide open.

"Of course, you will be escorted around by the guards. We can't invite and fox into the chicken coop without some contingences. I said that right, didn't I? I'm still getting my tongue around the surface language and accents," she asks, picking up her teacup.

"Yeah, near enough."

"What if she dies?" Aria cuts in.

Mala's hand stalls just inches from her face, and those bright eyes flicker between us, "then her debt falls to you."

I nod in acceptance. I never even thought about what it would mean if I didn't make it out of this alive.

"Mala, I cannot thank you enough." I bow my head, and she waves off the action, "but I must be getting on. I have something that needs taking care of."

Since the night previous I've kept my phone on silent. Too concerned with making sure Aria was safe to actually think about it at all. But I certainly wasn't going to turn it back on now.

The sky is as clear as any diamond that decorates the king's crown and the sun beats down heavily on the rooftops.

It's from there I see them. Talking quietly amongst themselves and packing the few beige boxes into the back of the car.

Some spy. I can all but hear Aria's voice ringing in my head. I'd seen those same boxes the day the intruder broke into our apartment, I've since found out the intruder was Aria, looking for evidence. I never thought about them again, if I had, we could've ended things before they got too deep.

She's sat next to me now but neither of us has spoken a word since leaving the embassy. She's agreed to help me with this, keeping Rich occupied whilst I deal with Declan. Not that I really want to face either of them right now. Not when my nose and arm are still healing. But it's best the rip the bandage off now, while I can still salvage the mission.

Declan claps Rich on the back and the two exchange the last few words between each other, before Rich climbs in the car and drives off down the street. I nod to Aria, and she gives chase, whilst I find a way back into the apartment.

Climbing down the drainpipe, I arrive at the white doors leading into my bedroom, still left on the latch. I shake my head at their stupidity.

Flinging the sheer curtains to the side I take in the peach room with the adjoining pink bathroom. A bedroom I no doubt would've loved to have had growing up living a normal life.

The front door opens and closes signalling Declan's arrival. My spine straightens. He mumbles incoherently to himself as he paces by the front door.

That all stops when I start walking over the threshold into the living room.

"Aella," he breathes, upon seeing me. The small smile that graces his face is like a gut punch. A knife in my back that twists and turns but I stay where I'm stood.

I watch him taking a few tentative steps towards me. "Elle what's wrong."

Dragging my eyes to his I pause upon seeing them full of hope and longing.

"I think you and I need to have a conversation."

CHAPTER TWENTY-SIX
A HOUSE MADE OF CARDS

"Where's Rich?" I ask. Of course, I know where he's gone. But I look to the front door even so, as if he'll walk through it any minute.

Aria is hunting him down now, as I stand here and do something I never thought I would have to do. Especially to the male in front of me.

"He's actually gone out looking for you. Elle, what's happened to your face?" Declan steps forward his face squinting to see the cut on my cheek and the purple bruises over my nose. I'd forgotten Aria had given me those after she told me what these two had been up to.

"Who did that?" His voice is hard and demanding.

I scoff.

"What?" he grits, his fingers curling into fists ready to hurt the person that hurt me, still believing as if I don't know.

My heart aches. An unbearable sort of pain had settled in as soon as Aria had said the words. My head not wanting to believe it and yet something in my heart already knew. The foolish organ always rushes in, only to come back with bruises.

"How long?" With my voice low and untrustworthy, I keep my stance high. I will show no further weakness to him.

"How long what?" He steps towards me, a little too cautiously for someone who is apparently comfortable around me.

"How long have you had your eye on me? How long did it take for you to come up with the plan the kill the king? How long did it take for you to figure out you wanted to use *me* to do it?" Keeping my voice as level as I can, I push off the doorframe.

Everything about him seems to freeze. Like he's been dipped in ice-cold water but in reality, he's been shown just who he is and now he will suffer the consequences. "Elle." His voice suddenly changes from quietly joyful, to broken and weak with just one word.

My calm demeanour bends to near breaking point. "Don't step any closer." A lethal smoke fills my aura, and he abruptly heeds my request. "You have lost the right to use my name. In fact, you have lost the right to a whole lot of things."

He stutters backwards a step as if I've slapped him. His breath stalls in his lungs.

"So, tell me handler Angelos, when exactly was it that you thought you could use me? The moment we met, on that battlefield. Perhaps when you found out my true identity when you took me to Kos? Or did it only occur to you when I was dropped off in Ellwey?"

"Elle you have to understand..."

"It's Three-Nought-Nought to you," I say, cutting him off.

"No, it isn't," he growls back, "it has never been your name because you are more than a fucking number." He rushes forward placing his hands on my cheeks, his hazel eyes searching my own. "Aella, you cannot shut me out. I messed up and I'm sorry. Just please give me a chance to explain."

The heat of his hands is soothing on my face, and his words threaten to make me melt like ice cream on a hot day. But my chest throbs and I pull his hands from my face.

"My whole life I have been used. As a weapon. For political power. Used as..." I trail off, not wanting those select memories to surface. "I have never been my own person. Everyone looks at me and sees what I can do for them. They don't see me for who I am and then I met you two and I thought," I scoff and roll my eyes, "stupidly I thought that I had found people who saw me for me."

"Elle, please, let me explain…"

"I'm not finished." I hold my finger up to silence him. "If you must know, I considered you two to be friends, actual friends." I scoff, "How silly of me. A Fury cannot have *friends*. She cannot have attachments and then we… grew closer and I thought it was real." I tilt my head to the side. "But now I know it was just another ploy to keep me close. To keep me wrapped around your finger, so that when the time came you would begin poisoning me against the crown. Enough to make me want to kill the king."

Declan's chest staggers and his face pales. His eyes widened, showing a look of pure horror that I had come to that conclusion.

"I would never… You have to believe…" He reaches for my face again.

"Do not touch me," I whisper, the sound damaged and broken.

He flinches back and his face falls. "Fine. If that's how you want to play it."

I grin knowing I've gotten him to finally drop his guard. He turns showing me his back, and I'm stupid not to take the opportunity to knock him on his arse. But I want to hear what he has to say for himself. He moves back over to the lounge but doesn't sit.

"Know this. What we shared wasn't real. At least to me. It was nothing more than an itch to scratch. A passing inclination. A moment of weakness if you will. Because nothing could ever come out of it, I could never love you. You're a murderer, an assassin without a heart. One of your kind killed my father. I have tried time and time again to get you on our side. Asking the right questions, only to get absolutely nowhere. I've tried to win you over. I've tried not to force you into this." Somehow, I actually believe that he doesn't want to make me do anything against my will. "But when needs must." He pulls a clear vile from his back pocket and I know instantly what it is.

"How did you get that?" I ask.

"Believe me when I say it was incredibly difficult. But nothing is impossible." In his hands is the serum. The very same used to alter the chemical brain function in the subject. "When you told us about this little concoction, I knew I needed to get my hands on it. Should you not be willing, I could always make you. Where there's a will, there's a way. Is that how the saying goes?"

"You're no better than the Director. Then the king himself if you think doing that to another person is ok."

"See that's where you're wrong. I'm doing this to save others. To free my country from his rule from his Stratos. But he has made this a lot easier than we all first thought. He has continued to allow the creation of weapons that will be his downfall." He waves at me, referring to the Furies.

I step back. I shouldn't be shocked. Hel I shouldn't feel this hurt. But I do. Like someone has reached into my chest, pulled out my still-beating heart and presented it to me on a silver platter.

I smile. Somehow, from somewhere deep inside, I find strength. "You're delusional if you think I'll allow you to do that to me."

"I wish I could believe that. But it's not about what you want anymore. I wanted this to go smoothly. I wanted you to see our side of things, to see what kind of monster he truly is. But it's about what needs to be done. And if you won't do it willingly." He wiggles the vile in between his fingers.

"You don't think that I know what he's done. What he continues to do. He's a poison. But believe me when I say you won't get away with injecting me with that crap and keeping me hostage." Thinking of Aria and how she'll be expecting to hear from me at least by the end of the day. I thank Madame for having sent her. It seems that even when I don't realise it, she's always there looking out for me. "The Fort will come looking for you and they won't go easy on you. You won't make it out of the country if they don't hear back from me."

"So, make this easy on me and submit," he drawls, tucking that vile away once more. "You don't want this. I can see it in your eyes." Something in his voice flickers to life and gives me pause.

"You have no idea what I want," I utter back, my gaze flickering between the door and him. I shift into my fighting stance knowing that I won't get out of here without us coming to blows.

I throw my knife deliberately missing his head by mere inches. He flinches to the side, and I see the blade embedded in the wall behind him. His response prompts my own. I charge, using the coffee table as a step, I launch myself into the air, propelling all of my weight into my right arm and fist, bringing it down to connect with his face. His body twists to the side but he's quick to recover. Charging me, he slams me down into the coffee table, breaking it. Splinters and chunks of wood come flying up and around us, falling on our entangled bodies. Kneeing him in the stomach, he rolls off me groaning and I take his distraction to elbow him in the nose. Satisfied only when I hear the cartilage crunch.

"For a commander of an army, you're not trying very hard against a dainty little woman."

"You're not dainty. Nor are you just any woman," he groans from the floor.

Reaching into his pocket I pull out the vile.

He uses his legs and plants his feet into my abdomen, flinging me over himself so I'm lying flat on my back. I roll before he has the chance to pin me.

"Aella, stop!" he growls, scrambling to keep up with me.

"You've lost the privilege of using my name," I snarl back, kicking out at his head. He dodges and grapples to grab my ankle, without success.

"I don't want to hurt you."

"No, you just want to use me like everyone else does," I yell, jabbing him in the ribs.

He pauses suddenly looking at me. Dropping his guard. I throw the vile on the ground smashing it. The action distracts him long enough that I run into my room, straight for the patio doors. He yells his frustration and stomps after me.

Without an ounce of hesitation, I jump over the railing into the water below, leaving them both behind.

Aria arrives back at the warehouse shortly after me. Whilst I have been dealing with Declan and finding out the truth behind their motives. She had the task of collecting the boxes and files from Rich.

In their desperate scramble to hide the truth from me, they had chosen to rely on Alex to dispose of their gathered evidence. They also forgot to check the apartment for the bugs that Aria planted in order to find all of this out.

She tucked the vehicle out of view from the street, before climbing the stairs to meet me. Pacing in front of the small office I cannot seem to control my own breath, my legs quake deeply and not from the exertion of the run. No, that was a breeze like it normally is, but from the sheer emotion running through my body. Now I understand why the guild made sure we couldn't feel. Why they tell us emotion is for the weak. It's taking over everything in me. I can't seem to function without thinking of hazel eyes. My heart seems to be calling out for him. My body wants to be wrapped up in his arms despite everything. The entire way here I tried not to stop, even though that's all I wanted to do. I wanted to cry and scream, and I certainly didn't want to leave. Wringing my hands through my hair once again, I continue to pace. Desperate not to cry. Once I start, I fear I will never stop.

"Are you going to mope all day or are we going to read through these files," Aria asks.

"Fuck off," I grumble.

"Now that's not very nice. I did help you after all. You could've done it on your own and lost it all."

I already have.

I groan an incoherent slur as I give one final tug on my hair before turning to face her. The look in her eyes tells me everything. She's been here before, in this position. Losing everything and then some. *I wonder what it was that she lost.*

"He's still alive, isn't he?" I ask her. Even after all they've done. I still don't want them dead.

"For now," she drawls. I know if she had it her way. He would have breathed his last breath without even noticing until it was too late.

The sound of gulls screeching fills the quiet as all three of us read through the stack up stack of files and various papers we managed to steal from Rich.

After our meeting point at the warehouse and Aria – almost literally – wanting to smack some sense into me, we left for the Salacian embassy.

The aching feeling hasn't lessened even as I concentrate on the inked words on the paper I hold. I keep being pulled back into my own head and wallowing in my grief.

Mala had joined us both not too long ago, bringing with her a team of servants who began to lay out an incredible spread of food, filling the coffee table. Aria had smiled and dug in, but at the sight and smell it was all I could do not to gag.

Sat back in the sunroom, where only yesterday, we had asked for aid, is where we sit now. Mala had some guards bring in a dining table and chairs, and that's where I'm sitting, with papers covering the surface.

The princess and Aria chat together the whole time, it helps to have background noise, to know I'm not completely alone.

"You've been awfully quiet Aella. Is everything alright?" Mala's soft voice is like a feather brushing against my ear, but it still startles me out of my mind. When I look up from the papers, I see her tropical ocean eyes filled with concern.

"It's nothing to concern yourself with, your highness." I give her a false small smile. The fact is I've never been in emotional turmoil. I've always been told to shut it all out and allow nothing to deter you from your mission. That is the main reason graduated Furies are made to go through the sterilisation ceremony. To make our job easier. I've tried my techniques, but nothing seems to be working.

"Do you want some food?" Her delicate voice chimes again, I shake my head and pick up one of the files I've been avoiding, since reading it that first time.

Declan Angelos.

The one beneath that is Rich's. Both are fairly self-explanatory. A few basic data entries, name; date of birth; height; weight; country of origin; medical history; and military history. It's no surprise that after, the Stratos they had fallen in with the rebels. Most of those with military history have done the same, having gone from working with the Stratos or for the king's guard straight into an open rebellion.

It's only when I get down to their notes that I understand why.

Rich had served eight years under his countries, Sormbay's, banner, to Declan's ten, under Anaphi's and had both met when Rich's group, fresh out of basic training, had been sent to the front lines to serve under Declan's command.

As Lieutenant of the thirty-first regiment Declan had risen quickly over his service and had gained his position by being ruthless and precise in just under two years. He and Rich became fast friends, and Rich had even become his trusted adviser.

The duo quickly became unstoppable.

In the years after Rich's arrival, they grew to become one of the strongest regiments in the army, having gained more ground back than any other ranking officials.

They were awarded the Red Cross, for valour, by the king himself and Theodore degreed that Declan and his units would become part of the kings' elite guard. Declan was further promoted to Brigadier for his efforts; some of the most ruthless men and women were part of this brigade of nearly three thousand soldiers and Declan was in charge of them all.

Coming up on nearly nine years of service, they had been sent orders to push the border further and take back a military encampment that they had lost in the first few months after the war began. Instructed to leave no survivors they had set out during the night to catch them off guard.

When the sun rose the next day, they found they had not laid waste to any part of Duranda's army, but survivors of the war that had been misplaced because their homes had been destroyed. Their commanding officers had used their mercilessness to their own advantage and had forced Declan's hand into killing innocents. For what reason neither Declan nor Rich understood, but they had become racked with guilt.

Crushed by his own obedience, Declan had disbanded his forces and deserted the army shortly after, Rich going with him. They were stripped of their titles, and they had been sentenced to death for desertion. They had escaped and fled to the Southern Colonies, where they met and young man, also hiding from his past.

Roman Garcia.

My heart stutters and my breath holds itself in my lungs as I read and reread the words over and over again, branding them into my mind.

"Are you alright, Siren?" Aria's voice cuts through my racing thoughts.

Clearing my throat, I fold the file back over. "Yeah," I mumble, tossing them aside and I pick up the next one. "Anything on Melanie?"

She seems to understand my shortened response. Understands that I don't want to talk about it, she flips the folder in her hands. Looking at Melanie's name stamped on the front. I haven't seen her since the night of the ball, I can only assume that she went back to her father's sector and faced the consequences of her actions to save me.

"Melanie Lincoln, one of the three 'high-ranking members' of Dawnya. Her mother served in the king's guard. It doesn't say how they met; I can only assume it's a wild story. Edward Lincoln was already the don by the time her and her mother, Elena met. Elena was killed in action a year after giving birth to Melanie.

Her father is now known as Eddie 'Blackfoot' Lincoln, a powerful lynx shifter and one of the most notorious mob bosses in Ansrutas' history, known for his ruthlessness and cunning." She lists everything off like she's reading a shopping list, but this is something I already knew.

"Although I will say, because of who her father is, she's not someone we want be messing around with," Aria says, pointing her chopsticks at me as she stuffs another crispy duck roll into her mouth.

"I've already been on the wrong end of those claws and believe me when I say, they're going to scar." I wave my left arm in the air, still covered in a bandage, something I need to change soon.

"Well, then you're an idiot and a dangerous one at that," Aria scolds, her usually soft brown eyes, turning darker as she looks at me.

"Tell me something I don't know," I mutter, "anything on Roman, Princess?"

"There is very little that anybody knows about him, no one knows who his father is, nor his mother. There's a brief description of him, but you've already met him. There's this picture." Aria leans across the lounge and snatches it out of the Princess's hand.

"Hmm, he's hot," she hums, chewing on a dumpling.

"How can you tell, it's blurry black and white CCTV footage?" Mala asks incredulously.

"I can tell." Aria winks.

"Anything on Alex?" Mala queries.

Alexander Nephus, the third and final highest-ranking rebel topping off the odd trio. An architect by day, a demolitionist by night.

The small photograph inside his file is clearer than any of the others that I have seen. I stare at his eyes, the shape and colour scarily familiar, the lines and curves of his face too.

Having served in the king's guard, taking after his father – who had given his life in service of his king – Alex served for close to fifteen years, before his own desertion.

He climbed the ranks taking on the role of Major, in charge of up to one hundred and twenty officers, and after his first three years, he had been deployed on yet another mission. He and his group had saved over fifty prisoners of war from a camp thirty miles behind enemy lines, where, coincidentally, he had found his first wife.

They had married about a year after he had saved her, and they had a baby girl. She died giving birth to the child and shortly after Alex had been deployed back to the front line. Duranda's army was pushing the border and had started to make headway. While he was gone, he had left his daughter with a family friend, and shortly after his departure, their neighbourhood was set ablaze. He went home to rubble and a deceased daughter.

The air is stolen from my lungs as I read further about this man who has lost everything. Reading on I find myself more and more, intrigued with his story.

His Lieutenant Colonel had tried to relieve him from service for time to grieve, but that had only made him fight harder.

'The guy is a madman, I wouldn't want him to be against us, his unfiltered rage has won us back the compound that we lost weeks ago. He doesn't talk, he doesn't eat with the troops anymore, the only life I see from him is when he is killing.' Lieutenant Colonel Kim had written on his notes to his commanding officer.

Colonel Wolff had replied, with minimal interest in the male's health. *'If he continues to win us ground, keep putting a gun in his hand.'*

My lips purse and a heaviness weight my insides down.

"There has to be something we are missing," Aria says breaking through the agonising silence of the room.

"Well obviously," Mala answers, rolling her eyes, sipping on her glass of water.

"Feel free to share with the class," Aria retorts with equally the same amount of sass.

I stare at the photographs of the known suspects, spread out in front of me. Each person is totally different and has their own motives, yet each has the same goal. Aria and Mala continue their bickering and it's nice to hear instead of the incessant flap of pages turning.

"What's up?" Aria asks breaking my train of thought, once again.

"Nothing."

"Well, it's not nothing. You've only made that face, like twice before but I still can't figure out if it's a rage face or a sad face."

I scrunch my brows.

"And you only do that when you're confused." She's beginning to freak me out.

"What in the Abaddon are you doing?" My voice rises, squeakily.

"Do you really not remember?" she asks and when I shake my head 'no' she continues, "Madame told us to be just like you. So, we all watched everything you did, copied your mannerisms and such, to become just like you."

The look in her eyes shows no trace of a lie. My eyes widen and I can feel the colour drain from my face.

"That look though, that one I haven't seen before."

"It's the look of terror," Mala says filling in the blank, stuffing some form of fried food into her mouth, "you've disturbed her with your truth."

"Both of you stop it!" I snap. Now thoroughly unsettled – mostly because I never noticed them watching – I turn back to the files continuing through Alexander's file, reading about his past only to find history had repeated itself.

He had met someone new towards the end of his service, they had another baby, only for him to come back from deployment to find them both dead. He had deserted the army shortly after, and stumbled upon a lonely traveller, with his own motivations.

Roman.

Again.

I send a prayer to the God of Death, Damien, to protect those souls, and place his folder back onto the pile. I place my head in my hands and take a minute to recover from the emotions running rampant through me.

"Aella, I didn't even ask before. What happened with your boyfriends? All you said was to steal these files from one of them," Aria asks, pulling my attention to her.

"They are not..."

"Boyfriends?" Mala nearly screeches and settles down just as quickly, looking at me quizzically. "Oh, the two shifters you were with at the ball. They were hot," she hums appreciatively.

"How was the ball? All I got to do was watch it from outside. In the cold. All alone," Aria drags out, trying to gain sympathy.

"AELLA! Why did you not invite her inside!" Mala asks, appalled.

"What! I didn't even know she was in the city, let alone watching me."

"Yeah, you really dropped the ball on that, didn't you?" Aria critics.

"How has this now become about me?" I sigh, annoyed.

"Oh! Yeah, we were talking about your boyfriends. What happened?" Mala questions.

"They are not my boyfriends, neither of them are," I repeat.

"So... they're available?" Aria draws out the question, teasing me.

"Yes! They are. But I know what you are doing and it's not going to work."

The door opens then.

"Adrian," Mala greets, her voice a pitch higher than normal, "I thought I had told everyone; we were not to be disturbed." Her voice sounded just like her mother's when she had called me out for lying to her. Even *my* spine straightens at her tone.

"My apologies my princess, your mother wishes to speak with you. I am to escort you to her." He bows low sweeping his arm across his torso as he does so.

"Surely I don't need an escort, in our own embassy."

He side-eyes me and Aria.

"Your mother requested it." Is his weak response.

I sneak a glance in his direction, not even feeling bad for the over-cautiousness. He stands there in a loose-fitting teal green linen shirt, which does nothing to hide the sculpted body beneath it, paired with black leather pants that hug to his form, and lace-up knee-high boots. His light blonde hair hangs in delicate waves just brushing the tops of his ears, and his eyes reflect the ocean and all of its many colours. I almost drool at the sight of the cocky grin that he gives me when he catches me staring.

Fingers snap in front of my face and I jump, having not heard anyone approach.

"I take it you've finished reading now," Aria says loud enough for the whole room to hear. Mala snickers, standing up, and smoothing out her dress.

Coughing to clear my throat, my cheeks flush madly, so warm I'm sure you could cook food on them.

"Y...yeah I also think I've figured out what they have in common."

"Oh?" Adrian says stepping closer allowing two guards to follow in his wake. Mala too steps closer to the table seemingly having forgotten about her mother.

Everyone crowds around the back of me Mala takes the chair opposite, watching me intently. Adrian and Aria hover over my shoulders, looking at the files but I can tell they are listening for me to begin.

"So, these are the notorious rebels huh?" he asks, his voice right next to my ear, as he looks at the photographs spread out on the dining table, his warm breath smelling of mint. "Come one then don't keep us waiting in suspense. What is it that they have in common?" he asks. Something like unease, squirms in my gut, telling me to keep my mouth shut, but everyone's looking at me. Waiting expectantly.

"Unfortunately, that is confidential information, reserved for the Fort and the Director only," I reply, closing the files and I place them back on the pile. Aria seems to agree, standing up straight, she gathers the files for me.

"What and the queen who is putting a roof over your heads, can't know?" he fires back, Mala although stays quiet, seems to agree with Adrian.

"If her majesty wishes to know. She can speak to me herself," I counter.

"Oh, I didn't realise we were in the presence of royalty. Your Majesty you look so different from when you did this morning," Aria jokes dryly, as she looks to Adrian, her voice devoid of emotion. I struggle to hold my laughter, seeing Adrian roll his eyes and plaster a smirk on his face, finding the humour in her words.

He points to the princess, "You are in fact, in the presence of royalty."

One of the armoured guards walks over to us carrying a wooden box, I open my mouth to ask Adrian what is going on when I feel a sharp prick in my neck.

"WHAT THE FUCK WAS THAT!" Aria yells as the world becomes blurry and my head feels as if it's been filled with cotton balls.

"Adrian! What is the meaning of this? What did you just do?" Mala screeches. I see her blurred figure stand, her hand balled into fists.

I hear the sound of a fist meeting skin and a thump against the floor, I try turning my head, but my muscles are so relaxed they aren't cooperating with my will.

"Your Highness, this is why I asked you to leave. I didn't want you to see this."

"And yet here I still am, and you will answer my questions. Or so help me, I'll have you dismissed." Her voice is laced with an anger I've not heard from the princess before.

Suddenly the world is shifting from under me and my head hits something soft, the plush cream carpet. Aria lies next to me, unconscious and I watch as the room spins.

I see the two guards, one holds Mala back as she screams and rages at Adrian, even as he tries to explain himself. Their voices are muffled and distant as if I'm underwater. The second guard picks up Aria, as the first manhandles the Princess from the room.

Adrian steps over me and leans down brushing some stray hairs away from my face, my vision fading in and out as I try to focus on his face. "Sleep Siren. Everything will be over soon enough." That's the last thing that I hear before the darkness claims me.

CHAPTER TWENTY-SEVEN
NEW GAME PLAN

Rich

The apartment is quiet when I walk back through the door sometime later. It's been nearly an hour since I set off to hand over the files to Alex. The streets had been quiet, so it had been more than a surprise when the passenger side window exploded and in swept a woman dressed all in black. She beat the shit out of me and shoved me out of the car, before driving off taking everything with her.

I'd been more furious that I'd lost everything if I wasn't in awe of her feat. Jumping into a moving vehicle through a window.

Blood is streaming down the side of my face from the cut on my eyebrow, and my nose might just be broken from where she slammed my head into the steering wheel. But damn if I didn't find that so attractive. Her strength. Her precision. Her natural agility. My cock hardens at the thought, and that's all before I've seen her face.

Walking in, the first thing I see is the shattered coffee table and a small splattering of blood.

"Declan?" I call into the room. My head throbs painfully, disorientating me. But if Declan is in trouble nothing will stop me from fighting.

"In here," he calls back. His voice is a little muffled.

Stepping closer to Aella's room I see him sitting there on the floor resting back against her bed, with a bloody rag pressed to his nose.

"I fucked up." Is the next thing he says to me. Silver lines his eyes. A deep purple bruise is swelling on his left cheek, blood has trickled from the small cut there and has dried soon after.

"What the fuck happened?" I rush to his side and gently pull the rag away. His nose isn't broken, just pouring still. Pressing it back to his face I look around the room. Aella's things are gone, and she is nowhere to be seen.

"Where is she?" I ask cautiously.

He waves his hand towards the open wooden doors in Elle's bedroom. The very same that overlooks the river.

"No," I murmur turning back to him. He simply nods. "Fuck."

"She gave me these on the way out." A faint toxic smell wafts under my nose staining the air. Leaving him where he is I follow it coming to a halt in the living room. Where a small pile of glass lies broken on the floor with liquid pooling around it.

"What's this?" I ask kicking around some of the glass, to see a label.

"The serum," he replies. Ice runs through my veins.

"What serum?" Never once had we talked about a serum and if he confirms what I think it is. It would seem he is more desperate than I thought.

"Don't play dumb, Rich. It doesn't suit you."

"Why in the Abaddon would you use that? Where the fuck did you get it from?" I growl storming back into the room. If Aella didn't beat enough sense into him, she can bet I will.

"I have connections that even you don't know about Rich. But does it matter now? It's gone. It was a once-in-a-lifetime find and it's gone."

Astounded. I'm utterly, utterly astounded and it shows on my face. I can tell by the way he looks up at me. I can see his shame.

"Like I said. I fucked up," he mumbles looking down. "I played the wrong hand. Hel, even as I said the words it felt like insects were crawling under my skin."

I sigh deeply. "So, she knows everything and we've just lost her. Lost months of trust building and work and what for? Your pride? Or were you just that impatient?"

"I get it Rich. You're pissed."

"Pissed doesn't even cover it, Dec. You aren't the only one who wants revenge for what he did to us." My voice is booming around the room, it's so loud he flinches under my anger. We have worked so hard for years with nothing to show for it. Our only hope had run for it, because of his stupidity.

When we found her amongst that pile of bodies all those years ago and we found out what she was, we felt like we would finally get the retribution we deserved. She was that first breath after drowning underwater. Taking our wild seemingly impossible dream to the right people felt unattainable. They wouldn't believe us. There was no way they would help us, it was too outlandish, but Alex saw something in the scheme. Roman, still young then, followed along with Alex, Melanie was introduced to us later when they accepted our wild plan.

"I need to talk to Alex," I scrape my hand over my growing hair. Through this whole business, between us driving to Lefki, Elle and Dec being attacked, and Elle being kidnapped by Eddie Lincoln, I haven't been taking care of myself. It's unlikely to change if she now knows everything. I've got to talk to her. I've got to get her to see our side and to not hate us for hating someone else. Even if it's a long shot.

"Just give me some more time. I'll find her and bring her back."

"It's too late for that Declan! You have shattered what little trust in us she had. She was already looking into our authenticity. From the first day, she didn't believe that we were part of the Fort."

He stays silent looking for the right words to say.

"Why did you do it?" I ask instead.

"I guess I was just growing restless..."

"Not tonight. Why did you sleep with her if you still intended to use the serum on her? To force her into killing him."

His open mouth snaps shut instantly, and I can hear the distinct sound of his teeth grinding together. "If only you could've done that tonight," I snap at him, referring to his silence, and I storm from the room.

"Where are you going?" he yells after me.

"To fix this shit that you put us in." The front door slams behind me and the only thing that I can think to do is talk to Alex. He'll hate me. He'll likely try to kill me. He put faith in our idea and now we have nothing to show for it. But he is also the only one that can help with our predicament.

Stepping out onto the street I see Frederick stepping out of his royal car. His chauffeur holding up the door and Elijah watching the street as if he could do anything to fight off someone hunting his prince. His stature alone would not allow him to pose a threat.

The prince himself seems surprised to see me.

"Who did you tango with?" he grins, nodding to my face.

"An unknown Fury."

The grin slips away, and I watch his throat bob with a swallow. "There's another?" He asks the most obvious and pointless question. I shift my stance and fold my arms over each other.

"Why are you here?" None of us have heard anything from him since the night of the ball.

"I came here to see Aella."

"She's not here."

His mouth closes at my tone. I'm in no mood for games right now.

"Where is she?" he tries again looking up at the windows as if she'll magically appear.

"At the moment I don't know. But all I can say is she's not here and you've had a wasted journey." I'm not about to pour my heart and soul out to the guy. He's still yet to prove to me he's not the absolute dickhead I think he is. He came off all sweet and charming when he was getting his way but the moment something went awry, he became a petulant child. I stand guard at the door as if it will stop them from forcing their way in.

"Now if you don't mind. I have somewhere to be."

"Can we give you a ride somewhere?"

Shocked that he would offer; I sceptically looked him over. Has he been hit in the head? You don't typically help someone who's treating you like shit. But until he proves himself, I won't treat him any other way. Not with how he was looking at Aella. He reminded me too much of his father.

"No thanks," I utter, the sound rumbling in my chest.

"Please, I wish to talk also." He steps to the side showing me the back seat. What did Elle ever see in the pompous fuck?

Rolling my eyes I slide in. Elijah joins the chauffeur in the front and Frederick closes the door taking his seat next to me. I give the driver the directions and sit back in an awkward silence waiting for Fred to begin.

"How has Elle been? I know my father's summons was unexpected for her but…"

"Wait what?"

"She didn't tell you?" He looks quizzically at me.

"No." my answer is clipped and short. He stays quiet for a long time. So long in fact I turn to watch him. His eyes are tired, and the skin of his face is losing its colour. "Have you slept?"

"Not much," he answers so fast it shocks me. I hadn't thought, with his eyes cast so far away, that he would answer at all. "I've been searching for a way to help her and with my father on my case, he's forbidden me from seeing her. I have come today at great risk; it's been difficult to search for a clean break for during the normal working hours." He gives me a soft tired smile.

"A clean break?"

"I'm trying to get her out of the Fort's control," he mutters, "so far. Unsuccessfully."

I cock my head to the side and see the immediate change in him. As soon as Aella is brought up, he brightens. It's not the first time I've seen it. It was also the reason for his frown when I told him she wasn't at the apartment. It clicks into place. "You're in love with her," I murmur.

His focus snaps to me and heartbreak flashes across his eyes. He clears his throat, "How can I be?" He exhales long and hard and paints a shockingly fake smile on his lips, shoving a false air of humour down my throat. "I've only worked with her once. For a few months." He mumbles the last bit, but his tone is what betrays him. When I do nothing but stare at him, he drops the act almost instantly.

"Have you ever been in love with someone, who doesn't love you back?"

My swallow is audible and so pressure filled that I feel like I've swallowed my tongue. *Yes.*

"Loving someone and not being able to have them, is the most maddening feeling. To not be able to wake up to them every day. To not hold them whenever you want, or even fucking talk to them, in my case." He scowls, rubbing at his chest, an unconscious action.

The car slows. Outside I see Alex's studio.

"I am not one for speaking my mind. But something about you allows me to feel open.

"Aella said the same thing once upon a time." I turn away looking at my shoes. The confidence she gained whilst being with us. The trust she put in me to help her. To protect her.

"This doesn't leave us, I trust?" he asks.

I nod.

He leans over me and pops the door open, "If you find her first. Lock her in her room and call me. I can move her somewhere safe."

"How do you know she's missing?" I jest, trying not to show the real terror that he knows more than he lets on.

"I saw it in your eyes. You're scared for her. She's either been taken, *or* she's stuck somewhere."

"You have met Aella, right? You know that she could get out of a locked room, even without having tools at her disposal?"

He chuckles. Some of the stifling air lightens around us, "That is true. She also finds herself in the strangest of places sometimes. But that can only mean she's been taken and that is even more troublesome."

I climb out and wonder just how readable I am. But I'm glad he hasn't figured out the true reason for her sudden disappearance. I doubt he would take kindly to the woman he loves being played into killing his own father. Even I'm having doubts about whether or not this was truly a good idea to begin with. It seemed so simple at the start. Get someone who was already trained in the skills we needed. Use her altered mind to do our bidding and then send her on her way. Because the more the serum broke down the more, she revealed her true self. The more I doubted I'd be able to ask this of her. She has dug herself into my heart and rooted herself in there. Like a thorned plant that will be agonisingly painful to uproot. Not that I see her ever leaving.

A bell above the door rings as I walk in and blue eyes meet my own within an instant of arriving, he stands next to his receptionist some files in hand, their conversation halts upon my entry.

"Keita," he greets with no warmth in his voice.

"Nephus," I greet equally solemnly.

Alex places the folders down on the desk in front of him and motions for me to follow behind him, he closes his office door after I enter and offers me a seat.

"Why don't you tell me what happened?" he suggests taking a seat on the opposite side of his desk, his brunette hair tousled as though he has run his hands through it a lot already this morning.

I don't know how he knows, maybe by the look on my face, but this meeting was in fact about our progress.

"Honestly I'm not sure myself," I sigh, rubbing my thumb and forefinger across my brows.

"What do you mean you don't know?" His face is completely relaxed. He sits back in his chair, his forearms resting against the arms of it watching me a little too closely. Like an eagle watching a mouse.

"Everything has been fine, going according to plan until a few nights ago. She disappeared for an afternoon and into the night, she didn't tell us where she was going. Declan managed to get a hold of her, and she said she was coming back to the apartment and never showed up. Next thing, we've packed the car, and I was driving to your apartment to drop it off." He nods understanding. "And then one of the windows in the car explodes inward and I gain this," I gesture to the cut on my face, "a female fae is suddenly beating the crap out of me. She pushed me out of the car and drove off." I pause, take a breath, dropping my head into my hands, sighing. "It's not until I got back to the apartment that Declan tells me that she knows about everything and that she left." I pause looking back up at him, his hard gaze hasn't changed.

"And?"

"And what?"

"There's more to the story, tell me everything or get out." His voice is just as icy as his eyes. The deep blue looks familiar, the hardened edge to them makes me feel like I've seen it somewhere before, but I can't put my finger on it.

"The crown prince stopped by, asking where she was. I told her she was out; he didn't believe me and is no doubt going out there to look for her."

He breathes in through his nose and out again, his nostrils flaring every now and then with the movement.

"So let me get this straight, *the Siren*. The best, *infamously known*, killer and spy, who not only has a reputation on her home ground but across the globe, now knows that the two of you are members of *Dawyna* and has taken every scrap of evidence to prove the claim, from under your noses. This same someone who not only has affiliations with the king, the crown prince but is also under the protection of Reuben Ostair and the entirety of the most prestigious assassin's guild?"

I swallow loudly, the lump in my throat tightening and swelling and tightening again. The sheer size of what we've done, comes crashing down around me.

"And *you* lost the best *asset* we had?" he hisses.

"She's not... Not exactly, I think I may know more."

He pauses observing me, deciding on whether or not he believes me, *or* whether or not I'm one misstep away from being thrown to the curb.

"Pray tell. Where did the Siren..."

"Aella."

The anger in his eye's simmers some, but the hardness remains.

"What?" he murmurs lowly.

"Her name is Aella. Not the *Siren*," I insist. It took so long for us to be able to call her that, I'm not switching back to her alias now. The colour drains from his face, surprising me.

Clearing his throat, he looks down at his lap. "What is her surname?" He picks some invisible lint from his white dress shirt, not looking me in the eye as he waits for my answer.

"I don't know, I don't think she even knows, she grew up as a number."

He flinches so subtly that I feel like I might have made the whole thing up, but instantly recovers and schools his face into one of indifference.

"She was in my apartment." His musing is so quiet, I understand that he is talking to himself, although the confession does still startle me.

"What! When?"

"About four nights ago. Broke in through my office window." His eyes widen. "Gods. I've met her."

"Excuse me?" He ignores me for a minute, typing on his computer and searching through files until he finds what he's looking for. CCTV footage of yesterday, evening.

"A young blonde came in yesterday. Annie Munroe." The name instantly rings in my ears. "Claimed she wanted a consultation about a house she just bought out in the country." Within minutes he's turning the screen around to show me and sure enough there she stands, smiling as she shakes Alex's hand.

"I knew her voice sounded familiar." He stares at the image of her as if he's searing it into his brain.

"What time was this anyway?"

He shifts in his chair, "around six thirty."

"That's around the time Declan got a hold of her. He said she sounded funny on the phone."

"So, between her leaving here and their phone call she must've found out."

We sit in companionable silence, both of us trying to think, how, in such a short time, she found out.

"Before our brains shut down, trying to get into the mind of a Fury. Tell me about your theory. Where did she go?"

I scratch the back of my head, and scoff, "Yeah. About that."

"So, you mean to tell me, that you made a deal, with the sea queen? To secure *our* asset and Melanie – not only approved the motion – but has been the mediator between the two of you," Alex says. "All without me knowing."

"Yes," I reply. Not really sure if he's impressed or pissed and his face, as always, gives nothing away.

"Did Declan know of this deal?"

I shake my head. "It seems we have both been hiding things from each other of late."

"What do you mean?"

"It's a long story."

He tilts his head to one side, "Well you've got a lot of explaining to do. If the relationship between them really was as deep as you say."

"Well, I don't... I think with more time it could've become something more. But Declan..." I trail off. "It doesn't matter anyway. I've got to get her back. What we've been doing, what we've been planning for her was a mistake. One I intend to fix."

"Does Declan feel the same?" The question stumps me. Does he? I don't know. Things have shifted so much that I couldn't even begin to understand what Dec is feeling. But I still wouldn't call what they had a relationship. But it was definitely more than it should've been.

"Your silence is more of an answer than you know." He shifts in his seat, "So what exactly is it you want me to do now? If the Salacian Government have her there will be nothing I can do," Alex states.

I knew that would be his answer but hearing it and believing it are two very different entities.

"But we didn't even get chance to explain why we did what we did."

"Keita don't tell me you've gone soft on her." I have. Of course, I have. She has shown us a side of her no other has seen before and after everything she has been through it's only right that that it's held to the same standard as a holy script. "Surely if she's got the files. She will know, by now, your reasons." He pauses, his eyes widening. "You didn't happen to have mine, did you?"

My lips thin and that action alone tells him what he wants to know.

"For fucks sake, Rich!" he sighs angrily, pinching his brows. I flinch and feel my heart sink further. I didn't even think it could.

"Alright," he breathes, "I take it you want me to speak to the queen and see about releasing her?"

I nod once. Despite knowing that she is likely safer in the hands of the sea court. I had hoped that it would only be used as a last resort. But there are only so many people in the country she trusts. Cordelia isn't likely one of them. But that's the only other place I can see her going.

"And you're sure she's there?" he asks, picking up his phone with his fingers hovering over the numbers.

I sigh, "Not one hundred per cent but try it anyway."

He raises a brow at me and then types in a number I don't recognise. I watch him as we wait for the line to connect. His blue eyes look so similar, but I can't seem to remember where exactly I've seen them before. His scent too. I've smelt it somewhere.

All thoughts of where are gone when he opens his mouth. "Connect me with her majesty. I believe she has something I want."

The phone call was tense and halfway through Alex had ushered me from the room. All I had to do now was talk to Declan. Mostly to see where we both stand after everything. But I also need to tell him about the deal I made.

Anxiety has curled its way into my heart and settled heavily in the pit of my stomach. Each step up the stairs to the apartment felt like an added weight to my own body. It was a struggle to not just turn around and figure this out myself.

Walking in the broken coffee table has been tidied away, as has the blood. Declan sits but the window overlooking the river. Looking at him now, I can see the changes the mission has brought over him, his hair has grown longer, his natural curls are starting to come back through; the wind blows through them ruffling them into a frenzy. His beard is growing back, he looks tired and beaten down.

He turns when he hears me enter. The purple bruise on his face has darkened and swelled, but at least the blood has stopped pouring from his nose now.

"What did Alex have to say for himself," he asks turning back to the view.

"He is surprisingly going to help us."

"Fuck me. What did you say to get him to agree to do anything for us?" He grins.

I share the smile, "It took some convincing."

"I don't doubt it."

My smile falls. "Before we move forward. I think we need to have a chat."

"Gods, you sound like Aella. She said something similar before she beat the crap out of me."

"I don't doubt you deserved it."

He sighs heavily, "There's no lie in your words. But can we stop kicking me when I'm already down?"

My lips kick up at on corner and I nod. This was going to be a difficult conversation. It's not that either of us is any stranger to each other. Quite the opposite. We've been partners in many things for so many years. Sharing stories, families, women. There's very little we don't know about each other. For years after our own trauma, Declan would wake with nightmares. Still believing that we were the monsters they made us out to be and I was there to hold him through everything. I was his shoulder to cry on. His advisor. His friend. His brother. There was a reason he closed himself off from everything.

Until Elle came around. Without even trying she began to break down those walls he so meticulously built up for years. I've never seen him act like this with any of the women before. Most of the time they have only ever been a release from the torment that he puts himself through daily. Never once forgetting the faces of those who have died at his hand.

Elle always believed that we signed up for the army, and for the most part, we never tried to sway her understanding. We were drafted because the king wanted bodies to stop Tinos from crossing the border after Duranda began to break it down. It wasn't about saving his people from foreign invaders; he simply didn't want to lose land to his enemy.

"I know," I sigh. Declan never has much of a talker. Over the years I have gotten used to reading his expressions and watching for signs that he's hurting or needs comfort. "Which of us is going first?"

"Where did you get the serum from?"

"Me then," he scoffs, "I made a friend whilst we were at 'the academy' training to become guards at the Fort. He managed to slip into the lab and procure a vial for me. At great personal cost because if he were caught, they would have killed him."

"A friend. Really? You don't have any friends," I snicker when his mouth pops open.

"I have you, don't I?"

"You're stuck with me there's a difference." He nods agreeing.

"What about you? What have you been hiding?"

I sigh and my anxiety spikes. I'd been dreading my turn. But this needs to be said and whilst I can still look him in the eye, I need to get this off my chest.

"I made a deal with the sea queen that she would apprehend Aella should she not take the news of our intentions well. That is the reason they are in the city. Not for the king's celebratory ball for his daughter."

The room falls quiet.

I turn to see him staring at me, and for the first time in years, I can't read his expression. There is no sadness, no anger.

"Ok." He nods looking at the wall in front of him, "Two questions?"

The air seems to flood back into my lungs and it's because I was holding my breath, waiting for his reaction. I had assumed he would blow up and rage around for at least a few hours. But I'm thankful he has taken a calmer approach to it.

"Shoot."

"How the fuck did you get her to agree? And how did you get in touch with her?"

"I told her she wouldn't get her own retribution if this didn't go to plan. That she would need to become more involved if she wanted us to continue to be partners. As for the second question, Melanie is due to be wed to a Lord in her court. An arranged marriage between the Lord and Eddie Lincoln. She batted her eyelashes at the Lord and got herself an audience on my behalf."

"Fucking genius," he mumbles, and I grin.

We sit for a few moments in silence both of us allowing the other's confession to sink in properly.

"You really didn't think I would fly off the handle at you, did you? I can't do that when I think what I did was so much worse," he mumbles.

"It's not about who did what anymore. At least I don't think it is. I think we both fucked up and now we both need to fix it," I conclude.

"Now what are we going to do to get our girl back," I ask him. His eyebrows scrunch.

"Maybe we don't," he utters, surprising me. But there is no way I'm leaving her in their hands, even if the whole thing was my idea. I have quickly understood that not all my problems can be locked away. "Maybe we just think of a new plan with Alex. She's safe with them for now, away from the Fort away from the royals. We can figure a way to get her out when the deed is done. They would just let her go at that point. She would no longer be a problem."

"If you think that, then you really are delusional. Because there is no way they would release a Fury back into the world. They would kill her where she stood if they haven't already," I counter, "That doesn't bother you?"

"You forget, they killed my father." And there's the old Declan. Holding back from really truly opening up. Using his past as a shield to never truly care for someone.

"You don't know that it was them. It could've been another guild from another continent," I snap. "You can't tell me that after everything, that you don't care for her."

His lips thin and the skin around his mouth goes taut.

"I know you want your revenge for your father's death, Dec. But you could be sentencing an innocent woman to death for something that wasn't even her fault."

"She's hardly innocent, and don't forget who put her there." He waves his hand at me. Guilt lashes through me like the crack of a whip at the reminder.

I know at the moment there won't be much that I can do to dissuade the queen, she will want her payment for the favour I have asked of her, but I can at least try. Declan has proven my early thoughts about him caring for her might not be as true as I thought.

It shouldn't surprise me. He never has cared much about the women he beds. But I had thought Aella was different.

All I know that *I* will not be leaving her behind.

CHAPTER TWENTY-EIGHT
TRIAL BY SHADOW

Aella

My eyes shoot open, and I cough up mouthfuls of salt water, right onto the tiled floor below me. My throat is raw, and my head houses an excruciating throb, so disorientating in its pressure, that what little light is in here, is too painful for the eyes. Nausea roils through my gut, and it takes everything in me not to throw up what little is left in my stomach.

The constant drip of water fills the space, long after my coughing and groaning have died down.

"You, ok?" I hear from behind me. Aria.

"I think so, you?" I croak back.

"You tell me." I turn my head to look over my shoulder and see her one swollen and very purple eye.

"Ouch," I say, she scoffs and turns away. I take my time taking in the walls and ceiling around me. "I think it's safe to say we aren't in the embassy anymore," I mumble.

Aria shouts a laugh, "Any more bright ideas?"

I turn to her, annoyed by her tone. But I don't stay mad. It was my suggestion that we go to Mala for help and while she didn't have a hand in this, she didn't protect us like I thought she might

Algae, in colours of orange, red, and green, cover most of the stone tiles on the floor and even up the natural rock walls. Clusters of coral and even patches of seaweed grow from the crevices in the walls and a wooden bench hangs from one side, held up by flimsy-looking chains that are covered in moss and slime, but the bench itself is the only bone-dry spot in this hovel. Thick black bars close off the front of the cell, allowing me to see into Aria's cell adjacent.

My limbs are cold and stiff, and I feel weak, too weak, whatever they gave me must still be in my system, but it's not strong enough that I can't move. My stomach roils again, as I begin to twitch my limbs and joints awake, groaning as I haul myself up on unsteady legs before thudding down on the bench, the wooden planks creaking.

"That sounds promising," I joke half-heartedly, wrapping an arm around my middle, fighting to keep myself warm. "Has anyone been by?"

"A couple of guards have been into your cell, just to check you were still breathing, whatever they gave you was strong, you've been out for nearly half the night."

"Either that or I really needed the sleep," I chuckle hoping to lighten the mood. Aria responds in kind with a snicker of her own.

"I'm glad you find this predicament so funny ladies, it would be a shame to ruin such a blossoming friendship." Adrian's voice comes from somewhere else in the room, the scraping of chair legs grates in my ears before he comes into view, between our two cells, looking ever so slightly smug.

Damn, this fine-ass male.

"Would you prefer us to bawl for hours on end?" Aria asks, venom lacing her words. I can feel her anger from here. Given the chance she'd kill him and never once regret her decision.

"We might be able to arrange that for you if you'd like. Although I haven't properly cried in years, so it might take me a minute," I add.

Aria's sinister face splits into an equally terrifying grin.

Adrian tactfully ignores her and turns to me, "You never did share your epiphany, what was it exactly that you found out."

"That's probably because you stuck me with something terrifyingly more fascinating. What was it by the way?" I inquire, shifting my uncomfortable limbs, to lie down on the bench.

"A concentrated, experimental, vial of the hormone melatonin. It might have been too much in your case I've been sat here for a while watching over you as your slept," he replies, "now answer my question."

"What was it again? I'm afraid my brain's a little foggy," I groan, snuggling down on the bench, I lace my fingers together and close my eyes.

"I'm not here to play games, *Siren*. Tell me what you know," he hisses, hitting the bars of my cell, I don't so much as flinch at his sudden outburst.

"Why would I give you the pleasure of spelling it out?" I mumble back, "If you want the answers, you figure it out. I'm assuming you confiscated the files, and all of my findings so go ahead and dig through it all. I've done all the work for you; you just have to connect the dots."

"Can you two stop talking? Gods above and below, you are giving me a headache. More so than the after-effect of being punched in the temple," Aria snaps, glaring lethally at the back of Adrian's head.

Adrian opens his mouth to reply but I cut in first, "You can give up. I'm not saying a word."

He spits at me, the gob landing only a few inches away on the floor and hits the cell bars again.

"Bitch!" he hisses, standing up, the wooden stool he was sitting on flies back with the force, and he storms from the room.

Aria chuckles into the silence, "he's pleasant today, isn't he?"

"If you think being lured in on a self-assured niceness, only to find you're in an unimaginable danger pleasant, then sure.
He's *pleasant* today," I retort. I wait for a minute to make sure he is in fact gone before talking again.

"You figured it out, didn't you?" I ask into the room, quietly.

She scoffs but stays silent for a minute or two before responding, "Say I didn't."

I roll my eyes, which was a big mistake. My stomach flips and I gag.

"*Dawnya* has a common goal. They want the king out of power, whether he is elected off the throne, which would likely take months or maybe even years, or if he befell a terrible accident and died. Their combined motivation is revenge. Salacia's is probably the most prolific excuse, but still, we don't judge people on the state of their trauma.

"No, of course, we don't," Aria agrees. "So, what is Cordelia's deal?"

"Her husband."

"Excuse me?" I glance at her to see her looking quizzical. "From the moment I heard of her. I began doing some research on her history. I never read anything about a husband."

"That's because he's dead, and has been for about twenty-five years, give or take," I inform.

She rolls her eyes and huffs, "Get to the point, I wasn't kidding about the headache."

I chuckle and continue, "They want revenge on Anaphi for a war that wasn't theirs to join. So as retaliation, they're planning to start a new war over a dead guy that they can't bring back." I close my eyes and wiggle into the bench more trying to find a comfortable position.

"That doesn't make sense," Aria says.

"A few years after the war first started, King Theodore had sent word pleading with Salacia to send aid. He knew his forces weren't going to be quite enough to hold the border and he wanted to push further and begin his long-term plan to overthrow Tinos, as well as banish Duranda. He asked they send whatever they could give, whether it be supplies, medicine or soldiers. Queen Cordelia, being from the royal line, had refused at first, but it soon came to light that her husband, Prince Malik Delmare, had been close friends with Theodore Haakon whilst growing up, back when the surface world and the depths mingled before Cordelia closed the borders.

Malik was all too happy to help out his friend even after Cordelia had begged him not to go, he refused to abandon his friend, taking half of their troops with him. None returned, not even her prince. They'd paid the ultimate price for a war that did not even involve them."

The dripping water is the only sound echoing in the stone chamber around us, for a few heartbeats.

"And now the noble House of Salacia has joined forces with terrorists in an act of rebellion against Anaphi." My eyes bore into the porous ceiling, it too grows coral. "I still don't know Roman's place within all of this, but I know that killing Theodore, won't bring Malik back.

Since Adrian's departure — and my and Aria's conversation — four guards had come in with hot stew and slices of crusty bread. I asked what time of day it was and received no reply. I thank them much to their surprise and they leave just as quietly as they entered. Both me and Aria devour our meals in silence not quite realising just how hungry we both are.

"We need to figure out a way to get out of here." Aria thinks aloud, around a lump of bread.

"Agreed, how's the eye?"

"Fine," she replies, taking another bite of her food.

I look down at my bowl, and push my food around with the wooden spoon I was given, "are you sure?"

"Yes!" she snaps, looking at me with annoyance on her face.

"Are. You. Sure?" I repeat, slower and more deliberate. Her whole face scrunches as she thinks over my words, trying to find the ulterior motive.

"Oh! No. No, it's hot and itchy, I think it might be getting infected," she agrees, finally understanding.

I turn back to my food, "Well then, it needs checking, doesn't it?"

When the guards finally come back to collect our bowls about twenty or so minutes later, we politely ask for a medic to be sent for Aria, to which they grunt in response and leave us once again.

"Have you thought this through?" Aria asks, suddenly. "We have absolutely no idea, where we are, nor how deep underwater we are. We might be able to get out of these cells, but we'll still be stuck in this place. I doubt very much that they took us to the palace."

"Stop shitting on my idea. You think of the next bit then if you have so little faith."

She laughs, "I never said I didn't have faith. I was just asking about the second half of the plan. You can't have, like, twenty per cent of a plan."

I eye her suspiciously. "Twenty per cent of a plan?" I scoff, "Honestly, no I haven't thought about it. But Adrian's here, so I'm certain there's a way out."

CHAPTER TWENTY-NINE
LOCKED UP

A sound so obnoxious and utterly unnecessary clangs against our cell bars the next morning, waking both Aria and I from our slumber.

"Good *morning*, inmates! Breakfast time!"

My head unready begins to pound at the noise only one man can make, and the day hasn't even begun properly yet.

"And good morning to you too, Adrian," I reply, throat still clogged with sleep, I don't even bother to open my eyes to greet him properly.

He stops outside my cell, blocking what little light comes in through the one tiny window on the side wall. "You seem very chipper for someone locked in a cage."

I sigh placing my arm over my eyes, hoping that might help the impending headache. "And you seem entirely too relaxed for someone who is at the top of my kill list."

He barks a laugh as though that's the funniest thing he's heard in a while. His life must be boring if that's true. "Funny, but for that I'll decline to give you breakfast."

"You mean I don't have to eat the gruel you call food. Thank the gods!" I take a peek at him from under my lashes to see him glaring at me,

I grin, and he turns around showing me his deliciously muscular back with a skintight tee wrapped around it like a delicious treat, while he looks into Aria's cell. Damn all these males and their striking good looks. I've seen so many in such a short amount of time. Even if half of them are pricks.

"I believe you called for a healer. Something about an infection?" His voice is condescending. It takes Aria great strength to nod, without looking like she wants to rip his throat out, but — lucky for him — she manages to do just that.

Adrian is surrounded by at least six other armoured guards, and I almost laugh at their cautiousness. "Behave and you might still get yours." He nods to the still steaming, bland porridge on the wooden plate that another guard is holding.

Her unswollen eye glares menacingly at him, the other so heavily infected that it has puffed up more than initially expected. Turns out we didn't actually lie about that, well certainly not after she shoved some of the algae growing on the walls into the cut.

I groan and stretch my back and arms, standing to join the guards by my cell door. I lean against the bars my hands dangling down on the other side. Watching the scene unfold. This is the most interaction we've had from any of them since we arrived in this prison. Two males one with pale green skin and one with deep purple, clad in the silver armour of Salacian queen's guard, step into her cell, with their hands on their swords.

"Stay seated," Adrian commands, his voice silky smooth. He makes sure the two males before him have the situation in hand before entering himself. The healer follows after him, looking wary of her patient.

The girl is tall, with dark hair covered by a silken headscarf that matches her full-body, burgundy robe, which hangs loosely around her slender form. She looks mortal, with pale brown eyes, there's no trace of magic around her at all and yet Salacia doesn't usually let people in unless they can participate in their society. But she is a healer, someone who is always in demand, no matter the species.

"Step back," a third guard demands of me. Having turned and realised just how close I'm standing to him when I don't immediately move, he pulls a dagger from his belt and points it at my eye. I raise my palms and chuckle lightly, taking a step back to watch from a distance.

The healer's nimble fingers get to work straight away, assessing the wound, cleaning it, and finally adding an ointment meant to stop the infection and heal the broken skin. She doesn't say a word, but I know she's noticed how intently Aria is staring at her. Her caramel fingers tremble slightly under the oppressive glare.

Aria's one good eye flickers directly to me. Without words, I know what is running through her mind. I shake my head slightly, hoping no one sees the action or the silent conversation we are having.

The healer gathers her belongings, stuffing things haphazardly back into her leather bag, and rushes from the cell. Her breath rises and falls quickly, she glances at me once but quickly looks away. I see pure terror in her young eyes. She holds her bag against her chest like a safety blanket.

One of the guards stands to attention and walks her from the dungeons and into the corridor beyond.

Aria's head tilts ever so slightly as if to say, *'The odds just got better.'* Taking a deep breath, I analyse the guards in front of my cell, before replying with a head tilt of my own.

She stands quickly, grabs a hold of the guard's arm, she fastens it to his side while she kicks the back of his knees. He crumbles to the wet rock floor before she smashes his head into the wooden bench, she was just sitting upon, knocking him out cold. Grabbing a hold of his weapon. She turns pointing the narrow sword at Adrian, who has already drawn his own.

"Put it down," Adrian drawls, already bored.

I reach for the guard standing outside of my cell, wrapping my arm around his neck. He fights me as I choke him, but his thrashing only assists me, until he passes out and thuds to the floor.

Aria twirls, her foot connecting with second guard's elbow, kicking the sword from his hand. She reels back a punch letting it fly into his face with an audible crunch. She is only stopped when Adrian wraps an arm around her neck his voice hissing in her ear. A dagger digs into her ribs as a warning.

"Get them out of here!" he demands of the only remaining guard. He holds his face with blood pouring from his nose.

With his chest to her back Adrian drags her further towards the back of the cell, while the guard scrambles to get his unconscious comrades out of her cell and away from mine. I can do nothing but watch, hoping that dagger doesn't pierce her skin. Adrian keeps tight hold of Aria's neck until the guard comes back, blood still pouring from his nose, with his sword is raised at Aria, so Adrian can finally let go. The cell door slams closed and the key screeches loudly in the lock.

"If either of you try something that stupid again, you'll be going back to the surface in pieces," he spits. His rage-filled gaze flickers between us both. "No one enters this room for the next forty-eight hours!" he demands of the two guards standing outside the wooden dungeon door. "No food or water will be given to them in that time." He eyes us both smugly, "I hope it was worth it." He turns on his heel and storms out of the room.

The crushing silence is enough to make anyone go mad, I can't, however, do anything but laugh. I slump back down on the wooden bench behind me trying to catch my breath. The sound isn't forced but it is slightly maniacal. It takes a few minutes to calm myself down.

"Well, that did not go as planned," Aria states when I've finally calmed down enough.

With a snicker and an eyebrow quirk, I reply, "You think?"

Those seemingly never-ending hours without food or water were far more difficult than I originally thought they'd be. Aria and I haven't spoken much in that time, conserving our energy to make it through without complaint. Both of us are too stubborn to yield to begging.

The dripping of water as it falls steadily from the ceiling is maddening. I've read in certain corners of the world they like to use this as a torture technique. I can see why. It is certainly enough of an irritation to make anyone want to give up their deepest darkest secrets.

Hours have turned into days, but I don't know how many. Three? Four? I tried to keep track but with little to no light, I gave it up quickly. Guards have come and gone, mostly just check that we are both still breathing. All wearing this mysterious black armour.

I wouldn't think for a minute that they brought us to the palace but if not there. Then where in the Hel are we?

The lack of sustenance and energy has my otherwise fortified mind wandering back to Ansrutas, back to them. The sting of their betrayal is still present, I only wish now that I had handled things differently. I allowed my emotions to overthrow my judgment. Something I was always taught not to do.

"Do you think she'd be disappointed?" I mumble out loud, from my position on the floor. The bench had become uncomfortable after the first day. With my arms and legs spread wide I'm lying on the floor looking up at the ceiling. At the different shades of coral and algae that grow from the cracks.

"Who?"

"Killick," I clarify.

She seems to contemplate her answer before finally sighing, "Oh most definitely."

A curt laugh escapes my lips.

The wooden door to the dungeons swings open, loudly slamming against the stone wall behind it and in walks Adrian, looking ridiculously smug, "Good afternoon, inmates!"

Neither of us reply to him. In fact, I note we both go so far as to not even look in his direction.

"What's this? Moody silence? You females are all the same aren't you, no matter the profession."

"It would seem so are you males," I drawl back, tired of his attitude and his constant need to have the last word.

"Only because the queen has demanded that I feed you, will I still hand over these trays of food." He levels his stare and points a slender finger at me, "But talk back to me again and this will be your last meal." His voice is dark and ashen, and entirely too seductive.

He's flanked by two guards while two more stand in the doorway spears in hand. The guards shove the food under the bars and step back.

"I'll believe that when I see it, Adrian." I say, eye the food but neither Aria, nor I move towards it.

"What? You can't tell me you're not hungry?" Adrian mocks watching us.

The smell of the cheese, and the fresh bread along with a steaming bowl of soup wafting up into the air of the cells, makes my stomach rumble. And with the exhaustion I feel, I don't know how much longer I can hold onto this defiance.

But still, he stands there with his hands on his hips. "Don't tell me you are willing to far go a fresh meal in the name of petulance."

"I'm sure the queen would love to know how you're spending your time. Instead of serving her like you were trained to do. Why don't you bring her down here so she can see for herself." I taunt.

He scoffs, "She's ordered me to be here. Believe me wouldn't choose to stay in this prison longer than necessary unless it was a direct order for Her Majesty herself."

So, we are in an actual prison then.

A knock on the door interrupts us.

"Captain, you are wanted." A guard, stationed at the door, calls over his shoulder. Adrian sighs heavily as if he wants nothing more than to watch us lose our control.

"Who and why?" he all but snarls and the innocent messenger.

"There is word from the palace that requires your attention."

Adrain sighs again. "Eat!" he growls at us. He turns and saunters from the room, the two guards follow swiftly behind.

We wait for the door to close before pouncing on the trays of food, more than ready for our bellies to feel full. The soup burns my mouth and throat in my haste to rid myself of the hunger pains.

"It's a shame they didn't give us a metal spoon," Aria speaks, toying with her wooden utensil, stirring and stirring her soup, mesmerised by the action. Her eye has gotten better in those few days, the swelling has gone down. She can almost open it fully now. "I could've turned it into a shank."

I laugh, "And that's probably why they gave us wooden ones."

"I could still use it I suppose," she mumbles, stabbing the air with her spoon, making me smile.

A quiet takes hold of us, a suffocating blanket that makes me more uncomfortable as the seconds tick by. The remaining food on my plate looks suddenly off-putting. Already sitting on the floor, I place the tray down next to me, my appetite vanishing into the air. The slight tap of the metal bowl on the stone brings Aria's attention to me.

"You miss them, don't you?" Aria asks quietly. She too stops eating to engage in conversation.

"Who?" I answer, still watching the steam billow out from the top of the bowl, not wanting to see her knowing brown eyes.

"Don't kid yourself, you know exactly who I mean. I've watched you get that wistful glaze over your eyes these past few days. Not to mention that I watched you for about two weeks before this." She waves her arms around in the air motioning to the situation we find ourselves in. "I saw the interactions you all had. I saw your smile." The last statement is barely a whisper, and it breaks my already damaged heart.

I pull my knees up to my chest and wrap my arms around them, dropping my chin to rest on top. "It doesn't matter anyway. I let my guard down and it won't happen again."

The minute tap of her own bowl being placed down, and the shuffle of boots draw my attention to her. Her brown eyes are filled with sympathy. "I know that feeling. The feeling that you finally belong." Her gaze goes distant, as though she is remembering something and a soft smile tucks at her lips. "I had that with Surya."

I wince at the name.

At the voice ringing in my head, *I'll have the body collected later.*

Aria seems to hear it too; her face drops, and her eyes are downcast. "She was my safe haven, even after the beatings back at the guild she would always be there to help me pick up the pieces."

"I'm sorry, I never knew," I offer timidly, my heart cracks further, aching for her and her pain.

"No one did. We couldn't risk it. We found a slice of happiness in the darkest of places, and neither of us wanted to lose it. But we loved each other, I know that much, and when she died... I wasn't even allowed to mourn her..." she pauses and takes a deep breath, "I still don't think I have properly. There's this hole inside of me, that I don't think I'll ever fill." Her lips tremble, "it gnaws at me day and night. I don't even know where she's buried. I can't say goodbye. I didn't…" She stops just as the first tear falls from her eyes, "and now it's like she never existed." She shakes her head. I don't know what to say. There is nothing in this world more painful than losing someone you hold so close. I would know, but this isn't about me. It's about Aria, about acknowledging her feelings and allowing her to grieve her loss.

"You aren't alone anymore, Ria." I smile and wish I could reach out and hold her hand. She smiles back, watery, and weak, but still a smile all the same.

"Back at the Fort after you left, everyone was put into overdrive. More training daily, harsher punishments. It was like they were preparing for war."

My face pinches in confusion but she speaks again. "Even some of the Furies on overseas missions were shipped back, some were even pulled off assignments early and others were cancelled before they began."

The clatter of armour hitting the floor interrupts our ever-darkening conversation and the door to the dungeons opens. A large figure whips inside making me stand up immediately, my hands balled into fists at my side.

"Fury?" an unfamiliar voice rumbles through the room. Deep and masculine. I look to the door and stand up, Aria mirrors me, our fists clenched. The circumstance is very familiar of when Declan found me in the City Hall. My heart thunders thinking Declan has come. He's come to get me out of here.

The figure is large, similar to Declan's stands looming in the doorway, completely in shadow, light only illuminating their silhouette. My hands loosen, my fingers uncurling. Hope, foolish damn hope, rising in my chest.

The figure steps up to my cell and my breath stalls in my lungs.

It's not Declan. My heart, my stupid little heart falls.

This male look similar with tanned skin and curly hair so dark it looks black, cut short, with matching brown eyes. A strong jaw and ungodly long eyelashes. He could be Declan's brother – if you squint a little. The mystery male doesn't hesitate to go for the lock on my cell. Surprised I step back until my back hits the wall at the far side, raising my fists.

"Easy Fury. Princess Mala sent me." He turns seeing Aria, equally as distrustful. "Yours?" he turns back to me.

I nod without using my words. The cell door pops open. "I'm going to open her cell as well, please don't hit me on the head."

He twirls and again begins working on the lock. Freedom has never felt so false. But this male is wearing the brown leather armour embossed with the crest of Her Majesty's guards.

Aria's cell door open before long but neither of us moves.

He stands there waiting for us. "Come on then. We don't have a lot of time," he urges. Still, we don't move. We look between each other and him.

"My name is Carlos and I work for Princess Mala. I have for a very long time. Now can we please just go before we get caught? I'm putting my job and life on the line for this..."

Aria links eyes with me once again. She nods once. I nod with her fae hearing she can hear his heartbeat, as creepy as I still find all that. But she knows he isn't lying. I take the first step out of the cell, looking over how rescuer.

"Where to then Carlos?"

He smirks, "Now that's more like it." He jogs to the door, pushing it open just enough that he can see the corridor outside. An unknown guard walks past the door. We all wait until he has rounded the corner before following Carlos out into the hallway.

"Princess Mala is waiting for us by the airlock. But we need to hurry. Adrian could reappear at any minute and if this place goes into lockdown we will never get out," Carlos informs us both. I share a glance with Aria and decide to trust this unknown male. If he can get us to the surface that's fine by me. We walk by a window and find it bordered by white glittering magic, keeping the seawater outside and the air in.

"Pure magic," I whisper in awe of the display. I reach out to touch it, the sizzle of power is electrifying the closer I get, but Carlos snatches my hand away.

"It's not like you'll disrupt the magic, but can we please our hands to ourselves until we leave here?"

I resist the urge to pout my lip but follow him silently.

This place is nearly deserted. Made from black stone and iron cells, each in their own block, this prison is isolating and where dreams seemingly go to die. With the cells in blocks of six in separate rooms, just like ours was, we luckily won't have to worry about people screeching and blowing our cover. The corridor is long and straight, wide enough for at least four people abreast, with arched ceilings painted with sea creatures and underwater landscapes.

Passing by the windows shows more and more stone walls expanding into the distance, disappearing into the gloominess of the sea. Fire lamps projecting light through other windows are the only indication that there are other parts of the prison are in fact occupied.

The whole place looks to be surrounded by an impossibly dark trench, which goes down so deep it mirrors an abyss.

Shadowing Carlos is easy and given his size and muscular build he is surprisingly nimble. It's his shoulders I'm looking at when he stops suddenly making me walk right into the back of him.

Aria snickers quietly behind me.

Carlos steadies me, seemingly unfazed, as he peers around the corner watching as another set of guards survey the corridors.

"We aren't far from the entrance. Princess Mala should be there," he whispers over his shoulder, following in the same directions as the guards. He goes slower now. Crouching lower. He stops dead when another, singular guard passes down the corridor ahead of us. It's only by the mercy of the gods that they don't see us.

"We are nearer to the guards' quarters. Stay low, stay quiet and do exactly what I do."

Needing no further instruction, we follow. He makes his way down the corridor first waiting for us in the shadows. I see his hand wave us over, as he keeps watch.

I push Aria in front of me.

"Scared to go first?" she teases.

"If anyone gets caught, he can at least get you out," I reply.

She eyes me, "I don't need a white knight thank you."

"I never said you did. But you're here because of me. Now go before we both get caught."

She takes a step and white light fills the hallway. The guards' quarters door opens wide, and the chatter of off-duty personnel filters into the corridor with laughs and cheers and the distant sound of a sports game that is playing in the background. Two guards file out and three more walk in. Aria melds into the shadows so well, that even I have problems tracking her. The door slams shut a moment later and I see her whispering with Carlos.

My turn. Following Aria's path, I keep away from any fire lamps and windows streaming with unnatural moonlight. Only unnatural with how deep we are underwater, the magic must help produce sunlight in the daytime too.

It's not long before I join back up with both of them.

"I hear yelling," Aria whispers.

Carlos sighs, "I told her to distract him. Not yell at him." I distinctly see an eye roll before he turns and leads us further into the labyrinth of cell blocks and even darker corridors.

"What is this place?" I whisper.

"It's our most secure prison. We send our worst criminals here. Ones that we can't keep with the city walls."

"So, we're not in Salacia?" Aria asks.

"Not quite," he answers, before silencing us with a finger placed over his mouth. Guards come walking down the adjacent hallway. The clink of metal chains accompanies them.

Carlos ushers us all into a nearby cell block, careful not to have the hinges of the ancient wooden door creak.

"You know I don't have long left here. I don't see why this is necessary."

They're transporting a criminal.

"Shut up and keep moving." I can hear the guy stumble like he's been shoved. Seconds later they pass by us.

"What's that?" They stop. Within inches of us.

"What?" The second, quieter guard, asks.

"That?"

They quiet, pausing to listen. The prisoner looks around, his eyes landing on the door that we are all hiding behind.

The sound of clothes shuffling behind us startled me. My spine straightens. I turn in time to see someone moving around in the cell nearby.

Collectively we hold our breath. My heart pounds violently in my chest. But this is what I live for the thrill of being caught. The chase not to mention the deception of it all.

I catch Aria's attention silent pointing over to the cell. She stares into the darkness; I know she can probably see whoever it is. All we can hope for is that they can't see in the dark as well.

Before long the prisoner looks away. Having seen nothing.

"That's Princess Mala."

"What the fuck is she doing here?" The two guards carry on their way.

"She not happy with Adrian bringing in those two Furies."

"We have Furies?"

"Yeah, I'll take you to see them later, after we drop this idiot off. Not as exciting as you'd think so don't get your hopes up."

I bite my lip to keep from laughing.

"Prick," Aria mumbles under her breath.

"Hello?" The prisoner behind us murmurs into the dark.

Carlos's head turns around and even in the dark, I can see the panic on his face. Not only has he risked his job getting us out, but he could very well lose his life on the grounds of treason for us. I slip out from behind the door with no sound, followed quickly by Aria and then Carlos brings up the rear, closing the door to as he does.

Taking point, once again, Carlos rushes us from the cell block up a flight of stairs, hugging the wall all the while.

The rough black stone is freezing cold and faintly damp. I begin to wonder just how long this prison has been here and how it's still standing. I know magic must have a hand in it but there has to be more to it. How much longer will it stand if water has already started to seep through the cracks.

"I don't like you, Adrian. I never have and I don't think I ever will." Mala's voice begins to echo through the corridors. "You have been my mother's guard for so long that I have merely tolerated your presence. But don't mistake that for actual affection."

"Princess, believe me when I say that I know. But I still cannot permit you to see them. It is an order from your mother. Not even you can overrule her orders." Turning the corner, we come to a room with a glass window, rippling with raw magic. It overlooks the lobby in which, a very angry-looking princess stands with another guard, in silver armour, his hand resting on the hilt of his sword, with several members of the prison guard, all dressed in black stand behind Adrian, who's pose shows boredom even with his hands behind his back showing some modicum of respect for who stands in front of him.

Despite her angry expression and tone of voice, she could still be the most beautiful woman in the world. Dressed in pale pink salwar pants and a matching bedlah top, decorated in mountains of crystals and sea glass. A diamond tiara sits upon her wavy black hair. The silver-plated guard – who looks vaguely like Carlos – behind her looks to be holding back a laugh.

He and Carlos catch each other's eye and give a subtle nod. The latter pushing us in front of him showing us which way to go.

Still in a crouch, we make our way across the room to a hatch that looks discreetly like a white bubble. With words above it in another language.

Carlos stands and turns the wheel on the front of the 'bubble door.' It opens with a groan.

"Climb in," he groans pulling it open slowly. His muscles bulging from exertion. When we hesitate, he sighs. "It's the airlock. Now will you please get in." Aria jumps in first then me, Carlos waits outside his hand still resting on the door.

A flurry of pink jumps in before I can really appreciate the veins on Carlos' arms, and another one of silver. Our rescuer jumps in last, sealing the airlock shut behind him.

"Easy, it's only me," the smaller figure says. Stepping into the gloomy blue light of the room. I turn to see a flustered-looking princess.

"Your Highness," I nod my head in respect, but my stare never leaves her face. "What exactly are you doing down here with the common folk?" I tease.

"I heard they were starving you." She looks us over. I don't know exactly what she sees but it's enough to have a frown tuck at her plump lips.

Aria taps my arm and gives me a particular look. Her mouth doesn't move. But I understand all the same.

"Are you sure we can trust these people?"

"Well, they did just get us out of those cells. What more do you want?"

Her eyebrow rises. But she doesn't 'say' anything more.

"You know we are standing right in front of you, right? Whilst you're having your little private conversation," Mala bites back, sassily.

Aria pulls a face.

"Alright." I roll my eyes getting her to stop.

Mala eyes Aria warily, but neither speaks further.

"You have to forgive our scepticism. Why exactly are you helping us, when your mother locked us in here in the first place."

"Because 'Dawnya' and my mother are about to make the biggest mistake of their lives. One that could potentially start a war with the surface world, one that we can't win. Secondly, I didn't put you in here, so you can't be mad at me. Thirdly, and lastly, I promised I would help you back at the embassy. This kind of covers that." She flips her hair over her shoulder and stares me down with her bright turquoise eyes.

My brow quirks again, of its own accord, but caution gives way to the brightness of humour.

The tension in the room becomes palpable, and I move closer to her. Waving towards the other glass, and magic, door showing nothing but the darkened ocean beyond.

"On your leave, your highness."

CHAPTER THIRTY
THE BIG BLUE

"Put those on, surface dwellers," the second guard mutters from behind the princess.

"Sebastian," Carlos growls in annoyance.

Aria narrows her eyes at him.

I turn to find two black suits, skintight with a zip at the back lying, folded neatly, on the floor.

"And what exactly are they?" I ask.

"Suits," Sebastian states unamused. "Look do you want to get out of here or not, because we can always just open the door and..."

Mala slaps him on the chest, cutting him off. "They are suits designed for a human to be able to withstand the depths. We are quite far below and bringing in a transport vehicle would bring too much attention. So, these should suffice until we get to Salacia."

"Should?" Aria questions. I too had picked up on how Mala's eyes wandered when that came up.

She stays silent and turns to Carlos for help.

"They haven't strictly been tested," he answers for her.

Aria's eyes find mine again and, once again, I can tell she's unamused.

'What do you want me to say?' I use my eyes to convey the words.

She scowls at me and doesn't reply.

"You need to change quickly before they realise you're missing."

I waste no time in slipping on the suit, over my other clothes. It's a little uncomfortable at first but the material is breathable and light. Aria is slightly more hesitant than I am. Mala then hands me a mask for my face with a rebreather built in along the seams mimicking gills. The implication of that isn't lost on me. She pulls the straps tight around my head and pushes me towards Sebastian.

"He will be looking after you out there, please do as he tells you." I nod to both of them and move to stand by his side.

Mala secures Aria's mask to her head and steps back. Carlos steps up to Aria's side.

"This is going to be a shock," he mutters, watching Sebastian open the hatch to the outside. The water begins to slowly filter in, hitting our feet first. I gasped loudly at the sensation. It's like being slowly dunked into an ice bath it's very uncomfortable but as more water comes in faster and faster it's suddenly hard to care. I began worrying about how easily one could become lost in the sea. Carlos clips himself on a line to Aria and I feel safer knowing that once the hatch is open fully Sebastian will likely do the same. At least that's what I'm hoping.

The water climbs higher, up to our chests, and I begin floating, travelling with it to the ceiling. I put my hands up to stop my head from hitting the roof of the small room until it's finally full of cold seawater. With the hatch fully open, Sebastian exits first, no doubt checking for threats to his princess. But that knot of worry tightens in my belly.

Mala leaves next, then Carlos and Aria. I follow, swimming timidly out into the open, blue, and black sea. Sebastian closes and seals the hatch behind me while I admire the sheer size of the ocean before me.

It's so quiet.

Its vastness is so overwhelming there would not be enough lifetimes to map out every crevice and rock formation, every trench and mountain.

It's both peaceful and entirely too calm. I can see what they mean when they say we are very deep beneath the waves I look up and I can't even see the surface. We are well and truly lost beneath the waves and I've never felt such freedom. I tread water just looking around at everything. Most things around are nothing but black splotches because of the lights from the windows but I can see more of the prison. It looks to be in the shape of a pentagon, and indeed there is a trench surrounding it. Looking down at the inky water below brings fears forth I never knew I had before. If something struck from below, I would be completely helpless to defend myself from it, yet there is a part of me that wants to explore it. To see for myself what manner of creature lives down there.

Sebastian grips my arm. I realise then I've started to drift from the group he clips himself to me and begins to swim back to the group.

He hasn't shifted like I thought he would. None of them have in fact. Not that I would know what their changes would be anyway. But I guess I expected something different. Sebastian pulls me along, faster than he should be able. Most definitely faster than any mortal I've ever met. The pace is a brutal one, one I know I would have trouble keeping up with if it wasn't for the princess' guard.

With the mask covering my whole face it gives me the freedom to talk a little, wetting my lips, "Aren't you merpeople? You know half human half fish?"

Sebastian laughs and an embarrassed blush warms my cheeks. Cursing myself for putting it so bluntly.

"We are, at least my brother and I." He nods his head to Carlos, "but our princess didn't think you would take too kindly to witness us 'up close and personal' just yet." He turns and gives me a wink and the embarrassment slips away.

"Why is that?"

"Because usually from the waist up a mer is what you humans call naked."

"Even the females?" I swallow.

He looks confused at that, "Oh yeah, you people have a modesty thing. I always forget your weird laws. But yes, even the females."

"So, are you classed as shifters then? Because you can be in two forms?"

"Most mer can shift between the two but no we can't shift into animals as some above-ground can. Only the seven royals can. One for each sea domain. Cordelia is the only one in the city that can. Mala thought she might have the gift passed down. But so far, no signs."

He focuses on the way forward once again, checking in on Mala briefly. But I focus on how his hair is blowing through the waves and the way the minimal light catches on his cheekbones. I faintly see stripes along his skin in the form of scales, golden and deep brown in nature flowing with the current of the water. It's an effort not to trace those stripes with my fingertips.

Using the tie strapped to both mine and his waist, Sebastian pulls me closer to him until my back is flushed with his chest. I noted Carlos has done the same with Aria and just as I'm about to ask why he twirls and drops down faster than I can imagine. My hair is bolt straight behind me we are travelling down that fast. The action has my stomach roiling, and it somehow drops even as we fall further into the deep blue.

Gripping onto Sebastian's arm I breathe deeply waiting for him to level out and mercifully after several hundred meters, he does once again level out. He lets go of me again to swim freely next to him. Whether it be my imagination or the actual feeling, the pressure from the water creeps up on me I feel heavier than I did only moments ago.

We swim in silence for a while, every so often I hear Carlos ask Aria if she's ok, or the trio – Sebastian, Mala, and Carlos – will crack a joke between them in a language neither I nor Aria has ever heard before.

"We are going to have to hurry up. There's no doubt that they've found your cells empty by now and they will have sent someone to the palace to report," Mala says out of the blue. She has been taking the lead for this convoy and has been fairly quiet for most of it. Her mind must be riddled with thoughts of treason. She's gone against her mother's wishes, and she's broken two very dangerous people out of an underwater prison. If she isn't experiencing at least a little bit of worry or guilt, then I'd think she'd have gone mad.

Sebastian scoops me up to his chest once more and I fear we are going to drop further, but it's instead to make us more streamlined as he propels us faster through the water. I can feel the resistance of it on my mask and I worry that for some reason my mask will slide off my face and I'll drown down here. I roll my eyes at the intrusive thought and grip his arm like I did before, running my thumb over those stripes feeling the bumps of the scales as I do. He gives me a little squeeze and I go back to searching the ever expanding, black, murky waters for anything. Any sign of life. Most importantly I'm watching to see if anyone is following behind us. Someone we may have missed. But I can't see very far in this darkness. The light from my mask is making me more of a beacon than being of any actual use for anything else.

Sebastian is in my ear a moment later "Keep your eye out on that big spot of blackness." He points to exactly that, a big spot of blackness.

"That's helpful." I roll my eyes, "We are literally surrounded by darkness." But he's right, it's not long before we make it past some sort of magical barrier, I feel it tingle across my skin as we pass through.

"Welcome to Salacia, surface dweller," Sebastian mutters in my ear again.

My mouth drops open at the city sprawling before me. Something that no mortal has lied eyes on before. A place so sacred even its location is held to a standard of divinity. Precious stones of all shapes and colours have been used as not only the foundations of the city but the use of such stone carries over into new buildings and towers. Towers, that are far taller than anything on land, they twirl beautifully up towards the sun – or rather for this time of night, moon – illuminated by soft blue and yellow lights that glow from within. Markets and smaller houses are scattered throughout the city there doesn't seem to be an immediate line between classes like there is in Larissa.

The Palace sits pride of place in the centre of it all, like a shining beacon made entirely of pearl. The stone gleams and reflects any light that touches it. The building itself appears angelic with an ethereal glow hovering around it.

Sea creatures of all manner and size dwell amongst the locals as we seem to fly above them.

Sebastian chuckles, "I've never seen one of your kind so quiet. I'm yet to meet one that isn't quite so talkative."

"Oh, you have now," Aria nods to me. I hadn't realised that the group had closed up so much that we were all now within talking distance, "Unless it's for information. She's not one for talking, that one."

"Interesting," Sebastian mutters, and although I can't see I can feel him watching me. I keep my eyes on the approaching city. At all the lights and colours of the buildings it's like an artist's dream and the opera house sits close to the outer edge of the city designed to look like a conch shell, lit up from the outside and music plays loudly from within. Trees of coral line the mini streets. Although I'm not quite sure what mer need with streets when they can swim everywhere.

My mouth snaps shut, when I feel an ache in it from having it open for so long.

"It's like something out of a dream," I whisper.

"Which is why we have to protect it," Sebastian mumbles. I turn to him. His strong jaw and contoured cheekbones are illuminated by the soft glow of the lights coming from the approaching city. His gentle smile lights his eyes, and the crinkles around them are downright adorable. "You can't start a war without losing something in the process."

Mala slows stopping in front of us, her clothes flowing around her like ribbons.

"I think we should just head straight there. Wouldn't you agree?" She turns to Carlos, who nods.

"We won't get far into the city with these two without being seen. No offence girls."

"None taken," I reply before Aria can bite back.

Sebastian's grip tightens on me again and we drop. A girlish squeak burst out of my mouth much to the pleasure of my guide who rumbles a laugh as we descend.

"You couldn't have given some warning?" I groan, gripping his arm tighter than before so I don't slip from his grasp.

"You got your warning, Mala said we should head straight there." The cliff streams past us at a dizzying speed and we plunge further and further down into the depths. My suit begins to feel tighter almost oppressive, and it's getting harder to breathe.

Lights brighten a crack in the cliff towards the bottom of the cliff, which gets brighter and brighter on our approach. When we get close enough, I see it's actually an underground hanger filled with submarines and other cargo ships.

The moment my feet hit the floor I feel almost too heavy. Like my steps are weighted, and not just from the water. Aria, even with her fae heritage seems to be struggling with the pressure and with walking.

"It's the suit, it's helping to hold you down, so you don't float away. Let me know if it gets too much," Sebastian fills in the unspoken question.

"Can you read my thoughts?"

He laughs, "No. I saw the confusion on your face and the pathetic leg raise you just tried to do."

I grunt trying to take another step I succeed in lifting my leg, but it's used all my energy. It slowly sinks back, and I've gained no ground. I'm panting and sweating, the pressure of the water is too much for me.

Suddenly I'm lifted into thick arms, "How do you mortals do anything? Like I mean *anything*. You're so fragile."

"Are all merpeople such arrogant bastards?" I snap.

"Oh, you're feisty."

Aria watches us from the side of her eye.

"I could just drop you and sit back and watch as you try to stand."

"You wouldn't dare."

"Oh, believe me, Aella, he would," Mala's voice chimes from in front of us. "If you don't mind waiting here, I need to speak with the captain."

We don't actually wait by the submarine; Sebastian leads us into it as Carlos follows his princess. An unexpected pleasure to find down here is that the sub is filled with air and movement has never felt so easy. Aria and I have finally been given the green light to take off our suits. The mask, while being a lifesaver, was starting to feel a little uncomfortable.

Sebastian is now giving us a brief tour of the machine that would carry us back up to the surface, in only a matter of hours.

Each doorway we walk through has a high step and low ceiling, and my thighs burn with the delicious heat that I've missed from my training.

We pass by empty bunks after empty bunks all neat and tidy, but I don't see any personal belongings anywhere. Not that I should be all that surprised. A Fury doesn't get that type of luxury either.

"These are for the crew, they are on the most direct route to the control room which is where we are headed now," Seb explains waving to the rooms as we pass by. It's been very amusing watching him kick his leg up so high and bend his head down to squish himself through the doorways. He's massive, much like his brother, in such a confined space a submarine. Thankfully Aria and I only have high knees to worry about.

"How do you know you can trust this crew of yours?" Aria asks of Sebastian.

"Why would we not? These are our people."

"Doesn't mean they don't have their own agendas."

"Are you always this mistrustful?"

She falls silent as we walk into the control room. It's the only part of the vessel that has signs of life, people busily from side to side, talking to each all trying to get the tub ready for launch. The odd few people glance over at us but they only wave to Sebastian in greeting.

"And this is where the magic happens," Sebastian smiles, his arms wide presenting the room to us.

The room is similar to that of the mission's room back home. Blinking lights and dials on control panels fill displays throughout, interspersed with radar, a communications console, sonar, everything one could possibly need to operate a machine of this size.

The hair on the back of my neck rises and from across the room, I can sense eyes on me. I turn to a darkened corner, and I see exactly why.

"Roman?" I question, my voice a little too high. But my confusion is very real. I knew he was in Salacia. I hadn't thought he'd be on the same damn boat.

He walks over and Aria puts herself between us just as he steps up to me.

"That's hardly necessary," I mumble.

"And yet I'm doing it."

"Nice to see you again, Siren," he greets.

"Siren?" Sebastian chuckles, "The mythological mermaid that lures pirates to their deaths?"

"I didn't exactly give it to myself," I mumble, for the first time in my life I feel a little awkward about the name. Given that it's a myth about his people.

"Do you have like, water powers then, or?" he crosses his arms over his broad chest and leans down ever so slightly.

I look down to my hands turning them over as if I've never seen them before. "Not that I'm aware of, but that would be so cool."

He smiles and seems all the more intrigued until Her Highness walks into the room. He stands bolt-straight with his arms behind his back.

"Ah I see you are aware of our other precious cargo," she says by way of greeting. "Sebastian if you wouldn't mind could you show them to a room, I want to let our crew know where we are headed."

"And we don't get to know?" Aria whirls on the princess.

"Watch your tone," Carlos grumbles, pointing a finger at her. The glower in his eyes makes me feel a little defensive of the stubborn fae at my side. I grip her arm squeezing it in warning. I turn and see the whole room has stopped working and is watching the interaction.

"Should we maybe go somewhere private to finish this conversation?" I surmise.

"I was just going to suggest the same," Sebastian agrees.

Mala nods, "Seb show them the room. I'll be there in a few minutes. I want to give the crew their directions and coordinates of where we are surfacing."

He nods and leads us from the room. I can tell Aria is still angry. I can feel it rolling off her like a roaring fire. One misstep and any one of us could be burnt by it. I don't know whether she is more upset with the princess or if she's simply angry on my behalf. But either way, we will soon have the answers that we want.

The clank of our combined footsteps against the metal floor fills my ears, but not my thoughts. I can't possibly imagine why Roman is on board with us. But I know keeping him confined underwater in a steel capsule with me is not going to end well for either one of us.

The room can only be described as a small office, with a desk on one side and locked glass cabinets on the other, filled with book and trinkets. Only two chairs sit in the room and Mala takes the one behind the desk, Carlos at her side, his hand resting on his weapon. Aria pushes me down into the other, her arms across her chest. Her trim muscles flexed under her clothing.

"Care to explain?" Aria insists, her face devoid of any sort of familiarity.

"Aria," I snap, "Enough." She doesn't turn to scowl at me like I thought she would instead she keeps her heated gaze on the princess, who returns the look in kind.

"You know why I'm pissed about this Aella. Don't pretend you don't. He shouldn't be here and it's for *his* safety more than anybody else's."

"I'm not sure I understand," Mala drops her gaze to mine across the desk from her. "What is she talking about?"

I open my mouth to explain but nothing comes out. Only a strangled sort of sound until I snapped it shut once again. Aria steps away from the table to stand at the back of the room, leaving this up to me, despite her dropping me in it.

"It's a sort of a state of mind that we have no control over," I start, "It's difficult to explain but it is something that the Fort has taken years to perfect, a chemical enhancement serum is injected into the bloodstream, usually monthly but for those going on long missions they get a stronger dosage to make it last longer and for it to be more effective. Even when the body has broken it down over time. The serum, as we call, becomes reactivated when in the presence of our target. As though it can sense them through proximity. It's like the body gets another dose and all humanity we had shuts down until our mission is complete. We'd kill our own best friend if they got in our way, and we wouldn't know it until it was already done. The process makes our waking life painful until we accomplish our goal."

I play on my own personal pain. Dragging up a particular skeleton that is undoubtedly going to dredge up others with it, ones that I'd buried years ago in a lovely iron lockbox and dropped into the farthest reaches of my mind. But to get my point across it's important Mala understands what Roman being here means for me.

"And you've just put hers in a steel trap, a few thousand feet underwater with next to nothing to stop her from completing her mission," Aria snaps from behind me.

We are met with a deafening silence and terrified faces.

"I didn't realise..." Mala begins but trails off.

"What that we didn't actually willing go about killing people?" Aria snaps back.

"Ria, don't," I utter, placing a hand on her arm.

"Don't abbreviate my name, it's already short. Don't be lazy," she turns to me, I see the humour in her eyes, most would mistake it for a sinister delight.

The joke seems to lift some of the thickening tension from the room. But not so much that we all forget the seriousness of the situation that lies before us.

"Now that we have explained our tragic life. Why don't you begin explaining why the Hel is Roman is here?" Aria's already small grin drops, as she turns back to the still-stunned trio.

The sub churns to life the noise deafening, cutting off all conversation. We all sit there, our gazes flickering between each other uncomfortably.

It's several minutes, and some mild turbulence later, that we finally find some smooth motion. "WE'RE CLEAR!" One of the crew shouts through from the control room, letting us know we are out of Salacia and that there is definitely no turning back.

"I will only say this to you once more before we really start to have a problem. You will watch how you talk to the princess," Carlos warns Aria one last time.

"Is there more to what you are telling us about this 'state of mind' as you put it? It seems like you may be holding something back. I'd like to know what we are in for should this occur. Despite the fact that I have seen you change a shade of emotion since seeing him."

My mouth opens and closes a few times trying to find the right words. "You will not like the details. They are traumatic and unethical."

"Try me," she challenges.

"Ok. But remember this is all we have known. It is vital you know, so you can find ways to prevent Roman's death."

Mala's eyes harden, she shifts to be more comfortable in her chair and weaves her fingers together, resting them on the desk, ready for my explanation. I hear both Aria shift uncomfortably behind me and Sebastian moves to stand at the other side of the princess. In my eyeline for the first time since this discussion started.

"Understand what I am about to tell you is highly confidential and dangerous. This is not for the faint-hearted. We have already told you more than we probably should've." Carlos shifts from foot to foot and clears his throat. But doesn't leave the room. When neither says anything, I turn to Aria. She hesitates, I can see her mulling over what I'm about to say. I won't do it without her permission. This is not just my history and trauma that needs to be accounted for.

She nods and I continue. There's no more stalling. "The mindset you will witness is something the Furies have taken to calling *'the final call'*. It has earned its name because once a Fury spies her target, she will become nothing more than a predator hunting its prey. It is like a basic animalistic need that takes over and it won't be satisfied until the target is killed. It is near impossible to ignore, and when it fully takes over control, there's nothing anyone can do to stop it. As you can imagine, it is degrading and debilitating to experience. But something the guild thought was a necessary experiment that they wanted to make into a reality." I take a deep breath and look at Aria. She shows no signs of discomfort, so I continue. "It is a mindset that is literally conditioned into us from a young age, enhanced by the serum. To achieve the desired state, we are subjected to extra doses of the serum and electro-shock therapy, simultaneously to adjust the body's chemistry."

Mala sits back up in her chair, her joined hands falling to her lap. She looks as though she has just swallowed her tongue and wants to throw up both at the same time; her bright eyes widen in shock.

"So, what you will witness – if it does occur – is essentially my mind shocking itself into submission, in order to carry out the orders that I have been given by the guild. You will witness me in total surrender to the guild. You will not be looking at Aella anymore. But the Siren. The monster they made me." I keep my eyes locked with hers, choosing not to look away. I need to show her that my words are truth and not some fairy story that has been made up.

Her previous curiosity is washed away and is almost replaced with shame and sadness. For me? I hope not. For the others still at the Fort and still going through it? Maybe. But it doesn't matter regardless. She can't do anything about it. Not that I would expect her too anyway.

I cannot muster an ounce of pity for myself and the things I have gone through. That has simply been my life, something I have grown accustomed to. I have never felt anything for the torture they did to me, and I will not start to feel sorry for myself now.

I look to Aria who stands tall like a pillar of strength, and I can't be anything but proud as I look at her. Two of a kind, both of us. Having undergone all of the same treatment, yet here we still stand.

I stand up shaking out my legs just to give myself something else to think about, and Aria steps forward. "Now you know more about our catastrophic lives. Why is he here?"

Mala blinks rapidly, tears have welled in her eyes, but she doesn't give them a chance to fall. Carlos' eyes bore into the side of my face. They have since I began talking.

"He came to us about a week ago, just before the ball asking for sanctuary from you." She points at me, her voice wobbly with emotion, "and of course, my mother jumped at the opportunity, despite my obvious objections to the very idea that she get involved with surface world problems. We had to keep him hidden of course. So, we dressed him up as a guard that night. Better to keep him close than leave him at the empty embassy for the night, ripe for the picking if you'd figured it out. He was brought to Salacia the next morning. So, I bided my time waiting for the right opportunity, we couldn't have a sub leave the city within a week of arriving it would be too telling.

Then word of your arrival in the prison reached the palace and I knew you'd be the ticket out. Roman had mostly free range of the palace and had council with my mother at least twice a week so it wasn't hard for me to find him again. I asked him if he wanted to return. I wondered if he missed his home. He had said he missed his brother but that was about it."

I scrunch my face. Nowhere did it say it had a brother. Not in any of his files or any government documents that he had. Which, to be fair, weren't many.

"Well, I suppose you should feel safe in knowing that I wouldn't have even thought about you harbouring him. I would've thought you'd want to stay away from surface problems as much as possible," I cut in.

"Believe me I've tried to steer her in another direction," Carlos drawls.

"I have only had to because of my mother," Mala claps back against her guard.

"That doesn't explain, why he's here on this sub though does it," Aria's patience is on its last legs.

"What did I say about that tone?" Carlos snaps, stepping forward pointing at her.

Aria shrugs, "I'm yet to see you do anything about it."

"I received a letter, from the crown prince of Anaphi a few days ago, asking me to return him to Ansrutas. Claiming he had found a safe haven for him," Mala says, ignoring both of them as if they're nothing more than misbehaving children.

"So, Roman is aboard this vessel as a favour to Frederick?" I surmise, still utterly confused.

"Yes," Mala answers without hesitation.

Sebastian also steps forward, partially shielding the princess from Aria's growing annoyance. His hand rests close to his weapon, he notes me glancing at the wickedly curved and deadly sickle sword, before eyeing me with open curiosity.

"OK, then why? What does Frederick want with Roman?" I ask.

Mala laces her fingers together and leans forward on the desk, "What do you mean what does he want? He wants to protect him."

"Why?" I insist, growing irritable.

Mala looks at Carlos; the pair share a look of confusion and disbelief. When her turquoise eyes connect with mine once again, I almost begin wondering whether or not I actually want to know the answer.

"How is it you do not know? Are you not close with Frederick?"

"Clearly not as close as you two are. Now if you please just answer the question," I drawl, growing increasingly bored of this conversation.

"It's because Roman is his younger brother."

CHAPTER THIRTY-ONE
THIS IS A TEST...
RIGHT?

I tilt my head to the side.

My hearing is gone surely because there's no way I heard her correctly. My lips thin into a line and my eyebrows pull down impossibly far as I watch the princess. I wait for any sign to say that she's only kidding or that maybe, just maybe, I've finally snapped and gone fully insane.

"What now?" I ask, leaning forward in my chair to get closer so that I can make sure I hear her this time.

"Frederick is Roman's older brother. Roman is the second-born child of Scarlett Haakon."

My lips purse. I can't believe it. Everything in me knows her words are true. Why would she lie about something so important? But my mind can't comprehend why he wouldn't tell me – except for the obvious of course.

"Why of just Scarlett?" Aria asks. I hadn't missed that either.

Mala shifts uncomfortably in her seat, looking between Carlos and back to me. There's something she's hiding I can see it. Something that a lot of people do not know. If any.

"Mala," I level my stare at her. "What are you not saying?"

Again, she keeps a tight lip. Her eyes don't stay in one place for too long before they flit over to something else in the room.

"This is not common knowledge." But thankfully the princess in front of us has more sense than anyone I've ever met. "So, this will not leave us." She points at both of us, sighs and rubs her forefinger and thumb along her immaculate brow.

"Did us telling you highly confidential information on the Fort not already clarify that enough for you?"

Carlos draws a dagger from his belt pointing it at Aria.

"Stand down, Carlos," Mala speaks, "they have a right to be pissed off."

"Nothing you say here will be repeated," I reassure.

She sighs again, "As you know King Theodore and Queen Scarlett haven't always gotten along very well. Their marriage was arranged by the former king and the fae king across the North Sea. They lived happily for a time, then Frederick came along, and the king was given an heir.

Anaphi and Tinos were talking trade deals and a small unit of Tinos' people travelled from their capital to Larissa. Where, coincidentally, Scarlett met her mate."

The word tings through me. Mate? I didn't know such a thing still existed.

"Mates are so rare now it's seen as a pure miracle if a pairing like that ever happens. But alas, that started their secret love affair. Of which Roman was born. Theodore didn't find out about it until after Iris was born and since then, it has been a marriage of convenience and not of love. They smile and wave politely for the people. But behind closed, I believe from what I've heard Frederick said, they have separate wings of the castle to each other now."

I knew that last part already. From my time having spent as Iris's 'handmaiden' whilst we worked on kicking her habit of Mica Glitter. But the secret son thing, now that is an interesting tale.

"So, the queen had a son with another?" Aria concludes.

"Yes," Mala answers.

"Holy shit."

"Holy shit indeed."

"Is Iris his? Theodore's, I mean," Aria asks next.

Mala opens her mouth but it's me who answers, "Believe me when I say he wouldn't treat her nearly half as well as he does if there was a chance, she wasn't his."

Aria asks a few more questions, things I already know, but I'm guessing she is trying to take advantage of Mala's loose tongue for the moment. I sit there in silence, my eyes glued to the desk in front of me. Still trying to comprehend all of this information. Staring into space. I can see and hear things happening around me, but I can't find it in me to care. I've never been silenced with such effectiveness before and it's only when a warm hand rests on my shoulders that I come out of my own thoughts.

I see Mala and Aria have gone for a wander; Carlos will undoubtedly be keeping the peace.

"You doing, ok?" It's Sebastian. He's standing at my side looking down at me with concern in his chocolate brown eyes. A place one could easily get lost. At this angle, he looks so much like his brother. Except for his boyish charm. Something that Carlos does not harper.

I hum back in response; my mind still hasn't caught up properly.

"It can be hard trying to comprehend something like. I understand, especially when it directly involves the people you trust."

I place my hand over his on my shoulder, giving it a gentle squeeze. I appreciate his words, but I don't think, for the moment at least, that I can talk about it too much.

"Where did they go?"

"They wanted to give you some time. But they are also talking about ways to keep the two of you apart for the next few hours. I just think you could do with a guard." The answer is so simple in his eyes. I'd love to agree.

"And I'm guessing you volunteered?" I grin up at him.

"Naturally. Aria didn't seem too impressed though."

"Is that right?"

"Hmm, something about being inappropriate. Not quite sure what she means."

I giggle, thankfully for his humour. I give his hand another squeeze and stand. "I'm assuming there's a room I'm due to be locked in."

He dramatically bows at the waist, "Right this way, my lady."

I follow him in silence, although he cracks joke after joke, trying to lighten my dullen mood. All this time I had been chasing Frederick's brother. No wonder he had been so protective. The king's attitude towards all of this now made complete and utter sense, even if his methods for getting rid of the problem are questionable at best. I wonder how Scarlett is taking all of this. Does she even know that her husband is trying to kill her son? What happened to her mate?

Mate. Gods above, this has been so much more complicated in such a short amount of time.

"And here we are," he announces, showing me an empty four-person bedroom. Two bunk beds one on either side and lockers at the front for any personal belongings.

"Thank you, Sebastian," I smile up at him. I move and roll onto one of the bunks sighing at finally having at least a semi-decent place to rest my head for the first time in about a week. I wiggle trying to get comfortable.

"A bed snob?" Sebastian asks, from the other bunk beside me. Dressed still in his armour it's a wonder he even fits in it, with shoulders so large.

"Oh, you bet. I've slept in some places that you couldn't even call a bed. But recently I've been sleeping on a very cold hard stone floor, so my back is a little messed up."

"They shouldn't have put you in there," his voice is low. Filled with lethal smoke, he's angry at his own people for locking someone like me up. It's probably the least I deserved considering.

"You need not try to cheer me up. You can't tell me you wouldn't have done the same in their position. I am what I am, and I'm feared, rightly so." I turn to him in time to see him shrug.

"We'll never know."

We both lay there for some time talking about nothing in particular but it's so refreshing talking to someone who doesn't know my past and it's not long before I've fallen asleep content for the first time in a few weeks.

When I woke again the news still hadn't sunken in. Sebastian has been replaced by Aria who sits across from me watching me like a hawk.

"Ok freak, can you turn away now?" I croak out, my mouth dry.

"There's water on the table next to you."

I take several gulps almost draining the glass, that time being starved has really come back to bite me in the arse. I see there's a small plate of food next to it as well.

"Your new boyfriend is just outside don't worry; he hasn't gone far."

"Gods above," I roll my eyes, eating through the food. "Not all guys I meet are somehow in a relationship with me. Will you cut it out?" I scowl.

She raises her hands in defeat, "It seems very easy for you to have them wrapped around your finger is all."

"Probably because I don't scowl at them all the time, nor do I give them attitude every time I talk."

She simply shrugs as if she sees nothing wrong with it. I'm inclined to grin. "You look better," she says out of the blue.

"Shouldn't I be saying that to you?" I nod to her eye.

"Probably but you haven't said anything else so I'm assuming it's healing just fine."

"What makes you say that anyway?"

"You don't look as sad anymore." And there is that void in my chest that I'd managed to forget. If only for a few days. Sucking all life into it.

"Thanks?" I answer placing the now empty plate back on the table.

"You ever think that we got the shit end of the stick?" she asks suddenly.

My brows pinch together, "What do you mean?"

"In life. You cannot tell me, that with the amount of people we meet – when out on missions – that you haven't thought about how good it would be to take their identity and disappear into nothing. To finally get out."

Her words stun me. It's not until recently that I have thought about it.

This is a test... Right?

Two years ago, to be exact, but I'd squashed those thoughts, for fear that they would be found out. It was two years ago when I began fearing that they could somehow hear my thoughts. I had begun to question whether I was the only one, with these treasonous thoughts. I grin despite the suspicion that swims to the surface.

Lying back down I ask, "Do you remember your family?" Avoiding answering her question directly, I instead question her end goal and satisfy my own thoughts that this could all be a trick. She is still, after all, a rival Fury.

"Not really. Just the colour of my mother's eyes and that's only because I see them every morning in my reflection," she replies solemnly.

"We've worked together for so long and yet this is probably the longest conversation that we've ever had."

"Yes. Well, spotted," she quips.

I spit out a rough laugh.

The groaning metal shell of the sub cuts through the entire body of the machine deafeningly loud. Both of our attentions turn to the door as if it will magically open. By pure coincidence the lock turns, and the door swings open, revealing Sebastian with a bright smile on his face.

"Morning sunshine," he greets. "Carlos is on his way and so is Mala."

"Ok," I draw out the word sitting up slowly, "why?"

"Protection," he answers nonchalantly.

On cue, Mala comes into the room in a flurry Carlos next, he looks as if he's had to run to keep up with her.

"Everything is fine," she speaks first, loudly and in a high enough tone that I don't quite believe her words.

"Are you sure?" I laugh.

"Roman wants to speak with you."

"Absolutely not!" Aria yells, standing. She steps in front of me.

"Why? What does he want? Also are you ok with this?" I ask of Mala. "You're the one putting everyone and everything at risk to get him to his brother." A shiver runs down my back at the name.

"I don't want it to happen, but he seems insistent. Even after I told him what you could do." Aria and I, as if a mirror image of each other, rear our heads backwards.

"You did what now?" I ask, a little stunned.

"Sorry. I didn't know how else to keep him at bay." I can't actually fault her for that.

"It doesn't matter regardless because it won't be happening," Aria snaps again.

"What won't?" All heads in the room whip towards the door to see Roman standing there grinning smugly, seemingly oblivious to the danger he has thrust himself into.

Sebastian steps in front of me also so I'm completely covered by both of them, unable to see Roman at all. My bloods heats and the twitches begins.

"Aria," I manage to snarl out right before, my mind goes dark and my vision glazes over, rage builds in my chest.

"What the fuck are you doing in here?"

I feel something cold and metallic against my throat, keeping me in place.

"I've come to talk to her." His voice is soft and calm, cutting through the wrathful beast wrestling for control of my body.

"Well as you can see, she's not exactly up for visitors at the moment. With you being at the bottom of that list."

"It's OK," I grit, through my teeth.

"Are you crazy?" she argues.

"Just make it quick," I snap.

Carlos draws his sword, pointing it at me, "Sorry," he murmurs. I can barely make a nod to show there are no hard feelings. That darkness within starts speaking, drowning them out. I don't even think it would matter much to listen to what Roman had to say, because I don't think I would hear him anyway.

"I had hoped to speak to her alone" I hear him say.

"Well, that isn't going to happen, is it? I told you why you could not," Mala snaps.

Someone is calling my name and something warm is holding my hand. But my fists are clenched and the instinct to kill is making me shake. The darkness is whispering in my ear tempting, urging me to complete my task. Cold claws circle my throat and shadows brush the back of my neck like a deathly promise. I shiver in answer wanting to concede. I can't remember why I am fighting it at all.

All of a sudden, the darkness clears. The door to the chamber is locked tight. I am standing in the middle of the room and Aria has her fists raised an intense pain blazing through my temple.

"Fucking Hel," I groan as a crumble into a crouch clutching my head. "What did you do to me?"

"Cognitive recalibration," she states factually.

"Oh, cool. Yeah, thanks," I sass angrily.

"You surprisingly didn't put up much of a fight. You were fighting the demon more than me," she notes, sounding impressed. "How are you feeling."

"Like I just got hit really hard in the head. But I suppose I'm fine."

"OK, good. Can you please elaborate on why Roman seems to think that you made a deal with Frederick?"

"A deal?"

"A promise then. If you don't want to call it a deal." She's angry. I can see it in her eyes and at how even though her hands are back at her sides once more, they're still bunched into fists.

"Oh. Right. That's because I did."

"Fool!" Aria yells, clapping me on the back of the head.

My brain rattles in my skull when it jolts forward. "Thank you, again, for that," I growl, rubbing that new sore spot now instead of the first. "I said it in a way that meant I would buy him some time to get Roman away from me. Whilst I figured something else out."

She's quiet for a long time, "You're not serious?"

"Is that your new catchphrase? When am I not serious?" I retort finally looking back up at her. I sit back on the bunk seeing the sheets dishevelled, no doubt from the fight I put up. I cringe at the knowledge that not only Aria had to see me like that but the two brothers and even a damned princess, not forgetting Roman.

Her chocolate gaze softens, "You care *that* much about the half-fae, that you would be willing to do that for him?" She moves to sit on the edge of the bunk opposite me, while I sit on the floor.

I'm silent for a moment, letting the words hang in the air.

"You don't understand what he has been through and how that has defined our relationship. You forget how long I spent in his company; we were closer than we should probably be. He confided in me, things that not even his mother knows."

"Did you know the connection between the two before today?"

"No."

"So, you can't have been that close," Aria points out.

"Yes. I realise that." I glare at her through my eyebrows.

She shakes her head, lowering her eyes to the floors. "You could've gotten yourself killed; I hope you realise that and with you gone, who would stop *him*?"

Her words stump me. *Him?* The King? why does she think I am the one to stop him? Why does everyone seem to think that?

"Who?"

"Reuben," she speaks quickly. As though she'll lose her nerve if she waited another second. Our gaze connects once more, her eyes lined with unshed tears, "he needs to pay for what he has done."

We share a silent moment and I understand exactly what she's saying without having to use the words. My teeth clenched together so hard it hurts.

I am not the only one he did it to then. Those 'private lessons.' Gods only know how many other young girls have fallen prey to those deceiving smiles and endless eyes. How many childhoods he has ruined, only for those girls to release there is no escape from his torment, except for death.

My breath comes out heavy and deathly calm. The temperature of the room drops with it.

There will be no more fighting against the darkness within me.

No more writhing against the bonds I've placed around myself.

No more fire fuelled duty burning through my very bones.

There is only the cold kiss of death.

A call that will not go unanswered.

This is a test... Right?

Rich

It's been a week and three days since Elle was taken. Or left as Declan claims. Alex got no further than a very tense phone call one that the queen rejected answering. He yelled at the servant who answered for several minutes only to be hung up on.

We still haven't thought of a way to actually help her out of wherever they have taken her, because the one thing the servant did say was that she was not in the palace. That panicked me more than anything. Because that was our agreement, that she would be within the confines of the city protected from everyone and everything. Only for Cordelia to go and change the parameters of our deal. That made my blood boil.

But that's not why we are currently here standing in Melanie's house after she demanded a meeting with both me and Declan, but also Alex.

"You're lying. There's no fucking way," I reply to Melanie, who almost immediately had begun to accuse each of us of somehow, locating Aella and breaking her out, all within a matter of hours. She'd gone quiet after I explained how stupid it all sounded. That was the only word we had of her was that wherever she was taken, she was now no longer there. Apparently, it was a massive security breach. That doesn't really surprise me when it comes to Elle.

"Well, she got out of that prison somehow. My source intercepted a letter from the Queen herself this morning."

"Prison?"

"Don't play coy," she sneers back at me. I'm *this* close to knocking her on her arse.

"So, she's coming to us," Declan mutters, to no one in particular. He's sat on the fancy white leather lounge to one side of Melanie's extravagant office. With glass shelving, behind her matching glass desk, filled with ornaments and books. The interior is white and natural wood, a calming space in her otherwise chaotic life.

"Not necessarily," I reply to him. He looks up and I swear I see a glimmer of disappointment dulling the iris. Yet I can't help but feel like that isn't a good thing. Her coming back after such a short time, is sure to have consequences and we'll be at the top of her list.

"So, what do we do with a pissed off Fury? Not forgetting, of course, the second one that was brought in..." Alex chuckles in disbelief, "...who have both been in an underwater prison for a full week. Who probably still feels the sting of betrayal?" His words are like a slap to the face. Not that they aren't deserved but they still make me physically flinch and I see Declan do the same.

"Run?" Melanie says weakly. I'm not so sure that she even believes her own words.

"They'd find us. That was what they were trained to do." Alex looks deep in thought as he replies to her.

"As opposed to what? Confronting her and getting killed on site?" she spits back. "At least with my plan, we'd have a little bit more time above ground."

"She might find it less cowardly to confront her. If we go to her and confront her face to face, she might at least respect us again," I muse, looking at Declan.

"She won't show leniency if that's what you're thinking," he replies.

I think for a moment, "She might make it quick if we go to her instead of turning tail and running?"

Declan spits out a laugh, "That's wishful thinking, Rich."

"Maybe," I trail off again trying to think of another way around it but come up with nothing.

"How are two making jokes and not at each other's throats? You remember it was Rich's idea to send her away in the first place, but it was also yours to use her to begin with." She directs her question at Declan himself and I watch him deflate. "Have you all forgotten why we banded together in the first fucking place?" She's angry, understandably. "And you!" She points at Alexander, "Why are you so suddenly more interested in the Fury than the mission? The mission you wholeheartedly believed in only a matter of days ago, and now look at you. What changed?"

"My business is my own. But it is imperative that we get her back to continue with the mission. She has more insight into the royal family and the palace than we were led to believe. She can blend in and make herself so invisible you wouldn't even know she was there until you already had a knife to your throat."

"You are all fucking mad!" she yells, standing up "She has you bewitched!"

"Melanie calm yourself..." Alex tries, stepping forward cautiously.

"No! I will not. That monster killed my mother! You all seem to have forgotten the ones you lost because of him, but I have not. If you won't help me, I'll kill him myself!" she growls storming from the room. The door swings open and slams against the wall so hard it leaves an indent in the plaster.

Her father's armed guards watch her leave, before turning to us with scowls of disdain across their faces, their hands casually clasped together in front of them. The pair contrast with not only each other but themselves as well. The one with white hair, on the right of the door, has tanned skin and is littered with gnarly scars, wickedly dark eyes, and pointed ears of the fae. The one on the left is fae also, with smooth, pale skin, ice-blue eyes, and dark hair. But both look equally enraged.

"I think it's time you all leave, don't you," the white-haired fae snarls and suddenly, I couldn't agree more. I'm the first to make a move heading for the staircase, I can hear Melanie barking orders from somewhere in the back of the house but choose to avoid her at all costs, not that I would get far. Her father — she told us — sent more men to her house after Aella had 'attacked' her in the temple, and she had been dealing with being watched day in, day out ever since.

Declan and Alex trail behind me, each time we pass a guard they stare us down. The feeling is akin to us being rabbits caught in a wolf den. None of us speak until we are outside.

"Well, that was uncomfortable," Alex chimes up, stating the obvious.

"What are we going to do about Melanie? She seems pretty serious about doing it by herself," Declan asks.

"I wouldn't worry about Melanie. She's done this before when something hasn't gone her way, or if Roman and I have found a more efficient way of doing things, she storms off in a strop like a petulant child. She doesn't possess the resources or the freedom to do it. Her father is too in her business for her to pull it off without him interfering."

"So, what now?" I ask, puffing out a breath, watching the people pass us by, going on with their day. Totally unaware that two, very dangerous, and likely very furious Furies is on their way back into the city.

"Well, I would say go back home and wait, but she'll know where you are. I'm not taking you to mine because I don't want your blood on my walls. In fact, I probably shouldn't return there myself," Alex explains and then sighs, "You've really fucked it up for everyone you know that." His face is devoid of humour, all except for a faint glimmer in his eyes.

"I think it might be best to just face it head-on," Declan says, turning to me. I nod in agreement.

"She'll kill you," Alex tries to persuade us otherwise.

"Maybe," I reply, "but that might just be a risk we have to take."

Aella

My mind is still swimming with Aria's confession. We haven't spoken for some time, in fact, I told her it might be best if she left for a little while, to walk around the sub and get herself together once more. Not before tying me up to a chair, provided to us by Mala. After what happened with Roman just walking in before, none of us were willing to risk *the final call* happening once again. So now I can do nothing but stew in the knowledge that the Director, the one who is best equipped to keep us safe, has been the worst danger of all. A predator in an enclosure full of prey.

My own experiences surfaced after she told me in detail about her own. How he would love to be too close to me. How he would find any excuse to hold my hand or smell my hair and of how he made me promise not to tell anyone about what happened after our first private lesson. A shiver runs down my spine that spreads outward into anger. A vengeance that will be paid. One way or another.

So, here I sit, still lying in the small bunk contemplating every little detail of my life. I finally begin to understand what has happened to me, hasn't been a normal existence. Not as I once thought it was.

This mission has pushed me to see more than I bargained for. It has led me to believe that not all things that are taught at the Fort are true.

This is a test... Right?

There are things that they don't know about people, how resilient they can be, or how brave, how wit and wisdom are more profound than fear and pain. How kind and gentle they can be whilst also being protective and fierce.

My mind flashes to Declan. His hazel eyes consume me, as does his smile. That lopsided grin he would wear whenever I was talking, something he didn't think I'd notice, or the way he was so protective even when it wasn't necessary. I think about how we had left things. The fight we had. The vial he had acquired. None of it was real, no matter what I want to tell myself. It couldn't have been. He said it himself that it wasn't. I was nothing more than a means to an end for him a pawn in his games. To fulfil his wishes on killing the king finally. After that I was to be turned loose. I'd have no home to go to. I couldn't exactly stay at the Fort after deserting them for my handlers. That's if they didn't kill me before then.

"You want to go for a walk?" Aria suddenly asks. Drawing me from my thoughts once more.

"I think it's best she stays where she is, given what we've all just seen," A husky, truly masculine voice rumbles from the doorway.

Both of us turn to see a bare-chested caramel-skinned male leaning against the door frame, water droplets run down his well-toned chest and disappear into the waistband of his dark, leather slacks.

My lips purse at the sight.

"Sebastian," I greet, a little too breathily.

"Why are you wet?" Aria snaps.

"I've just been for a swim," he shrugs as if the notion is completely normal. When we are in an air-tight vessel leagues under the waves.

"And you couldn't have put some clothes on before coming in here."

"I have shorts on," he deflects.

Aria rolls her eyes.

"We will be surfacing, just west of Lefki, far enough from the city that it won't cause trouble. We have a mutual acquaintance awaiting our arrival there," Mala informs us walking in ignoring the knocking etiquette, with her personal guard not more than three steps behind her. "For now, just sit tight." Both Carlos and Sebastian snicker.

"Thanks, Mala," I sigh, wiggling my hands from under the bonds.

"Oh, poor choice of words," her cheeks flush. "Sebastian's, going to guard the door, properly from now on, no more visits from Roman." She turns and points to him, he bows his head to his princess.

"Before that, he's going to put on a shirt," Carlos mumbles, rolling his eyes.

"Ah yes, of course," Mala stutters, having not realised he was in fact half naked in her presence.

"Is nakedness so common in Salacia, that even the princess herself forgets to notice it?" Aria questions, taking the words right out of my mouth.

"More than you realise," Her Highness mutters to Aria over her shoulder, keeping her eye on the two brothers. Carlos is scowling at Sebastian, and Sebastian couldn't have a bigger grin on his face even if he tried. The two, if Carlos hadn't already confirmed that Sebastian was younger than him, look so similar they could easily be passed off as twins.

"Right! Out, the pair of you. We have things to do." Mala chases them both from the room, and turns back to us, her slender hand resting on the doorknob, "If either of you need anything, just let us know." She smiles and closes the door behind her.

Aria turns to me, "he is entirely too cocky."

"Is he? I've not noticed that. He just seems playful to me," I utter back.

"That was probably because you were too busy following the water droplets gliding over his abs. He was grinning the whole time you did that."

"Shut up," I chirp back, unable to hold the grin from my face.

There's a pause for a few heartbeats as we observe each other.

"One each though, right?" I say and begin cackling. Aria does the same.

CHAPTER THIRTY-TWO
THE CALM BEFORE THE STORM

"Aella." My name falls from his lips in such a way that it racks my very soul with disgust.

He'd called me up to his office some time ago for one of his 'private lessons,' and I'd been stood here motionless ever since.

Madame K was quick to help me learn how to disassociate from myself after she forced the truth from me, when I came back from his office as white as a sheet, after the first time he'd done this. As soon as I was summoned tonight, I knew what it was for and as if automatically I began to stray from my conscious mind.

He sits in his chair looking at me through his lashes, his hand is pumping up and down steadily as he takes me in, in my nearly naked form.

He demanded that I keep on my undergarments finding satisfaction in my hidden barely there curves – even though he has seen them already. His face is flushed, and his eyes never leave my body as his hand speeds up. He groans through his release, his head thrown back against the headrest of his black leather office chair, with a slack jaw.

His cheeks are flushed but it's the noise of his zipper that pulls me back to reality.

Shame and disgust roil all around me. It's an effort not to throw up right there on the floor.

Plucking tissues from the box at the edge of his desk, he wipes his hand, and takes a few breaths to collect himself before he gets up and saunters over to me. He places a hand on my cheek and leans in close to my face. "You're so very alluring, my little whirlwind. So very desirable. What's that myth? A siren? That's what you are to me. You draw me in and one day, I'm sure you'll kill me." He grins and that devilish glint returns to his eye once again. He places a kiss on the corner of my mouth. "Get yourself dressed and remember, not a word."

I startle awake and begin tugging at my arms and pulling my legs up, grunting with the effort seemingly unable to move even an inch. Sweat beads along my forehead my eyes flash around the room trying to find him. The threat to me and to everyone. My breath comes out strong but erratic until brown eyes meet mine.

Aria.

"Easy Elle," she shushes me, trying to keep me calm. She doesn't dare to touch me. She knows exactly what's going through my mind, "take some deep breaths." Aria helps me through it every step of the way, speaking softly and keeping her own calm demeanour, and she still refuses to touch me. Not even to comfort me. My eyes dart to the doorway where Sebastian stands with his jaw locked, his brows are lowered, and he seems to be contemplating something, but those fierce eyes don't leave mine.

"Ignore him for a second, as hard as that is for you, and answer my question," Aria urges my attention back to her.

"What?" I pant, confused. I hadn't even heard her speak.

"Why, when you woke up just now, were your eyes glowing yellow?" Aria queries. The sound seems so slow but in fact it's just my own mind trying to comprehend what's she saying. The words ring in my head and my heart skips a couple of beats. That isn't the first time I've heard my eyes have glowed yellow. Hel's even Eddie Lincoln noticed when he had me tied to a chair ready for torture.

"What?" I whisper, trying desperately to avoid the subject altogether. Since the question came out of her mouth, she changed tactics with me. Her hand wrap around my knees, keeping me grounded, putting a lot of faith in the knots in the rope that she herself made, to keep me in the chair. Ruby red marks blister my skin, I must have been thrashing in my sleep. She begins to loosen those knots once she seems satisfied that I've calmed down and finally lets me up. The instant she steps back I stand, my mind racing with flashbacks and emotions I can't fully control, so instead I pace the little room back and forth.

"Close the door," Aria snaps to Sebastian. The door slams shut not a second later and the lock grinds into place. Sebastian stands in front of it, his arms folding over his chest, watching us both with deserved caution and perhaps a hint of concern.

Having been confined to one room for hours on end has made my mind turn to mush. The need for fresh air is weighing on me. Claustrophobia has never been a problem for me before. But since waking I can't shake the feeling that I'm in danger in the submarine, as if at any moment the Director will pop out from round the corner and continue his sadistic games.

"Will you answer my question please?"

"I don't know what to tell you Aria. I've never seen or even known of my eyes to glow." That fact is true. My body has certainly changed over the years. Certain... abilities have made themselves known, but glowing yellow eyes, never once have I seen that. I have only been told, but I can't exactly take others' words for truth. But Aria being freaked out about it, is making that fever dream a little too real.

The look she gives me tells me everything I need to know. She doesn't believe me. But I also know that she won't push this conversation, at least, not in front of a stranger.

"Do you want to go for a walk?" Sebastian asks, following the path that I'm taking back and forth across the room.

"Please," I answer without hesitation. The need to do something, anything, even a simple thing such as walking burrows away at me, eating at my sanity.

We walk in companionable silence, just Sebastian and I, he has graciously shown me around the metal tube that we are trapped in, at least for another few hours, and I have since found out that the submarine is a multi-level vessel. We are rooming on the top level and having more space to explore has made that claustrophobic episode dissipate into nothing more than me fidgeting with my hands with mild anxiety.

"Do you get nightmares often?" Sebastian mutters from behind me. He had let me lead whilst guiding me on a path that would keep us going and seeing new places.

"My life is a nightmare," I joke but when he doesn't laugh, I stop chuckling myself and answer honestly, "Seemingly more and more."

He nods in understanding and just when I thought that was the end of the matter, and we turn a corner to begin walking a new path, but he stops me short with a hand on the shoulder. It happens so fast that my body goes rigid and my brain stutters for a moment trying to process. Strong arms wrap around me, and I'm engulfed in a hug.

He has forgone armour for this little soiree in its place is a soft cotton t-shirt and leather breeches. A mistake on his part, if we were to run into Roman at any point and my insane counterpart came forth, he could be seriously hurt in an altercation. But that's not to say that I'm not enjoying the view, especially with the leather breeches fitting snuggly around his rear.

His arms envelop me like a giant bear, swallowing me into his warmth. Once my brain had caught up, I wrap my arms around his waist a burrow further into his chest, his scent of dark spice and whiskey scent fills my nose soothing my racing thoughts.

"Thank you, Sebastian," I mumble into his chest.

"Please call me Seb," he murmurs soothingly. He holds me for longer still rocking us from side to side and I giggle at the sweetness of him. A guy I met only a few days ago who seems so happy in life that he simply wants to spread it around to everyone. Including a lost Fury who has no home, no family, and no future.

I pull away.

"Want to continue?" I ask him, smiling when he grins.

"Lead the way."

———————————

The submarine is due to ascend within the hour and Sebastian has decided to distract me with food. I don't know where this male has come from, but I love him. Especially when he shows me chocolate for the first time.

"I just can't believe you've never had it before!" he exclaims for the fourth time since I'd confessed.

I swallow my mouthful of chocolate cake, "I don't know how else I can explain it to you Seb. I just don't have food for fun. It's for energy and keeping myself at a healthy weight, it's never been for enjoyment."

He shakes his head in mock defeat those brown curls falling across his forehead, "crazy," he mutters. "Take as much as you want then." He pushes another slice towards me.

I laugh and blush, pushing it back, "One is enough, thank you."

———————————

We weren't given much warning before the sirens blared announcing the sub's ascension. Sebastian and I were still in the cafeteria, eating and talking when the lights went out and the red emergency lights started flashing accompanied by the sirens.

We both ran back to the control room, thinking we were under attack. The crew looked at us as though we had grown second heads but didn't say anything until Mala told us we had arrived.

Climbing the ladder up to the hatch of the sub feels like a walk to the gallows, a sense of dread and foreboding fills me.

The stars are twinkling down at us when we emerge, Aria first, I don't miss the groan she releases at the fresh air on her face, but I can't find it in me to care when I see the full moon lit so brightly in the inkiness of the night sky. The cold of the wind whips through my hair pulling my gaze to the sea behind us. I watch the moonlight bounce off the waves and feel a sort of serenity in the calmness.

A slap hits my arm – Aria – upon turning to her, I follow her gaze to the end of dock, to find Frederick staring at me. His mouth in a tight line but his eyes shine with hope. The rise and fall of his chest is steady but I can see him playing with something in his hand nervously.

"Our mutual acquaintance?" I ask Mala when she appears at the hatch entrance. She gives me a shy smile; I sigh and carefully make my way down the dock. Within seconds of me putting my feet on the rotting wooden platform, I'm enveloped in another set of arms.

"Hey," I murmur into his neck. The scent of fresh linen and crisp citrus that is so classically Frederick, invades my senses.

"You scared me, Elle." I can tell by the wobble in his voice that his words ring true. I just wrap my arms around his waist and hug him back, and he melts into it, heaving out a heavy sigh. His weight very nearly knocks me off balance.

"You feel different," Frederick suddenly says, pulling back to look at me.

"Excuse me?" My brow furrows.

"You smell different too."

My eyes widen, as he leans in, his nose brushing the skin of my jaw.

"Stop smelling me," I snap. I know he's fae and his senses are stronger but it's still weird to me, that he can smell a difference in my natural scent.

"Have you quite finished with your weird, sappy reunion? We've got somewhere to be," Aria snaps.

Frederick seems reluctant to let go so I step away first and move to the vehicles. Roman, accompany by a small army of guards climbs into the back of one. That overwhelming urge to kill him simmers beneath my flesh. Frederick shares a few words with both Mala and Carlos, hushed whispers that one could only hear if you were staying right next to them. When the crown prince finally turns away from them, he steps up to the same vehicle that Roman is in, offering me a solemn glance, like he doesn't want to go. Like he doesn't want to be separated from me. It's only on the urgency of his own personal guard that he makes that step up and the car door is closed. They don't hesitate to depart. Getting Roman as far away from me as physically possible is the best chance for his survival at the moment.

"Where are we going?" I hear Aria ask behind me.

"We're going back to Ansrutas. I think we all have some questions that need answers and a mission to save countless lives," Her Highness answers.

Aria leans into me, "Well that was far more dramatic than necessary." Nobody else speaks while we make ourselves comfortable. Mala and Carlos seat themselves in a different car to us. Sebastian joins me and Aria in the second, forcing me to be in the middle. Mostly likely to keep watch over me, like silent sentinels.

Ansrutas truly is a beautiful city. No matter the time of day you arrive it always looks so open and welcoming, despite its own darker history.

Some call it Faramond's City, given he is the God of Travellers, and the city itself is open to all. That and the fact that he has more statues here than anywhere else in the country.

It's the spires that make up The Circle that I'm watching as we approach the metropolis once more. It seems like a lifetime ago when I'd scaled the side of those buildings to have a private meeting with my oldest friend. I suppose I could in fact call him that. It's The Circle we come to a stop at when we finally do make it back into the city and both Aria and I are handed long dark-coloured cloaks.

"To conceal yourselves," Sebastian had said before leading us into the building using the back door.

The three of us use the stairwell, devoid of cameras, to reach the floor Frederick's rooms are found on. I hadn't realised that we still needed his council, but Mala claimed that she still had business to do with the crown prince and that, with us in her custody we should accompany her.

Of Fire and Shadow

The halls are long and empty, and mostly white, it reminds me of the Fort, clean within an inch of its life and devoid completely of warmth or any sense of life. But it's fitting for a place like that. It's a place of horrors. A place where dreams, and often innocence, go to die.

These towers are commonly known for their diversity, some floors are office spaces, others are apartments for the wealthy. But more common than not there are rooms made up for use as a hotel.

It's not until the door closes behind us that I finally let out the breath I'd been holding. The room is exactly the same as when I saw it last, all white furnishings and small coloured accompaniments. It's Frederick's room and not a thing is out of place from my first visit.

The lack of guards concerns me; I had thought his father had him watched after he had learned that it was me, his son invited to the ball. I turn to Mala, but Aria asks the question that was on the tip of my tongue.

"Why are you and Frederick working together?"

"We aren't... well not really, and quite frankly it's none of your concern."

"Then why help us," I cut in.

"It's purely selfish really, I need you to save the king. If he dies and someone connects it to my mother, which isn't a stretch given that she lost her husband – my father – then my people will suffer."

"Not to mention the fact that you are engaged to him," Sebastian answers sipping from a glass of water, as he walks back from the mini kitchen off to one side.

My mouth pops open but no words come out. Mala looks at me with widened eyes. Carlos sighs heavily and just looks at his brother with disappointment filling hie glare. I snap my mouth shut.

"It is not a union that either of us wished for, Aella. Our duty dictates this of us as prince and princess. Our parents arranged this from the moment we both took our first breaths."

I smile, "it has nothing to do with me who Frederick marries. Out of everyone though I'm glad it's you." It's not the information that I'm mad about. It's the fact that this is another thing that Frederick has kept from me and if he wasn't happy with the arrangement, we could have figured out a way to stop it from happening. I would've done anything to see him smile. But he has once again left me in the dark. Ashamed of what I am because it doesn't look good on him. Bringing me out only when it suits him to do so.

"Ha. Hardly," she chuckles, "it's an arrangement of convenience. Even my mother loathes the idea. She is merely playing house to the king's wishes. Showing face and pretending that there's no hard feels for the lack of a fatherly presence in my life, thanks to him." The curve of her lips lightens the load of information just dumped on me, even just a little. "Besides the male anatomy is not favourable to me anyway," she grins. Her admission surprises me but waves me off when my eyes widen in understanding.

"Ouch," Sebastian chuckles, looking down at himself, alight with humour. I do the same, biting my lip when I get as far as his abdominals. Even in his cotton shirt he still looks like a delectable little treat. Well, maybe not little. Scratch that. Definitely not little.

Mala clears her throat and moves to the bathroom leaving me with the two brothers and Aria who glares pointedly at Sebastian.

"What have I told you about watching what you say?" Carlos scolds, pointing to another adjoining room – Frederick's bedroom. Sebastian rolls his eyes. He knows he'll get his ear chewed by his brother but follows without complaint and the doors close behind them. Both me and Aria can hear the hushed whispers spewed between the two, but neither of us actually hear anything of interest and we move to the lounge and await Frederick's arrival.

Left alone with the only person who has shared the same life experiences as me. The only other person I think I'll ever be fully comfortable with, and she tried to kill me not long ago. But we share a similar mind. I drop myself down heavily onto the plush white lounge with a deep and long sigh.

"You, ok?" Aria asks, following my lead, but instead of dropping down, she gracefully takes a seat and turns herself towards me, resting her head in her hand.

"I'm tired," I breathe and lean my head back against the back of the lounge, closing my eyes. "So, fucking tired," I sigh. A silence falls around us, "and now we are being asked to save someone who would light us on fire the first chance he would get if he could."

I hear her clothes shuffle with movement, but she doesn't verbally reply. My mind is a minefield. It reels with everything chaotic and overwhelming with all of the things I have yet to do, things that I have left unchecked. But then there's the tiredness. The bone-deep ache that has me wanting nothing more than the curl up under a thick duvet and sleep until I've had my fill, all the while hoping that my problems fix themselves overnight.

But that will only ever happen in dreams. I do not live in such a perfect world where such good will overrule such evil.

An evil that I helped to create.

An evil that I enjoyed. Hel. Still, enjoy it from time to time.

"This is so far off mission, that there is no going back."

Aria bursts out laughing, "There's been no going back for you for longer than I think you're willing to admit. But tell me. Do you honestly still remember the mission? Even now?"

"Something about locating a terrorist and killing him, but now... now it's all fucked up," I reply.

"You really do lie so sweetly. It was never so simple. You were set up to fail I think." Something in her face tells me she believes her own words and I'm inclined to believe her too. So far, her judgment hasn't been wrong. "But yeah, find and kill a terrorist that is also your friend's brother, and listen to your handlers that want you to kill the king. Some mission," she scoffs.

Her words cut like a knife. Ones I need to hear. But ones that will make me bleed, nonetheless. I mull them over briefly. Wondering if Madame K knew. She must've, there's no way she wouldn't. But why not tell me? Unless she thought the truth would've killed me.

"I guess I now understand what you meant when you asked if I'd ever thought about getting out. In truth, about two years ago I thought about it for the first time, and every day since, around the time when I met two extraordinary males who I knew nothing about. But the fact that they would help someone they didn't know, was fascinating to me. Without an ounce of hesitation, they charged forward and rescued friend and stranger alike and again, without being asked they took care of me and when they eventually worked out what I was and what I did, sure they were understandably pissed but at they stayed. Well, Rich did. He supported me anyway," I say unprompted. "I couldn't say it before..."

"Because you weren't sure you could trust me. I get it, we've never been allowed the freedom to trust in each other before," she answers for me.

"It's always trust in the code, isn't it?" She nods in reply, her eyes cast away as if she is reliving a memory, "It's the assignment first and foremost. Always the damn mission."

I nod in agreement.

Her words, next, are as quiet as I've ever heard her go, "Have you thought about what I said?"

I turn to her opening my eyes once again to see the worry in hers, "Yes." In truth I haven't stopped thinking about it. It's one of the thousand things that are battling away in my mind.

Her chest stops and starts irregularly, waiting for my full answer.

"I've got a plan, but it entails you being as far as you can get from the city in the next twenty-four hours."

"What do you mean?"

"I mean, Aria, that I have a plan in mind, and you are not a part of it," I state plainly.

"Don't be a martyr. It doesn't suit you," she retorts.

"I'm not. I'm doing what I should've done from the start. I'm putting others first. Doing this won't undo the years of pain I've caused but it's something I can do right by you."

"You sap," she grins.

"Shut up."

"You're wrong you know."

"About?"

"You did once. You have put people first. It's one of the things that they couldn't kill in you. Your humanity. You are the best of all of us. But not for the reasons the Director believes. Your heart is what makes you strong. Not the torture they put us through," she mutters.

"And look where that got me," I mumble back, taking in her words but I can't let them change my course. I know what needs to be done. Not to mention the conversation change is not something that I actually want to talk about especially not now.

Hannah was a good friend. My first even. Until the monthly fight when both of us got chosen. She'd been brought in shortly after me, and we grew up together. She was much like Surya, always found the light in a situation even when I fumbled through the dark, she was my guiding light. She would drag me from my doubt, my sorrow, my pain, and I'll never forget that same light leaving her eyes as I was forced to wrap my hands around her neck.

She didn't even fight.

She knew.

She gave me a small smile as she choked on her words, I forgive you.

I didn't forgive myself, I still don't. There is nothing in this world that I can do that will ever make me forgive myself for killing her. She was my friend. The closest thing I ever had to a sister and now I can't even think about her without that shame drowning me.

It's nothing short of what I deserve.

But I won't allow that to happen to Aria, not when she still has a chance at a normal life.

"Promise me something," I utter, my voice wobbling as I replay images of Hannah, her dark chocolate hair, her angled dark eyes, and her happy smile.

"Anything," Aria matches my solemness.

"If there's a way, to get them all out. Promise me you'll find a way to do it. That you'll stop at nothing until they're all safe."

"Why are you making it sound like you won't be there to see it happen?"

"Just promise me?" I shake my head grinning. I catch her eye and there is a faint sadness there.

"I promise."

The morning comes quickly. Quicker than I'd like. I spent most of the time tossing and turning until I gave up and sat out on the balcony to watch the sunrise.

Fredericks had arrived last night so all five of us talked, getting to know each other more. We had mostly talked about Salacia and the upcoming rite that takes place in the spring. The three had been looking forward to it. That is until they broke us out of prison and essentially made themselves fugitives of their own home.

The others started to rise after seeing the first few rays began peeking through the curtains. The key turns in the lock and in walks Frederick, his manservant Elijah and a handful of his most trusted guards. I don't get up to greet him, I keep my eyes glued on the sea, but I hear Aria greet him before quieting quickly.

Footsteps sound and she's by my side with her hand on my shoulder. I grunt a welcome and she squeezes the joint.

"He's here."

"I know."

"He's brought a small army with him."

"I know."

"How?"

"The sky is darker today," I reply solemnly.

"Are you usually this dramatic, this early in the morning?"

I scoff and wrap the faux fur blanket tighter around me. "Not usually. Only when he is around."

"He's here for you. You know that."

"Of course."

She takes a deep breath, "So what are you going to do?"

I finally take my gaze from the sea and direct it at her. I had been thinking about this for most of the night. It was the reason I couldn't sleep. I know deep down within me there is only one way to proceed from here. So, I turn to her a say the words I thought that I'd never say in my life. "I'm going to kill Reuben Ostair."

CHAPTER THIRTY-THREE
FURY PERSONIFIED

"You cannot be serious?" Frederick exclaims as I tighten the gloves around my hands.

"Why does everyone seem to think that I'm not serious? Have I shown anyone at any time that I'm not?" I ask genuinely confused.

"I don't want you to get killed. I have done everything in my power of late to avoid that at all cost, Aella! Don't do this, please." His voice is fierce and firm, and his words cut deeper than he can ever know.

"I'll never be free until he is dead and others like him are as well," I reply, sighing. We have been arguing like this for what feels like hours. Only because I'm drained and irritable, but I am already over the concern for my well-being. I don't plan on dying by Reuben's hands. But if the gods deem it my time, then I will gladly go knowing I'm taking him to the Abaddon with me.

"And it's fair for you because?" He tries again, even though he's already asked this.

"I'm not having this discussion with you again, Frederick," I snap back, waving him off. "I am doing what needs to be done. The future of those young girls who needn't go through what we have just because of who they are. I am doing this for all those who have lost their innocence to the male and all those we have lost along the way. You wouldn't understand any of that because you've never had to lose someone. You've never had to know the pain of torture of the debilitating nature of being drugged and forced to kill people. So, you do not get to speak on this."

"I will know the pain of losing someone if you go ahead with this!" he yells. His eyes were blown wide and cheeks red with rage. He shakes with emotion, he tries to hide it by running his fingers through his hair, but I catch that shake in his hand. He takes some deep breaths as he paces back and forth in front of his bed. "Can we please just discuss this with Rich and Declan first?"

"No." I snap, leaving no room for argument.

"No. You don't get to be selfish now, Aella. They have a right to know that you plan to get yourself killed."

"They won't care!" I yell in anger and desperation, "They'll probably fucking celebrate. Dance of my fucking grave. So, no. They don't get to know anything."

He's shocked and looks entirely too lost when he speaks, "What makes you say that?"

"Does it matter? I'm doing it. Nothing, not you, not them, is going to stop me. This is bigger than me. Bigger than any one person."

He sighs and I can see the sadness in his eyes when he finally comes to terms with the fact that I will not be stopped. His body physically deflates, and he sits on the edge of the bed and drops his head into his hands. I move around the edge of the bed to stand in front of him, placing my hand in his hair. I sigh and play with the strands.

"He's not allowed to get away with it anymore Fritz. I cannot stand idly by and watch as more girls get snatched and used in the same sick and twisted ways."

"I know. You've always been purer of heart than you believed." He mutters resting his head against my stomach. "Before you do it. Can we maybe just offer some aid? Or at least come up with some kind of plan?" I move my fingers in his hair and sigh. I agree if only to put his mind at rest.

Stepping back into the apartment I called home for some time has never felt more alien. Sebastian walks in behind me, offering me support. He has been the only one who has not tried to deter me from my plan. He dislikes what I must do but understands nonetheless that this isn't about me and my life. It's about the others that followed and even more to come.

The whole company of us headed out to do this. The two royals, the two brothers, both Aria and I, and even little Elijah. All of us file into the apartment that seems smaller now than it did when we first arrived. We all stand in before Alexander Nephus, Declan Angelos, and Rich Keita. Who in turn appear a little more than startled to see me in one piece. I spare each of them a single glance and move to stand in the small kitchen, Sebastian, ever the guardian, stands with me, watching over everyone in the room as they sit and discuss plans to get out of the city now that Reuben is here. There is no mention of the plan to kill the king and thankfully Frederick doesn't bring up my own plan, despite yelling at me for a good forty minutes.

Sebastian offers his own muttered commentary in my ear when arguments break out making me laugh even when I don't want to. Much to the apparent annoyance of Declan who glares at the mer each time he makes me smile. I glare at him in return, daring him to try something.

"Reuben arrived this morning," Frederick suddenly says, drawing my attention to him and the room falls deathly quiet.

Three sets of eyes flicker between me, Aria and Frederick, with a mixture of pity, panic and caution.

"He has come for the Furies I suspect," Alex concludes, his warm honey voice still soothes me in a manner I've never known before. It's both unsettling and entirely recognisable.

"No one knows why he is here, but it is an easy assumption to make, yes," Mala speaks. "But that fact that he is, is not good."

"Well, he can't have them," Rich growls in defence. Naïve defence but he's the only one who's tried.

"That is not for you to decide." My mouth moves before my brain can register the words. "If it is the only way to ensure Roman's safety then it is a risk we may have to take."

"No." The singular word comes from the person I thought would be least likely to say anything on the matter at all.

"She's right," Alex chimes in.

"Why is Roman's safety more important than your own?" Rich directs at me. I eye Frederick who stays quiet. "Do you want to tell them or should I?"

He nods giving me the go-ahead.

"Roman is Frederick's younger brother. The person I was sent here to kill," I drawl, not bothering to wait for their reactions, "so his safety is of utmost importance because Reuben has brought guards and undoubtedly more Furies. So even if we hand ourselves over it is unlikely, that they will be leaving without the task being complete. So, we are here today to secure a safe passage for him to get out of the city. Before it comes down to sacrificing ourselves."

Aria shifts uncomfortably. She doesn't want to do it. What she doesn't know is that she will not be doing it. But for now, I need her to have a drive to get a plan into motion. Both she and I can figure out a way to keep the Fort and Stratos off our tail until Roman is secure, whilst everyone else in this room makes a hasty escape.

"You won't be sacrificing yourselves. Because that will not be happening." Declan growls.

"Enough!" Mala shouts, "We are not here to discuss this. Everyone here has put everything on the line to ensure Roman is safe. We need to do it one more time so that not only he, but everyone else can make it out alive."

I breathe a sigh of relief for the princess. I did not need to have an argument with Declan right here right now over something that died with me when he betrayed me. Something between us that I don't even think can be fixed.

Aria and I had moved over to my bedroom, the sun lowering in the sky casting lengthened shadows across the apartment. We are sorting the room out for the princess to have the bed since she will be staying the night. I start trying to find blankets and pillows for the others staying the night. Frederick and Elijah have decided to leave still feeling hostility from both Declan and Rich, much to my surprise. I wouldn't have thought they would still care about his treatment towards me, given their own blatant disregard.

Mala and the two brothers are staying. Having nowhere else to go, they cannot go back to their embassy after having broken us out.

Each of us understands the risk of being alone, especially with a shark lurking in the depths. Not knowing if he'll strike in the night or wait until morning. Alex too, is staying, sleeping on the floor in Rich's room.

I move over to my weapons bag. Something Sebastian had brought with him after I was taken from the embassy. He has already told me about his nosiness and how giddy he was when he looked over the selection of weaponry I procured from the armoury, back at the Fort.

"Reuben thinks he has the element of surprise, and we need to take advantage of that before it's too late."

"You're calling him by his name now?" Aria asks, her arms full of blankets.

"To refer to him as the Director is to make him powerful. Is to make him hold power over us." I pause and turn to her, "That is no longer the case." She opens her mouth to argue the fact, but a knock at the door stops her.

I know who it is without having to look. The door creaks open slowly and his brunette hair peeks around the wood.

"Elle." His voice comes out timid and weak, nothing at all like the Declan I have come to know. But then I suppose I never really knew him at all.

"That took you longer than I thought," I answer.

He steps inside wearing a black t-shirt and slacks and his usually immaculate hair is in disarray. His gaze flickers between me and Aria, warily trying to get her to leave without saying as much.

"Aria, can you give us a minute please."

Aria bristles narrowing her eyes at Declan, "I'll take the first watch," she grumbles leaving us alone, even when I don't particularly want to have this conversation yet.

Pulling out my holster from my bag I begin to strap everything around my waist, adjusting where I need to.

"Going somewhere?" he asks, his voice closer than before.

"What do you want, Angelos?" I ask, still refusing to meet his gaze. I don't want him to know how his betrayal pained me. I was trained better than to let my emotions get the better of me. I let my walls fall only to have been stabbed in the back, and now I must be the one to build them back up again. Brick by aching brick.

I'm securing the last buckle when he reaches out for me, his fingertips brushing the skin on my upper arm. Mala had lent me and Aria some fresh clothes, a pair of breeches each and form-fitting tank tops. Declan flinches back when he sees the cuff marks on my wrists.

"What happened?" he whispers, gliding his fingers down over the raw skin, gingerly, wincing when the heat from the bruises becomes prominent. The touch sends goosebumps across my arms, something I can't hide when the hairs stand on end along my arms. I pull my arm away from him.

"Do you need something from me, handler Angelos?" The name makes him visibly flinch. "If that is in fact your real name."

"Aella." He draws my name out with a pained sigh. His dark eyebrows pull together and settle low over his eyes. The usual chips of amber in his hazel irises are nowhere to be seen, not even a whisper of it circling his pupils, like all those days before. The corners of his mouth are turned down in a frown.

"Can we talk?" His voice is but a whisper.

The sight of the male before me looks nothing like he did when met all those months ago back in Ellwey. Days-old stubble grows fiercely along his jaw, dark circles pull his eyes downward, and unshed tears shine on his lower lids. His breathing deepens and time seems to stand still between us. Standing so close together our chests almost touched with each inhale and yet neither of us dared to move away. Scared that this moment is all we have and to break it would be to accept the reality of something we barely even had. Something that was never fully tangible and yet felt so real all the same.

His hand cups my cheek, the roughness grated deliciously against the softness of the skin there, while his thumb wipes away the tears I didn't even notice had fallen.

"Declan," I whimper, my voice breaking. That void inside of me cracks open further, and I step away shaking my head.

Despite his own pain, he lets me take those steps.

I clear my throat, "Is there anything else, handler Angelos?"

"Stop calling me that," he snaps, without any real anger. I tilt my head to the side and place my metaphorical mask back over my face, securing it tight. "Don't do that." Declan grasps my face in both hands, his eyes boring into my own. "Don't shut me out. Don't shut yourself out. Talk to me, Aella." A grumble is present in his tone, and the amber sparks back to life in his eyes.

A part of me wants just that. To fall into his arms and to talk everything out, to understand why me, why lie to me. Why use me the way he did? But the other half, the part of me that feels the overwhelming grief and pain that his betrayal caused has me, shifts me back into my old habits, back into my training. Becoming the faceless weapon that they made me into and there's nothing I can do to stop it.

Of course, I have been betrayed before, by informants who think they could get one over on a Fury, but those people have been easily dealt with. I could never hurt Declan, not even if I wanted to. Nor Rich.

"I have nothing to say, handler Angelos. Now please let me go." My voice sounds meek even to my own ears and I hate the sound. I hate everything that has led up to this moment.

His hands fall reluctantly from my face.

"Elle please don't do this," he begs.

With my face devoid of emotion my eyes flicker to his, "I'm not doing anything more than what you've already done to me."

There's a pause of breath between us. He looks like I've slapped him in the face the blood rushing from his cheeks.

"If that is all," I bow my head slightly and walk away. Away from the hurt and they only person I thought understood what it was like growing up with missing pieces of your own soul.

But clearly, I was wrong.

My own words ring in my head. Haunting me, coupled with the hurt on his face. He hadn't tried to stop me when I turned away. He didn't say anything else actually, he just let me go through the patio doors of my room and climb up to the roof.

The air is quiet up here, the smell of the sea still heavy in the air. I can hear the group settling in for the night, lying on the floor in the living room like one giant sleepover party, and yet I've never felt more alone than I do now. The stars twinkle above me, and I find some solace in knowing that they are there watching over me on this night. The night that might just be my last. I pulled my phone from my pocket; another thing Sebastian had confiscated for me. I pull up a familiar number, still looking at the cloudless night sky I dial, waiting for the receiver to pick up.

"What do you want?" Her irritated voice crackles down the phone at me.

"Hello to you too, Melanie Lincoln."

"Can we get this over with? It's freezing out here," Melanie complains, not for the first time, and I'm sure it won't be the last.

The stars gave me an idea. Not a good one. But an idea is better than nothing at all.

Melanie agreed to meet with me, on the condition that we call a truce, and tell her where Roman is. I had also agreed, but only because I needed her equipment. I can't very well go breaking into the Ansrutas PD, weapons locker now, can I?

Sprinting over the rooftops as quickly and quietly as I could, I found myself back in the Black Pines territory of the city within a matter of minutes and that also explains why Melanie is only, once again, in a lavender chiffon nightgown with matching fluffy slippers on her feet. Standing in her back garden, with her arms crossed over her chest.

"I'm going to need you to calm down. It's not that cold," I mumble back for the umpteenth time, rummaging through the bag she brought me.

"What do you need all this for anyway?"

"What did I say about asking questions?" I pause looking up at her to see her rolling her eyes.

"The less I know the better," she recites. "And what am I going to tell my father when he wakes up and finds all of this gone?"

"That it went to a better cause than terrorising innocent people?" I quip back, pulling the bag up onto my shoulder. The weight of the cargo inside pulls me down.

She eyes me for a moment. The scrutiny is sceptical at best and downright catty at worst. "What's wrong with you anyway? You're not at all the Fury who ambushed me in my own temple."

I roll my eyes sighing heavily, "And here I thought we called a truce. Things have happened since our unfortunate first meeting, and I need these items to fix it." I slap the bag on my hip, "that is what this is for and before you ask no this is not for Roman. He is safe elsewhere." Cutting her off as she opens her mouth, she visibly relaxes upon hearing my words. "If you wish to know, more get in contact with his brother." I turn to leave.

"So, he told you then?" The question is quiet, timid as though she doesn't wish for anyone to overhear us.

"No. The princess did," I answer over my shoulder.

"Wait!" she calls after me.

"Don't worry, Melanie Lincoln, this will likely be our last meeting." I turn to face her, bowing with my arm across my chest like I have done for years at the guild. The action is just as fluid as the day I started this tradition. "Thank you, for your cooperation." And with those last words, I turn, leaping over her garden wall and dashing into the shadows. Into the comfort they bring, and away from the Black Pines.

Aria

The first watch is always the easiest. At least I don't have to be the one waking up and trying my damnedest to stay that way.

Aella's handler, or Rich as he introduced himself. Said he would take the second. Trying my hardest not to wake the others I gently tap him with the tip of my boot.

"Oof. What have you got in there? Rocks," he groans rubbing at his side.

"It's a steel-capped boot," I state back.

"Well don't go shoving them in people's ribs next time yeah?" he grumbles, throwing the covers from his body.

"And yet that is precisely why we wear them." I know the grin I wear is terrifying. I can see it on his face, but the low light of the room, must make me look downright savage and I can't help the chuckle that slips through my lips. His scared expression pleases me in a way I cannot describe.

"Good night, Rich." The single syllable rolls off my tongue like liquid silver and I see his tense posture loosen at the sound. Biting his lip to hide his own smile, I leave him in the dark and pad through Aella's bedroom door, only Mala lies in the room. Aella's makeshift bed on the floor doesn't look like it's been touched, and the outside doors are propped open, the sheer curtains waft gently on the breeze.

I storm across the apartment before the thought has even finished forming. A white door is the only obstacle between me and my target. Sleepy grumbles about being quiet are lost in the roaring rage coursing through my veins. Someone yells, but my fingers curl around a soft white tunic and the body I'm shaking wakes with a start.

"Where is she?" A growl ripples past my lips. Something throaty and menacing, something I've never done before.

"Who?" Declan's eyes are lit with terror and anger, and I don't know which to follow to get the answers that I want. "Aella! She's not in her bed, where she should be."

I swear I hear his galloping heart stutter and start all over again. "What?" He's out of bed before I can ask more questions, pushing me off to the side in his haste to determine that my word is true.

The other sleeping residents are awake now and Rich is in Declan's doorway, his arms crossed over his chest, glaring at me. I scowl back, there's no time to be angry at one another.

I push past him without a word, but he grabs my arm instead, "Watch yourself *Fury*." Silver chips lit in his eyes, blazing with hatred. The sight is enough to make any mortal weak in the knees. I am no such mortal.

"Do you speak to Aella with such contempt?" I sneer, snatching my arm away I follow his compatriot across the wooden floor of the apartment. The others in the group rubbed their eyes and yawned at the noise. Each glares at me as I pass. Mala jumps awake when the door to Aella's room bangs against the wall.

Declan forces the adjoining bathroom door open, frantic.

Placing my arms behind my back, I observe him a few minutes more. I can see all the possibilities and outcomes racing through his mind. His face is like an open book, and one simply has to know how to read it to understand that he didn't know she left.

"She was last with you." He startles at my voice. "What was said?" Rich steps up behind me, his vanilla and sandalwood scent assaulting my nose, and his own panicked breath beating down on the skin of my neck. Mala moves to the living room where her guards have been sleeping on the couches, not wanting to be caught in the middle of this. Not that I can blame her.

Declan drops down onto the bed, placing his head in his hands and weaving his fingers through his ruffled hair, pulling at the strands.

"Dec..." Rich begins behind me when the former begins bouncing his leg.

"Do not coddle him," I cut him off. Thriving on the feel of him bristling. I can practically feel his hackles rising.

"It's not coddling if it's genuine worry. You don't know what we've been through to get here," Rich snarls.

"On the contrary. I do and I clearly remember better than you." I turn back to Declan. "Where is she?" I've never been one for mollycoddling, it sickens me to even think of touching another person in such a tender way, just to bring them an ounce of comfort. I need precision. I need a strategy. I need people to be strong, even when they are feeling weak. If not for me then for themselves. The world will swallow up the weak.

With a sigh, he points to the open doors.

"She left out of those. She likes to sit on the roof and watch the sky. I didn't think she would go far. But I guess not."

"You never quite knew her then." I roll my eyes and rummage through her weapons bag. Her mask and vest are still resting at the top. Along with her unique combat blade and two of her assault rifles.

"Who else can acquire this kind of weaponry?"

Another more annoyed sigh comes from the doorway. The older mortal man with piercing blue eyes and a deep brunette beard stands there with his thumb and forefinger rubbing over his brows. "It doesn't take a scientist to guess where."

Aella

I've been here before.

In this position I mean.

Hanging from a balcony by my fingertips.

It was some months ago now, but the fear is still the same. The pounding of your heart thundering through every pulse point, makes it feel louder and all the more deafening. The salty sweat begins to coat the skin making your grip even weaker. The daunting drop below you, which can only lead to certain death, is always something that makes your mind spin. But it makes me feel alive.

Certain death awaits me if I fall.

Certain death also awaits me inside the building I'm hanging from. But the sky. The night sky is calming. Even my roaring heart slows its racing pace as I find peace within the stars above me.

Of Fire and Shadow

I left in the night. I didn't want to fight. Nobody will stop the inevitable even if I wanted them to which a part of me did. I wanted someone to find a way out for me. I wanted nothing more than to be taken care of instead of me making sure everyone else was OK first. Some may call me a coward for not wanting to face my truth. For not wanting to face Reuben Ostair. Maybe it does make me one. A coward. But still, I'm here taking in the last few minutes of the sky whilst I still can.

He is the reason that I, once again, find myself climbing the northmost tower of The Circle, reminiscent of my first week in this unknown city when I climbed these same balconies to have a private meeting with our country's crown prince.

I know Reuben will be closer to the higher level of the tower. It's where they keep the higher-ranking officials when they come to visit and since he thinks so highly of himself there is no doubt in my mind that he has taken full advantage of his title.

Pulling myself up and onto the balcony, I shimmy the bag from my shoulders and pull out the equipment Melanie provided. A bulletproof vest, and face mask. Exactly the same as my old ones, minus the Fort's markings an assortment of pistols, knives, a few hand grenades, and even an assault rifle. I couldn't risk bringing my own gear it would've been more susceptible to discovery if anyone walked into the room to see everything missing. Not to mention the, currently dormant, tracking devices I have implanted in there from the Fort.

As quietly as I can, I gear myself up, before popping open the patio doors into a room, similar to the room Frederick occupied when I met with him. Just not quite as grand. The carpet beneath me cushions my steps, the plush white marred by the dirt coating my boots. Male guards are no doubt on duty with Reuben's selection of deadly Furies walk the halls, the echoes of their footsteps resound through the otherwise deserted room I find myself in. What little moonlight that lights the room, guides me to the door connecting to the hallway beyond and with bated breath, I slink across the floor like a cat stalking its prey.

When my gloved hand reaches for the handle, footsteps stop outside the door. I hold my breath as if that will stop me from being heard. They're waiting. Waiting for what I don't know. Voices turn a corner, muted by the distance until they stop outside the door.

"The Director wants you upstairs guarding his door. Four-Seven-Five." The familiar voice of Callum slithers into my ears. Four-Seven-Five also known as Enyo Bazin, a girl who was destined to advance into my group some years ago. Despite beating her opponent in the end-of-month fight, she never did join us, and it was never explained why.

I steal myself and raise my chin higher. Just as Madame taught me.

There's no reply on her end. There doesn't need to be. She simply marches away, leaving Callum and another guard to themselves.

"You ever thought how Three-Nought-Nought and Four-Five-Seven, look alike?" The unknown guard asks.

Callum scoffs, "Don't get too curious about it. From what I heard Three-Nought-Nought's gone rogue. She won't leave this city alive."

CHAPTER THIRTY-FOUR
THE STORM

Aria

Rich volunteered to drive me to this Eddie Lincoln's territory. Leaving a disheartened Declan behind. It's better that way. I'm one obnoxious comment away from throttling the life from him. His affection for her has allowed her to undoubtedly run into danger and without her tracking device, there is no way for us to determine whereabouts she is. I know of course. Given what we've talked about recently, I know. But if I can stop her before she, does it, I'll sleep better. If I can't change her mind. Then I go down in a blazing glory with her at least.

Neither Rich nor I have spoken a word to the other since we have been enclosed in this space and that suits me just fine. I'd rather not get to know this male at all. Something about him makes me uncomfortable. Not in a life-threatening way. But in a way that seems too familiar, considering we met only hours ago.

The sky begins to grey above us, and the stars seem to burn brighter because of it.

"So, how long have you been at the Fort?" he asks, tentatively.

"We do not have to speak," I reply and from the corner of my eye I see him press his lips together and something I haven't felt in some time lashes through me. I sigh, "since I was young. Maybe about three. I don't really remember. It's been all I've known for a very long time."

He nods clearly unsure what to say and the quiet fills the car once again.

With the roads being so quiet at this hour, it's not long before we reach the Black Pines. My finger naturally twitches towards the weapon at my side when I feel eyes watching us trundle down the otherwise deserted street.

"Easy. It's going to be uncomfortable but don't forget why we are here," Rich reassures me and although I don't sit back in my seat again, the words bring me some comfort, nonetheless.

We pull up to an unlit sandstone house. The stone was meticulously cut to match the others around it despite it obviously being a newer build.

Guards step out of the front door guns drawn as we unfasten our seatbelts, dressed in fine black suits and they eye us with malice.

Rich places his hand on my forearm stopping me from drawing my own weapon. Something tingles beneath my skin at the contact and unlike earlier I feel reluctant to turn away. It's only when he exits the vehicle that the connection is lost. His hands are raised as he walks forth. I'm quick to follow. Aella cares for this male, and I'm sure she would be disappointed with me if I didn't try my hardest to stop him from dying.

"We are here to speak with Melanie," Rich speaks plainly. Seemingly uninterested in the multitude of guns pointing at his chest.

A sigh comes from behind the white-haired guard, protecting the doorway. "I thought that you would be visiting me next."

A slender brunette steps up behind the guard with dark eyes, dressed in a lavender nightgown and a sheer dressing gown with fur lining the cuffs and collar.

"Melanie," Rich greets, his tone is level and unamused.

Her glowing golden eyes latch onto mine, and I can practically see her lynx pacing back and forth. "You. You are new."

"And a friend. We only need to ask you a question," Rich defends.

She rolls her eyes. "I know. Come in." She disappears into the darkness of her house and despite the invitation, the guards still do not put down their weapons.

"Please don't do anything stupid," Rich murmurs to me.

"I'm offended you would even think that," I counter stepping in front of him, following after this mysterious Melanie.

"I bet." I hear Rich mumble under his breath, but he's quick to follow me.

Aella

Callum and the guard move along swiftly, and I take the opportunity to slip out into the corridor. The light is nearly blinding in contrast to the darkness I've been hiding in but that won't stop me from reaching my goal.

Rifle drawn between both arms I pull it up, peering down the scope, I pad gently down the corridor. Two guards turn the corner, completely unsuspecting and unaware of my presence. I squeeze the trigger and their bodies drop to the floor before they've even drawn their own weapons. The shots muted by the silencer attached to the end of the barrel, not that it matters since I won't be moving the new corpses, it'll take too much time. Instead, I step over them as no more as an inconvenience and continue on.

That void in my chest expands leaving me empty, its all-consuming and scarily dark, but it keeps me centred as I drop another three guards. Their blood pools on the white tiled floor, the red running in the cracks and expanding further. Droplets run down the beige walls.

That iron chest within my brain rattles and jumps, begging for me to remember my training. To stop the massacre that will ensue against my own people. To be the ever-glorious Fury, who has spent years building her reputation into something no one could possibly hope to reach. But my blackened heart is reminding me of everything lost. Of the life I could've had. Of the parents who I never knew. My gut twists at my indecision. So, I follow my darkness and push forward. They will no longer control me.

The staircase is empty as I ascend to the floor above. Either they are slacking tonight, or they are held up in one room awaiting my appearance.

Each noiseless step begins to feel more and more like a violent death sentence. I keep my gun raised, tucked into my shoulder, the weight a comfort despite what is to come. I stop just before the door to the next floor. My heart pounds in my ears and I tuck myself into the wall. Listening, waiting. With shallow breaths, I wait for what feels like an eternity and still nothing moves.

A yell comes from downstairs, and I hear a thundering of boots as the male guard's scramble to get themselves organised to begin the search for me. I push the door open to the much quieter upstairs, and darkness greets me.

Taking a solid breath, I step into the hallway. Within seconds something drops at my feet. I turn and jump to the side, covering my eyes, as a flash bomb lights the hallway. I hit the tiled floor with a back-shaking thud and the air is knocked from my lungs. I scramble to stand, and my boots thankfully find purchase, propelling me forward towards the closest room.

"Three-Nought-Nought." His slimy voice slithers over the speakers lining the ceiling. "You disappoint me."

"Good!" I bite back, shouting into the darkened hallway. Exhaling I slam my shoulder into the random door, charging through the wood and breaking the lock as the Furies, previously hiding in the shadows, open fire. "Fuck!" I cry, landing on the floor on the other side with arms come up to cover my head. I quickly twist my hips trying to roll out of the way gaining a graze from a bullet through my thigh.

The shooting stops briefly and I'm granted time, however little. I gather myself, tucking up close to the wall next to the ruined doorframe.

"Stand down!" I yell over my shoulder, "I'm not here for you. Only he needs to die."

"Oh! My little whirlwind," His voice comes through again. "I knew there was a reason you were my favourite. You do have such a way with words." He cackles and the sound grates on every nerve, like they've been lit on fire and shoved through a meat grinder.

"Coward!" I scream, pulling out my handgun, I shoot into the darkness. The wet smack of a body hitting the floor is pleasing, as is the pained groan that accompanies it. The last thing I want is to go up against my sisters. But there is no way to reach them. They have a mission. Protect the Director, and I'm their target.

"Last chance!" I call again. Listening for approaching footsteps.

When no one replies, my heart sinks. I was hoping beyond hope that at least one would have taken the escape. But instead, I'm left with no other choice. The sweet release of death is better than continuing to live in this torturous existence that has been chosen for each of us.

"Fine," I hiss to myself, bracing for the onslaught. Readjusting my rifle, I tuck it tightly back to my shoulder and step out from behind the wall. Releasing a shower of bullets down the hallway. The doors open from the stairwell and the guards come running to their deaths, their own guns are drawn but none get more than a few steps into the hall before they fall to the ground.

The formerly darkened hall is now lit with the warmth of gunfire. The hues of yellow and orange flash menacingly from my rifle, and smoke falls eerily to the floor, coating it in a deathly glow. Red splatters across the white walls running down in waterfalls.

The Furies are quick to retaliate, opening fire. Through the darkness, I can see figures taking cover behind the walls and tables that have clearly been pulled out of countless rooms for extra protection against me. They must have known that I would come. But how?

At least twenty people stand between me and my target. It would be a simple feat if they weren't Furies. I'm no stranger to these fights. But my heart flies all the same, staying lodged in my throat until it's all over. Adrenaline floods my blood in droves and it's that I use to steel my shaking fingers. A whip cracks against the floor and I can hear the retreat of footsteps.

"I always knew there was something wrong with you." Madame Tuli. Her voice is thick with disgust as it slithers down the hall, right towards me like a snake ready to strike. "Three-Nought-Nought. You were always so odd. You knew more than you let on. But your time has come to an end. There will be no more mistakes. Once you are gone, we will hunt Fury Three-Five-Nine and that will be the end of the old ways. Are there any last words you'd like to have forgotten?" I can practically see the terrifying grin on her face by the sneer in her voice alone.

Green lasers track the room in the darkness, the room I'm finding it increasingly difficult to hide in. The lasers trail from wall to wall. One brushes the outer of my leg, not enough to give me away but enough to double back and check. Sliding my leg to the side gently that is exactly what the male does — checks and rechecks the corner I'm hiding in.

Madame Tuli steps forward, her feet light as a feather, in her leather boots.

"Hel hath no fury like a vengeful woman," I hiss, coming out of my hiding space. I fire off a few quick shots, Madame drops to the floor to avoid the spray, but I manage to take out the guards behind her.

I make a run for another room, careful to avoid Tuli as she stands as see me bolt further down to corridor, making small advancements on where I think Reuben is hiding. I just have to take all these guards and Furies down to get to him. Great.

"Madame Tuli, teach this one a lesson for me," Reuben speaks through the speakers, "and then bring her to me. I'll be waiting." With that, the speaker system cuts off and Tuli rises.

"Come here little bird." The malice in her voice used to scare me as a child. Her stare too, like a bird of prey watching from the skies for vermin running amongst the grass, waiting for you to slip up. and once you did it was game over. You'd be eaten alive.

If K has taught me anything over the years is to never give into the fear. Kill the innocence and become they fear. Become the nightmare, and I'm about to make Tuli rue the day she ever became a member of the Fort of Ajay.

I quickly detach the rifle from my vest and pull out a combat blade. Placing my handgun in my other hand. She steps into the room, searching the shadows. I don't want to get too close, but feeling her body go limp and seeing the light leave her eyes is better than simply shooting her dead. This woman tormented me for my whole life and while I respect her for staying true to herself, I can't wait for her to die, so she's one less problem in my life.

"Little bird, there's been a secret that not even the great Director has shared with you. Something I'm sure you'd like to know." She spins so fast it makes even *me* dizzy. She cracks her whip into the shadow I was occupying only moments before.

Swiftly I duck behind one of the armchairs at the centre of the room, listening for her movements, flexing my fingers around the blades handle nervously.

"It's about your parents. Wouldn't you like to know what really happened to them?" The slither of the whip on the ground fills my ears, as my heart my foolish, foolish heart stops, skips a beat and begins pounding at double its strength. Closing my eyes, I force myself to believe that my parents are dead. She's only doing this to throw my off my game, to give my hope when there is none.

I tuck around roll behind the couch next trying to make it to the door. If at all possible, it would be best not to engage with Tuli. She was trained by the best assassins to the East she is much faster and stronger than I. But my anger at her words says otherwise.

She pulls out the chair and the whip cracks again, slicing past me.

"Gotcha!" she cackles.

Cursing under her breath she pauses in time to see me leap from behind the cream-coloured couch. Using it as a platform I throw myself at her, wrapping my legs over her shoulders, locking her head between my thighs, and use my weight to twirl us around and drag her down to the ground; something pops at the abrupt turn.

"I don't care what deceitful things you try to use against me. I will kill him, and you will join him." Struggling with her for a few moments until she pulls out a small blade and tries to stab me in the leg. I release my grip and roll away from her and regain my footing, raising my fists in front of my face I watch her stand, one leg turned outward.

She doesn't put any weight onto it. I've dislocated her knee. It take no satisfactions from it, "surrender now and I won't have to kill you."

"Like you could," she snarls through clenched teeth, she hobbles back a step, but her arm moves so fast that I don't even know she's released her whip until it slashes across my cheek, my head snaps to the side trying to avoid it, but still, she draws blood from me. Recoiling it, she draws back again ready to whip me again. Reminding me very much of the times she was ordered to do it before when I stepped out of line.

I rush her, tackling her to the floor, she lets go out the whip which I don't hesitate to snatch up. The leather binding is warm, and I stand once again. I've never been trained to use a whip. It's one of the things that is unique to Tuli, but it's never too late to try. She throws that little knife at me missing completely while I twirl to avoid it and the whip follows, I let it fly towards her, it just misses her head as she ducks out of the way, stumbling to the side on a leg that won't cooperate. I try again, opening the skin of her upper arm. She doesn't so much as flinch when blood starts freely flowing from the newly opened wound.

She pulls out her blood-red kukri blade and charges me.

Neither of us says anything more. No more taunting words, not sly comments to rile the other up. Just pure focus from the both of us. We equally want to win this fight. Her to prove herself to Reuben. I to prove that I'm capable of killing him. Sweat beads along her forehead while she slices the blade through the air. Even whilst she's injured it takes everything in me to dodge each of her attacks. She catches my side, just under my ribs and I drop to the floor, a punch her dislocated knee. She howls in pain and backs off, if only to let me catch my breath.

The windows bring in pure moonlight, that shines along the floor revealing us both covered in an unhealthy amount of blood and sweat.

"You want to know how I got this?" Her sneer suggests nefarious means, while waving the menacing blade around.

"Not really," I clap back, throwing a cushion at her from the couch. She slices it and feathers explode into the room. I kick her other leg out from underneath her and jump on top, my knees on either side of her, pinning her to the ground. Thus begins a desperate scramble for control of the blade. Both of her hands are tightly holding onto the golden hilt. My forearm is braced in front of me using my weight to hold off her advance, whilst my other hand is trying to pry one of hers off the handle.

"You won't win," she hisses at me.

I pant heavily, ignoring her, until I gain control. The red blade twists in the air and a wet sound reverberates in the room. Tuli lies stock still in shock. Her own knife protrudes out of her rib cage, puncturing through her lung.

"You really shouldn't underestimate me," I snarl back. I know my eyes are glowing yellow again by the way her own widen.

"What are you?" she stutters. Blood pours from the wound, warming my fingers and the back of my hand before it starts to soak through the carpet.

Tuli's eyes widen further when I pull the blade out, her breath is sharp and quick, trying to keep the air locked in, to no avail. I wipe the metal on her clothes, before tucking it into my belt.

"You don't deserve that." Her throat is raw, edged with death and pain. Her head turns quickly, breaking our eye contact, she begins to cough violently and blood splatters on the shaggy white rug.

"Maybe not but you can't tell me you did." I step over her. The sounds of her choking on her own blood are like a melody in my ears as I walk away, exhausted and bloodied from our fight.

The hallway is empty when I step into it, only Madame Tuli's chocking follows me through the otherwise silent building. I pull out my handgun once again, holding onto it like a safety blanket waiting for someone or something to jump out at me.

"It's just you and me now, Reuben." His name feels like ash in my mouth, and it's a fight to utter the sound. My conditioning pushing me to use his title not his name; it goes against everything I've ever been taught. "Come out, come out wherever you are," I taunt. I don't need to yell anything, I know with his fae hearing he'll be able to hear me even if I didn't speak, but this at least gives me some solace to know that I will draw him out and he won't jump me and get the upper hand.

The speaker's overhead crackle to life once more.

"Where did it all go wrong, my little whirlwind?" He drawls, as if this is no more than a lazy Sunday afternoon, sitting out in the sun drinking cocktails. "Hmm? We had such a good thing going."

I listen to him talk, still inching down the hall, waiting for the Furies to pop out at any minute, "if you call kidnapping and torturing girls a good time, then sure, it was a *blast*," I reply, the words dripping in sarcasm.

"Was it him?"

That gives me pause and my heart drops to my stomach.

"Ah. So, it was." The sound of pages flipping comes through next. "Declan Angelos." He drawls out his name, like it tastes so sweet he has to relish in its flavour. "No matter. He'll be dead before the sun rises."

It's at that moment something charges into me from the side and I go stumbling into a wall. My head smacks against the concrete rattling my brain.

A dark-haired Fury dressed similarly to me, with the Fort's branded vest and mask, stands there brandishing a knife that glints in the low light; her fingers flex around the handle while she stands there staring at me. Not even remotely out of breath.

It's then that I begin to wonder where the rest have gone. There was so many before. But now they seem to have vanished. Still, I need to focus on this singular one in front of me. If I can get through to her, she may be the first of many that I can save.

"Please don't make me do this," I plead, raising my fists all the same. She tilts her head to the side and doesn't give me a second longer. She pushes forward her knife cutting through the air with deadly precision. She cuts through the top of my arm and blood instantly pools there before flowing down my sweat-soaked skin. Dodging her attacks is harder out here than in the room with Madame Tuli. The hall is much narrower. Swiping up the curtain hanging in front of the window, I step to the side trying to take her off guard. She takes the bait and missteps, and I take the advantage to wrap the cloth around her neck. In her rush to remove it from her, she steps on my foot and both of us go tumbling to the floor. With her on top of me. My grip is tight on the cloth as I hold it firm around her neck. She struggles violently, trying to free herself. I hear the clank of the blade as it's discarded in favour of her hands. Her nails dig into my skin, drawing little drops of blood in the shape of crescent moons.

Her fight begins to weaken, and the struggle becomes more of an acceptance of what awaits her beyond this mortal plain. Until she stops altogether. I kick her off me and untie the curtain, checking her pulse.

It's weak, but it's still there.

"Do not worry about her, my *Siren*. She has failed me." I'm panting so hard, that I almost miss the slight ticking I can hear. I search her body quickly trying to find the source. When I see a red flashing light coming from her neck. I turn her over quickly and the ticking intensifies. The blinking light is under her skin, and beeping so fast all I can do is duck and cover.

The light is nearly blinding even as I'm tucked under my arm. My ears ring from the sudden explosion. I give it a few seconds before checking the damage.

Her head has been blown clean from her shoulders. Chunks of brain matter lay scattered across the floor, along with masses of blood and chips of her skull and upper spine.

My stomach roils but I have to resist the urge to gag. The explosion was so vast it took out part of the outer wall and a window, the wind howls loudly as it finds it way inside. The early morning silver light has broken over the horizon, it too squeezes through any available crack it can find.

Despite the chaos around me, I take some solidifying breaths, calming my abused and racing heart to take in the sunrise. Likely the last I'll see.

"Is this thing still working?" His voice crackles from further down the corridor, into one of the other speakers. The obnoxious tapping he's doing in the microphone grates on my very last nerve. I curl my fingers into fists and take one last glance at the fallen Fury beside me. I crouch down resting my hand on her chest.

"Safe journey, into the beyond. Sister." My heart weeps for her. At the life she could've had I want to cry for her. I want to hold her until I can do so no longer. But I still have a job to do. To stop this from happening again in the future. To stop more girls falling in the name of power. I stand allowing the first and only tear to fall. I steel my resolve once more and turn around.

"This ends with us, Reuben. Come out and face me. Only one of us needs to die tonight."

There's a casual shuffle of boots behind me and I whip around to see him standing there completely unfazed by the body lying at both of our feet.

"Well, sweetling I'm here." He raises his arms as if he's a gift from the gods. "The question now is, what are you doing to do with me?"

Rich

"I don't know what you want me to tell you Richie boy. She dropped by but she's not here now and before you ask me, *again*, no. I don't know where she was going. She elected to leave that part of her scheme out," Melanie repeats, swirling the ice in her whiskey yet again, looking completely unfazed by my panicked questioning.

"We are wasting our time when we could be out there trying to stop her," Aria drawls from my side, rolling her eyes dramatically as she does so. If Aella wasn't missing, I'd find her attitude amusing.

"And you are?" Melanie claps back. Aria had done well to heed my warning before entering the house. She mostly kept to herself and kept her questioning to a minimum. Until now.

"I'll be your worst nightmare if you carry on giving me attitude, shifter," she snarls back baring her fangs. The action sends her hair blowing back, revealing her fae ears.

"You know where she is," I turn to Aria. Melanie had urged us into her study to have this particular meeting. The space is decorated from floor to ceiling with bookshelves, and wooden mahogany desk and two wingback chairs, situated in front of a grand fireplace.

"I know where she is," she answers.

"Then why not speak up before now?"

"I thought we could stop her before she gets there, and you asked me to be quiet, so..." she shrugs.

"Sorry, I couldn't be of more use to you," Melanie interrupts clearly wanting nothing more than to go back to bed. The tone sounds like a genuine sadness resides in her words. Her guards guide us back to the front door, and out onto the street where thankfully our car still sits. Not that I was necessarily expecting it to go anywhere.

"Well, that was fruitful," Aria's tone is bored. And the statement finally makes me snap.

"Where is she?" I snap, thoroughly pissed that we have wasted so much time.

"She went to him," she replies. The tone hollow and totally detached.

"What do you mean. She went to him?" Something drops within me, and panic slowly starts to creep in.

"I don't know how I could possibly spell this out for you. But we had a discussion. I told her not be a martyr about it but clearly, she didn't listen."

I stay quiet wanting her to continue, we pile into the car, but I don't turn the key. When she finally notices, she turns to see me staring at her like I've seen a ghost.

"I think you should go back to the safe house and pack up. Allow me to go and dig her out of whatever mess she's made."

The car rumbles to life, and panic fills my body. I need to get back to the apartment I need to warn them that we need to leave now. Turning the corner onto the main road that stretches from Weet to East, it's pretty much a straight shot to The Circle's five towers. Those same pillars shimmer like a thousand pearls as the sun begins to rise.

"Where. Has. She. Gone?" I spit out, sick of being left in the dark.

"What's that?" Aria asks, ignoring the question once more, pointing to the one furthest on the left. The North Tower. I lean forwards closer to the window to see she's pointing at a section of the building that looks as though there has been a hole blown into the side. Dust falls in clumps from the gap. Slamming on the brakes I turn to look at Aria who is still staring at that gaping hole in the side of the building.

She says the words that I'm only thinking. Words that I wish weren't true. "She's gone to kill Reuben Ostair."

Aella

His wolfish grin matches the sharp angles on his jaw and cheekbones. He always did look more skeletal, with his slightly gaunt cheeks, his sunken eyes that cast a wicked shadow over his eyes; his ivory skin that's pulled tight over the bones of his face. His nose is pointed like a bird beak, with thin lips and pointed fae ears and fangs.

"Come on, sweetling. If you come with me now, we can forget this whole thing," he bargains in a voice that is all too sweet for the cruel, calculating male in front of me. He holds out a hand to me as if I am merely a child that he is coaxing into following him.

Cold rushed through my veins, heavy and jarring. It makes my knees feel weak and my fingers shake as I battle to regain control. My eyes travel up from his hand, up the length of his arm wrapped in a well-tailed suit, to his face. His smile has softened his features, but it's his eyes that betray him. There's a vile creature lurking within them. One that will no doubt delight in my screams as he tortures me to death. There is no redemption for what I've done. I almost swallow my tongue at the thought. No words come to mind, only my training. Eliminate the target.

I raise my gun, and suddenly everything clicks into place.

The cold of my limbs begins to thaw, and my anxiety leaves me, my muscles harden, ready for the fight to come.

His smile drops and all that's left is the raging, writhing animal fighting to claw the flesh from my bones. "You disappoint me, Three-Nought-Nought."

Something tumbles down at his feet a flash of cream, sprawled on the floor.

I drop my gaze and find Madame K lying there, bleeding from her temple. That coldness returns, keeping me frozen in place. Making me a mere bystander in my own body. He crouches down, and that smirk is back in place.

"Say hello, Yvonne." He pinches her cheeks in one hand and turns her to me. Revealing her other eye that's completely swollen to the point that she can't open it.

Her one icy blue eye locks onto mine. A pain I've never seen in them is present now. Begging. For me to run, or for the mercy of death I do not know which. But what little piece of my heart is left just shattered into pieces.

"Let her go," I command, my voice wobbly with emotion.

Her eyes flash with something unrecognizable.

"Fine." He drops her face, and she barely catches herself with her hands. "See I can be reasonable, Siren. You've just never seen through to the core of me."

Yvonne begins to crawl towards me, through the mess of the Fury's sudden execution. Blood soaks through her white blouse, her fingernails are broken presumably from putting up one Hel of a fight, her usually kempt hair tangles down in waves around her ears and across cheeks.

My eyes stay fixed on Reuben and his on me.

"You are stronger than this Aella," K's voice is gravelly and uneven, "your heart is pure. You may not see it, but it is." Reuben's smile is malicious and teasing like the words he's hearing are a part of some joke. "There has always been a light within that not even the harshest of training could dim." Yvonne pulls herself up next to the body and from the corner of my eye is see why she's not walking. They've broken her kneecaps and her legs at all different angles. There's a flash of something and a quick motion, making Reuben flinch and step away. Madame has pulled a throwing knife from the Fury's utility belt and hit him square in the shoulder. He stumbles back a few steps in shock.

Using that to my advantage I squeeze the trigger, bullet after bullet pierces his chest. I keep going until I've emptied the clip.

I watch in relief as his corpse hits the floor with a wet smack.

I drop before me to Madame, pulling her up to the wall.

She gives me a weak smile, "You were made for more than this," she utters, fighting to keep herself conscious.

"Please don't," I whimper, holding onto her cheeks, I can already see the light begin to leave her eyes.

"My time has come, my love. I'm sorry I wasn't better for you." Tears pour from my eyes. "You are stronger than you know, Aella and it has been a privilege to guide you and I would protect you all over again, even if it resulted in the same ending." Her words are but a whisper, and I can't help the tears that fall. "But I've lost too much blood and I'm in too much pain. I'm just grateful I got to see you one last time." She starts to put more weight into me as she speaks the words slowly letting go, trying to tell me, everything before she does. "We are out of time. But Aella, you will rise. Stronger than before." Her hand covers one of my cheeks as I cry. Until her head lulls to one side and her eyes focus on something that I cannot see. Her chest falls one more time and doesn't rise again.

"No!" I scream at her. For her. The lump in my throat expands, there's no fighting the tears at this point. I pull her head into my chest. Although she may have been cruel and downright abusive at times. This fae has been the only mother figure I have ever known. I'd be lost without her. In fact, I'd likely be dead without her protections and guidance.

Sitting on the floor, with her head pressed tight to my chest, I rock back and forth, as if that will give me some comfort. Even if I know that she will not come back. The final piece of my heart cracks and that void expands once more swallowing everything in its path. Making light into dark, shadows expand along the floor as I scream out my pain. Smoke clogs my throat choking me with my own sorrow and pain.

I turn to Reuben's body, not entirely myself, something clinks on the flooring having rolled out of his limp hand onto the tiled floor.

Placing Yvonne gently on the floor, I tuck her hands together on her chest, and touch one of my hands to both of hers, "safe journey into the beyond. Yvonne." I whimper her name, and my lip trembles as I look at her paling form. It takes everything in me to rise and walk away. But I do. I found the strength she said I had and stood before my former Director.

My worst abuser.

But I will no longer be a victim.

I look at what was in his hand, a blinking panel. The light flashes red with a timer, counting down.

Ten seconds.

"Oh fuck!" I run back to Yvonne desperate to get her out of there. Between my injuries and her weight, I don't get far. The hole, blown open by the Fury's death, shows each level of the building has been rigged with bombs. The very foundations shake as the top being to lose balance.

The explosions get louder and louder the higher they climb. I barely stand before the floor cracks below me. A hole opens up taking Reuben and the headless Fury.

Five seconds.

Dust and rubble erupt all around me. I can't see within an inch of my nose. Another explosion, this one louder ringing in my ears.

Four seconds.

The wall to the outside completely crumbles blowing out. The structure crumbles and the tower collapses in on itself.

Three.

Fire comes rushing through the hall. Lighting the dusty haze around me.

Two.

I drop down covering Madame's body with my own.

One.

Another explosion above brings the ceiling down upon us. Concrete slams onto my back knocking the wind from my lungs and everything goes black.

Zero.

EPILOGUE

'Captain' Cornelious Anderson

Upon hanging up the phone, or rather slamming the fucking thing back into its place, no thoughts swirl in my mind, just a buzzing white noise. The naked redhead sat up on the desk in front of me, her legs spread wide, all but forgotten, except for the taste of her on my tongue and even that sours in comparison to the words I've just heard.

The Director. Dead?

Rueben Ostair.

That fucker was indestructible. It's a lie. It has to be.

It can't be true.

The female looks disgruntled that I've stopped my efforts to please her, but the scowl on my face says enough, she slowly slides from the desk, gathers her things and leaves, the soft click of the door seems to echo in her wake.

Reuben, my lifelong friend, dead?

All because of that bitch.

The one he favoured.

The one he gave a gods damned nickname. *The Siren.* Rage boils in my blood, and my fingers turn white as they rest in my lap. Hands curling into fists.

I stand with such force my chair hits the wall behind me.

Campbell told me she died with him, but that is not enough to quell this rage. She won't get away with this, none of them will.

I will kill everything and everyone she loves until my anger is satisfied. My animal begins to surface, his vengeance matching mine, but I can't lose control. Without another thought my hand is reaching for the doorknob.

"Joel!" I call, so loud that even the whimpering inmates quieten down.

Footsteps sound seconds later, he's running. Good. There's no time to waste. The dark-haired boy is before me quickly; his grey eyes shine with an inkling of fear that is terribly masked over with false confidence.

"Yes sir." He bows his head, with his arm across his chest.

"Bring me the *key*," I hiss. My anger is not directed at the boy before me, but I won't hesitate to lock him up in one of these cells should he ever disappoint.

"Yes sir," he replies, running off back down the hall. I don't miss the utter terror his face showed at my words. I like it when they are afraid.

Within minutes he's running back down the hall towards me, a black wooden box in hand.

"With me," I utter. He nods and hesitates slightly to follow. I don't miss the utter stench of his fear as it rolls off of him in waves, filling my nose like clotted cream.

"Calm yourself boy, or I'll leave you in there," I growl. He nods shakily once more but becoming composed.

We walk down the long stone halls, and through a set of steel doors. Guards positioned there, haul the heavy metal open, the hinges grind so loud it's deafening. All the cells beyond this point are empty. Used only for the worst of the worst. Except for one.

"Joel," I mutter, waiting for him to heed my silent command.

Fire, of the most brilliant orange bursts from his hand, encircling his hand and forearm, like a serpent wrapping around its meal, and the old oil torches begin lighting one by one.

The stone is black, iridescent, and naturally jagged on all four sides.

A perfect unbreakable cage.

Cell after empty cell stream past us, all made from the same natural rock, with a torch nestled in between each set of bars, lighting the stone so it almost looks like a deep purple.

Our steps echo off the stone and reverberate back to us, I fight the shiver that creeps up on me. Even I hate coming down here. But my thirst for blood will not be deterred.

We come to a halt outside the door, and Joel holds out the wooden box. His skin is pale, and completely taut across his sharp face. His slender, scarred fingers work the lock, and he opens the lid to reveal the key. A black iridescent stone, matching the corridor and cells around it. One key for countless cages.

Stealing my breath, I place the key in the lock and turn, listening to the many locks click and grind under the surface of the thick door. The gears all click and pop before the door swings open.

The cell is dark, but nevertheless, I know he's in here. There's nowhere else for him to go.

I nod to Joel and place the key back into the box before stepping inside.

Sure enough, there he sits on the stone bench, his elbows on his knees and eyes downcast on the floor. His dark hair blends into the darkness around him. Joel provides the only light, in the form of his flames that curl into a ball in his palm.

"Look alive," I call, cringing as it echoes back louder than I intended. I school myself and stand taller, clasping my hands behind my back.

"Prisoner Six-One-Six, I have a mission for you."

ACKNOWLEDGEMENTS

I would like to first say that this has been an experience. I have enjoyed every minute of writing this book for you and the journey it has taken me on is something that I never thought that I could endure.

Before this I had only dabbled in writing when an idea struck me for a plot point, and I took it from there and it rapidly snowballed into something that I didn't think I would ever be able to do. So, the dedication to this book was not only for you, the readers, but I suppose a little bit for me too.

With that being said, I would like to thank everyone who has been a part of my book, you know who you are. Those who have been there to support me when I struggled with finding a way through writer's block or for those who simply listened as I rambled on about where I could take the story, I can't thank you enough.

To my sisters who have help me with editing and giving me a few plot ideas, helping me along when I wasn't sure where to take the story.

To, Emma my fantastic artist who illustrated the cover for me. You have made the whole process so easy and enjoyable. I hope we will continue on our journey for any other books that I may or may not have in the works. You made the process so easy and understood exactly what I wanted from the get-go.

And of course, to you, dear reader, for buying the book and believing in a story written by someone who is as much of a fan of fantasy and romance stories as the next guy. I am forever grateful.

Printed in Great Britain
by Amazon

42938558R00303